Scribner's Best of the Fiction Workshops

1998

Guest Editor
Carol Shields

Series Editors
John Kulka and Natalie Danford

SCRIBNER PAPERBACK FICTION
PUBLISHED BY SIMON & SCHUSTER

SCRIBNER PAPERBACK FICTION
Simon & Schuster Inc.
Rockefeller Center
1230 Avenue of the Americas
New York, NY 10020

This book is a work of fiction. Names, characters, places, and incidents either are products of the author's imagination or are used fictitiously. Any resemblance to actual events or locales or persons, living or dead, is entirely coincidental.

Set in Monotype Baskerville
Designed by Brooke Zimmer
Manufactured in the United States of America

1 3 5 7 9 10 8 6 4 2

Library of Congress Cataloging-in-Publication Data is available.

ISBN 0-684-83836-2

Copyright information continued on page 399.

For my parents,
Arleen and Richard
N. D.

CONTENTS

PREFACE

SCRIBNER's Best of the Fiction Workshops, now in its second year, is an annual anthology collecting the best short fiction from graduate workshops in the United States and Canada. The series aims to introduce to a larger audience the exciting new voices coming from these programs, and to provide workshop writers with a publishing venue. What makes this anthology different from others on the market is that the writers represented here are all new, unfamiliar talents, most of them previously unpublished. For the most part these are young writers, but all of them—regardless of their ages—are at the beginnings of promising careers. It is gratifying to learn from editors and agents that a few of the writers from last year's anthology have now gone on to sign book contracts.

Last year, as envelopes containing nominations for the debut volume, *Scribner's Best of the Fiction Workshops 1997*, came pouring in, we opened them eagerly, certain that we were going to discover fresh and exciting work; that expectation was fulfilled. This year we faced those same envelopes with trepidation. Could it be that the graduate writing programs had sent us a backlog of their best work that first year? Would we find ourselves choosing stories from the same schools? Were we to be caught in a sophomore slump?

Happily, the answers turned out to be no, no, and no. This year's submissions are as varied and innovative as last year's. Moreover, there are some noticeable differences between the two groups of stories. This year we saw more experimental work, more language-driven stories. And there was more magical realism, with settings in the Southwest or Latin America. While last year there were several stories located in Prague—bolstering that city's reputation as a playground for American students—this year's graduate students seemed more connected to southeast Asia. As a whole this year's crop of stories was much more international, and characters tended to benefit from well-defined ethnic identities.

Despite the greater number of less traditional stories this year, the majority of the stories we received were still told in a realistic mode. And as might be expected, many of the stories were related in the first person. The long shadows cast by Hemingway and Faulkner were still evident in some of the stories, especially in stories by male writers. But the influences of less likely models were also visible: Franz Kafka, Bruno Schulz, I. B. Singer, Gertrude Stein, Sinclair Lewis, Don DeLillo, Thomas Pynchon. Many of the writers seemed influenced by other mediums—film and television primarily. A few of these writers made use of television or film as extended metaphors for creativity.

While one writer can boast of having been published in both this year's and last year's anthology, and while a few writing programs are represented here again, we made our choices without regard to school affiliation. Writers in this year's anthology come from a diverse group of programs. Many of the programs listed in the table of contents this year appear there for the first time. Columbia University is represented by two writers, a notable achievement indeed.

So many worthy stories came our way this year that unfortunately not all of them could be included in the anthology. In fact, almost another volume could have been filled with good stories. One hundred nineteen workshops participated in the anthology, forwarding to us what they felt were their two best stories from the previous academic year. In total we received 234 such nominations. (A few schools opted to send in only one story.) Guest editor Carol Shields has selected twenty-two stories for the 1998 anthology.

Carol Shields proved a diligent and conscientious guest editor who provided astute readings and suggestions. We would like to extend to Carol our sincere thanks. Thanks also to the program directors, program administrators, and students who worked so hard to make this project a continuing success. Our editor, Penny Kaganoff, played an integral role in the creation of this book and supported us with professional advice as well as warmth and humor. We would also like to thank Penny's assistant, Diana Newman, Jeff Wilson in the Simon & Schuster contracts department, and our families.

—John Kulka and Natalie Danford

If you are a director of a graduate creative writing program in the United States or Canada that was not included in this edition, please send a brief note with your name, university, address, and phone number to:

Penny Kaganoff, Simon & Schuster,
1230 Avenue of the Americas, New York, NY 10020.

INTRODUCTION

by CAROL SHIELDS

IF A SOCIETY IS the sum of its choices, of all we admire and select and consume, then we ought to be able to take the temperature of our immediate state-of-the-moment culture by consulting the major best-seller lists: the ten top CDs, movies, TV programs, and, most tellingly perhaps, our top-selling books. The easily accessed literary index, showcased each week for us in the press, tells us what reading material is in current demand on our continent, what book lovers are thinking about and expecting when they make their choices and plunk down their dollars. Here, registered in the words of established, successful writers are the clues to our society's modes of expression, its appetites, its concerns. This is where we are, what we have jointly chosen to become.

But if we want to know where society is going in the future, we would be wise to look at the work of our emerging artists. Whether young or middle-aged or unapologetically old, those who are just entering their creative lives are often freer of skepticism than their experienced, publicly sanctioned predecessors and more open to forces beyond a tightly drawn artistic premise. Anything goes, their work seems to announce. Dare me. Trust me this once. I'm at the beginning of my writing life, but right now I've got things to say.

Many of today's fledgling writers absorb their fundamental skills through the medium of creative writing programs that are securely lodged in our colleges and universities, sometimes attached to English departments and sometimes proudly independent. Here apprentice writers meet others who are struggling with the same narrative conundrums, and here they hope to find a constructive response to their early efforts and the companionship of similarly directed minds.

Creative writing programs are often associated with the sixties and with certain varieties of counterculture initiatives, but, in fact, they have been with us since before mid-century. The Iowa Writers' Workshop was launched in 1939, and in 1940 Johns Hopkins established its acclaimed writing program. And so when we talk about teaching creative writing, we are speaking about an "idea" that is sewn into our educational fabric today. The concept of teaching writing is no longer flaky or frightening, though its worth, even now, is sometimes questioned.

Can you really teach people to write, it is asked. In response, one might pose a parallel question: do we really teach people to be philosophers or mathematicians? Don't we, instead, hand over to our budding philosophers and mathematicians a few basic tools that permit them to self-evolve?

Perhaps what we really mean when we say we can't teach writing is that we can't teach someone to be Virginia Woolf. On the other hand, a number of our most accomplished writers were, early in their lives, enrolled in writing courses: Eugene O'Neill, Tennessee Williams, Arthur Miller, Wallace Stegner, and Flannery O'Connor, to name just a few.

Ah, but writing is God-given, it's often said, the implication being that the writer is also God-protected and superhuman, an uncomfortable assumption for most of us these days. Those who reject the God-given thesis sometimes believe that Bohemia is the place to learn to write. But Bohemia, that mythical realm—meaning freedom from compromise and convention, an excited, open state of mind, a portable set of liberties that fertilize the ground from which writers spring—has not much flourished in North America. Something else was clearly needed, but what?

Writers are romantically believed to be seekers of solitude, but in fact they have historically gathered around centers of power. Today in the United States and Canada the university has become one of those power centers, delivering encouragement in the shape of course offerings and informed tutoring. A center of learning, it can be argued, is an appropriate venue for the teaching of writing since it also possesses libraries, bookstores, accommodation, staff, classrooms—and, most important, people who know how to write and who are willing to share their knowledge and intuition with those who are learning. Haven't writers always, in fact, functioned this way—teaching, coaching, mentoring, advising, editing, and influencing other writers—in garrets or coffeehouses or the courts of kings or in country houses, through correspondence, or by the simple dissemination of their books? The place of interaction has shifted; a slight and gradual formalization has occurred—but the process is not radically different from what it has always been.

The early writing programs, perhaps in order to defend their legitimacy in the university, were often rather traditionally organized, using textbooks and assigning letter grades for weekly assignments. They were, in fact, institutions that ran on the gas of criticism rather than creativity. Gradually the workshop evolved, becoming the cornerstone of most creative writing programs, and there are some who believe that this manner of teaching has influenced the way learning has come to be shared in other enlightened—that is, nonhierarchical—disciplines. Basically, workshopping in creative writing programs means that the work of students is read and critiqued by members of the class and by the teacher/writer who acts as a sort of group leader. Ideally, students are not asked to memorize set information; instead they are drawn out, cajoled, persuaded, questioned, nudged, niggled, and encouraged to make a new and personal set of criteria.

If this methodology sounds vaguely, nostalgically familiar, it may be because it gestures toward the methodology of the medieval or even classical university. Obviously, students are not taught *how* to be original, but they are made aware of nonoriginality and they are exposed, though not perhaps systematically, to certain skills involved in writing: setting up a scene and furnishing it, situating a narrative in time and space, controlling the flow of information, creating a mood, and deciding who is telling the story and why.

In 1973 all the teachers of creative writing in colleges and universities in the United States were invited to a conference in Washington, D.C., hosted by the Library of Congress. Five hundred writer/teachers attended, among them such luminaries as John Barth, Wallace Stegner, John Ciardi, and Ralph Ellison. Out of this meeting an official organization of teachers of creative writing was formed—a positive step forward—and the animated discussions between the participants brought to light some disturbing revelations.

The first finding was that only about one percent of creative writing students became writers. The second finding: ninety-nine percent of students were "lured by the glamour of the profession or the desire for money and fame." (I can only suppose that these numbers were arrived at anecdotally rather than statistically.)

Three other discoveries came out of the 1973 meeting. 1. No one knows how to teach writing. 2. In particular, no one knows how to teach the talented. 3. The talentless can be taught only a little.

It might be thought that these dismal conclusions would spell the end of creative writing teaching in America. Exactly the opposite occurred. Despite such alarming perceptions and despite the shrinking markets for fiction, courses in creative writing proliferated, writer-in-residence programs were established in all corners of the country, writers' retreats (often with a writer/teacher available) flourished, and degree-granting writing programs grew in number and in power, and their presence was more and more seen as a sign of prestige for their mother institutions.

Creative writing courses are often the only place in our society where writers can come together. They are our salons, our Left Banks, our wine bars, the laboratories of our literature. Creative writing classes give to students of literature a glimpse of how literature is made, how difficult the process is, and how fragile and fleeting the creative impulse. A certain sharpening of critical ability occurs in these classes, at least some of it self-directed. In addition, writing courses seize upon that compulsion most young people have to write a poem or story, to say something in words that will be entirely their own.

The descriptions of writing courses in college catalogs are often brief and vague, probably deliberately so. For most courses there exists the merest trace of a syllabus, no textbook, no exam, and no attempt among those teaching different sections of a course to standardize the content. This, you might think, is a fairly slippery business. Students registering for creative writing courses are often unaware of what exactly they are buying into and what pedagogical procedures will be followed.

In addition, writing classes tend for some reason to be less homogeneous than other university classes, and so new and unexpected accommodations must be reached. How will an eighteen-year-old youth, fresh from a suburban high school, find something in common with a fifty-year-old man who has been fired from his engineering job, who is freshly divorced, who is a single father, who has recently been hospitalized for a nervous breakdown? (This sounds like a collision out of a soap opera, but it nevertheless occurred in a course I once taught.) Will a twenty-year-old woman, a lover of Stephen King and a fundamentalist Christian, be able to comprehend an ironic, cryptic, emotionally charged short story written by a sixty-year-old woman, the wife of a psychology professor, a woman who has wanted to write for thirty years but felt blocked, blocked even before writing a single word? Will a young man who has written a gothic horror story in which the hero dies by being flushed down the toilet have anything to say to a young woman who has produced a dozen short exquisite prose pieces about the fantasy, the seduction, the necessity—so she says—of her projected suicide?

These random cross-connections serve a social function. Writing classes are, after all, small and intense, and deal frequently with highly personal material. Certain standards of kindness and respect must be established and adhered to, and the civilizing virtues of tact and trust incorporated in the classroom atmosphere. The human transactions that take place are enormously useful, more useful in the long run perhaps than aesthetic transactions.

A total of 234 stories were submitted this year from 119 writing programs, with each program asked to submit the two stories considered the "best." With this kind of rigorous selection, it is no surprise that all the featured stories in this anthology transcend what we normally think of as apprenticeship writing. As I read I wondered about the ages of the different writers. The fact that several of the stories deal with parents of young children may point to slightly older students, those who have "been there."

There may have been a time in our history when student fiction reflected a commitment to philosophical or political forces, but the stories in this collection tend to be about the self, the lonely or misunderstood self, and the way in which that self fits or fails to fit into family or communal relationships. The superb "Your Own Backyard" by

Adam Marshall Johnson takes us into the heart of a father who has a profoundly disturbed son. Judith Claire Mitchell's "A Man of Few Words" describes just that, a father who learns too late—much too late—how to talk to his children. And "Forager" by Natasha Waxman follows a young man who slowly disengages from mainstream society. On the other hand, the ability to communicate is what rescues both characters in Timothy A. Westmoreland's "Near to Gone," a deceptively simple story of two strangers who share a cup of coffee and a few joints. "Breathe In Breathe Out" by Colleen Conn Dunkle examines the sharp jealousies and ardent love a divorced father feels toward his ex-wife and teenage daughter. The story is funny, moving, well constructed, but with some nicely roughened edges. Melanie Little's "Apnea" is a road story, a father and a seventeen-year-old child attempting to know each other and to set each other free.

Tenaya Rahel Darlington's "Relevant Girl" concerns itself with the obsessive imaginative narratives that live side by side with our real lives, curled up there like a sleeping animal, and impossible to get rid of. In Christopher A. Pasetto's "Waiting for a Crash," a high school student wonders whether his obsession with the paranormal might officially be considered strange. And Athena Paradissis's "Clean" is a story of obsession as well: an ex-alcoholic mother attempts to take control of her life by acts of excessive cleanliness, scrubbing away her uncertainty and learning a new patience. Carolyn Moon's moving story "Through the Timber" is an account of two brothers and their struggle, and ultimate failure, to please a difficult father. Aimee LaBrie looks at two sisters in the painful "Visitation," and the way in which they resent and yet need each other.

Several of these stories are situated in places outside the United States, but there is little sense of calling on the exotic for color and fantasy. Such stories as Christina Milletti's "The Retrofit" (Mexico) and Kiran Desai's "The Toilet and Rampal the Government Official" (India) are embedded in their cultures, and breathe naturally the air of their surroundings. Naama Goldstein's "Pickled Sprouts" is solidly set in Israel, while "Durian" by Sheldon Robert Walcher places an American couple in Asia, where their sense of dislocation threatens their already tenuous relationship. Foreignness in this story is disturbing, disorienting, a counterforce to reason and order.

It is a gift to be able to make a reader feel at home in the unfamiliar; a friend of mine once said she couldn't read about different cultures unless she was first given an understanding of "how people move around in a house," an observation that I find remarkably astute. In Nelinia Cabiles's story "Waiting for the *Kala*," we are introduced to a troubled Filipino family living in Hawaii, and are made to feel and know the texture of their home life. Julie Otsuka's wonderfully patient "Evacuation Order No. 19" finds its space in a Japanese-American household.

It was a pleasure to discover how many of these beginning writers document the importance of work in our lives. Work, though it occupies most of our waking hours, is often left out of fiction; dramatic events are relegated to weekends or evenings, and a character's job or profession noted but not felt in all its particularity and dailiness. Andrew J. McCann's extraordinary "Zenith" is a genuine work story with the details of a machinist's task made utterly convincing. It is also about the way in which we relate to work and to that old orthodoxy of doing a good job. This writer dares to write about the pleasure of working well, of making something that no one else can make, and how this passion forces one man to the margin of his work society.

This batch of twenty-two stories shows us dozens of carefully described job holders. A policeman who works in a zoo. A taxi driver and tour guide. A man hired to guard a live wire. An actor, an obstetrician/gynecologist. A fisherman, a podiatrist, a lawyer. There are farmers and civil servants and a cafeteria cook who is a death camp survivor. Their work does not define them, but it does give them context, and at the same time thickens their sense of being alive on the page.

Two stories, Greg Changnon's "How the Nurse Feels" and Wendi Kaufman's "Helen on 86th Street," share, by coincidence, similar subject matter: participation in school plays. But the stories take different directions. "How the Nurse Feels" illuminates the nature and mystery of roles and how one can imagine one's way to a braver place. "Helen on 86th Street" is about a child whose immediate wish to star in the school play is granted, but whose real longing for her absent father is denied.

There was a time when teachers of creative writing, myself included, took out their chalk and drew the traditional narrative arc on the blackboard, the old familiar line of rising action, and then the denouement. Students dutifully copied this design into their notes and attempted to analyze their stories, guided by the correctness of its curvature. I can't remember just when this pattern began to feel false. One day I was drawing the diagram on the board and it suddenly looked like nothing more than a bent coat hanger. Perhaps it was the cry of feminist writers who rejected the traditional model, describing it as the ejaculatory method of storytelling. Or perhaps I began to see so many fine stories that allowed themselves completely other shapes.

One such story in this anthology is Daniel Noah Halpern's "The Golem's Record." Four people sitting at a card table are deconstructed before our eyes into the broken and buried stories of the past. The bright threads of lost narratives flash on and off an imaginary consciousness—which gives them coherence. The story is daringly told, as though the writer has decided he can trust his reader to jump with him through a series of fanciful hoops.

Richard Elson's "The Shooting" also breaks rules. It is the story of a boy who accidentally shoots and kills a friend. Traditionally, the point of view in this kind of story would be confined either to the guilty boy or to the father who comforts his dying son. Here the narrative eye moves back and forth, almost as though the boy is imagining how the father is thinking. The extremely subtle conflict in this story is not between people but between states of consciousness and degrees of forgiveness. The writer's risk pays off in emotional power.

Christina Milletti's brilliant "The Retrofit" embraces humor, irony, satire, and sadness, and although it is a "well-made" story with a beautiful sense of rondure, it breaks the rules by placing one foot in the real world and the other in the land of fable. The story's form becomes a container for the idea it holds, and the reader arrives at the end grateful to have spent time in the hands of a genuine magician.

We are almost certain to be hearing more from these twenty-two beginning writers. Their work winks with intelligence. The voices are fresh and vigorous, and the narrative lines push boldly against traditional imperatives. These are stories we can settle into and, at the same time, stories that will change our lives.

Judith Claire Mitchell

University of Iowa

A MAN OF FEW WORDS

Only minutes after he died at age seventy-eight Ike Grossbart had come to understand he could enjoy, one more time, a pleasure from his life. It was up to him to choose which pleasure that would be. Ike was surprised and grateful. He had been expecting earthworms and dirt. Instead—or at least, first—here was a squirt of whipped cream to top off his time on earth.

He mulled over the various joys and delights he had known. He did not want to choose precipitously. But deciding was difficult, and made even more so by a conversation he'd had only hours before and could not shake from his head.

"Ike, remember the knishes they had at Zalman's in Flatbush?" his brother-in-law had asked. "Wouldn't you love one of those now?"

"One of those now would kill me," Ike had said. His voice was near gone. He'd never imagined he'd use up his voice over the course of his life as if it were ink in a pen. Thank goodness he'd been a man of few words. "All that salt and fat," he managed to rasp. "Anyway, the best knishes were from Dubin's."

"Dubin's?" Ike's daughter asked. "Was I ever there?"

His wife had looked up from her crossword puzzle. She was sitting in the recliner the orderlies had dragged in so she could spend nights in the hospital room. "What are you saying?" she said. "Are you saying the best knishes weren't from Yonah Shlissel's?"

Yonah Shlissel's. Of course. The two men murmured the name

out loud, and sighed as if recalling the most beautiful woman they'd ever laid eyes on. It was a sigh of fond remembrance but also of regret. The beautiful woman was long gone, and Ike and his brother-in-law so old they had to be reminded she'd existed at all.

"What made that place so good?" Ike's daughter asked.

"I heard Yonah had a secret ingredient," his wife said. "Once I heard oil imported from the old country. Another time I heard potatoes from some farm out in Jersey."

"Nah, it was water they pumped in special," the brother-in-law said. He was the kind of man who had to let people know he was smarter than they were. Ike had never understood how his sister endured this man's blather. Nevertheless, she had, and so, though his sister was gone, the man remained family.

Ike had shrugged. "All I know is my wife is as usual right. No one matched Yonah Shlissel's potato knishes."

It was a few hours later—the brother-in-law gone home, the daughter in the cafeteria having a late-night snack, the Grossbarts asleep—that death came for Ike. *Yitzchak ben Moshe,* death sang like a rabbi honoring a congregant by calling him to the pulpit to bless the Torah. Ike left the hospital room quietly, obediently. He was thankful he hadn't been asked to say good-bye to his wife; he could not imagine anything more difficult.

Now he wishes he could ask her advice. She'd been the wise one, the expert on emotions and pleasure and pain. "Life is so full of heartache and loss," she used to say to the kids. "Whenever the chance for happiness comes along, I want you to fill both hands."

Ike's hands are empty. It's not that there's a dearth of pleasures to choose from. He just doesn't know which one to pick. He considers weddings, his own, his son's. He considers Bar Mitzvahs, his own, his son's. Birthday parties, even days with the family at the beach. But knishes keep pushing these memories out of his head.

You are spending far too much energy chasing knishes away, he scolds himself. Don't be so frivolous. Food has always meant far too much to you.

Although he was gaunt when he died, he had the clogged arteries and overburdened heart of a fat man. He had always loved to eat. From growing up poor, he supposed. Columns of gingersnaps, spoonfuls of peanut butter, and the skins of barbecued chickens, which he'd pull off the birds and roll in his fingers as if he were rolling a cigarette and then noisily slurp down the way the kids sucked spaghetti.

Jewish food, the food his mother used to make, was his weakness. He once encountered an anti-Semite who called Jews not kikes or sheenies but bagels. You goddam Jew-bagel, he'd say. Ike had found it hard to take offense. After his second heart attack, only days before, he'd offered the floor nurse five dollars to sneak a bagel to him. I'm at death's door, he thought when she refused, what can it matter? Finally, when neither the nurse nor his wife was looking, his daughter brought him a jumbo deluxe from Weinstein's, the crusts sticky with brown onions and the soft-toasted middle smeared with at least an inch of cream cheese. The two of them had shared it. It had been a foolish thing to do. His daughter was already fat enough and just look where it had gotten him. Still, that had been a nice moment, maybe as nice as any.

Can a dead man blush? Apparently, yes. Shame on you, he thinks. He will not go out a glutton, a pig. He'll select a meaningful moment of his life to enjoy again, a memory sweet enough to sustain him through eternity. If now is not the time for meaningful memories, then someone should tell him when is.

Yet as he reflects and ponders he realizes his difficulty in choosing is compounded by the number of precious memories that sustain him already. He has not made love to his wife in fifteen years, for instance, but now, when he thinks of her, he feels sated and sleepy as if they last lay together moments ago. He can taste her mouth, feel her soft, round belly and the breasts that, as if he had been granted a wish by a genie, had grown larger with each of the children she gave him. To seek even one more time with his wife strikes him as greedy and, in a way, superfluous. She is with him still. Leave well enough alone, he thinks.

He considers, too, reliving the day his youngest was born—the boy, a son. As the baby came into the world, Ike had paced in the waiting room down the hall. He smoked a few packs of Luckies, ate three or four Hershey bars. It was what men did in those days. He was glad for it. He had no interest in participating in birth the way fathers had to now—catching the baby, cutting the cord, seeing one's beloved wife open and as red as the meat of a plum. But to go back once again to the waiting room, that might be nice. To hear once again *Mr. Grossbart, it's a boy.*

Yet just thinking about his son's birth causes the same explosion of pride beneath his ribs that he experienced forty-one years ago. An explosion he had not felt when his daughter had been born seven years prior. An explosion, he now realizes, not all that different from a minor heart attack. *Mr. Grossbart, it's a boy,* and his heart twisted like a wrung dishrag. He felt fear and pain; he felt small and inadequate—mortal. It was as if his body, aware that his head and his tongue were too stunned to thank God in words, began to express his awe and gratitude through trembling and aching and terror. And then, as if God heard and responded to his body's prayer—for that's what it had been, a prayer spoken by flesh and bones—Ike's heart had been soothed. Comfort and hope and optimism had rested on his shoulder like a reassuring hand.

It was the most powerful moment of his life. Perhaps for that reason he does not want to live it again. If his son could overhear these thoughts, Ike knows, he would feel only rejection. He would resent Ike's decision to choose a different moment to return to. He would not understand the love in this decision.

Other good days—the birth of his chubby, uncomplicated daughter, the day Hitler got his, the morning in the middle of the Depression when Ike found a twenty on a subway platform—none of those other good days have faded for him, either.

He is getting nervous now. What if there is only so much time in which to choose? Maybe a buzzer will go off soon. An egg timer might ring. He racks his brain. It's still full of knishes. Perhaps, he thinks, there's a reason for this.

So at last he decides, why not? Why not choose a Yonah Shlissel knish? That overstuffed pillow, yellow as gold, salty as sea air. Why not choose to relive the simplest pleasure of all? He'll have a knish, but before he does, he'll bow his head, recite the proper blessing so God will know he is thankful for even small pleasures. And then he will call it a day.

The Lower East Side has been given over to colored people. West Africans and Haitians and Jamaicans, dark-skinned Cubans. The buildings shake from drumming and radios and languages. The sidewalk is broken, and the street with its potholes resembles the soles of a poor man's shoes.

When Ike was a boy, the air here smelled of garlic pickles and sauerkraut. Now the air reeks from fumes expelled by idling delivery trucks and city buses. When Ike was a boy, the stores here sold felt derbies and fresh fish and used books. Now they sell knock-off designer sneakers, vinyl leather jackets, and T-shirts with dirty sayings across the front.

This is why he has avoided the area for decades. He feels discouraged now that he's here, a little downhearted as he keeps walking east. He thinks about the other, better choices he could have made—even the day Kennedy squeaked by Nixon might have been better, even the first time he watched TV he felt more excitement. How about his first car, the gray Plymouth, that boat.

Then suddenly, his feet stop short. If he'd been the Plymouth, his brakes would have squealed.

"*Kineahora*," he whispers.

He is standing in front of Yonah Shlissel's. It's there—here—right where he left it, right where it ought to no longer be.

His no-good heart pounds. He hesitates. In his head, he counts to three, and on three he pulls open the dark heavy door. He steps tentatively into a vestibule with a wooden slat bench used not for sitting but for piling. Even now it's covered with stacks of Jewish newspapers and political pamphlets. He takes a breath. With a trembling hand, he turns the mock crystal knob of the next heavy door. He steps inside. It's the same. It's Yonah's.

If earlier that day his wife had challenged him to describe Yonah Shlissel's, Ike would have replied that he couldn't remember what he'd had that morning for breakfast, much less the interior of a restaurant he last saw fifty years ago. But seeing it now, he knows every detail is one hundred percent correct. The wooden floors, scuffed and warped. The round wooden tables, each with a waiter's pad shoved beneath one leg to quiet its rocking. He remembers that—yes—there were no windows, yes, the place was dimly lit, yes, the waiters ran about in clean white aprons and confided the customers' orders to Yonah in the kitchen as if they were passing along government secrets.

Is it an illusion? A gag? Ike knows hair continues to grow after death, but do dreams continue to spin? He reaches for one of the mints in the bowl by the cash register and chews it cautiously. It's stale. It tastes more like soap than mint. It's the same as ever. The mints, at least, are real.

And now here comes the frowzy, fat hostess in her polka-dot dress. She wears a brown wig meaning she is married, this battle-ax, maybe to Yonah himself. In those days the married women covered their hair when they went out in public. He'd nearly forgotten, but now he remembers and remembers, also, his mother's wig. He remembers it suddenly, fondly, and then with tears that shine but don't fall. His mother's wig also was brown, always askew, and so cheap he could see the stitches holding the strands to its net crown.

"Party of, what, only one?" The fat woman is annoyed. Ike remembers this woman now as clearly as he remembers the wobbly tables and soapy mints. When he was a child she frightened him. Now he is a seventy-eight-year-old dead man and she still gives him the heebie-jeebies.

Why is she so aggravated with him? Did his wish to return here disturb her own rest? Had she been forced to rouse herself, stretch her bare bones, tunnel up through six feet of beetles and ruin, all the while bobby-pinning that wig to her head, just so she could get to Yonah's in time to seat him, this negligible party of one?

"Poppa, why are they so grouchy here?"

"Did we come to make friends or have lunch?"

Yes, Ike thinks. Yes, he is only one. Yes, he's alone. We come in alone, go out the same way. God knows he wishes that wasn't how it worked. God knows already he misses his wife, wishes she were at his side. Or no, he doesn't wish that. That would be wishing her dead. He wishes he knew what one had the right to wish for under these circumstances. He might have wished not to go back into his life but forward into his death where his loved ones who'd left him might be waiting.

He says nothing, of course. He is too shy to speak, too tongue-tied. And what would be the point of philosophizing with Mrs. Shlissel? The woman has been dead at least half a century. To her nothing he could say about death would be news. To him everything about death—even the fact of it—is a revelation. It came as a shock. Of course all the time he knew. All his life he knew everyone gets old, sick, dies. It wasn't exactly top secret. But somehow all along he figured nobody really meant *him*. Not him, not little Yitzchak Grossbart. But of course, that's just who they meant. The proof was in the pudding. Here was little Yitzchak Grossbart standing in a building demolished during the Korean conflict, talking away in his head to a fat dead lady.

She does not even look at him. She waddles to an empty table near the counter intending for him to follow. As he does he thinks that today a woman with such a rump would never wear that skinny cloth belt nor those big white polka dots. His daughter always wore big shirts that skimmed her tush, covered the thighs, and always they were black. "Am I ever going to see you in anything but mourning rags?" he'd once heard his wife ask. A similar comment would have hurt his son's feelings, but his daughter had laughed and said she liked to be comfortable and that black didn't show dirt. Maybe he should have said something then. He didn't mind a girl with a fanny on her. But it had not seemed proper. It had not seemed like something a father should say.

A waiter comes, places a wooden bowl filled with slices of bread—seeded rye, black pumpernickel, braided challah—onto the table. "You need time?" the waiter asks. Ike nods. He needs time.

He cranes his neck so he can see the long cases beneath the counter. A wall of food under glass. Kishke, kasha, kugel. Herring. Greek olives, black and wrinkled like the skin on the hands of the old man sweeping the floors. Lox as pink as flamingo, gefilte fish pocked and slimy, and rows of white fish still sheathed in their gold scales, their dead eyes like opals. And, then, in another case, meat. The salami and franks, the corned beef and pastrami, the tongue. Agents of death all looking as benign as a schoolboy twiddling his thumbs.

The knishes have an entire compartment to themselves not in respect of any dietary law, but rather the same way royalty is given a private box in the concert hall.

Ike sighs. He truly is at Yonah Shlissel's again. It's a miracle and a blessing. It was, he thinks, a pretty good choice. It reminds him of his boyhood, his father, even of something his daughter had said when she'd split that bagel with him. She'd been violating not only the rules of his diet that day, but the rules of her own as well. She was perpetually starving herself, that one, never with any discernible results. She'd inherited his appetite and God knows whose metabolism.

"I'm so bad," she had said, but it was clearly a fine moment for her, maybe the moment she'd return to someday. She'd rolled her eyes and licked her fingers. "Oh, God," she'd said. "I've died and gone to heaven."

His time is up; the waiter is back, tapping pencil against pad. "I haven't got all day, mister," he says. "You want to order before it's tomorrow?"

Ike remembers the waiter now, too. Abrupt and arrogant. A Shlissel for sure. Always acting like there's somewhere more important he has to rush off to.

"Pardon me," Ike says. "One potato knish."

The waiter scurries off. Ike looks around at the other customers. Are they props, are they real men, or are they his comrades, other dead Jews who have chosen Yonah's? They are mostly old men, he sees. Many of them are reading the *Forward*. The newspapers smudge their fingers and conceal their faces. It's from seeing their hands that Ike knows the men are old. Brown spots stain old hands the way rust stains old cars.

When they were youngsters, he and his sister had called such hands old lady hands. Old lady hands, as if a man's hands never withered, never wrinkled, never became bent and blue with veins. After a bath, he and his sister would show their wrinkled, pruney fingers to each other. His sister's singsong taunt: *Yitzchak's got old lady hands.*

He'd held her old lady hands when she died. She'd passed a decade ago, beaten by the same ailment that got him years later . . . minutes earlier. A heart whose muscles sagged from working too hard for so many years until it could no longer beat, and slowly came to a stop. It was how hearts were designed, like old-fashioned windup toys.

He had held her hands and thought about singing her song back to her: *Look now who's got old lady hands.* Not as a taunt, of course. More like a lullaby. He hoped she'd remember the time they were so young they could bathe naked together, laugh at old age. *Wisenheimer,* she'd maybe have whispered. *Ishkabibble.* These were the worst things she'd ever called him. Much nicer than asshole, which is what his son used to call his daughter when she teased him too hard.

Ike had not sung to his sister. Something had stopped him. He'd worried she might not have remembered. It would have been terrible had she taken it wrong. So he'd kept quiet. What does one say at such moments? Is anyone so wise they know? Certainly not Ike, not some-one like Ike. As his sister passed on, he squeezed her hands and thought, She looks so much like Mama. This had comforted him. Anyone in heaven who took one look at his sister would know just who to direct her to.

Again there are tears in his eyes. He is able to blink them away. He tells himself to stop. You are squandering your moment, he thinks. It's supposed to be a moment of pleasure.

So he focuses on the task at hand. He prepares for the meal to come. He gets up, goes to the sink in the corner of the restaurant, washes his hands. In his own home he and his wife were never so observant, but here it seems fitting. He returns to his table and tears a piece of challah. He considers his life. He'd lived it as right as he knew how. He loved his wife, had a daughter who was good-natured and smart, had a beloved son he could name after his father. He had grief and loss; he had modest pleasures and joys. He never would have asked for more but now he has been given more, just a little bit more. He recites the blessing for bread.

Twice a year his father took him to Delancey Street to buy a new suit. Once in the fall for Rosh Hashanah; again in the spring for Pesach. And then after, as a reward for not bellyaching during the fitting, his father would take him to Yonah Shlissel's. Just the two of them, father and son, twice a year. Just the men in the family.

Like the old men here now, his father hid behind a newspaper. Ike, six or seven, pretended the paper was a shield that made persons on either side of it invisible and invincible.

Six or seven, he ate his knish with his fingers. He peeled the thin crust apart and then, like the boy in the nursery rhyme, he stuck in his thumb. But he did not pull out a plum. He merely pulled out that same thumb coated with hot mashed potato. Nor did he say, What a good boy am I! He knew this was not something a good boy would do. He would not have done this in front of his mother. But his father, absorbed, never noticed.

His table manners were never what they should have been. He was the child of immigrants, unschooled and unsophisticated. If he'd grown up during his son's era instead of his own, he'd have blamed this shortcoming on his father. *I'd stick my thumb into a knish and you wouldn't say boo; how was I supposed to learn better? No wonder I was never asked to join a fancy men's eating club.*

No one cares about table manners at Yonah Shlissel's. Everyone here slurps, sighs, grunts, belches. We are descendants of peasants, Ike thinks not without pride. Children of immigrants, adventurers, survivors. And this our reward for feeling no shame. This place of our people. This wonderful repast. Manna from Yonah's. Something his children have never tasted, will never taste.

His daughter would have loved it here, he thinks. She would have run about, pressing her nose to the glass cases. *What's that? What's that? Let's try some of this.* He never brought her here, though he remembers one time taking her to that same children's clothing shop. His son was an infant with the croup, the Holy Days were around the corner, and the girl needed a new dress. Ike remembers sitting in a chair feeling useless and bored while his daughter emerged from the dressing room in one matronly purple dress after another, baby fat distorting the lines of each one, her head lowered—sulking only emphasized the double chins—and the saleslady shaking her head. "She has a bit of a belly, doesn't she?" the woman had said, and Ike had shrugged.

By the time his son was old enough both the clothing shop and Yonah Shlissel's were gone. It didn't matter. His son would have despised Delancey Street. His son despised his own heritage. It was too bad, then, that it had been his son who inherited Ike's face, the same face Ike had inherited from his own father. The huge ears that winged from the head and had been ridiculed even during Gable's heyday. The narrow horned beak rising between bushy brows, bestowing a cross-eyed and angry appearance. Those three faces repeated generation to generation had proclaimed, probably too loudly, their lineage. Those faces had gotten each of them beaten up, one time or another, by tough Catholic boys in prim navy blue uniforms.

Still, it had never occurred to Ike to try to change his face. He'd never really tried to change much about himself. When he married his wife he had warned her. He was not a plant who, with water and sunlight, would bloom and grow into a flowering thing of beauty. He was a homely, hard-working, straightforward man who felt silly saying honey bunch or sweetie pie. He called his wife *fleegle*— Yiddish for chicken wing.

His son believed in change. His son changed his name from Grossbart to Garner. Then he changed his religion. "So what should we call him now?" Ike had asked his wife, "Mahatma Garner?" His son had changed even his face. His son had his ears pasted back. He had his nose shaved and trimmed as if it were a mustache rather than hard bone and cartilage.

The boy had shown up at their house one Sunday modeling the new face, preening like a woman in a hat. Ike had said nothing. He left the kitchen, shut the bedroom door with more noise than required. "It's my money," the boy hollered after him, "and my face."

Ike lay on his bed, turned on a ball game with the remote. He closed his eyes.

He didn't object to the way his son spent his money. But the rest of what his son had hollered up at him . . . how could the boy think his face belonged to him only? When his son studied his new reflection, whose child did he see?

When his wife joined him in bed that night, Ike said, "You know, *fleegle*, sometimes, I catch a glimpse of myself in a mirror when I don't expect to, and I think, 'Hey, that guy looks like a member of my family.' I like that. I take pleasure in being from this family." A veritable speech, an outburst.

His wife had said, "And why are you telling this to me?"

"There's a point in telling him?" Ike never mentioned it again. He said nothing about it even though it hurt to look at that face. Revised, his son looked not like a Grossbart, not like a Garner, not like a Jew or the Hindu he claimed to be, but like an owl with a big round head, angry yellow brown eyes and, lost in the middle, a tiny snipped beak.

And yet, in the end, it was the boy who refused to look at Ike. During those terrible months after the boy's marriage ended and he'd moved back home, he refused to sit at the same table with Ike.

It was his table manners the boy objected to. "It's disgusting," Ike heard his son say. "He just sits there and shovels it in. No wonder he can't make conversation, with his mouth stuffed like that. It makes me sick. I'll eat in my room."

Like a servant, Ike's wife carried the boy's plate—the boy; the boy was thirty-six—up to his old bedroom, where once again he was living, holed up like a hermit, the room a mess as it had been when he truly was a boy, all his clothes on the floor, dirty Kleenexes and rotted banana peels overflowing the trash basket, and the mattress he slept on bare, not a sheet, not even a pad, and yet this was where he wanted to be. Sometimes he did not come out for days, at least not while Ike was awake.

Sometimes the creak of floorboards, the snap of a light switch woke Ike before sunrise. He lay in bed and told himself that another father would get out of bed and go downstairs. Another father would pull up a chair, pour two strong drinks, get the kid to open up. *Talk to me, son, tell me what's wrong.* But after that, what does one say at such a time? Besides, as the father of this boy, Ike knew getting up and going downstairs would be futile. There was nothing anyone could say to this boy. Not even Ike's wife knew what to say. She'd say, "You want at least a mattress pad, honey?" and the kid would look at her like she'd accused him of child murder.

Ike had been grateful for whatever snippets of time his father had managed to give him. At Yonah Shlissel's, Ike sucked potato off his thumb. He blew air through his straw turning his glass of celery tonic into a bubbling caldron. His father said nothing. Ike balanced on two legs of his chair and worked up some jokes, the funniest being a variation of an old one that, to set the stage, he now told his father. "Hey, Poppa." A grunt. "Poppa, what's black and white and red all over?" "What?" his father asked, still hidden behind the newspaper shield. Ike gave the answer. He gave it loud so his voice would penetrate newsprint and Yiddish. "A newspaper." "Mmm-hmmm," his father said. "Hey, Poppa." His father grunted. "Hey, Poppa. Over all red and white and black is what?" A second grunt. "The Jewish newspaper," Ike said. "Get it? On account of you read it backwards."

"Very good," his father said. "Be quiet. Eat your knish."

Whenever Ike felt sad because his father was not conversing with him, was not asking about school or laughing at Ike's jokes or telling a few of his own, then Ike would think the following: *the two men shared a companionable silence.*

From what radio show or dime novel he had gotten that phrase, he had no idea. But it made him feel better to think it. It was the way men behaved together. Not like his sister and mother who babbled endlessly, clucking chickens. Not like women. Men shared companionable silences.

But the silence he shared with his son had not been so companionable, and he thinks now of his grown son returned to the narrow bed of childhood, where he keened like a lost goat, cried to Ike's wife what a terrible father Ike had been. Distant, his son wailed. Withholding.

Like a drill his son's voice bored through the walls of the house Ike had worked his whole life to pay off. Like a jackhammer, the voice of his son—his heir, his devisee—shattered walls into splintery fragments. It made Ike hate the house. It made him see it as flimsy and cheap. "He never played catch with me," Ike's son wept. Crash, a wrecking ball knocking down plaster. "He never took me fishing." Boom, a sledgehammer punching holes in the framing. "He never talked to me about women. How was I supposed to know what to do when Dinah got so unhappy?" Thirty-six and bleating like a goat. "Never once did he say he loved me."

"He's angry?" Ike asked when his wife came to bed.

"At the world," she said. "Don't take it personal."

"Did your parents ever say they loved you, *fleegle*?"

"I'd have dropped dead twice from shock, *fleegle*." She hesitated. "But since he wants to hear it, what could it hurt?"

He couldn't sleep. Had his own father ever tossed him a ball, ever taken him fishing? And he could only thank God his father had never talked to him about women. It would have been excruciating for both of them. His son had seen too many TV fathers on the TV sets Ike had bought through the years, the black-and-white consoles, the big-screen colors, the miniatures you could hold in your hand as you lay on your naked mattress and bleated like a goat. Fathers in ties spouting philosophy whispered into their pasted ears by a team of professional writers.

Nobody fed Ike dialogue. Growing up nobody fed him delusions.

His father had been too busy working double shifts in a factory to be a television father. A teacher in Poland, in Brooklyn Ike's father worked in a dye factory. He came home late and exhausted and his fingernails were tinted blue as the summer sky.

Ike got out of bed. He knocked on his son's bedroom door. No response. He went in anyway. "You really don't know I love you?" he asked. "I know I'm not the father you wanted, but you have to at least know I love you. You have to know that. You're my only son."

"How does a person know what he's never been told?" his son had said. His unfamiliar face was pressed into a bare pillow with a small tear in the side. Little white feathers floated from it, lighthearted and comical.

By the color of fingernails, Ike wanted to say. But he did what he had come to do. "I love you," he said.

"Too little too late," said his son.

The next time Ike saw his daughter, he felt obliged to ask her if she knew he loved her. She shivered and said, "Oh, Pop, please don't." She brought up the time he'd taken her to Delancey for that dress. "Remember how that heinous saleslady kept harping about how fat I was?" she said. She reddened a little. Ike was not sure if she was embarrassed or angry on behalf of the chubby little girl modeling purple. "And I was so miserable," she said, "until finally you jumped up and picked out that beautiful ivory smock with the shirred bodice and scalloped hem? And I remember thinking, My father knows how to make me look pretty. My father knows what I look like. No one else in this world saw me the way you did. That's how you told me you loved me."

Ike tried to remember the day. He remembered the chair he sat in, he remembered checking the clock on the wall, he remembered the ball game he wanted to get home for, to watch on TV.

"It was such a special moment for me," his daughter said, still red-faced, a girlish blush. "Really, the best. I have that dress still. Can you believe it? In a box in an attic, the way some women preserve their wedding gowns." She was looking at him smiling, expecting something.

"Still, I hope someday you get married," Ike said.

It was a nice speech she made. Maybe she'd make the same speech over his grave. Later that same day his memory finally dredged up the dress. He'd been impatient. He wanted to get home to that ball game, to his new baby boy. The ivory dress was the only one left on the rack she hadn't already tried on and rejected.

At last. The waiter has placed the knish before him. It sits on a pristine white plate. It glistens with oil. Ike pierces the center with the tines of his fork. From the pricks in its belly come perfume and heat.

He cuts off a piece with the side of his fork, carries it up to his lips. It is steaming. It is too hot to eat. He blows on it. His breath is not yet chill enough to cool it.

He could have brought the girl here. The day they picked out the dress, Yonah Shlissel's had still been standing. They could have walked here, her dimpled hand in his, and he could have bought her one of these potato dumplings, could have called her potato dumpling, a little joke between the two of them. He could have told her jokes.

It had never crossed his mind. Yonah Shlissel's had been for the men in the family. It had not crossed his mind. There was a ball game on TV he wanted to watch. He was waiting to take the boy. By the time the boy was old enough, Yonah Shlissel's was gone.

The boy would have hated it anyway. Even had he brought the boy here, the boy never would have returned on his own, certainly would not be here now.

Ike blows again on the knish. He thinks, I had a boy who heard nothing in silence that was rich with meaning, and a girl who heard everything in silence that was nothing but silence. Which child was more foolish?

Which child, he wonders, was he? He remembers visiting his own father weeks before the old man's death. His daughter, a teenager then, had come along. His father, who lived in a not-so-hot neighborhood, had complained he couldn't sleep. "It's the *blue-ers*," he grumbled, "up all night playing their radios."

"What's that, a *blue-er*?" Ike's daughter had asked.

"Well, you can't call them *shvartzers* anymore," his father said. "They know what it means."

The girl had smiled. "We'll buy you earplugs," she'd said. "You can't stop people from playing music. You know what God says. Make a joyful noise unto the Lord."

"He says, too, 'Be silent and know that I'm God.'"

Ike had considered engraving those words on his father's headstone. He is certain the pleasure his father chose to reclaim had been silence. Perhaps the late hour when the kids on the street finally turned off their music. That moment of peace before sleep comes. Ike knows at least this much—his father had not returned here to the site of their twice-yearly father and son lunches. He has already scanned the room for blue fingernails, hoping, finding none.

In the reverent quiet of Yonah Shlissel's, Ike puts down his fork. It chimes when it touches the wooden table. The waiter looks up, comes over as if summoned. "Something wrong with your knish, mister?"

Ike gestures for the waiter to lean closer. "I think I made the wrong choice," Ike whispers.

The waiter clearly has never before heard such a thing. He frowns. "You can never go wrong with a Yonah Shlissel potato knish," he tells Ike.

"I completely agree, but I think maybe still I want something else."

"What do you mean something else? You already ordered."

Ike wishes again he knew the rules of wishing. Who makes the rules? Is there someone he can talk to? What is the point—this is what he wants to know—what point is there in experiencing again a joy from a life now complete? Better, one should be able to return and rectify an error. One should be allowed to meet with departed loved ones, brainstorm, figure out how to improve things for the grandchildren. Better yet, one should be able to hover over loved ones still living and guide them a little.

If he could do that, he'd return to his son, steer him toward simple pleasures. He is concerned that the boy will have no pleasurable moment to return to someday.

Not true, Ike thinks. He remembers his son as a child—baseball games, roller skates, Schwinns, picnics. Pleasure after pleasure. Sitting in sunlight. If Ike had made a mistake, it was not his failure to shout his love. It was his failure to teach the boy how to say "Boy, oh boy, that sun feels good on the back, doesn't it?"

Now a short man, a bald-headed man in a stained apron is walking Ike's way. He is muscular and sweaty, a man with glittering eyes and a scowl, someone who, despite his scant height, Ike would not wish to anger or fight.

"I hear you don't like my food," the man says.

Yonah Shlissel, Ike thinks. He has never laid eyes on Yonah Shlissel before. He is in awe. It's like meeting a celebrity—Joe DiMaggio striding up to your table. At the same time, there's a part of him wanting to laugh. He is picturing the Shlissel family, this stunted chef, the fat woman in polka dots, the crotchety waiter.

"It's not that I don't like your food," Ike says. "God knows it's not that. It's just that I was thinking I need to be somewhere else."

"What, you got an appointment with Roosevelt to bring world peace?"

Ike shrugs, tries to smile as if he and Yonah were pals, joking.

"You got a cure for the common cold maybe? You have to run and share it with all of mankind?"

"You're the one with the cure for the common cold," Ike says. He means to be ingratiating, disarming. "Your matzo ball soup, right?"

It works. Yonah softens. "So, just to make conversation, where do you think you should be instead of my place?"

"There's this kid's clothing store around here," Ike says. "Somewhere near here. My daughter is trying on dresses. Or will be. Or might be. I don't know. I got to go there in case. I need to hand her an ivory smock."

"She can't pick out a smock herself?"

"She's a kid. She needs me to find it for her. She doesn't have the sense of herself that I do. You know what I mean."

Yonah shakes his head. "I'm not one for fashion. I'm a cook, plain and simple." He is considering. Then he says, "You'd rather hand a kid a dress than eat my food?"

"I want to see the look on her face," Ike says. "I want to say how pretty she looks."

At that Yonah laughs. It is not an especially pleasant laugh.

"All right, all right," Ike says. "You're right. It would never come out of this mouth. I've never been Mr. Smooth. But I want at least to look at her like . . ."

He wants to look at her with love this time. He doesn't want his daughter to end up the foolish one. But Yonah's laughter has made Ike self-conscious. He can't think. Words stop coming into his head.

He can't form the thought. Just sits there and feels it and doesn't know how to say it.

Yonah sighs. "The customer," he says, "is not always right." He takes the white plate back to the kitchen.

Ike sits very still, not sure what to do next, aware that now he has nothing.

Then the waiter returns with two packages—white butcher paper, a bit oily, tied with red-and-white string, the kind of string that came wrapped around the box when Ike's wife brought bakery cake as a present for friends.

"From Mister Shlissel," the waiter says. He sounds crabby and put-upon. "Potato knish to go. He says you should give one to your daughter, she should know how good they are."

The waiter holds the packages out to Ike. Ike takes one in each hand.

Out on Delancey Ike walks past stores and loitering youth. He doesn't remember the name of the dress shop. Pinsky's, he thinks. Maybe Pincus's. He's not sure if he will find it or when or where. He has no idea what time it is, whether he sat in Yonah's for minutes or decades. He doesn't know what else to do now but walk. It's a nice enough day. The smell of the gift-wrapped knishes he carries is stronger than the bus fumes. The smell of good simple food envelops him. The promise of tasting it sometime soon gives him the strength to go on forever.

Kiran Desai
Columbia University

THE TOILET AND RAMPAL THE GOVERNMENT OFFICIAL

Rampal thought there was no sight more pleasing to the eye than that of two young ladies riding their bicycles home from the government school. Their uniforms were such a dazzling white, so crisp and starched; their *dupattas* flew out behind them in swollen, undulating waves; their hair was shiny and braided into beautiful, stiff loops about their ears. Aluminum lunch boxes were fastened onto the seats of the old black bicycles that they pedaled. They clattered and thundered up and down the slopes, between the banks of spicy ginger lilies and blazing poinsettia. *Tring. Tring.* They pressed hard on their metal bells, twisting and turning the handlebars to avoid the steaming cowpats.

Although he had almost reached his destination, Rampal advised the taxi driver to slow down. "Why must you always rush. *Paaaaw. Paaaaw. Paaaaw.* Blowing your horn everywhere. Giving me a headache. Where is the hurry? Please think a little before you do all your Rambo-style driving, otherwise, you wait and see, both of us will be sitting crying together in the gutter."

"*Arre!*" The driver threw up his hands. "First you tell me go fast.

Then you tell me go slow. One minute this. One minute that. Hoooo!" he snorted and spat out of the window. But Rampal only leaned back out to enjoy the sight of these two women who so delightfully avoided his smiles and winks, fixing their eyes upon the rows of hills that climbed layer upon layer, way up into the sky.

"Hello, Dolly!" he shouted out encouragingly. "Hello, Sweetie! What are your names? One. Two. How are you?"

As a newly employed member of the Indian government, he made it a point not to shout at young women on their bicycles, but today he was jubilant. He thought of the others who had just joined the Department of Administrative Service, all his colleagues setting off, just like him, on their first postings as junior members of the staff. Rintoo. Pintoo. Micky. Pappadum. Leaving the comfort and excitements of New Delhi. The college samosa stand, the Gaylord Restaurant with its mango-flavored ice cream and its spring rolls, the motorcycle trips to Lodhi Gardens for cigarettes and beer and karate practice under the silk cotton trees, the embarrassment of the ballroom dancing on Friday nights at the club. He thought of them making their way to their assigned towns, stranded in the vast, barren dustiness of the plains, far from everything but the summer sun that blazed always directly overhead. "You are the one with all the luck," they had accused him bitterly. "All the connections, too." Rampal breathed in the clear mountain air, his lungs so full of its lightness, his heart so full of joy he would not have been surprised at all had he found himself rising like a cloud to puff up and sail triumphantly over the mountains. Unusually fortunate, the Rampal family could boast of three sons and, determined not to be outdone by any other family of good name, it had been decided with unanimous approval from the whole clan that one would be a doctor, one an engineer, and one a government official. The two older sons had passed every science exam with such nonchalance and ease that it became inevitable that Rampal, with his report card crowded with C's and D's, was destined to join the Indian Government Service. His uncle, his father's best friend, and his brother-in-law all worked in influential departments; Rampal had slipped in easily, his file slithering from a pile of hundreds into the right pair of hands. It was entirely natural that he should join them and even more natural that he should be sent not to some dreary, miserable town, but up high in the apricot orchards of the Himalayas, where the monsoons were plentiful and the climate benign. "No running water, of course," they warned him, "but the cook will get it from the spring every morning in buckets."

"Electricity at least there must be?" he ventured. "Ha, ha," they had laughed delightedly and slapped him on the back. "What electricity? *Arre, yaar. Citywallah!* No electricity. No light-wyte. No disco party. No movie-shoovie. Whenever the wires are put up there are so many illegal connections, the whole line goes phut. Or the rains come and boom, everything goes."

But to make it as comfortable for him as possible, they sent him off with the car trunk full of cans of ham roll and baked beans. Also in his bags were ointments for sprains and mosquito bites, tablets and tonics and remedies in brown, red, and yellow for disorders of the stomach, for coughs and colds, for headaches, sleeplessness, and lethargy. Bottles of whiskey and rum too, bought especially from the English Wine and Beer Shop. "Nothing but local liquor there, *yaar*," they had promised. "Don't touch it. Bloody soap and water."

Armed with his supplies, looking at the towering peaks, Rampal felt his spirits rise with every turn of the car up the mountainside. The dubiousness that he had felt grew thin as vapor and disappeared. Surely he was not himself in that vast garbage bin of a city, amid his loud, hee-hawing friends, the mess of people, cars, buses, bullock carts. The noise. The heat. The smell. He needed some peace. Some quiet. And it was only in the villages, he agreed with the prime minister's latest television speech, that one got to know and understand India. He looked out over the hills in front of him and thought how calming the greenery was to his eyes tired of the city's harsh yellow dust. Every face he passed in the village was separate and distinct. Here, people could be appreciated, noticed, and acknowledged with pleasure without being drowned in the blur of a crowd. When they had wound their way up to the top of the mountain and reached the government bungalow, Rampal was pleased to see it was exactly suited to the position of a government employee. It was pink, with sloping tin roofs and a porch crowded about with trees—British hill-station style. It was only later, as he sat relaxing outside, that Rampal thought of looking for the facilities. He finished dipping his Marie biscuit in his milky tea and slurping it up with loud, pleasurable sounds, then ambled into the house poking his head around corners and opening doors. He discovered the bedroom with its water-stained, musty walls. He came upon the storeroom with its rows of brass containers filled with split peas and brown lentils and rice. He confronted the large eyes of a spider clapped against the wall of a closetlike room containing two plastic buckets and an old, dried toothbrush.

At the very end of the corridor he found the kitchen, cavernous and charcoal blackened. The cook was seated in its sooty depths chopping away at vegetables, slice upon slice of radish falling onto a growing pile. "Bathroom?" he answered to Rampal's inquiry. "Vhat room?" He led him to the bedroom and then, seeing the shake of Rampal's head, he opened the door with a flourish upon the two buckets and the spider and the toothbrush. "Yes sir?" Rampal frantically tried to explain, making noises like a fireman's hose, and his face brightened. "*Ai ai ai ai ai ai,*" he said, happy to understand, and led him out of the house, down past the pumpkin plants, the cowshed, and the sour plum trees, pushing the bushes and the overgrown bamboo to reach the very edge of the mountain where stood a wooden shack built on stilts off the side of the cliff. Horrified, Rampal stepped inside as it creaked and swayed alarmingly. A large wooden hole was cut out of the floor. "Very clean, sir," the cook insisted. "Everything is getting washed by the rain down the hill. No problems." The shack was smaller than a closet; dark under the creaking bamboos; but through the hole Rampal, squatting gingerly over it, could see the ground falling away beneath him, bright in the sunlight. He felt dizzy and disoriented, and being the right sort of weight for an imposing government official, with a comfortable round stomach filling his shirt, he lost his balance and went pitching forward to hit his nose on the door. Being hit on the nose, of course, is unpleasant at any time, but Rampal having undertaken a long journey suddenly felt the entire day's fatigue descend upon him and he exploded in a violence of bad temper and sulkiness. "A government bungalow with no toilet," he shouted out in the bamboo grove. "Tell me which government of which other country provides for its employees like our beloved Congress?" The cows that were grazing nearby tossed their horns and backed away. "Am I a bird that I should sit on a twig, swaying above all civilization?" he asked. How dare they treat him in this manner? No water. No electricity. All right. He wouldn't complain. That he wouldn't mind. No hot shower. No TV. No cinema house. No matter. But no toilet! Never would he have imagined such a state of affairs. He stepped into a cowpat and angrily aimed a handful of pebbles at the nearest cow.

Even later, swallowing gulp after gulp of his whiskey, he could not rid himself of his irritation. He tried to think of how beautiful the night was, large, soft, and warm, crowded with stars. He tried to relax his body, to lean back in his lawn chair, to breathe in the scent of the magnolia blossoms that loomed large in the darkness of the nearest trees. He tried to think of the terrible city nights, blazing with tube lights, filled with the dull roar of the night lorries, the sound of the neighbors drunk and quarreling, or sitting out on the rooftops shaking their legs together in time to the evening program on the transistor radio. Here there was silence and only the light of a few kerosene lanterns set in a dim cluster below him where the village houses were. He tried to savor the warmth of the whiskey down his throat, the feel of the grass, tender and soft beneath his toes. But instead, his mind returned again and again to the outhouse over the side of the mountain and to his bathroom at home, pistachio-colored tiles and a commode in smooth, baby pink. Once again, before he slept, he made his way past the pumpkin plants already weighted down by the night dew, to hunt amid the bamboos for the shed: a string of biting, whining insects trailing his kerosene lantern. He promised himself that the very next day he would make an official complaint to the District Commissioner.

Six weeks later, the District Commissioner had not yet replied. The postman crawling snail-like up the slope brought no news to Rampal, waiting anxiously at the top. He was looking thinner. His spectacles loomed over his red, worried eyes. The outhouse floated through his dreams, black holes through which he fell, far, far down, his heart dropping into his stomach that gurgled and sloshed in the throes of indigestion. His appetite had begun to dwindle. The digestive tablets had none of the effects advertised on the back of the package.

It was not long before the outhouse began to emit a stench that rivaled, Rampal thought, the smelliest bazaar of New Delhi. The neighborhood dogs gathered beneath it, intrigued. Often as he perched miserably on top he could hear their squabbling above the buzzing of the bluebottles that, dizzy with excitement, dived in and out of the hole in the floorboards, into the walls, and smack, into him. His shins were raw and scratched from wading through leaves rough as sandpaper, from being entangled in branches that stretched out on purpose, he was sure, to capture him. In the little cubicle, he held his nose and shuddered, hoping he would not faint, bursting out at a gallop when he was done, jumping and leaping to shake himself free of the smell.

The villagers perplexed him greatly with their descent into the terraced fields to relieve themselves every morning, laughing and teasing each other like the flocks of mynahs that also visited the fields at this time for their daily gossip. "Perhaps today my marriage has been settled, perhaps today I shall know the answer. Oh, my heart misses a beat, for today Mr. Pinto has invited me to tea," sang the schoolgirls, happy as bumblebees in the gooseberry bushes, ribbons bobbing cheerfully as he watched from the porch. "Don't understand it," said the missionary from the Mennonite International Caring Committee, M.I.C.C., waiting for signatures on shipment permission slips. "Just two years ago we thought we'd build a whole row of toilets up on the mountain there. Nice and clean, in gray cement. But they wouldn't hear of it. It would be claustrophobic, they said. The atmosphere would be all wrong. Why sit in a box instead of in the open air, among the trees where you can watch the birds and observe the weather?"

The next day, determined to change things with or without the District Commissioner's approval, Rampal ordered a large western-style, Italian model toilet from the shop in the big town down in the valley. It was delivered immediately by the plumber, fastened onto the back of his motorcycle, its polished exterior gleaming, plastic seat flapping as it roared up the mountain, making such a grand entrance into the village that people rushed from their houses to see what the noise was about. "What is it? What?" the children begged and the milkman, who had visited the city on several occasions to see his brother in the factories, demonstrated how one was to sit upon it and what one was to do till they doubled up with laughter and screamed for mercy.

For Rampal it meant comfort, security, decency. The end room with the buckets that opened out onto the sunny back of the house was enlarged and the toilet inserted. With much discussion and deliberation over many, many cups of tea, it was decided that a pipe would be laid leading down into the tank from the water spring where the whole village collected its water, twenty minutes up the steep slope from Rampal's house. Another pipe was to run beneath the pumpkin plants and the cow pasture straight out over the side of the cliff in order to dispose of the waste. Within a week Rampal heard the first *pit, pit, pit* of the water trickling into the tank accompanied by the sound of the children cheering and clapping outside. That evening, with the workmen gone, Rampal sat joyfully on his toilet seat. The last of the sunlight lay in a streak across his knees. He sat a long time in the luxurious quiet, looking out of the also newly installed windows upon the light emptying from the landscape, at the blue darkness crowding in. He waited until the mountains turned ashen and gray, till they were mere shifts in the shade of the sky and watched till the bats detached themselves from the shadows of the trees to swoop ragged and squeaking before him.

The next morning he felt happier and more rested than he had been in months. As he yawned and stretched catlike amid the blankets, he thought how wonderful it was not to have to face the morning dew outside, the damp chilliness of the mist that descended during the night, that moved through the bamboos, with a beauty he felt was meant only for the Hindi movies where the hero called and searched, desperate in the shifting gray to catch a sight of his beloved, his voice echoing and reechoing, lonely and heartbreakingly sad. Rampal ruffled his hair and smiled at himself in the mirror. He saluted "Yes, sir," and sat down on the toilet seat with his newspaper, as was his preferred way of starting the morning. It was last week's paper, for the postman had left to attend his sister's wedding in the neighboring town. Consequently, the entire delivery system had broken down, much to everybody's annoyance, but in accordance with all their expectations. Such little problems, however, did not worry Rampal, and contentedly he read of the rise in the price of rice, of the Hindu-Sikh riots in Punjab, of the corruption of the Home Minister, of the Prime Minister's Swiss bank account. While thus indulging himself, he suddenly became aware of the fact that he was not alone. Looking up he discovered a whole gaggle of little schoolboys staring at him, their mouths open with astonishment. "*Hai Ram, Ram, Ram, Ram, Ram,*" he said, waving his paper angrily. "Stare so much and I'll pull your eyes out. Wait and see." But transfixed by the sight, they stood rooted, unable to budge. Dull, thick-headed hill children! "I'll come after you with a stick. One and two. Good and hard. I'll give you such a spanking that from here to Delhi they will hear you yell." He leaned out of the window, wrenching at the pom-pom bush as if attempting to break off a branch. Finally they backed away, slowly at first, still staring and then turned their backs on him to run, flustered and squawking down the hill like a bunch of chickens. No sooner had they disappeared than Rampal caught sight of another group of observers. Women this time, stopping on the way to the spring, giggling and nudging each other with their water canisters.

Every day there were new problems. Far from becoming bored with this new addition to the village, day after day new wonders were discovered, new advantages, new uses for the toilet. The cook, grown lazy, discovered the flush made garbage disposal a pleasure. No longer did he make the treks with his bucket to the rubbish heap. Instead, he sent his vegetable peels and fish heads down with a marvelous rush of water, whooshing over the side of the cliff with lightning speed. When Rampal stormed after him waving plum pits and leaves of spinach that he had fished out of the depths of the toilet bowl, the cook protested his innocence loudly. "No. No. What do I have to do with the bathroom? How do I know where the garbage comes from? Every day I am taking it out myself, sir. Promise." But the trouble continued and even worse, Rampal began to find the water tank of the toilet mysteriously empty day after day. He was certain the cook had discovered the true use of the toilet and, bold in his new interest, had begun using it when Rampal was out of the house. "Do not try and tell me you know nothing about this," he confronted the poor man. "Tell me right now, where does all the water go?" "What, sahib? What do I know of these modern-podern things?" A few days later, Rampal, hiding behind the bathroom door, caught the cook red-handed, in the process of lifting up the lid.

"*Arre,* sahib," he trembled. "One time, two times, I took a little water from the tank to boil the potatoes and to make tea. That's all." "That's all!" stormed Rampal. "Every day now I find the tank empty. Your job, I see, is of no importance to you." "*Aiyaah,* sahib." The cook was pained by Rampal's harshness. "With my arthritis it is difficult to go up the hill in the morning. And the tank is filling up and filling up. No problem."

"Filling up and filling up," Rampal said. "Next time it fills up I will put your head in it with the lid on top."

But it was not only the cook. The news of his discovery spread throughout the village and the women realized too the conveniences of this tank that was fed from the very heart of the spring where the water was clean and fresh, unmuddied by trampling cattle and bathing men. Instead of making the long, steep walk up the hill they took to waiting in the shade of the magnolia tree till Rampal left the house and then, pushing in front of them the milkman's daughter, whose slow, sly smile turned the cook's heart to putty, they wheedled their way into the house, into the bathroom.

The children, not to be outdone, discovered joy in the descending water pipe upon which they swung and played with such relentless energy, whooping and jumping, that within weeks the pipe began to spring leaks up and down its entire length. Though the cook was sent to do his best with gummy resin, cloth, and string, he was unable to stop the flow of water and soon a miniature stream, fed by the many holes, was flowing past Rampal's bedroom. The bullfrogs followed it downstream, croaking and delighted to enlarge their territory, to keep Rampal awake all night with their ugly chorus.

The poor man couldn't get a single peaceful night's sleep, a single opportunity to build up his reserve of strength before he faced the trials of the day. "This is not a water hole," he shouted. "You cannot cook and clean at the toilet. You cannot gather to gossip here. You cannot watch through the windows." But his distress made no impression on the villagers. The women, the children, the cook, the frogs all seemed to have a personal grudge against him and his happiness.

The monsoon rains, when they finally arrived, were almost a relief. Their ferocity, their darkness, their explosions of lightning and thunder kept people at home and indoors. Rampal delighted in the roar of the drumming on the tin roof, the hammering, the furious pelting that scattered trees like matchsticks, that shook the little village till it swayed and rattled. When the cook came rushing in frantically during a particularly bad bout, his clothes drenched and spattered with mud, Rampal, cozy on the sofa and in good temper, smiled and teased: "Oh-ho, why so fast? Scared the lightning might catch you? Aren't enjoying the rain as much as the frogs?" But the cook shouted out, "*Hai! Hai!* Come and see, sahib. Come and look at the bathroom." Following the cook to the end of the hallway, Rampal was horrified to see the door open onto no bathroom at all, but a river of mud that whirled down the side of the mountain in a landslide that almost knocked the cook off his feet as he stood knee-deep in its midst, wringing his hands. Thick and chocolaty, the current swept by in huge surges of liquid earth, rising, it seemed to Rampal, higher and higher every minute. This current that had torn down the wall, that had swept over the side of the cliff the buckets, the toothbrush, the spider, and his beautiful new toilet. Rampal could not speak. He watched with his heart stopped in frozen disbelief. To have his efforts thwarted in such a manner! He was not the sort of person to whom such things were meant to happen. He should have refused this posting the minute it was offered. This dreadful town, this backward place out in the middle of nowhere, these devious, plotting people devoid of normal human behavior. His place was not among them. Already he could see the villagers converging from all sides upon the house, drawn like bees to honey by the noise the cook was making, hurrying to join in this new drama. Little boys, oblivious of the rain and soaked to the skin, were the first to arrive, rowdy with delight. The men gathered with rust-spotted, leaky umbrellas or plastic sheets held over their heads to deliver their advice with unashamedly wide grins. The women came too, tittering and giggling behind their hands.

It was the little boys who first caught sight of the toilet emerging at the edge of the cliff. Rampal watched as, coated with dirt, it appeared for a single, poised moment, defiled and humiliatingly exposed, before it disappeared over the edge to the sound of loudly expressed exclamations and the cook's funereal wail.

That night, when the storm had passed, Rampal sat silently on the porch with his whiskey bottle. The air was clearer, softer, more fragrant than ever before, and in the garden, the velvet blackness was full of fireflies. Hundreds of them. Little, whirring creatures. Busy with their winking lights. On-off. On-off. On-off. He remembered they were always more plentiful after the rains, coming alive along with the trees, the creepers, and the bushes that tomorrow would have overtaken the little village in a jungle of green exuberance.

Adam Marshall Johnson
Florida State University

YOUR OWN BACKYARD

It is the oily tang of tiger fur that startles me awake, and the first thing I do is look for my son, whom I dreamed of at top speed. The scent is gone before I even open my eyes, but a quick pulse still pants in my wrists as I sit up to see my boy watching *CHiPs* reruns with the sound off. Ponch and Jon ride their motorcycles on the beach while wearing mirrored sunglasses.

I have taken to sleeping on the couch because it is summer, and Mac is a boy with too much time on his hands and a day-sleeper for a father. Last week I woke to find his hands on my belt, lightly twisting off the key to handcuffs I hadn't even noticed were missing. We looked at each other. "I have the right to remain silent," he volunteered, *for the record,* and I watched him roll out into our south Phoenix neighborhood, headed toward wherever my handcuffs might be. But today, he seems satisfied with *CHiPs*. I pull off my khaki security guard shirt from the zoo last night and rub my eyes against the midday sun through the windows. Today he's just a normal boy again, a little Indian on shag carpeting, legs crossed, shoulders hunched, reading Ponch's lips.

Sue says he's been telling kids in the neighborhood his father's a police officer again, that they better look out, which only adds to her theory that my quitting the force made things even worse for him. It's hard to know what to do about this. She is at the end of her rope with the board exams and a boy like Mac. She is reduced these days to studying with a stopwatch and speaking in two-word sentences: Room, *now*. Toys, *away*.

I see Sam moving under the carpet and watch him slowly cross our living room. He's a Mexican boa, five foot, that I inherited from the zoo one night. There's a hole in the carpet behind the couch where he gets in, and in the summer heat he roams the whole house, a prowling shape between the cool padding and shag. The other pets are unsure of him, including my Dalmatian, Toby, so things work out. Sam runs into the side of Mac, who doesn't move, who's gotten used to this dark-roaming shape. Sam is also indifferent to what might be out there; he turns and swims off toward the television set, where Ponch and Jon now appear on a five-lane freeway. With their white bikes and round helmets, they are like bowling pins, a seven-ten split. "You think that's really them riding those bikes?" I ask.

Mac knows how I feel about this show. He doesn't even take his eyes off the screen. "I want my shoes back."

"Those bikes have never even taken a real turn. There aren't even scratches on the foot pegs, and those side covers are spotless. They've never been down."

"They catch a lot of bad guys," he says.

"They catch old movie stars, has-beens."

"At least they're out there riding," he says, "and not code nine at home."

I try not to escalate this, especially over a show Mac usually says is for "dildos," a term whose meaning, at nine years old, he seems sure of. "What makes you an expert on code nine?" I ask him.

He turns back to me for the first time, a little too proud that I can now see he has picked up yet another black eye from somewhere. "You," he says with enough drama to make me think he's heard the term somewhere and assumes it means more than merely off duty.

I try not to be coplike about all this. I watch Ponch and Jon pull over a limo with a Jacuzzi full of bikini-clad women. The girls bounce and throw handfuls of bubbles on Erik Estrada, who feigns a mock defense, and I tell you I'm really trying.

"Come on," I say. "Let's cut that hair."

"For the shoes."

It's dangerous to give him too much leverage here. "One day. No more, okay?"

"Affirmative," Mac says. "Roger that."

Aff-erm-tive, I hear from the kitchen. It took me a year to teach that bird to say that. But you can't unteach them once they've learned.

In the kitchen I grab Sue's veterinary shears and open a pack of hot dogs she's left on the counter to thaw. Taped to all the cabinets are her anatomy lists and dosage scales. On the fridge hangs a chart of the parasitic cycle. I snap off a half-frozen hot dog and crunch on it while I wonder how much animal science Mac has picked up the last four years when I was on night patrol. Only now, as a rent-a-cop, do I think about how many times he's reached for the cereal, the bowl, the milk and read the secrets of animal husbandry. Slowly, unknowingly, he must have picked it up.

When he comes into the kitchen, I get my first good look at the shiner, a deep purple-brown that swoops and fans out to his cheekbone. He doesn't say anything about it and neither do I, which is our version of life after the bomb. The first black eye was last year, and he learned the worst possible lesson in the world for an eight-year-old: it didn't hurt nearly as bad as he'd expected. Next time, I knew, he would punch first. The boy's been punished, rewarded, tested, and medicated, and here we are, *postbomb,* as Sue says, stealing our son's shoes.

We had long ago made a deal, and it was supposed to go like this: she'd do most of the child-raising work while I made it through the academy and the first three years on traffic, then I'd watch Mac while she made it through vet school. Well, Mac is nine now, Sue's exams are here, and I am no longer a cop. I am no longer the same kind of father that once thought Mac was a good name for a boy, who used to describe motor-throwing car crashes to his son over dinner each night, who referred to hurt people as occupants and ejections and incidentals.

He snaps one of the cold hot dogs off the pack and sticks it in his mouth like a cigar. Though chewing frozen hot dogs on hot days is a habit he inherited from me, I am confronted with a portrait of him in what seems to be his natural state: bored, bruised, and sullenly indifferent to anything an afternoon with me might bring. I take a breath, open the door, and step out into the summer heat.

Out back I set him on a stool so he can watch his haircut through the dog slobber and paw prints on the sliding glass door. I hook up

Sue's grooming shears and then stand behind him, a sweating father and his black-eyed son reflected in an Acadia door. He is too large for his age, with bully-sized shoulders and thick hands that already have a hunch about how to get their way.

"I hear there's been some trouble in the neighborhood," I say and flip on the shears.

He simply shrugs and bends his head forward, chin to chest, waiting for me to start. I palm the curve of his head and roll it side to side as I run the buzzer up the back of his neck. Toby trots up with the desert tortoise in his mouth, an object he carries everywhere, and he shows it to Mac and me as he eyes first the buzzer and then the half a hot dog in Mac's hand. The tortoise has long since resigned itself to this fate and even lets its legs hang out, funneling slobber.

"Mom says you've been telling the kids I'm back on the force." I say this and I'm suddenly unsure if I'm going about this the right way, but his head feels loose and pliant in my hand, the hair soft and short like when he was young.

"So."

"So, is this true?"

"Mom told me you didn't turn in your badge. She says you can go back anytime you want." As easily as he spoke, he waves the hot dog back and forth before Toby, who sways and drools but can't figure a way to eat without letting go of the tortoise.

"You know that's not true."

He shrugs.

I spin his head halfway around so he can see me out the sides of his eyes. "I'm not going back there, so it doesn't matter. You listening to me? Believe me on this. That's over." But even as I say this I see he's messing with the dog. He's shaking Toby by the nose, pinching the dog's nostrils so his cheeks puff out around the tortoise. "Let go of the dog."

He does this and then I let go of Mac's head, which rolls back down to his chest.

"Brad's dog. You can hit it with a brick and it won't even blink."

"I'm serious. I'm not going back on the force. You hit a dog with a brick?"

"I'm just saying," he says and scratches the stubble drifted down to his arm.

"Did you?"

"What?"

"Throw a brick."

"Mom says you're lazy, says you want to be code nine."

Code nine, he says and I can feel his lip curl, sense the slouching indifference of his shoulders, and suddenly I don't want to keep shaving him. Suddenly, I can see him in a not-too-distant future, a tattoo on his arm, an earring maybe, wearing a black concert shirt with a wallet on a chain, and I don't even want to touch him, because for a moment I know this kid. I have arrested him a hundred times.

I flip off the buzzer and tell him to go hose off.

"What about my hair?" he asks, but it is not a question. "This sucks."

"Hose, *now*" is all I can say as I point him away, toward the hose and the algae-green dog pool beyond.

You'd be surprised how many animals get killed at a zoo. We cull old ones, young ones, sick ones, extra ones. I cull them. Yesterday, I spent most of the night scooping baby scorpions out of Desert Dwellers. They'd gotten out of their glass enclosure through the vent tube and were all over the atrium. I used a fishnet to scoop them up and drop them into a bucket of water, where they sank like dull pennies. The night before that I fished all the newly hatched alligators out of Reptile Land with a long-handled pool skimmer. I dumped them in a feed tub and then placed it in the big cat meat locker till they were hard as tent stakes. I cull the overbred carp and the pigeons that swoop in from the capitol. I'm the one who harvests the ostrich eggs, and unless you've entered a dark pen of nine-foot birds, armed only with a pole and a flashlight, to try to take their eggs, you don't know what I'm talking about. An ostrich can put a man's ribs out his back, which is something I've seen, though not from a bird. Last week I shot a tiger.

But tonight is the kind you find only in Phoenix, only in July. The moon is rising over the Papago foothills like some distant drive-in movie, and I will forget about black eyes and roughed knuckles, will swing wide of the empty tiger pen as I roam the zoo's dark paths in my zebra-striped golf cart. I have tonight's list of the animals I'm to cull stuck to the cart's visor, and beside me on the seat are my son's dirty Converse sneakers, a temporary measure I know, a faint hope that tonight at least he won't get too far from the house while I'm gone. It would be dangerously simple to get in the habit of day-dreaming on a job like this, to let myself ponder life amid a sleeping zoo, to speculate on the animals on that list, to keep looking at those shoes. I know that trap already, and tonight, I have decided, there will be nothing in the world beyond the cart, nothing but the luft of stale, warm air up my shirtsleeves and four more hours of dark. I will hum through the exhibits, roll through my list, and later, hopefully, remember nothing.

In the distance I can hear a big cat scratching against chain link. From somewhere come the soft thumps of a great owl hovering in its small aviary, and I sink into the kind of feeling I used to get back when I was a police officer and would cruise through residential neighborhoods. I could meander through dark cul-de-sacs for hours, head back, one thumb on the wheel, using only cruising lights, as I passed homeowners' neat lawns, their sprinklers snapping on to hiss in the dark, their security lights occasionally sensing my patrol car and shocking an upturned Big Wheel in the drive or an empty swing set. There would be nothing at all but the green glow of my dash gauges; beyond my windshield, the world became a series of dark houses that blended, and my mind would go blank.

I keep my headlights off now as I did then, but tonight, it's because of the rabbits. They make their way down the empty Salt River bed from the city dumps, and the zoo is overrun with them. Pink eyes are everywhere, ears swiveling in turn, and the sudden sight of me racing through the zoo is enough that they can throw themselves into the bright lights of trouble. You can't believe what they're capable of. When they get into the Oasis they'll eat whole flats of hot dog buns at a time. They end up in trash cans, air ducts, gummed up in water pumps or zapped in electric fences, and even if they find their way into a place like Sonoran Predators, it's not good because they're dump bunnies, raised on rotting food, full of worms.

I cruise into the night scent of wet eucalyptus, roll through a fun-nel of bugs humming under a floodlight, and I stare straight on because I don't want to get to know the animals the way some people would. I don't name them or follow too closely their movements. Back on patrol, when I rolled past houses and through alleys, I never looked in those windows or wondered if the sons were in their beds, because if you let up out there, if you let your thoughts start to wander, there wasn't one house you couldn't picture without chalk lines in the drive or yellow tape across the door. This isn't nostalgia here, not the voice of an ex-cop with a wife and a boy and nine years on the force. My goals these days are less ambitious. I am a security guard now, lucky to get this job, and tonight, as the rising moon blues the asphalt before me, I am hunting only rabbits.

I've got a little Remington .22 semiauto, but it's unwise to shoot at any distance in a zoo, so I'm driving around to check a set of heavy-mesh raccoon traps I put out on my first rounds. The zoo is nestled in the Papago foothills that slope into the shallow pan of south Phoenix, which is where I used to patrol. Occasionally, through breaks in the trees, I can see the bright city grid expand below, and every street corner, every alleyway comes back to me in the orange glow. I know these spots in my nightly rounds where my old life appears suddenly and all too bright, and so I have trained myself to look at my coffee in its little holder on the dash, at my hands on the plastic wheel, because it has happened before that I have seen silent red-and-blues out there and let myself wonder, *Is that Ted or José or Woco?* out there running something down. Then it's all too easy to start wondering about the runner, *How old is he? What's he running from?* What's he running from.

No, I try to keep focused on the task at hand. Sometimes high school kids try to jump the gates and occasionally there's a problem in the main lot because of the adult bookstore down the road, but other than that, it's best to stick to rounds. Mr. Bern, the zoo director, is still a little leery of me, so we talk through Post-It notes. I come to work, peel my note off the guard shack, and do what it says without thought. Speculation won't change the animals on the list. Dwelling won't bring my son in from the parking lots and canal roads below.

I wheel the cart around in the soft mulch of the Petting Zoo and head uphill to an exhibit called Your Own Backyard, which contains species of lesser interest like donkeys and javelinas, animals most people forgo because of the hike. At the top, it happens like it always does, the zoo gives way to a wash of Phoenix light, wavering unsteadily in the heat. It makes you look, look away, then look again. At the highest point in the park, the zoo also is reduced; it is now only the tops of trees, a rising breath from the green, and for a moment I feel for these rams and sheep, to whom this dangerous city appears brilliant and alluring. From below, there is a faint call of lemurs, and the thought crosses my mind to turn the cart around, to check the trap in the morning, because honestly I can stare out into that city for hours. But then I near the trap, and the sight makes me stop and set the brake. I turn the headlights on and grab the semiauto.

There is a full-sized dog in the raccoon trap, its bony haunches pressed against the gate, and this, too, is part of my job. The dog is wedged in so tight it can neither sit nor stand, and it is frozen there, silent, as if in midleap. Its gray fur juts through the mesh on every side, and the bridge of its nose and forehead are pressed flat against the far end of the cage so that it appears to be in deep contemplation of its paws below. I bend to look for a collar but there is none, only the slightest of quivering on its breath. I walk around the cage to view it from all sides, and the dog knows this is not good, that things have gone forever astray, but it is wedged in so tight its eyes can follow nothing but my shoes.

That this dog cannot fully see me is a small relief, though it is not enough to stop me from wondering if, when it happens, his body will have room to go limp, or whether it will behave as if nothing happened, and be just as hard to pull out afterward. The thought is neither sentimental nor cold. My snake was a Post-It note. So was my bird. But I already have a dog, and eventually you have to decide how much you can afford to care. A couple years on traffic will teach you that. They put you on traffic first, so you got used to such things. On traffic, you'll see pelvic wings unfold against steering columns. There'll be breastplates you can see light through, dentures imbedded in dashboards. Stuff you need kitty litter to soak up. Kitty litter was standard procedure. The older cops said you could even get used to the sight of kids getting hurt, though I pretty much quit before that. Regardless, I lift my gun. The dog will be easier to get out after, I decide, and turn my back to the city lights as it stares at the old police shoes I have quit polishing.

This bothers me though, this dog staring at my shoes, so I swing around to the back of the cage and figure I'll do it from there. But right away I know this is a mistake because I see its haunches and wonder how hungry a dog has to be to worm into a cage for rabbit feed. I see its tail jammed in the trap spring and start to think about my own dog for a moment, am bending down to loosen its tail even before I consider if this is best. I release the spring catch with my thumb, and the only reaction from the dog is a light trickle of urine. Standing, things only get worse for I am suddenly faced with that great bank of city lights.

Before I can realize what a minute of wandering thoughts will cost me, I am held fixed for a moment, mesmerized, because nearly all the people I care about in the world are out there tonight, including my son, Mac. I stand, mouth open, held, until I come to my senses, until I remember the dog and my finger feels for the semiauto's safety. The way you shoot a tiger is the way you stick your head into the smoking cab of a traffic rollover. It's the way you kick down a tenement door or pull the covers to shine your Maglite on the sheets of a rape scene. You just take that breath and go. It's how you drive your son home from school after he's broken another boy's fingers, three of them, for no reason, he says. It's how you keep from thinking what it means to have this dog's piddle on your worn-out cop shoes. You just take that breath. You go.

The next day, Woco and his new girlfriend, Tina, show up in the late afternoon to barbecue. I have already hosed down the patio furniture and stoked up the grill, and it is still hot enough out that the smoke doesn't want to rise. Sue is silent as she chops vegetables. She has been in the library all day and still has that fluorescent glow on her skin. The neighbor has informed her that Mac's eye is the result of his "arresting" and "detaining" two of the younger boys down the street, and coming home to the news we're having company is yet another ambush in her eyes. She could care less about my plan, she says as she goes at the carrots, whacking them down. She hasn't shaved her legs in a week, she adds. In the midst of all this is Mac, standing on a kitchen chair repeating mumbled words over and over to the African gray parrot. About his hair, Sue won't even speak.

So it is with caution that I answer the door when they arrive. Woco does a finger quick-draw as he comes through the threshold and Mac spins and drops to the kitchen floor. Sue shoots Woco a wicked glance over the salad spinner as I watch my son jump up and smile after his near-death experience.

"Look at that hair," Woco says, his voice booming through the kitchen. "No wonder the kid's got a shiner with a haircut like that. What's next, you going to make him wear a dress?" But even this gesture seems forced, and Mac doesn't quite buy it.

In the backyard, I put on hot dogs and pass out beers. We sit around a picnic table in the shocking heat, Sue leaning against a post with her feet in my lap and Tina massaging Woco's shoulder. It could be pleasant, this scene, but after the initial greetings are over, uneasiness settles. Sue takes soft pulls off her beer. Tina feigns interest in the empty yard behind me.

Woco opens his mouth a few times, but always pauses and thinks better of it. He is unsure these days of what's safe to talk about, and without news of holdups or hit and runs, there is little to say and we are silent. These are the dangerous moments in my life lately. As the hot dogs sizzle and our eyes float around the yard it seems we're all wondering how many more of these fumbling evenings we have left in us, how long before we're all at a loss. On the force, there were two levels of response to things: one and ten. It was either a polite *Are you aware this is a school zone?* or you were reaching for the thumb break on your holster. On the force there were no in-betweens. What I have learned in the past year, since the time my son first felt a finger break in his hand, is that life on one is the harder of the two.

Sue finally breaks the silence. "Are you going to tell him?"

Woco smiles and looks from her to me and back. "What?"

"Go get the paper plates," she says to Mac.

He just rubs the shaved back of his head. "What for?"

"Kitchen. Counter," she says and glares at him until he's inside and the door is shut. She leans back again and speaks to the porch roof, not quite bitter, but more or less resigned. "He's got a plan. He thinks if he gives you all his old uniforms in front of Mac, it will solve everything. He's got them dry-cleaned, in the hall closet, ready to go. His big plan. Uniforms."

Woco looks to me for confirmation. Listening to Sue describe the scene I can see it for the foolish notion it is. *The grand symbolic act*, she'll be calling it, *his solution to the bomb.* I shake my head at Woco.

"What can hurt at this point?" I ask him. "I mean, it's worth a shot."

"Worth a shot," Sue mutters to the roof.

Tina speaks. She hooks her hand around Woco's neck and takes a drink off his beer. "What's this all about?"

Woco pats her leg under the table. "Kid's got growing pains."

"It's more than growing pains," I say as Mac comes out the door eating a carrot. He walks with the other hand on his belt buckle like it's a light he's shining in your eyes, a habit picked up from me. Orange mouthed, he's grinning, so I know something's up. I watch him all the way to the bench, where he tosses the paper plates, facedown.

Inside we hear the parrot screech twice. Then it says, "Code—nine." What was Mac's silly phrase yesterday now has me by the collarbones, a sudden anxiety that stuns me until I realize the parrot has the perfect scratchiness of a radio dispatcher. *Code nine*, the parrot repeats and a knowing smile so obscene it scares the shit out of me comes across Mac's face. I watch him silently mouth, *Fuck yeah.*

I feel myself moving toward ten. "Did you teach that bird to say that?"

Mac blankly chews his carrot.

"It's going to say that forever. Do you know that?" All of us are watching now, and suddenly it's not so easy for him to smile. His face is bunching up, getting flustered, and I want this. I want to get through to him. I want him to stand in the hot glow of ten. "Forever. Did you think about that?"

"Okay," Sue says, "enough."

"Answer me," I say. "Answer."

But then something strange happens. There is a splash in the dog pool, a sharp plunk. Something bounces off the barbecue, sending sparks out the dome. Then I see it, a short hail of rocks sailing in from the alley. There is the crunching of feet in the alleyway and the stones bounce off the roof and skitter onto the porch as a group of kids yells and taunts Mac.

Mac is moving across the yard before I know it. With one high step and a leap he's over a six-foot fence and all I have of him are streaks of pumping arms through fence slats as he begins his pursuit. Sue shakes her head like I should get up to follow, but I don't. I will not chase my son like a fugitive down our alley.

"So much for the grand solution," she says.

We sit there in the quiet, looking at each other through the smoke of burned hot dogs, listening to the sounds of disappearing feet. On the force things would be easy. On the force I would know what to do. But now, there is no procedure, and I can only close my eyes and try not to think.

After a while he appears, breathless, through the side gate. His ribs are heaving, his feet a throbbing mess. "I need my shoes," he declares and then puts his hands on his knees, breathing deep. "I need shoes." Sue glares at me.

At the zoo the yellow square of the Post-It waits on the guard shack. I don't look forward to these notes, to the extra duties Mr. Bern has waiting, but it's best to just plow onward and get it over. Though tonight I pull up short. Mac is in my thoughts, has been since he pedaled down the drive at sunset, and as I picture him weaving off into the dark neighborhood, I can't help feeling a connection between my son and a distant note I can't quite read, though I know what news it will bring.

It's foolish, I know, standing here in the parking lot, afraid of a note. For the first time I think I'd rather Mr. Bern told me in person the animals I was to cull, that one night he'd follow me around to see what it takes to make these notes good. But, like I said, he's wary of me, and it was only because Sue's veterinary professors put in a good word that I was hired at all. When people find out you used to be a cop, you can see the options run in their eyes: couldn't hack it, not good enough, crooked. Or worse, they imagine some tragic life-and-death scene that makes you quit, that changes a guy forever. The stray bullet that hits a tourist. The kid with a toy pistol. People never pause to think that such scenes can stop being tragedies after a while.

I tell you, the only thing I ever shot on the force was a cow, which was one of the reasons Mr. Bern hired me. Still, I don't think he's ever shot anything. I'd like to tour him around on traffic for a while, show him how to take that breath before you crawl underneath the axles of a tractor-trailer underride. If everyone did a year on traffic, we'd all speak another language. My wife and I wouldn't end up silent in the kitchen, at a full loss. There would be no need for yellow notes.

In the distance, a caribou ruts his horns against a fence and calls in the heat. It is a lonely sound and I decide I will set no traps tonight.

I pull myself together, tell myself such speculation is foolish, will only make things worse. But before I take two steps toward the guard shack, I again reconsider things. Into my head comes the notion that maybe I was wrong, that nobody should have to go on traffic, that my son shouldn't feel he has to face the world, head-on, before he's even ten. And, of course, he's learned what's out there from me.

The note, though, is not what I'd expected. It simply reads: Mind the wolves. I examine it closely in the sulfurous floodlights. It's the first time I've been asked to look after an animal rather than put it down, and as I aim the cart around toward the lower zoo, I can't help feeling a little high. I drive faster than usual and flip on the headlights to get a glimpse of animals who swivel their long necks to watch me pass. As I'm rolling through Down Under, a wallaby bounds to pace me inside his fence. I sink into the light mist of Flamingo Island. Coming out of Sonoran Predators I see them, ruby bright eyes fixing me from a temporary enclosure near the Papago boulders that mark the end of the zoo.

There are three of them, Mexican reds, and I watch them all night, forgetting all else. I have never seen a wolf before, but I know these are fresh off the range. The enclosure is only a fifty-foot square of chain link yet the females manage to show little of themselves. But the male, he is magnificent, a coat of deep amber, slimmer, smaller than you might think. Soon I find myself running the outside of the fence with him as he lopes, bandy-legged, circling his pen in a rocking-horse motion that pulls up and freezes at the slight sounds of distant rabbits, now a little less sure about descending into the zoo. He is used to being pursued; I am used to pursuing, and we fall naturally into this motion.

His ears prick; he pauses. At these moments I stop with him. Earlier in the day he sprayed these new fence posts to mark them as his, as if to say, *The world can come no closer than this,* and in such a pause there is only the mutual huff of our breath, the musk of wolf spray rising like spilled fuel, and the absolute silence of rabbits. I kneel down at the fence, and the wolf does not know what to make of me. He stands wide and low, ready to be knocked down, but for a moment we speak the same language and he is unafraid. We seem to recognize we are both in from the range, to agree the chase can end.

At home, the house is quiet, unlit, and I look forward to a half hour in bed with my wife before she rises to go to school. I lock my gun above the refrigerator and slip out of my clothes in the kitchen. Naked, I make my way down the hallway. There is the slightest wolf smell on my skin and I am glad for it. In the bedroom, open books are spread along the foot of the bed and Sue, in her deepest sleep, is beyond peaceful. My dream about Mac will not come tonight, I know that now, looking at her. It is a simple dream, short as a school play, yet can come suddenly, lung-punching, like high-speed chrome.

I slide my leg under the covers and am drawn to the warmth of her back, the slightly sour smell of her hair. She is curled away from me but her head rolls back, craned to her shoulder. One eye opens. Wide and unfocused, the pupil slowly floats across the ceiling, moving through her puffy lids as if in seawater. "Baba," she murmurs. "Cum sle wis me." I wrap my arm around until my fingers fit the slots of her ribs. She hums a single, short note. At the scent of her shoulders and the sound of her sleepy talk, I know her so fully it loosens my jaw, makes me exhale deep.

Her foot drifts over to scratch an itch against the hair on my legs, and near sleep, I hear *Mind* the wolves. I say it to myself, now wondering if instead of *take care of* the wolves, it means *watch out for* the wolves. *Stay clear. Beware.* Suddenly, I wonder what Mac is dreaming under his Bart Simpson sheets. We gave him the street-side room when he was little and I picture him fitful and turning now as late-night cars drive by and headlights steal in his windows.

My eyes are drawn to the wall, to an unseen boy not twenty feet away, and I want him to be restless, to dream about his black eye, about bent fingers, but I know what is really true: he is dead-to-the-world asleep, eyes rolled back, sheets on the floor, sunk so deep in his unconscious he is lucky to be breathing. He was as easy with a fist as I was with a wolf, and I want us both troubled by this in our sleep. My hand pulls against the flex of Sue's ribs. "Gon a sle," she says as her hand finds mine, squeezes, goes limp.

I decide Mac's hair is best fixed by professionals, but a trip to the mall, it turns out, is a bad idea. Even at noon, on a weekday, we are forced to park a quarter mile away. Daytime is generally more difficult for me, and entire days one-on-one with my son have recently given me reason to be leery. Any lightness I felt last night is reduced to the uneasiness of walking on heat-weakened asphalt and the feeling of dark potential that can come from a sea of fuming cars. I have decided to be "up" today, a carefree father despite the fact that Mac now refuses to wear his shoes; he woke me up by announcing they were for "pussies."

This is how we move through the parking lot: I, holding his sneakers, walk down the middle of the lane, while he zigzags back and forth before me from the relative cool of one car shadow to the next, saying, *Ow, ow,* and this motion, it seems to me, in the oven breath of the mall, is the essence of our relationship.

Mac has never before had a store-bought haircut, and it is the tools of the trade which interest him. He leans over to pump himself up in the chair. He uses the vacuum hose to suck red circles in his arm. He smells the blue fluid the combs are in. The young woman cutting his hair says something to him and he laughs. He closes his eyes, rolls his head to grin toward her shoulder, and I can see in his reflection a boy who's forgotten his sullenness, forgotten his father the ex-cop is waiting with his sneakers.

But with a razor nick at the back of his neck I see his fists lift on instinct and I feel a pang in my gut that makes me want to curl. He sits stark, straight up, his head whipped around to glare at the girl with the comb. What you need to understand about this, what I need to make clear to you is that regardless of what Sue or anybody says, I've lost this kid, I've lost him. I can get him back, I know that. What hurts here on this bench, amid waves of passing families, is that I have no idea how.

At work, there are three yellow notes waiting for me on the guard shack, and I walk right past them to the front power panel, where I shut down every light in the zoo. I step into my golf cart and for a long time just stare through the windshield into a night I have blackened. A light wind, unusual for this place, floats down from the Papagos, bringing a taste of wolf scent like warmed ammonia, and I can feel those notes hanging on the guard shack behind me. Then I hear him bay. The wolf's voice rises and turns in the bowl of the zoo, curls down around me, and resonates in my bones. The two females join in and their wail rings from the rocks like dished metal, a clear, sonorous sound that hangs in the air and moves me long after they stop, and I hope the call rolls far into the city below, makes people sit straight up from their sleep.

I drop the parking brake and wheel the cart around, drawn to the lesser animals, the mule deer, the desert burros, to the spot where I shot the dog. A wave runs through me as I remember the swooshing thud he made as I grabbed his paws and swung him into the Dumpster. I feel the urge to stand on the spot where I first found him trapped, to look at it again. But I don't do that. What I do when I reach the top of the hill is sit and stare for hours into the brazier of city lights below, looking and looking.

Eventually I hear the short whoop of a police siren in the main lot and I cruise down the cart path until I can see Woco far below, leaning on his patrol car, thumping his Maglite against the front tire and watching the light short on and off. I hold up and observe from a distance as he approaches the chain link with a cardboard box from the crime lab, and I know they have finally cleaned out my locker at the station. He just stands down there, holding all my old gear, waiting longer than I am comfortable with, and it is like the barbecue last evening, the awkwardness, the distance, the desire to jump shotgun into his cruiser and race off with him, the silent waiting for him to leave.

Later, after I have read Mr. Bern's notes and done my work, I leave the zoo early and patrol old neighborhoods with my cruising lights on. I turn the Ford down low-lit streets and roll past residence after residence where homeowners raise their juveniles. I put down four kit fox pups before I left. The zoo listed them for three weeks on the National Animal Bank, but no one wanted foxes, so Mr. Bern must have decided today was the day. His note suggested I use ambutol on them but I didn't. It is a slow drug, painful to watch, and they deserved better. The fifth one is on the seat next to me, in the empty crime lab box, wide-eyed and unsure. Already his piddle has soaked through to the fabric. In a few months he'll begin marking the house with fox spray, which is some of the worst, and I'll have to get rid of him. But for now the world outside the car windows does not concern him; he just sits amid the passing darkness with his legs spread, trying not to fall down in the turns.

I find myself near home, two blocks from my street, when I see a figure dash from the road in the murk of street lamps—a blur of a boy, it seems to me, diving for the cover of bushes. I give chase. I pull down the alley and reach for the spotlight lever that is no longer there. I prowl the back streets of my neighborhood, figuring, following, until the fox is asleep, until it is my own house I patrol past.

At home Mac is in the kitchen eating cereal by himself. I enter and stare at him, at his hands and ribs and feet, as if some element of what I felt out there might still linger on him.

"What's wrong with you?" he asks and stretches, rubbing the sleep from his eyes, and I can't tell if this move is genuine, if he's a sleepy five-year-old or a devious fifteen.

"I almost had you," I say.

He squints at me. He lifts the bowl of sugary milk and downs it before rising and silently returning to his bedroom. "Here I am," he says from down the hallway.

It's when I go to put my gun away that I notice a chair pulled up against the cabinet, the footprints on the counter below the locking doors. The clasp and hinges have not been jimmied, are untouched, but I can feel his presence here, feel that he's been meditating long on what's inside, cheek to wood, and I decide here, in the kitchen, that he will shoot a gun.

I stride down the hall and, in his room, grab his wrist. Two more hours of dark, I think, looking into his seditious eyes, and his shoulder socket knocks as I tow him down the hall and out toward the car, still idling in the alley.

Past the zoo gates, he lags far behind as we cross the footbridge that will land us in the park. That is how I see him nearing me, a black outline against the bank of city lights behind, and as I grab the .22 rifle and two boxes of shells from the guard shack, I want him to look into the leukemia-yellow eyes of a tiger. But rabbits are all I have left to scare my son back to me.

Mac is sitting in the driver seat of the cart when I come out, and without speaking we are off, rolling past the Arizona Collection in what seems an underwhelming first driving experience. He's driving one-handed, eyes wide and unfocused, a style he's learned from me. I give him no directions because the zoo is circular, though he doesn't know that, and he heads best speed through unknown turns, clacking the pedal up and down on the floor, upset the cart will go no faster.

We pass through the main exhibits, and I kill the lights as we near the rear of the zoo and reach over to turn off the key as we pass the makeshift wolf pen, leaving Mac to coast us past the last reaches of the fences. Standing in the fields that foot the Papagos, the stars brilliant even for the city below, I show him how to lever the little bullets, the features of the safety and sights. He inspects the rifle like he is viewing it through the wonder of another boy's glasses. I make Mac click the safety off and on to make sure he can finger the operation in the dark, but this does little to reassure me.

I bring the cart about and set him up in front of it, Indian-legged on the ground with the barrel benched on the grill. He points it off into the black landscape.

"The lights will come on and you'll see the rabbits," I tell him. "They'll stand on their hind legs and then the eyes will light up." He looks from me to the darkness and back. "Aim only that way or the bullets may come back to the wolves or burros." I point toward the dark field, but he doesn't follow.

"Where's the wolves?"

"Over there." He turns to look but there is only the hood of the golf cart. "Are you sure you're ready?"

He's still straining to see the wolf pen. Then he looks up, his face blank, and the safety clicks off. "Affirmative," he says.

I walk to the power pole unsure if I've made a big mistake. *Grand symbolic act number two,* I hear Sue say. I take a breath for both of us and throw the toggle switch to the floodlights above. They glow a dull sodium orange before flashing to show an empty field, and slowly the rabbits begin to stand up and stare toward the light. The semiauto snaps to life as Mac levers eleven rounds with amazing speed, just the way I taught him: pump sight breathe squeeze, pump sight breathe squeeze.

Little patches of dust stand frozen in the distance as we walk together, our shadows long before us. Mac opens and closes the breech to smell the smoke. I try to read the expression on his face, and as the moment I've been banking on nears, the moment he sees what a gun is capable of, what he's capable of, I begin to change my mind and hope he has missed.

I am wrong. We find a rabbit sprawled beside a small outcropping and I realize the worst has happened: Mac is neither scared nor disgusted, only indifferent. He picks it up by its long ears as if he were handling a milk jug. It slowly rotates by its stretched skin. With his finger he inspects the little hole in its chest. With his finger he opens its mouth and looks inside.

"Maybe we could feed it to Sam," he says.

"Negative."

"Ten-four," he says, mocking me, and spots another a few yards away. It is larger than the last one and Mac picks it up and shakes it. "What about this one?" he asks, holding it up as if weighing it in the light. I watch its front legs circle in the air.

Jesus, I think. "Put it down."

"No. It's still good," he says and shakes it hard. Its body rocks some and then its back legs slowly rear up, as if charging, and suddenly tear down his arm. Mac drops it and moves to kick it but I stop him. I grab his shoulder and pull him, squeeze him to my stomach until I can feel my pulse in his back. The jackrabbit skitters away and overbounds into the dark and I am left pressing my boy to me while trying to think of a way to explain the difference between killing an animal and beating it.

I turn him around, but I can't deal with his sullen, angry face. Mac's arm is scratched pretty good, but I can't even deal with him. I take the gun, hand him the flashlight, and walk away for the first aid kit. I should bring him to the cart, to where the light is better, though honestly I don't want to see him any closer tonight.

Anger has settled to a kind of emptiness by the time I reach the cart. I find the aid kit and I start a slow walk back to Mac, my son, whom I will patch up with gauze and Bactine. I make my way along the edge of the open desert and I know in a little while I will have to call Sue to come pick him up because even here, in a simple field under the stars, I am ill-suited for any of this.

I reach the spot where Mac should be, and it takes a moment to bring my head back down to earth and realize he is gone. I do a slow turn before I see him standing down by the wolf pen, shirtless, with a rabbit in his hand. He is rattling it temptingly against the chain link while his flashlight follows in its beam the dim image of a wolf in the dark, more eyes than anything as it sidles, circling, on loping legs. Mac is saying things I can't quite hear. His free fingers hold the mesh, and he is bent some, talking in hushed tones.

I call to him but he does not respond. He seems to finish what he is saying and his awkward body stands up straight. The light turns off. Then his arm lifts to lob the rabbit over the fence and I am moving. I see the rabbit do two slow turns in the air and I am almost running. It lands on the other side, not four feet from where he stands transfixed, fingers wrapped in the fence. *Mac*, I call.

He rolls his head to look at me blankly and I slow some. Soon, I am stopped, breathing heavy and watching from behind. It becomes quiet, and as I notice the *shh* of late-night cars on Van Buren, I wonder what had me running a moment ago. Then it appears from the dark, cautiously, legs wide, watching Mac as it comes close enough to shovel the rabbit into its mouth before it is gone. Mac is glued to the scene, and the thought that he feels connected to this animal brings him closer to me in the one way I do not want.

And then the wolf is back. It is only a gray glow in the moonlight, but belly low it nears the fence again. It pauses and sniffs, then nears more, and I have never seen anything like it, this wolf and my son. Through the fence its nose runs up and down his jeans, and Mac seems almost to press himself against the fence as it sniffs, neck stretched to Mac's shiny legs. Then it turns away from him, as if to leave, yet pauses. At first I think it is smelling the spot where the rabbit had lain, but the wolf lowers its head and with a quivering of its hind legs sends three great blasts of spray and foamy urine trolloping down Mac.

He turns, mouth open, a mist coming off him beyond smell, and his is the kind of terror I was getting used to on the force. I move to embrace him with everything I've got, but when he sees me run at him, he is gone; his legs shudder then burst, a flash of a boy racing down dark paths.

I chase him. I take a breath and run, my keys jangling, my name tag flying off to scramble in the green-black grass. We are running for all we are worth, and soon he is losing me, soon he is only the glint of working shoulder blades and the white arcs of elbows in the moon, and I run. I run until the saliva puddles in my mouth and I am only following his scent. I feel my gun belt take on its familiar cantering rhythm, and I picture him hopping the zoo gate to blur down Van Buren Street under dim street lamps, chasing the traffic, running shirtless past the adult bookstore. I ditch the Maglite and revolver and belt and pull my shirt off until there are only the sounds of my breathing off the asphalt. I round into the wide open of Your Own Backyard, and I know he has gotten away from me. Suddenly I've chased this kid a thousand times. In an instant I am heading again down old alleys and yards, over hedgerows, across empty causeways, and as a stitch starts in my side all I can do is follow that awful smell on my son and hope it will never leave him because there's no other way I'll find him in the dark.

Timothy A. Westmoreland

University of Massachusetts, Amherst

NEAR TO GONE

I walked up the road to talk with the lineman who had been busy for several days watching a downed power line. Since my wife, Anita, had left for Buckland I'd observed him for long hours to see what it was a man with a job like this does. Not much, I thought. He drank coffee and read the newspaper, smoked cigarettes in the afternoon, and at night I could smell cannabis drifting on the air. His truck sat around a curve a couple hundred feet up the road from my house, but I could keep an eye on him from my bedroom window.

Heavy, wet snow barely fell from the sky. Ruts left behind by Anita's car were still visible in the driveway and on the road heading south, away from the house. It was an hour before dark, and I wanted to see what this watchman could tell me.

"How long before we get power?" I asked.

"I'm just paid to make sure nobody touches it," he said. "I don't fix them." The man wore a thick wool vest over his coveralls. He sipped coffee from the cap of his thermos. Brown stains seeped down the back of his deerskin shooting gloves. "Snow's near to gone."

"Foot and a half to two on the ground," I said, running the palms of my gloves together. "Tonight?" I asked.

He looked straight ahead, down the road. "Another day or two." He cranked the engine and turned a vent toward his face; sipped coffee.

I looked toward the sky and could see breaks opening in the clouds. "It's about over." I pointed upward.

He leaned his head out of the cab. His neck was thick and rusty with two-day beard. His forearms, bare below the turned-up shirt cuffs, were at the wrist the size of good kindling wood—delicately reaching into the glove's gauntlets.

"I can see my breath inside the house," I said.

He watched the line. "Bundle up. It's going to be cold."

"What's your name?" I asked.

He looked me in the eye. "I'm doing my job," he said. "They'll tell you that if you call."

"I don't mean that," I said. "Just wanted to know."

He was quiet. "Norm," he said, finally.

"Norm?" I repeated.

"Yeah."

I lied. I said, "Buzz," and I reached my hand out to him. The palm of his glove was warm from the coffee. "Live down at seventy-nine."

"Seventy-nine."

"How much runs through a line like that?"

"A lot," he said.

"How much?"

"Don't know. I just make sure no one touches them."

"So if I got hold of it, I'd really fry?"

"Sure," he said.

"How long would it take?"

"Seconds."

"Would I feel it?"

"Maybe."

"Just for a second?"

"Maybe. Maybe a little longer."

"Son of a bitch would hurt?"

"Probably. But not for long."

"What would it feel like, though?"

"Don't know."

I put my hand on the lip of the truck bed and leaned inward. A shiver ran up my back as the cold went through my glove and up into my arm. A blue haze ranged on the snow around us. The torsos and limbs of pines fell in black shadows across the road. I could hear the way everything was beginning to seize up from the cold.

I felt warm air from a heater vent meet my face. "Toaster-oven warm in there," I said.

"Not so bad." He raised the cup to his mouth.

I shifted my weight, leaned back from the truck, felt an aching in my leg. I glanced up the road toward the power line. Across the pavement, down a long ravine, I could hear that the Saw Mill River was still running hard. Brenda Clark's bluetick, Chalk, ran the wetland. You could hear his bellow echoing through the beech and hemlock.

"Cigarette?" he said. He tapped the pack on the steering wheel and offered one my way.

"Not anymore," I said. "Is this what you do for a living?"

"Not particularly," he said. He cupped his hand over a cigarette and lit it. "I do a variety of things."

"The electric company just calls?"

"When they need bodies." He paused, then asked, "What do you do, Buzz?"

"Not much," I said. I pulled my stocking cap down over my skull and balanced on my other leg.

"Want a seat?" He gathered newspaper up from next to him and tossed it onto the floorboard.

"I could take one."

"Come around."

I walked around the front of the truck and slipped into the cab next to him, the air stale with coffee and damp pulp. "Where you from, stranger?" I jested.

"You've got a limp."

"I know."

"New Hampshire," he finally answered. Smoke streamed from the edge of his lips and from his nose. "You?"

"Around," I said.

"You don't work?"

"Not anymore."

"You have?"

"Not very well."

"At what?"

"Mostly being lazy," I said. "I subcontracted roofing jobs and boiler work."

"I hate shingles."

"I never touched them."

"Coffee?" he asked. He tilted the lip of his cup in my direction and then took a sip.

"Thanks," I said. "That'd be great."

"All I got is Tupperware," he said as he shifted in his seat and reached back behind me. "It should work."

"You've done this before?" I asked.

"What?" He spilled coffee into the bowl.

"Watched power lines?"

"It's hot," he said, offering me the coffee. He leaned forward and turned off the ignition. "Yeah."

"Ever seen anyone fried?"

"Not yet," he said. "But I expect to someday."

"You expect to?"

"People will drive right past you. Road signs and all."

"They're grounded."

"Not when they get out." He turned toward me and winked.

I laughed and held the bowl tightly, afraid the weakness in my fingers would somehow let me down. I had numbness too, and wondered if the coffee might not burn through my gloves and scald my hands. I reached down and rested the Tupperware between my feet.

"If you don't mind my asking, what's with the limp?"

"Surgery," I said. I slipped my cap off and he looked at my head, then at my face, and then, without blinking, right into my eyes. "I go for Taxol twice weekly."

"That's tough."

"Sometimes," I said. I leaned down and brought the bowl to my face. "Good coffee."

"Got a Coleman in back."

"I was wondering—"

"Set it out late when the chance of traffic is slim," he said. "I cook up coffee, pork chops, and eggs. I like to eat well."

"Listen," I said. "At night I can smell something."

"How's that?"

"I mean, sometimes it's good for the nausea."

"Pork and eggs?"

"No. The smoke," I said. "I recognize the smell."

"You've got a nose."

"I do."

Between us there was nothing but darkness. The cloud cover was gone and moonlight burnished everything in black and white. The road in front of us, hunkered down beneath snow, was cut by the tangled power line. We could see each other's breath hanging in the air like dust. Norm cranked the engine and turned on the heat. He lit a cigarette and turned his window down a crack.

"I can spare some," he offered. He took a drag off his cigarette, then leaned over and turned on the dashboard lights. "You ever smoked?"

"A few times," I said. "Years back." I shifted in my seat, turned so that I might get an idea what was on his mind. He didn't carry an expression on his face that told me anything. He seemed to be without judgment.

"Well," Norm paused, staring in the direction of the power line. "Let's get the Coleman going." He reached beneath the seat and pulled his stuff out and tucked it into his vest pocket. I watched him hunch over for a moment and get the feel of the heat coming from the vents. He closed his eyes and didn't move, letting the warmth get deep into his body. "Ready?" he asked. He killed the engine and opened the door. "Let's move."

The neighborhood was dark and all I could hear was the sound of our feet in the snow and Chalk baying somewhere down by the Saw Mill. The air burned my lungs. Norm let down the tailgate and then stood and looked up at the stars. The stillness of everything had made us both go silent.

"Need some help with that?" I asked.

"You shovel," he said, pointing toward a spot near the edge of the road.

I grabbed a garden shovel out of the truck bed. "Listen," I said, "I don't mean to come down and panhandle."

"Don't think about it," he said. He lifted the Coleman from the truck. "You can watch the line while I cook." He moved gingerly, putting the stove to rest in the place I'd cleared. "You a bacon-and-eggs man?"

"Sure."

"Got pork chops, too."

"Bacon is fine."

"Maybe some of both?"

"Sure."

"How about some fresh coffee?"

"That'd be nice," I said.

Norm lit the stove and got a cooler from the back of the truck. "You should take some weight off that leg," he said. He brought me a camp stool from behind the front seat, opened it up, and offered it to me. Patting the vinyl, he said, "Warm that puppy up."

"You're a real Boy Scout," I said.

"Semper Fi," he said, giving a salute.

I paused. "Always be prepared," I corrected.

"Vietnam," he said without looking up.

I watched this man, Norm, while he removed a skillet, coffeepot, coffee, eggs, bacon, pork chops, a package of paper plates, and plastic utensils from the cooler. Norm was a man of practical leisure. He made a table, as they say, and it wasn't so bad. He was careful, orderly, keeping things clean, and in the heat from the stove I felt almost at home.

"Let's get a smoke before we eat," he said as if it were an order of business. He stood up from in front of the stove.

"Sure," I said. I leaned over and put my elbows on my knees.

"Keep your seat," he said. Norm reached into his vest pocket and pulled out a joint. "I plan ahead," he said. "They're tough to roll in this kind of weather. By the time dinner is done your hands won't feel like yours at all."

Norm put the stub between his lips and lit it and then squatted down in front of me. "Okay," he said. "Okay. Like this," he said. He took a drag and then held it in. He seemed to swallow something that was bitter. "Like that," he said, offering the stub in my direction. "Hold it in," he said.

I started with a small breath and let it out. Norm nodded to me and I took in some more and held it as long as I could. I felt a stinging in my throat and tried to hold back a cough.

"You'll get it," he said.

I took another pull and this time I could feel my throat and lungs open up and take the smoke all inside. I closed my eyes and tried to locate any change, even the vaguest hint of one, that might be happening to my body. I held the stub out for Norm.

"It's all you," he said, motioning for me to finish the whole thing.

Norm stood up again and took a walk out toward the power line. Then, turning, he looked back over me and our setup, toward my house. "You live there alone?" he asked, taking steps back toward the stove.

"Not always," I said.

He kneeled beside the Coleman. "Better than always," he said, smiling. He cracked the eggs with one hand, directly into a cast-iron skillet, tossing the shells out into the snow. He whisked the yolks around a moment and then shuffled the coffeepot a bit closer to the flame. Thoughts looked to be strolling around in his head. "So why not always?" he asked finally.

"Wife's gone for a while," I said. But the truth was Anita had left me. Gone to stay with friends; people who had a gas generator—lights, hot water, heat.

"With you lame?" he asked.

"Yeah."

"That's tough." He paused a moment to shift the eggs onto one half the pan. You could tell he was attempting to conjure up my story. He laid strips of bacon out on the skillet. "How do you get around?"

"Walk."

"I mean, to the doctor and stuff," he hesitated. "For chemo? To the store for food?"

"Don't know," I said.

He divided the eggs onto plates and draped more bacon on the skillet. "I'll get the chops last," he said.

"She's just gone," I added, in an effort to make sense of it for him. I turned sideways on the stool and tried not to let the roach burn my fingers. I was worried about this, about how not to look like I didn't know how to handle the situation. I took a drag and tried to pass it on. He refused and so I touched the burning end lightly into the snow.

Norm drained the bacon grease and forked several strips onto each plate. "Fuel," he said, handing the eggs and bacon my way.

"Thanks."

"For good?" he asked.

"That might not be long," I suggested.

Anita had left a few days back, the first morning we were without power. Winter had hardly come at all. Then I felt something in my leg, and overnight two feet of heavy snow settled in over the valley—early for these parts, the first week of November. The night before she left, Anita was driving me home from the hospital when the street lights went dark and along the road the houses sat like coffins. We drove twenty miles in the dark, over forgotten routes, between open fields just cleared of corn, and then into Buckland where even the traffic signals were out. We live over some hills from town, at the base of a range that rises up and makes the northern rim of a valley. I'd always felt like this was a good place to be.

Norm had a plastic bag with flour in it that he dropped a couple of pork chops into. He shook them around a bit and then fingered the meat into the skillet with a bit of bacon grease. The smell of fried pork swelled around us.

"It hurt?" Norm asked, pointing to my leg. He turned the chops.

"There's a rod in it," I said. "I can feel it get cold."

"I knew a girl once. Had lots of metal in her."

"Yeah?"

"Years ago, in high school." He put his hand out for my plate. "Biology teacher had her bring X rays to class."

"What happened?"

"We started saying things like 'Fat Amy's insides.' " Norm put a pork chop on my plate and handed it to me. "She'd walk by and we'd say that under our breath."

I shook my head, thinking how things like that happen when you're young.

"Those X rays though," he paused. "She had bones."

"I guess."

"There were all angles. Dozens of them." Norm swallowed. "Close in. Far out. Just the knee, where the bolts and screws and all kinds of contraptions were, and then the whole leg up to where there's the crease. They put some kind of something on her to protect her parts."

"A real *Gray's Anatomy.*"

"Yeah. Really."

"So what happened?"

"We looked at those snapshots for days," he shook his head. "I studied the close-ups. It was like all those shadows and curves—the bones—were people. Tight. Together. Doing things, you know."

I didn't know, but I shook my head like I understood.

"I got to where I wanted her," he said.

"From X rays?"

"Seeing her insides all the way up. That leg just really got me."

"What happened?"

"She got herself killed somehow. A few years back. Left two kids. A car accident."

"Fat Amy's insides?"

"Yeah."

"How fat?"

"Not too." He paused. "Just enough, you know."

"That got to you?"

"Those bones," Norm said. "Some nights I'd just run my hands down her hip, along her thigh. I'd just try to feel them."

I watched Norm close his eyes and figured he was back trying to locate what it was that made him want to look inside a person. He sat for a moment, hunched over his plate, and then he reached over for the coffeepot. "Warm up?" he asked.

"Sure."

He was delicate, pouring carefully into the bowl. "I saw enough in Vietnam to cure me," he offered. He managed the bowl with both hands, delivering it to me like a child.

"I was wondering."

"Enough bone to make a thousand bodies."

"You ever marry?"

"Sure."

"What happened?"

"I don't know," he said. "What about you?"

"She said I didn't know how to be scared."

"That—I could teach you."

"She was terrified."

"Kids?"

"No."

"Well—"

"It's not like I've got a choice," I said. I lifted the bowl of coffee to my face and held it there for a moment. The steam brought moisture to my skin. I took a sip and held it in my mouth.

"You should be scared," Norm said, almost as if he were asking me to do this for him.

"She began to be angry with me," I explained. "About the pain and the treatments. It was a lot for her. Driving me around and taking care of stuff at the house."

"I've seen a lot of bad things happening," he said. "It takes a lot to watch. I saw Amy's daughter for instance. I see her around up in New Hampshire. She looks like her mother did and she sees that herself every day."

"I don't see much."

"In Nam I watched people waste away. From the inside out."

"Who doesn't."

"It's frustrating," he said. "It's like they won't admit anything's wrong. Their silence—it's like being blamed."

"What's to say?"

"I don't know."

"There's nothing."

"Just saying you're scared is something."

"For the sake of others?"

"Why not?" He paused and took a drink of coffee. "That's what we want to hear."

Norm stood up and looked off in the direction of the power line. We hadn't seen or heard any cars coming up the road all evening. "Let's warm up in the truck," he said, offering to take my plate from me. I walked around the side and got in while Norm went across the road and dumped the scraps along the tree line.

"That dog'll get them," he said when he got in and cranked the engine.

"Chalk," I said.

"Odd sounding."

"Bluetick," I said. "They all sound different."

A cold blast came from the vents. Norm raced the engine trying to get the heater to produce something decent. I thought of Anita down in Buckland, keeping warm. She might be trying to figure things out, coming to an understanding, wanting to run her hands over my leg, along my spine, across my chest.

In the moonlight I could see the power line in a tangled mess. "Suppose you touched that," I said. "What would you feel for just that second?"

"Surprise."

"Yeah. But that's like a thought."

"A last thought."

Norm turned to face me. The heat was beginning to kick in and I could feel my body loosening up—the muscles letting go. My hands ached.

"I imagine carbonation," he paused. "The tiniest bubbles. You feel the tingle in your blood."

"No thoughts."

"No. Just knowing."

"Not the life-flashing-before-your-eyes thing?"

"More immediate."

"Tiny bubbles," I said, in a half-song.

"Wires."

"Really. Yeah," I said. "I think so. All your cells—for that less than a moment—one."

"There's that moment when you're both there and not there. In between."

"I guess that's what it means to want to get inside?" I said. "That point when you're not alive, not dead. We want to know that."

"Sure."

For a moment I thought I knew what we were saying, but just as quickly I realized I hadn't a clue. I was just talking, just saying things, words, that might belong to someone else. Norm was there, across the seat from me, staring like he was waiting for me to tell him something. We both went quiet. Norm turned the ignition and we sat and listened to the engine cool down.

In front of us I could see the silhouette of Chalk shuffle around the food Norm had left out—dancing, doing a jig, tail wagging in a nervous kind of way.

"Brenda would not like this if she knew," I said in a childish, instructive tone. Chalk carried pork a little at a time a few yards away and then chewed like he was snapping at air.

"Brenda?"

"His owner."

"Well, Brenda doesn't know."

"She keeps him fit," I said. "On a diet."

Norm reached between the seats and pulled out a package of dried beef. "I hate this shit," he said. He rolled down his window and tossed a handful out in front of the truck. Chalk appeared luminous, blue, darting in the moonlight to pick up the stalks of jerky. His speckled ticking hovered about the snow. He stopped as if on point, then went for a second handful Norm had pitched out of the truck. Norm began to laugh and check behind the seat, then in the glove compartment, looking for something else to throw. He came up empty-handed and seemed lost for a moment.

Then it was as if our senses struck flint—a flicker of light; a crack; a brief yelp, maybe not one at all—and we both called, "Ohh." A shadow drifted across the road in front of us and came to a stop along a snowbank.

"What the fuck—"

"Chalk," I said, letting my hand search for the door handle. We both sat motionless for a time and just stared at what we had not quite seen. I felt my insides turn cold.

You could smell burned hair in the soft breeze and down the hill I heard the river. I stood over the dog, looking up the way toward the line.

"Let it alone," Norm called. "Don't touch it."

"Son of a bitch."

"May be hot," Norm said, coming to my side with a rubber-handled gaff.

"Could he be alive?"

"No chance."

"Sure?"

"Very."

We both stood over the body, confused, amazed. Norm nudged the dog. "All this time and then this," Norm said. "I'm in deep now."

"What could you do?" I bent down and ran my hand along Chalk's face. He could have been sleeping. My own heart was beating strong, pumping in my ears.

"What *can* I do?" Norm asked. He wasn't interested in suggestions: His mind was made up. "I'll have to call this in," he said. "Where's this Brenda live?"

"Up the hill," I said. And then I suggested, "It was an accident."

"No such thing."

I got to my feet and I could feel my leg was really beginning to hurt. The rod running through the inside of my thigh was cooling off, or that was the impression it gave. I hadn't left the house to come down here for all of this—some dope, a watchman, and a dead dog. I'd come to find a few things out. Now we had a situation. I glanced at the power line and then turned and looked back over the truck toward my house, at the dark windows from where I could be watching. I considered the options.

"Don't report this," I said, finally. "Don't say anything."

"If I don't," Norm said, "she will."

"Don't tell Brenda, either," I said.

"She's going to notice the dog's missing."

"She lets it run loose. Something could happen."

"Something did."

"I noticed," I said, trying to smile. My thoughts were going flat and for the first time I realized the dope had put its fingers on me, but was now losing hold. I turned and headed back for the truck. I hated what had happened to Brenda's dog. Shameful. It pierced me somehow, got to me while I sat there in the truck with Norm, us not talking, just waiting for the warmth to emerge.

"Take him down to the river," I said.

"She needs to know."

"No. She can think he's run off. Or been picked up. The truth is she doesn't need to know."

"It's better knowing."

"Is it?" I asked. "Does it help you—knowing?"

Norm considered the question.

"He'll drift far enough before things freeze up."

"And if they look for him?"

"Who looks for a dead dog?"

Norm didn't try to answer. I watched him keep an eye on Chalk. Norm lit a cigarette and took a sip of coffee. A trace of blood ran in the snow, coming from the dog's body. In the light I realized I could see steam rising from the dog. I knew Brenda would call down the next day, or in a few days, and ask if I'd seen Chalk. She might even take the car through the neighborhood streets, looking. She wouldn't stop though, only slow down, study the landscape, keep driving. She could keep her hope up that way.

"Lend me a smoke?" I asked.

"Cigarette?" Norm said, surprised.

"I've never seen anything like that," I said, holding out my hand.

Norm hesitated then handed me the pack. "You scared?"

"Maybe of being alone."

"You are alone."

"You go through it like that dog," I said. "Not knowing much."

"There's no other way to do it. That's fear—no one in your shoes."

"I guess." I tapped a cigarette out of the pack and lit it.

"I was beyond scared," he said. "I'm talking Nam. Waiting."

"Hmm."

Norm frowned. He opened his door and emptied his coffee. "I knew a guy," he said, then halted. Reaching behind my seat he found the thermos and poured a fresh cup. "Lukewarm," he said after taking a drink. He handed me the cup to share. I took a swallow and handed it back.

"Spider," Norm said, "was a buddy in Nam." He paused, took another sip, and let himself fall backward through his thoughts; he slipped down into his seat, slackened. "A real gunner, I mean."

"A walker?" I asked.

"You couldn't hear him two-step across gravel. A genuine Jungle Jim."

"GI Joe."

"With balls."

"Okay."

"You've heard this story a thousand times, I'm sure. But listen."

"I'm listening."

"Incoming hit and I heard all kinds of wails. Inhuman kinds of sounds. I ran to see. Spider had bones poking out of him, some not even his. A dirt hole with just a mess of flesh. Couldn't tell how many men there were. The mortar just made a deep grave."

Norm was quiet for a moment and I could see his breath in the air. He was beginning to breathe slower, deliberately. I looked away from him, out onto the snow that was losing definition in the rush of moonlight. I stubbed my cigarette into the ashtray.

"I came up on Spider in that hole and I stayed over him. My mouth started watering. I just kept drooling. His bowels stank, the stench spilling out of him as he rocked side to side."

"Jesus."

"Spider said it was like seeing pussy for the first time, seeing it in the flesh, balls tightening up—" Norm halted. "Watching him, it was like everyone was the same person. Seeing his senses firing all at once like that made me go empty inside except for the fear."

"Did he tell you things? What it was like?"

"It wasn't like the movies. He didn't just close his eyes. Spider turned on himself, tugged at his own insides, wanted to be used up."

"What'd he say?"

"He looked to me, like he wanted me to be afraid. But his eyes, they were calm. I got so pissed at him." Norm closed his eyes. He seemed to forget his job, the power line, and the dog lying in the street, and me waiting to hear what he had to say. "I wanted him to die," Norm said, pausing. "I left him behind and went on."

I sat quietly, stared out at the trees along the shoulder of the road. I began to feel the mechanisms inside me at work—my anatomy going all cockeyed. My muscles pulled tight, my bones ached. "It's getting colder than hell," I said finally. Norm didn't respond. I imagined Chalk floating downstream, his body calm, forgiving. "This has got me by the short hairs," I admitted.

Norm let out a brief laugh. His cigarette had burned down to the filter; he lowered the window and tossed it out. A dampness settled at the corners of my eyes. "It's cold," he said. He cranked the engine and sat up in his seat.

"You take Chalk down to the Saw Mill," I said. "Make sure he doesn't snag. No one will know."

"We're going to take care of this one," he said. Norm reached into his vest pocket and pulled out the plastic bag and rested it in his lap. He put his hands up to the vents, warming his fingers, and then rubbed his palms together.

"Get the snow out there too," I said, pointing to where the blood had stained the ground.

After his hands were warm, Norm turned the vents away from

himself. He undid the bag, culled a paper, and began to roll a joint. I watched his fingers work, nimble and quick, practiced. In a few minutes he'd made up several. "Take these," he said when he had finished. He tucked them into my shirt pocket. "This'll get you through a few times." He tugged the zipper up on my coat.

With the engine running, Norm got out of the truck and walked to where Chalk was lying in the snow. He shook his head and bent down to examine the dog. For the longest time Norm just kneeled there, waiting for something to happen it seemed. I let the heat pour across my face and hands. I thought about joining Norm, offering to help. But he gathered the dog into his arms, gently holding him to his body. It was as if he had hold of a child, or a lover. I could see he was steady on his feet, looking down occasionally, cradling Chalk, shifting his weight for support, until I lost sight of him between the trees.

I stepped out of the truck and I tried to listen for the sound of Norm thrashing down toward the water, but all I could hear was the engine running and as I turned and headed for home that noise faded and the echo of the river made it up the bluff. Wood burned in a fireplace down the road. I could see the smoke, silvery in the light, coming from a chimney. Even after all Norm and I had consumed, I was bare. I had a hunger and my stomach turned. I needed something to eat.

The house was dark, but not as cold as I'd imagined it would be. I stood in the kitchen taking in the smell of vacant rooms and listened to water dripping from the faucet onto a stack of unwashed dishes. This and the boards that creaked under the kitchen linoleum were the only sounds I could hear as I shifted my balance, wanting to feel something in my leg beyond the cold. I opened the refrigerator and used a flashlight to look around inside. I touched the tops of jars and casseroles, packages of meat and a carton of milk; everything was damp, almost tepid. The freezer-meat was half-thawed. Everything inside was on the verge of going bad. I decided to save what I could and took the flashlight down to the basement and returned with boxes.

I began to empty the refrigerator. First, the milk and half-and-half that Anita used in her coffee, then deli mustard, tomato ketchup, jars of kosher dill halves, and Hellmann's mayonnaise. A smell, dead air, escaped the refrigerator. My thoughts were mechanical, measured by the dripping faucet. I focused on packing the box—half-jars of pasta sauce; a container of Cool Whip and Imperial margarine; a few cans of beer; and on top of this I spread packages of Parmesan cheese; Danish emmentaler; smoked turkey and ham slices; and a carton of eggs. I felt solid, a part of the thick mess this early winter had brought on. I worked with an even motion, emptying the beef round, shell sirloin steak, boneless chicken breasts, and pork ribs. I put the pie crusts into a separate box. In with these I put a half-full bottle of Lindemans Merlot and an unopened bottle of Mumm Cordon Rouge. I wrapped the boxes in plastic trash bags and took them outside.

Behind the house I kneeled down beneath the limbs of a chestnut tree and began to remove the thick covering of snow with my bare hands. I worked my fingers into the packed layers, lifting clots out into a mound until I could see a dark slip of earth, a space large enough for the boxes. I set each box flush against the frozen ground and then I paused to get my breath. Sweat ran down my back. In the moonlight, the hole in the snow appeared bottomless.

I wanted to laugh. It was all but done. I dug in with my feet, shouldered a bank of snow over the boxes, smoothed the surface until there was no sign of what was underneath. I worked until I couldn't feel my hands. Air scorched my lungs and my head felt on fire, burning from the inside, and my mouth was dry.

I lay back in the snow and watched my breath drift upward. Snow-covered branches creased the sky. Around me, everything was bowing under the weight. In the distance I heard Norm's truck engine stop and I imagined him sitting in the front seat looking out at the power line, drinking coffee, considering whether he should walk up to Brenda's place to tell her the truth. I listened to the quiet, to the occasional snap of branches, and for a while I thought of Anita. A hollowness opened up in my stomach. I had the sense of falling, a fear of being trapped in a small place, of moving so quickly that I could barely keep my eyes open.

Carolyn Moon

University of Arizona

THROUGH THE TIMBER

In the final days of the harvest Glen drove the combine. The temperature had fallen to winter's, and while there hadn't been snow yet, it had rained or misted most of November. He could see his older brother, Michael, waiting by the wagon. Glen drove to the end of the row, watching to keep the stalk-cutting teeth from driving into the moist ground. For Glen, this was what farming was. Till, plant, spray, harvest, till. Up one row and down the next. There were certain things that Michael wouldn't do, or couldn't do: he couldn't drive the combine or the planter; he wouldn't spray the chemicals; he wouldn't haul the wagons to the elevator in town. He was a good enough mechanic, though, and managed to keep most of their equipment running. In Glen's opinion, Michael wasn't a farmer at all. If none of the equipment needed fixing, he would wander through the timber, or between the barns, or disappear until their father pounded on his door to come outside. Michael would appear, ambling slowly, his eyes squinting in the light, shaking his head no, no, no.

Marla, Glen's girlfriend, drove into the field and parked next to the wagon. She got out with a cooler and went over to Michael, who pointed toward Glen. When Michael walked away, Marla followed him as if she might actually engage him in conversation, but he didn't stop. He climbed into the brown Chevy and drove away.

Glen left the combine running and climbed down. He liked that she seemed so out of place on the farm. She was bright, he thought. Not smart bright, but colorful bright. She was wearing a turquoise ski jacket and matching cap. Her hair was bleached blonder than it really was. She wore lipstick and eye shadow, which he didn't care for really, but it looked so different to him, different from the brown, gray, and green of the farm.

"Where'd Michael go?" he asked. He took her arm and led her back to the pickup and they both got in the driver's side door.

"I don't know. I think I scare him. As soon as I show up, he always runs off. He needs a girlfriend." Marla opened the cooler and took out sandwiches and a thermos of tomato soup she'd made from a can.

"I don't think that's his problem."

"Well, he needs to get out more. Let's invite him to go to town with us tonight."

"No."

"Why not?"

Glen opened the plastic wrap that had been neatly folded around a boiled ham sandwich. "Because I don't want to."

"But why don't you want to?"

"Because." He'd started to say "Because I said so," but Marla wouldn't have liked it. She needed reasons. She wanted to know what he was thinking about things, she said. "Because he wouldn't go anyway."

"It won't hurt to ask," she said.

"Please, Marla. He's very shy." He felt he had to struggle for the right words, that the real things he was thinking about why Michael wouldn't go would sound mean and insufficient. "He's a strange person. He likes to be alone."

"It's so weird that he's your older brother. He seems so much younger," she said.

"I think he seems really old." Glen ate a sandwich in four big bites and Marla turned the radio to a top forty station.

The first time Marla had met his family, last Thanksgiving, Michael had told Glen that she was pretty. Glen told Marla, and she'd been pleased. She liked Michael, Glen thought, because of that. His parents had treated her politely but coldly. After dinner, after Marla had gone home, he heard his mother say, "She's probably never seen a house this nice before. Of course she's crazy about Glen. She's probably never met a good man with a decent living in her life."

He imagined how hurt she would have been to hear this. She and her five brothers and sisters had grown up with their mother in a trailer. Her mother was an alcoholic, as were several of the kids. The men worked as farm hands, which was the lowest of the low, and the women worked in bars, except for Marla, the youngest. She managed the furniture section at Penney's.

His father, too, had warned him about Marla. "I know you really like her, Glen," he'd said. "But did you ever think that maybe she's just after you for your money?"

"I don't have any money, Dad. You have all the money," he'd said and walked away. It was true. His father paid them less than five hundred dollars a month. He could have made a better wage at any fast food restaurant in town. "Marla makes more money than I do, Dad. Maybe I'm the one after her money."

"You have your house, and half the farm when I'm gone," his father said. Glen couldn't answer. It was true that he didn't pay any rent on the house he lived in. He also didn't pay for the utilities, but with five hundred dollars a month, he paid for everything else. He would even have to borrow money to buy Marla a decent engagement ring if they got married. Besides, every time his father mentioned that he'd get half the farm, it always made him wish that his father was dead. He'd heard it so many times: the farm is worth so much money, and it can be yours if you just wait until I'm dead. Glen was twenty-five, his father only sixty. The old man would never retire and might live another thirty years. He didn't drink or smoke. He was strong as an ox. Then there was Michael, who would get the other half, though he didn't do half the work. The thought of sharing the farm and his life with Michael forever made him sick.

Marla poured a cup of tomato soup from the thermos. One drop splashed onto her jacket. "Oh, no," she said. "I just bought this."

Glen took a paper towel and licked it. He pulled the fabric toward him and scrubbed until the spot disappeared. She put her hand on the back of his head. Their foreheads touched.

*   *   *

After dark, Glen showered and then drove to Marla's house, which she rented from a farmer who owned more farms than he had family. The house was white and covered with aluminum siding dulled by unbroken wind and grayed from blowing dirt. Inside, though, the tiny house was warm and brightly colored, like Marla herself. She painted everything: tables, chests of drawers, picture frames, lamps, switch plates. In the kitchen she had painted the old refrigerator "canary."

The TV was on when she answered the door, but she had been sewing; a pair of slacks lay on the couch with pins sticking out of the cuffs. She sewed and knitted, made slipcovers for her furniture. She was busy and resourceful and Glen liked her for that. He felt inside of himself a dullness, which might run toward sloth if he didn't fight it. Right now, though, he was simply exhausted and could barely hear from riding in the combine for twelve hours. When she said hello, her voice came to him as if she were speaking from another room.

"I can't go out, Marla. I'm too tired. I'm sorry" was the first thing he said after kissing her.

"It's okay," she said. "It's pretty late anyways." It was eight and town was thirty miles away.

"You're not mad? I'm sorry sorry sorry. Tomorrow we'll go."

"Something weird happened today," she said after they sat down together on the couch. "Michael was here when I got home."

Glen felt the skin on his back flare and itch. "Why?"

"I'm not sure. When I came back from lunch with you I saw his truck, and then I called for him. I walked around to the side of the house," she said and pointed toward the window. Glen felt that if he looked, he would see Michael's face and red flannel shirt behind the glass.

"I thought I heard him behind the house. I think he kicked out my basement window," she said. "When I came around the corner, I noticed the window, and then he was in his truck and driving away. It was like he didn't think I could see him. I yelled, but he wouldn't stop."

Glen stood and walked through the kitchen. He unlocked the back door and opened it, putting the image of Michael aside. There was nothing there except the yard with an empty clothesline and an old barn. The yard was lit by a dusk-to-dawn light on a tall pole. He jumped down the steps and saw that the small basement window under the kitchen was covered by a loose board.

"I put the board there. I found glass on the floor downstairs and swept it up. It was creepy, though. Glen, could you ask him about it?"

"Are you sure it was Michael?" he said, though he knew she was telling the truth. Michael had broken into his house twice before. The first time, years ago, he had claimed to be looking for a tool. The second time Glen woke to hear Michael in his house, in the kitchen. Glen floated in half-sleep in his bed that night, hearing Michael open drawers and then shut them. He'd been afraid, and that fear must've made him unable to wake fully and go downstairs. The next morning he discovered one pane of glass in the side door was broken, but Michael denied that he'd done it.

"It was Michael, Glen. I don't like him coming here like that. Was he trying to break in? I mean, why did he break the window?"

Glen crouched in front of the board and tried to secure it. He would get some nails and tack it in for her. Tomorrow he'd have to come over and replace the window. His ears hurt. Behind him Marla was hugging herself with her hands tucked into the cuffs of her sweater and bouncing from foot to foot to keep warm.

"Let's go inside."

Later Glen went back out and sealed the hole by tacking up a blanket and then fitting a piece of plywood he had cut to the size of the window. He put up another piece of wood inside. Marla's basement had a little workbench that he'd built for her. Above it were two aluminum lamps suspended from the rafters. She had all her tools hanging from hooks on a pegboard and around each one was an outline: the hammer goes here; the wrench goes there; the screwdriver here. Glen stopped on the stairs to see what Michael had been after, but there wasn't anything obviously missing.

Glen bolted the door to the basement. Marla had made coffee. He hung his coat on the hook. The cold had made him even more tired, made him ache in the middle of his back.

"What do you think he wanted?" Marla asked. He couldn't help but notice, again, how neat her house was, how much work she'd done on this rental. He wondered at her energy. Still, though, there was something about her: she tried so hard. Sometimes when he saw the details, he thought he detected desperation: plastic flowers in a vase on the kitchen windowsill, tiny framed pictures she cut from a magazine and framed with wooden sticks from ice-cream bars, and all that color. Now there was Michael, who probably hadn't wanted anything—he hadn't taken anything of Glen's that he could ever figure—or if he'd said what he wanted, it wouldn't have made any sense.

"I don't know. He's just very strange," he said. "But he's harmless."

"I don't get it, Glen," she said. "I've never been anything but nice to him. And your whole family." She put her coffee cup on the counter. The kitchen was tiny. Glen reached out and tucked the hair behind her ear. He went to her and put his arms around her shoulders and stroked her hair; Marla gasped once and sighed.

"It's not you," Glen said. "Michael's strange. He's just strange. He's a little bit crazy, I think." He had no idea what was wrong with Michael. Glen had made a point to know as little as possible about Michael.

"Well, if he's sick or something, don't you think he should get some help?" she asked.

He'd thought of that, too. "I sometimes think that farming has driven him crazy. The isolation and boredom," he said.

Marla looked at his face and tilted her head back. They were still holding each other loosely. Glen felt examined. Marla said, "Really?"

"Yes. It's like he refused to be a farmer, refuses to be a farmer, even though that's what he is. He doesn't do his job, though, and nothing—not me or my father—can make him," he said. "It's like he's doing everything on purpose. I mean, I can say he's weird and maybe crazy, but I still feel like he's doing it all on purpose."

"Even coming here?"

"Maybe. I don't know. Maybe he's jealous. But it's like he won't let me have something he couldn't have. I always end up doing everything." Glen thought that he might cry next, but then he felt foolish for having said anything at all.

Several days later, while he was standing at his kitchen sink rinsing dishes, Glen saw Michael coming through the timber and heading toward his house. The trees were gray and bare, like pencil marks on a white paper. Michael's red shirt made him think of the plastic cardinals his mother hung from the trees in the winter for decoration. He wasn't wearing a coat. Glen could see the steam of his breath as he stepped over a fallen tree and headed into the shorn field, lifting each boot.

Glen put his coat on and went to meet him at the edge of the lawn. The three farmhouses were arranged in a triangle, with the timber in the center. Michael lived in the house south of the timber, Glen in the house on the northeast corner, and his parents in the northwest corner, on a rise. Glen could see the barns at his parents' house, but couldn't see Michael's house behind the timber at all. Glen didn't want him near. He didn't want him to feel comfortable coming to his house.

Michael trudged on, not looking up until he stopped his march nearly twenty feet away from Glen. He just stood between mounded rows of cornstalks. Glen felt sudden guilt and fear that Michael had sensed his thoughts or could read his face. He stepped over the edge of the lawn as if it were raised and went to meet his brother in the field.

"Someone's been in my barn. Someone's been there, probably tried my house, but couldn't get in."

"How do you know?" Glen asked.

"I saw them run away through the timber."

"I haven't seen anyone." Earlier he'd been unraveling wire behind his own barn. He would've seen anyone come out of the timber, which rested in low land around a tiny marsh.

Michael waited. Glen suspected he had only heard a noise. "They're gone now?" Glen asked.

"I don't know."

Michael was taller than Glen, and bigger, but he always seemed stooped, always kept his eyes to the ground three or four feet in front of himself. He seemed more like an old bachelor farmer than a man of thirty. Since graduating from high school twelve years ago, he had rarely left the farm. Glen thought about the window at Marla's, then about Michael in his kitchen that night a while ago. Since then, he'd replaced the window with plastic instead of glass. He'd also installed another lock on her door. He was going to buy her a dog. Michael was afraid of dogs, which is probably what this was about: some animal burrowing under his barn to escape the cold.

The barnyard at Michael's farm was quiet. The windows of the house were covered with cloudy, thick plastic people used to keep out the drafts in winter. Michael, though, never took his down. Behind the plastic, which was practically opaque, the house was dark. The yard was kept and mowed, but the shrubs had been shorn off at the ground, as had the few trees.

This was the house they'd grown up in. Nearly ten years ago, his father and mother had built a new, large split-level ranch house on another corner. Glen had been in high school then; he had moved with his parents across the field, but Michael had stayed. Their parents had bought new furniture and left the old for Michael. Glen hadn't been inside the old house in a year or longer.

"Where did you see them?" he asked. Michael pointed to the barn where the tractors with the augers, plows, and planters waited for the next till. Glen checked the locks on both doors, but they were unharmed.

"There's a hole on the other side where they've been trying to dig their way in," Michael said. A few crows flew past before landing in the field to scavenge the fallen kernels of corn, calling to each other. Glen noticed the sound of the wind as they turned the corner to find a small hole at the base of the barn.

"Looks like a dog or something was digging there," Glen said. He wanted to leave. He had come to prove to himself that he wasn't afraid of Michael, but now he just wanted to get away from him.

Michael put his hands on his knees and bent over. "I think they've been coming here for a while trying to dig their way in."

"Well, a dog might sleep under the floor, but I don't think any people have been digging at that hole."

Michael shook his head. "They could have been."

"Let's just fill in the hole." Glen bent over and pushed the dirt back. He put his hand on the barn to steady himself, and paint chips came off on his hand. He stomped the dirt down.

"They'll just come back," Michael said.

"Nothing but an animal has been digging that hole, Michael."

Michael seemed to be listening to something. Glen couldn't hear a thing except the wind, the crows, and the distant chugging of a neighbor's tractor on the road. His eyes swept past the silent dryers as he tried to see who was passing. "The dryers!" Glen shouted and reached out for Michael, who stepped away with his arms over his face.

Five drying silos behind the barn held all of their recent harvest of corn, constantly turning it and blowing gas heat through it. Their father was waiting for prices to rise after harvest, before selling it. Glen ran toward the silos, but each of them was as silent as if it were empty. No whooshing of the fans, no creaking of the auger that brought the corn from the bottom up to the top. Inside each control panel, he found the switches turned to off.

"What's going on?" he yelled as he ran from silo to silo, checking each one, turning each one back on and hearing it rev alive. Even as he did so, he could smell a rancid, fermented odor. How much was ruined, he didn't know for sure. There had been rains and the air was damp, but he couldn't know how long the dryers had been off. Samples would have to be taken and moisture levels measured, but even then . . .

"Why, Michael? Why did you turn them off?" he shouted over the roaring fans. Michael didn't answer. Glen pushed him, but he wouldn't fight back.

"They were going to catch fire. They were too hot," he said in a loud, dull voice. "The noise," he said.

Glen turned. How much of their year would be ruined? How much time had been wasted? he wondered.

As Glen drove past his parents' house he let his anger build. He wished all of the harvest were ruined. He wished it were all stinking and rotten. He drove past the new house on his parents' lot, then turned the corner and drove toward his own. All of their land was in this block, this perfect square with ninety-degree angles. Even the timber was square, though the trees themselves grew without organization, in sharp contrast to the rows of corn.

He parked the truck in his yard but didn't get out. He remembered a conversation he'd had with Michael when he was in high school, when Michael had already graduated. He'd taken a photography class and worked on the newspaper. He'd thought about becoming a photo-journalist and, in his excitement, confessed this thought to Michael one day while they rode in the combine after school.

Michael said, "He'll never let you."

"He doesn't own me." But Michael just shook his head.

A year later, Glen quit the newspaper when his father told him that he needed him for the harvest. He hadn't been angry with his father, though; he'd been angry with Michael, who had tipped the combine in a low spot near the timber and gotten it stuck in the mud two other times. All three times they'd had to tow it out with the tractor, and once it had been badly damaged. Michael was forbidden to harvest and was left to haul the wagons of corn to the dryers. Glen had to drive one combine while his father drove the other. He came home every after-noon to work. Michael ruined everything.

Glen wouldn't tell his father about the dryers—not because he wanted to protect Michael, but because he had wished the harvest were ruined.

The next week Glen was sitting on the step inside his small enclosed porch, when he saw someone appear suddenly in the window. In the split second before he knew the figure in the dark was his father, he felt a wave of fear thinking it was Michael. His father and Michael shared the same broad shoulders, thick neck and body, the same squarish head. His father burst through the door and was stunned to see Glen sitting on the step, one foot in a boot and the other in a wool stocking.

"The dryers are off. I went over to tell Michael to unload a silo and take it in. They were all off," his father said.

Glen looked down at the mat where his father stood. His boots were caked with mud and frosted with glittering snowflakes.

"How could they all break at once? Did the power go off here last night?" he asked Glen. He looked confused and pathetic. All five would never break at the same time, and the dryers were gas, so even a power outage wouldn't shut them down.

"Power's been on here. Where's Michael?"

"I knocked, but he's not there. He keeps the doors locked," his father said.

"Michael turned off the dryers," Glen said.

His father frowned, "Why would he do that?"

"I don't know, but he did it," he said. Glen stood and put his coat on. In the pocket he found gloves, and on a hook next to the door he found a cap that he pulled down over his ears.

The morning was still dark. There was no sign of the sun on the horizon, but the yard light lit the gravel driveway. The two men rode together to Michael's farm. Light snow covered the road. The fields were black around Michael's house and barn as the headlights from his father's truck swept across the empty rows. The house was dark. Glen went to the back door, pounded, yelled, shook the handle, but Michael didn't appear and the lock didn't budge.

The dryers next to the barn were still silent. His father hadn't turned them back on after discovering them off, and now the two men walked through the crackling frozen grass to get them going again. All the while, his father seemed to move too slowly and by the time he had turned on one dryer, Glen had started all the others. They stood at the edge of the dark field, looking for Michael, the whoosh and scraping sound of the dryers behind them.

"His truck's in the drive," his father said. "I don't know where he could be."

"Dad, Michael turned off the dryers. He did the same thing last week. I turned them all back on. He admitted it."

"Why?" his father asked.

"He said he was afraid they would catch fire. He said he was afraid of the noise."

"Why?" his father asked again, and Glen wondered if he meant, Why didn't you tell me?

"He's crazy," Glen said. "Michael is sick."

His father reached Michael's house before Glen could catch up. He was ten steps away when he heard the glass breaking from his father's gloved hand. His father was unlatching the knob lock and then the bolt.

"Dad," Glen said, touching his shoulder, but his father ignored him and yanked on the door, which opened half an inch and slammed back shut because of another bolt at the floor. "Dad, let me." Glen managed to push his father aside and cleared broken glass with his fisted hand. The shards fell inside, tinkling on the floor. He hoisted himself through the frame and unlocked the last bolt.

Once inside they both called to Michael. They turned the hall and kitchen lights on. The kitchen was dismantled somehow. Glen remembered it from when he was young, the same wallpaper with the tiny flowers hung on the wall—though yellowed and dingy now from the propane that fired the stove. The cabinets were all open and empty and their contents were stacked on the counters. Pans, dishes, pots, kitchen towels were all arranged neatly, covering the space. On the kitchen table were rows of silverware, and then around the perimeter outward-pointing rays, creating a perfect circle of shiny forks, knives, and spoons. Glen recognized them as the same utensils they had used every day for twenty years.

Glen went to the window to see if Michael was in the barn, but what he had thought was the black night sky was black plastic taped over the inside of the window. He followed his father into the dining room. The windows there had also been covered by blankets nailed to the plaster. The furniture was stacked in a corner. The simple chandelier was wired up to the ceiling and the carpet was covered in plastic.

All of the rooms were similar to this one. In the perpetual night created by blankets and plastic, things seemed to be waiting for movers to come and haul them away. Each room was familiar and nightmarish. Glen's old bedroom still had the old posters, which he'd abandoned there when they'd moved across the field. In one corner were some clothes he must've left. They were folded neatly and lined up against the wall. All the rooms were dark. The lightbulbs had been removed or burned out and never replaced. They searched in an eerie silence broken only by his father's "My God" or soft "Michael? Michael?"

As they were walking down the stairs, Glen told himself that it was over, that he would leave, get out of this life and farming altogether. It was too much, what with Michael out of his head and his father getting older. All that land could be sold to someone else; he didn't want it.

Light appeared in a thin, yellow line at the horizon as Glen and his father unloaded the first silo. The smell of the corn reached them in short bursts, sharp and alcoholic, dull, then stronger, like a glass of vodka being raised. With the corn pouring from the hopper into the truck, Glen watched his father hold some in his hand, make a fist, and rub it between his palms, which came away damp. They let the hopper run longer to take a sample from lower in the silo. Glen shook his arms to warm them and then hoisted himself into the truck. His father handed him a little machine, like a hand-held calculator with a test tube attached, which measured the moisture of the corn.

After testing layers of the silo and finding them all too moist and rotten, they drove the truck through the frozen field to the edge of the timber. Again he thought that this was all his life had been for ten years. He might become a delivery person or a truck driver. He tried to imagine how far he could have gone if he'd traveled in a straight line. The harvest was over, and now the corn was ruined. This truck-ful alone represented two months of labor, and most likely the other silos were rotten as well.

Without speaking, Glen reached down to pull his father up into the truck bed and then handed him a shovel. Each shovelful of corn was heavy and wet like snow. Shovelful by shovelful, they dumped the rotting corn from the back of the truck and into a bright yellow pile. Glen calculated each shovelful as an hour, a day of a life he'd spent on the farm, hating each kernel as a second of his life. And if the corn had been dry as a bone, he wouldn't have hated it any less.

His father stopped to rest and unbuttoned his coat. He cupped his hands around his mouth and yelled for Michael, but the timber and the fields were silent. Glen looked out into the timber and could see a spot of red, like a cardinal in a tree. He dropped his shovel, jumped from the truck in a run, and fell on the uneven clods of dirt and the tangle of cornstalks. He crawled up and ran for the timber to find Michael.

Until January, Glen and his father barely saw each other. Glen stayed at Marla's most of the time. Her house was small enough that he felt her presence every minute. Nothing drew him back to the farm in the winter months. On a trip to his own house to get clothes and check his mail, he noticed the wood of the barn door had cracked and a board had popped out, but he didn't fix it. Another time, he noticed a window in the barn had been broken, probably from a sudden freeze or a stray rock thrown from the gravel road.

Back in the early winter, when Glen had reached the tree where Michael was hanging, he had tried to climb the trunk by holding it and inching his way up, but there were few low branches, and he couldn't manage. Michael must have pulled himself up there while holding the rope. He'd climb all the way to the high branch, which splintered off the main trunk. After Michael's funeral his father had said to him, "The farm is all yours now after I'm gone." Glen didn't answer, but he nodded. He should have told him, but didn't. Now his absence from the farm was the answer he ought to have given.

His father called late in January. Glen listened to the answering machine tape of his father's voice, slow and bland with grief. The next day there was another message when he got home. "The snow melted on the rotten corn," his father said. "I've seen rats and we should probably bury it somehow." There was a long pause and then he said, "We need you here, Glen."

"You can't just ignore him," Marla told him when she came home from work. "You've got to face him. He needs you." She had been so kind since Michael's death, but his constant presence had begun to frustrate her. She pressed him about his plans, but he couldn't think. He didn't have any plans. He slept when he was in the house alone, sometimes for ten hours at a time.

"I don't want to go back," he said. "I don't want to farm. I've never wanted to farm."

"Well," she said. "What do you want to do?" Her face was calm, but she scratched at the place mat and waited for an answer.

"In a way, this is my fault," he told her, avoiding her question. "I knew that Michael was getting worse."

"You're not responsible for Michael's death," she said and put water on to boil. Glen knew she did this when she was irritated or frustrated with him. She busied herself.

"No, that's not what I meant. I mean I'm responsible for the corn rotting."

"Who cares about the corn rotting?" She turned quickly and folded her arms. "Doesn't anyone care what happened to Michael? Isn't he more important to you and your father than the damn corn?"

"I'll talk to him. I'll go over tomorrow morning," he said, knowing this wasn't what she wanted. She sobbed, and he held her with his eyes closed, seeing Michael climbing the tree in the timber in the early hours of the morning as he and his father loaded the rotten crop.

In the morning, before light, Glen showered and dressed in his work clothes and sat on the edge of the bed. Marla had pictures of a canopy bed taped to her mirror. She wanted things, a particular life, that he'd never even considered wanting. The one thing he'd wanted—to be free of Michael—he had gotten, but now he didn't want that either.

This was the second day of a warm snap, though when he checked the thermometer next to Marla's kitchen door it read only twenty-five. The temperature was forecast to rise to forty-five. The road was clear and dry from the warm sun of the day before as Glen drove to his parents' house in the dark.

The kitchen light was on, and his father moved around inside. Glen watched him fill the coffeepot at the sink and disappear to the stove. The trees in the yard were small and their trunks were wrapped in paper to protect them from deer and drying wind. The house was pleasant and hopeful with new paint and new shutters. His parents had made a life here. Each Saturday night and some Fridays, his father put on a sport coat and his mother put on a dress and high heels. His father opened the door of their car to help his mother. They drove into town to the Twinkle Star Ballroom where they'd held their wedding reception long ago. They talked with their old friends, and his father gently held his mother's hand in his, and they waltzed in broad, graceful steps. Glen hadn't seen them dance in years, but something about the way his father had turned away from the sink had reminded him. He and his brother had sat oafishly at the table during weddings while his father held his mother's back and turned her around the floor. His father and mother had been happy, he thought. They had another life. He and Michael had toppled under the weight of the farm, but his father and mother had not.

Glen stood at the door and knocked quietly. His father let him in and hugged him. He seemed smaller, even his shoulders and chest seemed smaller, more like Glen's now than Michael's. Awkwardly, the two men patted each other on the back, and then his father put a cup on the table for Glen, though neither sat down.

"Michael and I sometimes had coffee in the mornings just like this. He would sometimes be here with coffee made when I came down," Glen's father said. "I wondered why you never came over."

The thought of them sitting in this kitchen together made Glen ache. He hadn't known, he wanted to say, but knew he wouldn't have come anyway. The rumbling of the boiling coffee relieved him from having to respond.

"I wanted to talk to you, Dad," Glen said. "I want to get another job and move in with Marla." He hadn't asked Marla and suddenly wondered if she would let him move in for good.

"You and Marla could move to your house," his father suggested.

"I mean that I want to leave farming."

His father sighed. "I hope this doesn't mean we'll never see you again," he said. It wasn't what Glen had expected, and it made him feel petty and small. Glen looked at him, at his thin face and the way his pants were gathered around his waist, as if the part of him that was Michael had been removed from his body, as if the loss had surgically cut him in half.

"We'll see you all the time," Glen said.

Out in the field next to the timber, the piles of rotting corn emerged from the scattered, melting snow and black dirt. They might have sold it to someone for silage, Glen had considered, but when he suggested it, his father said, "We'll just spread it out in the field and till it in. It's good for the soil."

They took their shovels and dipped into the mound. The top was crusted with frost, but underneath the decomposition had warmed the corn. It was heavier than when they had dumped it in the fall. All morning they shoveled the corn back into the wagon. When the wagon was full, his father pulled it with the tractor to the far corner of their farm, and Glen dumped it out the back with his shovel. They returned to the mound for another load.

As they ate lunch in the field, the sun was high. They talked about Marla's job and what Glen might do in place of farming. He noticed that his father seemed alive out here with his coat off and his back wet with sweat. "Marla's a great girl," his father said. "I've always admired her." Glen agreed that she was, but doubted that his father had always thought so. After lunch, each lay back in the empty wagon and dozed with the sun in his face. Glen woke to the sound of his father's shovel throwing the corn next to him in the wagon and rose to help.

By late afternoon the pile had nearly disappeared. They attached the snowplow to the tractor and spread the remainder into a circle in the field.

"I'll till it in tomorrow. You go home," his father said, but Glen didn't want to quit until the corn was under the ground. He felt tired, nearly exhausted, but his exhaustion cleared his head and he wanted to finish the job today.

"Tomorrow may freeze again," Glen said. "You go on, and I'll till it in." His father nodded. He was too tired to continue and walked away toward his own house. His father's steps were hard and sure as he plodded through the rough clods of the field.

When the sun was low, the wet ground sparkled, then turned a reddish brown. Finally, the night turned black, and bright lamps on the tractor's nose and tail illuminated a circle around him. He pulled the tiller in neat rows while sitting sideways in the seat. For half the night he watched the metal disk pull up black dirt and drop it over the dead corn to make it rot and, years from now, disappear completely.

Richard Elson
University of Alaska, Fairbanks

THE SHOOTING

On a cool and lovely Indian summer day when he was nearly thirteen years old, Pierce Bracken shot and killed his best friend, Ethan Veer. It was an accident, of course. The two boys had been hunting grouse along cleared edges of oak and horse chestnut in eastern Connecticut, near Coventry, where they lived. That morning Ethan's dad had reviewed again the strict and precise rules of firearm safety with the boys, proper loading and unloading, as well as correct and incorrect techniques for carrying a loaded weapon while walking on uneven terrain. Mr. Veer was framing a house on a two-acre parcel that abutted a large tract of forested land, and it was in these woods that the boys did their hunting.

The shooting happened suddenly. While they were walking side by side, guns at the ready, Pierce tripped on a tree root and discharged his unsafetied .22.

Mr. Veer was nailing two-by-fours when he heard Pierce's scream for help. He stood and unfastened his tool belt, then broke into a sprint. As he ran, what flashed through his mind was that it was Pierce who was calling out, not Ethan.

He couldn't see Pierce at first, could only follow the direction from which the shouts were coming. It was a crisp, sunny day with shafts of light angling through the leafy canopy. Old downed limbs that lay crosswise on the ground snapped underfoot as he ran.

"Here! Here! This way!" Pierce called to him.

Ethan lay heaped on his side, breathing in shallow, rapid strokes, his sandy hair brushing the dried, leafy top layer of the forest floor. Pierce knelt by his side shaking him, imploring him to come to.

As Mr. Veer got closer he called out his son's name, then dropped to the ground beside the dying boy. Pierce fell back to give them room.

"I shot him, Mr. Veer. I shot Ethan. I tripped, it was an accident. It was an accident, I didn't mean it."

As Mr. Veer turned Ethan onto his back, Pierce saw a small, thick fountain of blood gurgle out of his friend's mouth. In one deft motion, Mr. Veer lifted his limp son into his lap. Blood leaked from the small exit wound between the spine and shoulder blade. Blood was everywhere.

Mr. Veer was talking now in a low, soothing voice, saying things over and over, trying to comfort the boy.

"There now son we're going to get you help don't you worry yourself about a thing everything is going to turn out just fine there now that's my good boy there there."

Pierce could see Mr. Veer squint as he looked back through the trees toward the truck, trying to gauge the time and distance required to carry Ethan to the pickup. He could see Mr. Veer running heroically, Ethan in arms, leaping over small granite outcrops, could see him putting Ethan on the bench seat and driving him to the nearest hospital about fifteen miles away, the car flying swiftly over the paved back roads, picking up a police escort along the way, hospital attendants ready to pump serum back into Ethan's veins as they dashed him up to the operating room. But just then Ethan's body shuddered in his father's arms. The place where the bullet had entered, through the shirt pocket, had turned into a broad, deep circle of brick red.

"Ethan son it's Pa that's a good boy there now there can you see me son can you it's Pa that's my good son there now."

Ethan's eyes rolled slowly in their sockets, as if suddenly able to move independently of each other. His lips fluttered, trying to form words, but unable to.

Mr. Veer glanced over his shoulder and said to Pierce, "You'd best get over here and say good-bye to your friend."

The light in the woods was mottled. Each event—their walking side by side, then tripping, the gun firing—fit neatly, in Pierce's mind, one on top of another like a stack of flip cards that had to get played over and over again. Not one card could be added or subtracted.

"Come on," Mr. Veer insisted. "It's the best thing."

Pierce came closer and knelt again beside Ethan.

"Ethan, son, look who's here. It's Pierce."

Ethan's eyes tracked together and fell on Pierce but couldn't lock, so they wandered off again as though searching for something that couldn't be found.

Mr. Veer could feel the time slipping down and down, could hear and feel Ethan's breathing change, become more labored.

"Hello, Ethan. It's me," Pierce said. His own words came to his ears as if from on far, as if spoken by the trees or the air itself.

Again the eyes tracked together and focused on Pierce for just a brief moment. Pierce could see the constricted pupils dilate, trying to take in the available woodland light to look at the face hovering above him. Ethan's lips again moved, saying something that looked prayerful, less than a whisper, like lips that moved silently while reading. Then suddenly Ethan consolidated enough strength to speak, but the effort instead produced a spasmodic cough that forced out a projectile of blood onto both his father and his friend.

Pierce gasped and drew back. He looked down at his shirt and could see that the blood had become the next card in the sequence, inseparable now from the rest. The father seemed unfazed, though the blood drenched his arms and shirt and lap, and he continued to drone on to his son. "There there you don't need to speak if you don't want to everything is going to be just fine there now you rest my son there now there."

"It was an accident, Ethan," Pierce said. "I didn't mean it."

"He knows that Pierce he knows he knows there my son my good son," Ethan's father said, a wan, incoherent smile forming across his eyes and lips, as though the bulk of his own life force were draining from an unseen portal. He turned the boy just slightly to allow the windpipe to clear itself. "He knows he knows Pierce is your best pal right Ethan there now there my son my good son Ethan Pierce is your good friend there my Ethan there."

Pierce began to cry, and Mr. Veer rocked gently as though he would be able to ease his boy into sleep.

Ethan's hand came up just then and brushed Pierce on the forearm, just a brief and gentle swipe like a leather glove across the wrist, and Pierce felt himself enter a territory that before had been impossible and unthinkable.

"It hurts, Pa," Ethan said, his voice carrying the odd, disconnected squelch of an old man with a tracheotomy. "It hurts real bad."

Mr. Veer squeezed him closer, tighter. "There now there my son give me your pain give it up to me let it go into me I can take it for you there now Ethan that's good you just rest my son my good son—" and with that Ethan let go and died in his father's arms.

Mr. Veer and Pierce sat very still for what seemed like a long time. The breeze rustled the leaves overhead, and an occasional nut fell to the ground with a soft *thup*. A few shafts of dusty sunlight streaked through the canopy and reached the forest floor. The colors of the leaves were brilliant, vivid. Mr. Veer felt strangely calm. He was playing out in his mind a dialogue between himself and his wife. He was trying to explain to her what had happened, while she was drifting toward hysteria, demanding to know every detail, every piece of the puzzle as if she could lock onto one jigsawed fragment and dismiss it as impossible, show that it could not fit, prove to her husband that he had figured wrong, that if he would just retrace his steps back to the woods it would turn out differently this time. They argued back and forth, Mr. Veer trying to convince Ethan's mother that it was so, Mrs. Veer yelling at her husband, "No, no, how could you let this happen, how could you," swinging at him with both fists until she collapsed into his arms and cried the cry that Mr. Veer thought might never end.

Pierce felt a kind of calm as well, his tears exhausted for the moment, though his breathing was still irregular, punctuated by soft, cathartic hiccups. He tried to fight against his certainty that Ethan was dead, against the fact that he had seen that small, final shudder—as though something unseen were peeling away from the body. As Pierce watched his friend—the matted hair against his father's chest, the back of one hand cupped upon the humus layer of soil—his heart felt hopeful, or wanted to feel hopeful, that at any moment Ethan would revive. His mind, though, knew no hope, saw through the heart's ploy.

The breeze through the trees ceased, and the entire world went silent. Pierce's eyes stayed down, taking in the texture of leaves, the irregular shapes of downed branches, the sight of his own hands. A thrush's fluted call spilled through the air like liquid silver. His thoughts had already jumped forward to his return to school on Monday, though part of him saw this as something foreign and remote that could never occur. He would be face-to-face with an entire school that knew he was the one—even though it had been an accident. The teacher would remind them this was the case, would take his side, would demand order and try to return their attention to the lesson on reviewing the multiplication of fractions. Pierce thought how strange it was that when you multiplied a half by a half you got a quarter, and then a quarter by a quarter yielding a sixteenth, the answer growing smaller and smaller, toward nothing but never going away, never becoming zero. He wondered whether it would be better if they took Ethan's desk away like it had never existed, or if they just left it idle and empty in the classroom for the rest of the term.

Pierce recalled stories about time travelers who go back in time on a mission, but are not permitted to change a single event or move the smallest blade of grass for fear of altering the rest of history forever. Everything must happen just so, not because it was all good, or even because any of it was good, but because the direst of consequences would follow if anything were to change. But Pierce thought that it might be fair if he got a second chance, not to change everything, but just one thing. He would step over the tree root this time. It was an act so small that it was almost nothing at all. If he could just change that, the earth would not stray off course. Ethan would still be himself; he wouldn't cease to exist.

Once at the county fair near Manchester, Pierce had played a game in which you fired a squirt gun into a clown's mouth, thereby inflating a balloon atop the clown's head. The first to pop the balloon won a prize. And he had won! But when the man behind the counter gave Pierce his prize, he didn't pull one of the large, nice stuffed animals off the pegboard; instead he reached under the counter and gave Pierce a small key chain in a plastic wrapper. Pierce didn't know what to say. He looked at the man and could see that he wasn't even a man, he was just a kid, a teenager, the kind who probably smoked and maybe even drank. He could see at the time that this would turn into some kind of lesson his father would later explain to him about how the world really was, the kind of people there are, the disappointments that are possible.

What were his parents doing just then at that very moment? His dad might be mowing the lawn or raking the leaves, his mom baking the cookies he loved. Only now he had no appetite for cookies or anything else and probably never would again. And after his parents had heard the news and had wept or yelled or whatever they would do, the uneaten cookies would sit on a plate, reeking of impossible sorrow, a type of ache that could not be discarded or consumed or burned away but could only sit there on the table, unapproachable and persistent, day after day for as long a time as he could imagine.

A small gust of wind rattled through the trees, stirring up freshly fallen leaves. Then silence again. A ruffed grouse stepped from its cover and peered at them cautiously.

"Come," Mr. Veer said, "it's time to go." And with that he stood, lifting the dead child with a barely audible grunt, one of Ethan's arms dangling loose and jumpy toward the ground. "Gather up the rifles."

Pierce looked up at him.

"I didn't mean it, Mr. Veer," he said.

"I know it. Come along."

Pierce looked down and saw the two weapons, his own where he first had knelt, Ethan's a few feet away where it had fallen. He lifted Ethan's, checked to see that it was safetied, then slung it by its strap over one shoulder. He then picked up his own. When he opened the chamber, the empty shell flew out in a small arc to the ground. He then flipped the safety latch, and put it on his other shoulder. Mr. Veer hadn't waited for him, and Pierce had to walk briskly to catch up with him. Together in silence, Pierce walking behind Mr. Veer, they headed through the trees toward the half-framed house where the truck was parked. When they arrived at the truck, Mr. Veer took the rifles from Pierce, unloaded the remaining cartridges, then placed them in the space behind the seat.

Pierce climbed up into the bed of the pickup and sat on a roll of canvas beside the toolbox. Mr. Veer had an upturned wheelbarrow in the back, held in place by two weathered gray ropes fixed to the tie-downs. Pierce looked to these things for assurance, wanting to take refuge in them. He sat alone now, occasionally peering in through the musty rear cab window, but mostly sitting straight and looking out behind, or not looking at all.

Mr. Veer drove with one hand on the wheel, the other on Ethan, partly as a way of staying close and being together with his child one last time, partly to keep Ethan's body from falling off the bench onto the floor. At intersections and stop signs, Mr. Veer let go the steering wheel with his left hand and reached across to shift, rather than allowing himself to remove his right hand from his son's body even for an instant.

Mr. Veer navigated the truck with great conscious effort. Some summer nights he and his wife would go for drives on these very roads, watching the sky darken, looking for deer along the edges of fields. Driving could be a peaceful thing. He knew the roads well enough that he could go by rote, not think about where the curves were, where to turn, where to slow. But now he acted in precise fashion, paying careful attention to each movement. If I shift into third at thirty, he thought, my rpms will be near three thousand. I could go faster but for the boy in the back, I can keep an eye on him from here with the rearview mirror. Here is a turn, ease up on the gas, put on the blinker, watch for cars, yield to oncoming traffic, okay go, shift, accelerate, there we go.

Pushing hard at the edge of his thoughts was his wife, unknowing, still unaware, and pushing harder still, like a river at a floodgate, was grief. If it came forward it would swallow him, rip trees from their root systems, upturn cars and houses and barns, ruin crops ready for harvest. But still, with unfailing effort, Mr. Veer kept his wife and his pain at bay by braking, shifting, clutching, accelerating. Check the rear mirror, check the side mirror, look both ways at intersections, obey every sign, every rule of driving, every action, every gesture brought forward and made large before his eyes by his swimming brain.

Pierce wondered if Mr. Veer would go straight to the hospital in Willimantic or would stop at home first to tell Ethan's mom or maybe even stop at Pierce's house to drop him off. All three choices had their own logic to them, though Pierce hoped most of all that the truck ride would last forever or as near to forever as could be, because anything other than riding along the county roads, the sun flickering through the trees like a stick along a picket fence, would lead to something very final, something or someone impossible to face. The drive and the way the tires clicked over the tarred expansion segments and the warmth of the sun hypnotized Pierce. For the briefest of moments, he was disoriented and didn't know where he was. They passed a gas station and an ice-cream parlor. Out front, several bikes were chained to the bike rack with red flexible wire-locks, and Pierce wondered what kids they belonged to.

Maybe Pierce had drifted toward sleep, because he jumped with a start when he thought he heard a gunshot. He looked around and saw that he was still in the truck, the gunshot just a sound that had arisen from inside his head. Pierce turned and looked in. Ethan's body was limp and still, quivering ever so slightly in rhythm with the jostling of the truck cab. The body looked like nothing that had ever been animate. It might just as easily have been a sack of potatoes.

He slumped back into his spot on the canvas tarp. The sights that retreated from him as he looked out from his rearward-facing position distracted him. The broken center line emerged from beneath the truck with persistent regularity. Pierce tried to count back along the receding string of white dashes, but quickly got to a place where they ran together, their spacing no longer visible. A Buick sedan with Rhode Island plates passed, and that pleased him. He could see a man and a woman in the front seat, and he wondered who they were and where they were going, if they had any children and what their house looked like. It felt important to him that everyone have a house, a place where they belonged. Pierce tried to picture his own room, the bed and quilt, the shelf of board games, the tackle box, the clock radio, the oaken mirror above his bureau. These things helped make him who he was, and at that moment he needed more than ever before to place himself on a graph of the world or the universe with a pair of x and y coordinates to mark his position. It seemed critical to him just then to be someplace precise, not approximate.

Before long, the truck turned left and pulled into the hospital lot, coming to a halt under an overhang marked EMERGENCY.

Mr. Veer opened his door and stepped out.

"Wait here," he said, and went around to the passenger door and slid Ethan out a little ways by the feet then carried him in his arms through the hospital doors.

Pierce saw how blank and remote Mr. Veer had become as though he had receded into himself. He was pretty sure that the pain of a father differed from that of a best friend, but wasn't sure how. Pierce felt chilled and sat alone in the truck bed shivering, but very soon Mr. Veer appeared again beside him. He no longer had Ethan in his arms.

"Come on," he said, and Pierce climbed over the side and jumped down.

The light inside was unnatural and unpleasant, and the air felt stuffy and smelled like illness.

"Sit here," Mr. Veer said, and put his hand on Pierce's head. It was a tender gesture, though Pierce could feel how weak and trembly Mr. Veer's hand was. "I got to go in there for a while. Be good."

"Yes, sir," Pierce said. As he watched Mr. Veer walk away, he thought he could tell from behind by the way his shoulders moved that he was crying now. He watched him stop and stoop and through a force of will pull himself back together from the thousand fragments into which his insides must have shattered. Mr. Veer walked through two swinging hospital doors and was gone.

Behind those doors there was now nothing for Mr. Veer to do but call his wife, though she seemed as remote as another continent. He had delivered his son, his dead son, to the doctors and had asked a nurse to go speak to Pierce, and now he leaned against a cold wall and broke down. He went over again the instructions in firearm safety as if the boys stood before him. He reprimanded them, warned them, schooled them, drilled them so that all their behavior in the woods would be natural and automatic. Here is when to safety, here is when to unsafety, I told you, I told you! But you didn't listen, did you! My son is dead now and there's nothing to do and you did it! You did it! But these thoughts derailed and there was nothing but pain, and Mr. Veer knew that he couldn't blame the boy. He could blame only himself, and his hurt was as wide and deep as a desert in which he might wander a lifetime without finding shade or water. He put his palms on the thighs of his pants and felt how stiff they had become with blood.

The magazines in the waiting area were for adults, and the box of toys in the corner was for little kids. Pierce watched a boy whose nose needed wiping push a toy car about the room.

A nurse came over and knelt beside Pierce's chair.

"You must be Pierce?" she asked.

"Yes, ma'am," he said.

"You're Ethan's friend, right?"

"Yes, that's right."

She reached over and brushed back his hair from his forehead.

"Come with me," she said and stood up.

She led him into another room where they were alone together.

"Give me your phone number and we'll call your mom and dad."

He knew he had to, but knew also that doing so would make it too real for him. He wanted to tell the nurse that he could make the call himself, that he was a big boy, almost not a boy anymore, but it was too much effort, too easy to just let her do it for him. He didn't want to be treated like a child, but he was glad for her now and glad that she would tend to him.

"They're going to want to see you and know you're all right and take you home, right?"

"Yes ma'am," he said and gave her the number.

The nurse went to her desk and dialed. She spoke in a hushed, serious voice into the receiver. Pierce could imagine his mother nodding and saying "Yes" several times as though she were responding to questions. He could picture her in the kitchen, sliding into a chair while the nurse told her the news, told her it was an accident, told her it wasn't meant to be but was and couldn't be made any other way. He'd learned in math class that the answer to a problem might not be just a single number but a set of numbers instead. He wished that could be true now, that there might be other numbers, other answers. But there weren't any other numbers this time, just a single number. A single number can be a set, but then it stands alone within brackets, and with no substitution.

The nurse then set the receiver down on the desktop and came over to Pierce.

"Your mom wants to talk to you," she told him.

He looked up at her, but didn't say anything. The walk across the room to the desk seemed a long ways. He lifted the receiver and spoke softly into it. His mother asked him if he was all right. He wanted to tell her that it had been a terrible thing, something awful, an accident that he wanted more than anything to undo but couldn't.

"Yes, Mama," he said and started to cry.

His mother told him that they were on their way and would be there soon for him.

He could no longer speak he was shaking so. Every number can be a set unto itself, and there can also be a set with no numbers and that is called the null set, and in it was nothing, not zero, nor even infinity but, he thought, something that was the opposite of infinity, a nothing that went on and on. The nurse came and took the phone from him.

Again she spoke to his mother, telling her she would take care of the boy and watch him until they arrived. He heard the sound of the receiver being placed back on its carriage.

The nurse turned to Pierce and put her arms around him. He relaxed into them and allowed himself to be embraced. It was a warm, bosomy hug, and Pierce let himself cry in her arms. She held him close and whispered things into his hair.

After a few moments, he could feel his crying wane and then felt himself take a big shuddering sigh that seemed to mark the end of this one wave of grief.

The nurse asked if he wanted something to drink, and Pierce nodded that he did. She took him into yet another room, a little kitchenette with a stove and a small refrigerator. She poured him a tall glass of red punch, which he drank right down. The oversweet punch tasted good to him and seemed to fill something that had hollowed out within him. His thirst was strong, and filling it was satisfying.

"Better?" she asked. "Good. There's another thing, though."

"What is it?" Pierce asked.

And she told him that two police officers were coming over to talk to him and ask questions about what had happened.

A sense of panic overtook him. He hadn't meant to do it, they should know that. He couldn't understand why they had to talk to him. They could get all the information they needed from Mr. Veer, though Mr. Veer hadn't really seen what happened. But nothing had happened really, just that he tripped and the gun went off. He hadn't even seen it happen himself. It had all been so quick: the stalking, the fall, the discharge of his .22. His parents had always told him to tell the truth, and that was what he would do now since there was nothing to lie about anyway, nothing the police could get him in trouble for.

The nurse took him into a small room with a desk and two chairs.

"Pierce, I've got to go take care of a couple of things that won't take too long. I'll be right back."

He had heard her say to his mother that she would stay with him, and that was what he wanted. He liked her, but now she had left the room, and he felt cut loose, drifting toward what he couldn't say. Pierce remembered when he was six and his parents had taken him to the drive-in. He had wanted candy and had told his parents that he was big enough to go to the concession stand by himself. They let him, but he got lost on the way back; it was hard to tell the colors of the cars at night and he couldn't see in through the windows clearly. He walked up and down, from one row of cars to the next, certain that he would find his parents again. But he didn't, and a terrible feeling of trying to swim upstream overtook him. Finally his dad came and found him, and when they walked back, there was their car, just where it had been before, so obvious now with his father in the lead. "Where'd you find him?" his mother asked, and his father replied, "Oh, I found him in a reed basket floating down the river," and they laughed. Pierce didn't understand this and didn't see anything funny about it and was angered by his parents' way of joking.

In another room, Mr. Veer sat alone. He had spoken to his wife and now sat and waited, his head against the cold wall upon which he found himself depending. This wall and nothing else could prevent his being from getting washed away as if by some tide. Mr. Veer put his cheek to the wall's surface. It was solid; it was real. It was now the only thing left that was real—all other things that once were real had been swept away. The wall felt cool and sound, a solid thing, he figured, with twenty-four-inch spacing, studs of good, sound fir, and half-inch Sheetrock, not three-eighths, and not eight foot high like in a residence, but taller, ten feet for commercial use. A wall is what is important, he thought, a wall that supports a ceiling, that shelters one from the wind and rain. A wall is critical, integral. A hospital orderly had brought Mr. Veer a scrub shirt to change into, and he sat with his own bloodstained shirt clutched in his hands.

When the nurse returned to Pierce, she was followed into the room by two police officers in uniform.

One of the two came over and touched Pierce on the arm, while the other stood at the threshold and didn't say anything.

The friendly officer sat in the chair next to him.

"Ethan was your friend?" he asked.

"Yes, sir," Pierce told him.

"Can you tell us what happened?"

"We were walking in the woods. And I tripped." Pierce looked down between his feet. "And the gun went off."

The policemen were quiet. The one at the door was writing on his pad.

"It was an accident, wasn't it, son?" the policeman asked.

"Yes, sir."

"An awful thing to have to go through."

Pierce nodded.

"Sometimes awful things just happen like this. You've got to just shake it off and go on, all right?"

"All right," Pierce answered.

"Is there anything else?"

"Like what, sir?"

The two policemen looked at each other and shrugged. "I don't know," the one said.

Pierce looked at them and could see they thought there was something else that someone should say, but neither of them knew what.

"Your mom and dad ought to be here soon, son," the one officer said.

"Okay," Pierce replied.

As they left the room, one of the policemen said to the nurse, "Take care of the kid."

Pierce could hear their talking grow fainter as they walked down the corridor.

Mr. Veer still sat in the other room and waited. He found that beyond his pain was more explanation, more review of gun procedure—sitting the boys down and emphasizing his words with his index finger so that not only would they hear them, but they would see them as well. Beyond gun handling, though, was fault that could not fall on the shoulders of a boy but could only fall upon his own, which were broad enough, except that when he braced himself to receive the load it was more enormous than he could ever have imagined and he thought he might be crushed. Soon his wife would be here, and it confused Mr. Veer that he felt her presence would be no comfort, but would surely bring the weight yoked on his own shoulders more fully down on him alone. Although he had already been swept as far down as seemed possible, he realized he had much farther yet to go.

When Pierce's parents arrived, they had Mrs. Veer with them. His mother was crying, but Mrs. Veer was not. His mother led Mrs. Veer to a chair and told her to sit, which she did. She looked to be a woman in a trance who had sleepwalked to the hospital, her eyes glazed with a knowledge that was set firm on the surface but had yet to filter through to a deeper place. His father stood silently with his hat in his hands. Pierce saw him twist it as though to wring excess moisture from it. He saw Mr. Veer come out from behind the swinging doors, a shadow of his former self, an egg whose contents had been blown out leaving just the shell. His mother went and hugged this distraught figure, and he fell into her arms with all his enormous weight, his shoulders heaving up and down. Mrs. Veer still sat in the chair and stared straight ahead.

"It's my fault," Mr. Veer said. "I never should have let them go on their own."

"Don't say that. Please don't blame yourself," Pierce's mother said.

"If I had stayed with them, this never would have happened."

Pierce's dad came over and put his hand on his shoulder.

"Don't torture yourself about this," he said.

Mrs. Veer looked up serenely at her husband, and said in a very soft voice, "I need to see him."

"Oh, Nancy," he said, "I don't know. I mean he should be cleaned up first, don't you think?"

"No," she said, rising, "I really must."

Mr. Veer looked at the nurse, who nodded. He looked at those double doors through which he had already passed twice—once to carry his son, another time after he had escorted Pierce into the waiting area—and through which he would now pass a third time with his wife to let her see their son. Mr. Veer could not look at her directly. The three of them, Mr. and Mrs. Veer and the nurse, left the room together.

Pierce's mother came and knelt by him.

"You okay?" she asked, raising his chin so she could see his face.

He nodded.

"Such a terrible thing," she said.

"Are we going home now?" Pierce asked.

"Is that what you'd like?"

He shrugged his shoulders. "I don't know. I guess."

"Are you hungry?"

"No, ma'am."

She looked at her husband, who stood and put his ball cap on. He offered his hand for Pierce to hold. Pierce took it, and the three of them headed toward the door.

"Where's your rifle?" his father asked.

"Behind the seat in Mr. Veer's truck," Pierce told him.

He wanted to see the nurse again, but she was with Ethan's parents. The room hummed with emptiness.

Outside, afternoon was fading into evening. Cars went by. A streak of deep blue hung above the orange glow where the sun was setting. He watched his father take the .22 from the cab of the pickup, then watched him open the stock to see that it was unloaded. His father then placed it in the trunk of their car.

Pierce sat alone in the backseat. His parents were very quiet. He watched the sky darkening, the headlights of oncoming traffic flying by, the porch lights glowing yellow on the houses that they passed. He counted lampposts for a while, then counted the number of times he breathed in and out, then counted nothing and just sat and let his eyes unfocus in the gathering dusk.

As they pulled into the driveway, his mother said, "I think I'll make pork chops for dinner, Pierce. You want creamed corn or applesauce with them?"

"I don't care," he said.

When his mother knocked on his door later to tell him supper was ready, he pretended to be asleep. She kissed his cheek and pulled his comforter up over him. When she turned off the light, he could see how dark it was outside.

She left the room, and Pierce was alone again.

He put his hand on the beige wall covered with shadows. He supposed that adults thought about what lay ahead, and that was one thing that made them different from children. He knew that Ethan's death didn't make him grown up, but he could faintly see that it had left him stranded between two shores, neither of which seemed reachable. It couldn't be said that Pierce understood much of what he saw, save that it was not something that could be negotiated, nor was it something that could be put off, nor, lastly, was it something he could prevent himself from embracing.

Early in the morning before the blackness of night had disappeared, Pierce woke. He thought he could dress quietly, and then he realized he was still dressed. He wanted to get on his bike and go for a long ride, so he quietly went into the garage.

Propped in the corner, where his father had placed it, was his .22. Its gray barrel looked cool and liquid in the sparse street light that shone through the diamond-shaped garage windows. He stood poised for a long time, puzzled, looking at it as though he had never seen it before. He went over close to it. Pierce thought maybe he'd stopped breathing, and it wasn't until he heard the morning paper clap against the front door that he felt himself inhale again.

Natasha Waxman

Texas Center for Writers

FORAGER

Under the overhanging cliff ledge, they have a fine view of the savannah that smooths away toward the flat painted hills. And they're so happy, what with this wild piglet they've netted. The older woman is sitting on the ground, scraping a hide that lies flat over her legs. She pulls her small, wedged ax head up again and again, pulling off the fat and membranes. Later she'll lay the hide out flat on the grass to dry. The younger woman's compact, lean-muscled, *perfect*. She sits cross-legged, holding a distinctly simian baby in the crook of her arm; with her free hand she's winding a strip of hide around a digging stick. She's making herself a new one because she broke hers digging up wild potatoes this morning. It's lying broken by the fire. The man is using another, larger ax head to cut up the piglet. You can tell he's never worn shoes by his huge splayed toes, their nails horny as talons. This is a man who can walk fifty miles in a day, no problem. As he hacks the wild piglet, he looks to the side, grinning. Why? Probably because another man, unseen, is walking toward them, and from the look of delight on their faces it seems clear he's got something pretty good. The fire's all ready for the piglet. In a minute the delectable smell will start wafting, and they'll joke about how long they can hold on before plunging in. Later, glutted, they'll let the embers burn down, listening to the night wind in the grasses. This is a fine time, they don't even know how fine; for them it's always today, and there is plenty in the world.

Pressed against the glass, Jason is knocked out again and again by the scene.

His main job is defleshing. The animals come from all over, deep frozen and swaddled in plastic, and they go back again clean, mainly to other museums and university collections. *Northern badger. Spotted fox. Tarsiers. Gibbons. Squirrels. Felix felix.* There are hundreds more waiting in the freezer, sent to the lab for preparation. Frozen at the pinnacle of dying, before the frenzy of decay can set in, they shine like dark, prickly rocks through the thick plastic. He loves the inscrutable instruments. Picks. Calipers. Scalpels. The silky ribbons of tape measures marked off in millimeters. He has no head for half of what goes on here, science seems beyond his thick skull, but he can deflesh animals like nobody's business, nobody bothers him here, and for now that's plenty. In the clatter, he can forget the chittering, taunting voices, the one in particular that gravels: *hurting your mother, throwing every goddamn opportunity in the garbage.*

Today, Jason pulls a spotted African tarsier from the freezer. After he's unwrapped it and put it on the thawing tray, he takes up a badger that's been thawing two days, and brings it over to the workbench. The hide is stiff and clumped from the freezing, but workable. First, he draws a hard little line, plunging down with the scalpel through the pale skin below the belly, where it's thinnest, and draws it upward. Where the blade has been, a widening wake opens up, revealing the pale maroon of stiff musculature, encased in a filmy membrane. Another cut across the thorax, toward the underside of one forward leg, pulling the skin away where it bunched underneath the shoulder. More cuts to each of the legs in similar fashion. Once the frozen animals are thawed, the hides come off like gloves, with gratitude. After it's peeled, he'll place it in the Thermo-clav, which is basically a large pressure cooker, to loosen the flesh.

Across from him, Zoe's already flipping through printouts, making clicking sounds as she gnaws her pen. She's a tiny primate herself in her overalls and baseball cap, sexy as hell. She's working on her Ph.D. in biology and one of her many jobs is supervising Jason. She tells him for the millionth time, "The hides are going in the garbage,

Jay. You don't need to be so anal about it for God's sakes." But when he glances up at her, she's grinning. Between teaching and research and classes, she's always in a hurry. But he's not, and treats each animal as a challenge because nothing intrudes when you're concentrating that hard. The other lab techs, like Ozzie, who extracts bone fossils from rock with dental picks, claim to be disgusted by the smells and sights of defleshing. They close the door to their part of the lab whenever they can, which gives him a small thrill of satisfaction, because the smell doesn't bother *him* at all.

After several hours in the Thermo-clav, the flesh is tender, spongy enough to lift out in chunks, shaving with the scalpel near the bones. Jason watches his hands peel lemurs, tarsiers, gibbons and gibbons and gibbons, watches the knife go through the tight-packed strands of tissue, lifting and peeling. Because the specimens are all so similar under the skin, he has the sense that he is living the same day over and over. Weeks have piled into months like this; this is the longest he's stuck at anything in his life.

Zoe asks, "Can you change the solution in the—"

"I already did."

"Did you remember to—?"

"Christ, I'm not a complete moron!"

"Hey, relax, don't bite my head off!" she snaps. He has a sudden vision of biting a tiny head off. Friendly again, she asks, "What's up?"

"Nothing. Nothing." In addition to his so-called girlfriend Stacey's increasingly frequent mantra *When are you going to go back to school?* now she's after his hair. Whereas she *claimed,* when he dropped out, to understand perfectly about needing a break. Whereas she *claimed* that his dreads were cool last spring when they met. Now they're "skanky." *Whereas* any fool knows that you don't wash dreadlocked hair, you just hose it down every once in a while. Shampoo is bullshit, as he'd suspected all along. *Furthermore,* according to her they've clumped together at the back of his head. But he likes it, likes the feeling of his head being thatched on top. Protection from inclement weather. There's no way he's getting a haircut. He's firm on that, no matter how much sex she withholds.

Stacey doesn't want to hear about the clean room, or Acheulian axes, or the fascinating contortions of muscle and bone hidden inside dead animals. This morning, at her place, her roommates were both talking premed, prelaw, blah blah blah, and Stacey jabbed a thumb at him and said, "*Some* people are career-minded *at least,*" and told him she couldn't see him tonight, she has too much studying to do.

Schroeder bounds over, wielding one of his axes.

"Look at that, huh? This one's almost too beautiful to send out." And it is. The stone has flaked in one long sheet on both sides, a wedge narrowing down to a very sharp point. Schroeder, the head lab technician, is also an artist. He specializes in making replicas of Stone Age tools, using Stone Age methods; he has literally carved out a reputation for himself, and his creations are sent to collections around the world. He started in art school, he told Jason, but canvas was too flat to hold the interest of a Renaissance man like himself.

Jason hefts the ax, which has no handle. It's about the size of a girl's shoe. Schroeder will regale anyone who'll listen with stories about his Acheulian axes, and Jason is more than content to listen. About how the Stone Age tools dug up all over the world paint a picture of humans surviving for most of their history living off roots and nuts, scavenging carcasses killed by other animals. He tells it so you're there in the bushes, watching the lions with a growling belly.

Schroeder's participated in dozens of digs from Israel to Kenya, and has dug up hundreds of the axes he loves. Schroeder's favorite, "liberated" from a rich dig in the Jordan Valley, is a small one, but what he loves about it is the notch in the blade. A notch caused when some great-great-great ancestor brought it crashing down on bone or sinew.

"Just feel the power, can you feel it?" Schroeder asks.

By late afternoon, the badger's ready for the clean room. Because no matter how much you scrape and cut away, you can't get all the bits of muscle and cartilage.

Every time he goes, he remembers the first time, when he followed Zoe's high tight ass down to a security-locked door in the basement. "You'll puke for sure," she said, acting tough and winking.

Behind the door is a small anteroom with a metal counter and a sink. He fills one of the spray bottles on the counter and, taking up the broom from the corner, he pulls open the next door, which looks like the door to a walk-in refrigerator, pulling it shut quickly behind him. Inside, it slams into him: the thick, bitter reek, dense as fog, a puking smell. It's hot and damp and bright in here, and he savors the slow shimmer of movement around his peripheral vision, the fuzzy, rustling sound, which is them all eating. The maggots. He uses a broom to sweep a path through the ones on the floor, but they're mainly concentrated on the animal carcasses lying in open metal drawers all around the walls. He begins misting them, using the spray bottle. That first time, she'd told him, "They like it wet, so make sure you really soak them," and he always thinks of that when he's down here. And how it was somehow erotic, the two of them together in all that damp, amid the specimens and the incredible stink that encased them in barely breathing stillness. He didn't puke that time or any other; Zoe said it was some kind of record. The clean room is the reason they've lost every other lab grunt they've ever had. But he can take it, doesn't mind it at all. It turns out to be the one natural talent he possesses.

"That place is a time bomb, Jay," Zoe's told him. "If one of those little fuckers gets out into the displays, that's it." And there is something slow-acting and explosive about it. More and more, he sees them under his eyelids when he blinks, big as berries and moving slowly. They bloom behind his eyes sometimes when he's walking, or with Stacey, in bed and thrashing. It calms him immeasurably.

Zoe was only too happy to turn the clean room over to him. The trick is just to ride the smell, not to fight it. This will come in handy, of that he's sure. When he sprays the carcasses, the mist settles in delicate droplets that shimmer under the fluorescent lights. They gnaw with such dedication, crawling slowly over immense landscapes of bone, and when they leave the bones are clarified. The knobby articulated joints, the delicate bumps and sudden pits where nerves and muscles were once inserted, attached for life. From this, the immaculate cleanliness of the displays upstairs.

He slides the badger off the tray and onto an empty shelf, withdrawing two scoured gibbons to take upstairs to be mounted. In the elevator, he sniffs, but there's nothing left on the bones, not even scent. It awes him, somehow. Holding the tray, he sees bugs—glossy-backed and crawling slowly—when he closes his eyes.

*   *   *

Its gotten so that wherever he goes in his apartment, he can hear it, sometimes louder, sometimes softer, but always there. The cuts and snips contending against each other in air, an invisible sword fight.

When he finally realizes what it is, he has to throw them all out: the wall clock, the one in the kitchen, even the fat-bellied Big Ben alarm Gramps gave him. His landlady, Iris, who lives in the main house up the alley, comes roaring out after him as he leaves them in a pile by the sidewalk.

"What are these out here for?"

"Oh, I didn't need them."

"Really? Hey, this one's mine! It goes with the apartment."

"Could you just hang on to it? I'm involved in an experiment. Scientific. Very hush hush."

"I guess . . ."

Jason remembers that his father once gave him something called a Day-timer, which he called "the key to success." It had pages for every day, marked off in hours. He had to buy a special pen, with a point as fine as a hair, to write it all down. Where he went, who he talked to, what he said, how much money, etc., etc. He finally had to stop.

Throwing them all out gets rid of the aggravating noise, but it also frees him. He lives the same day over and over again anyway, that's why he loves the museum so much. After Burchman *Gibbon*, he writes in his lab book: *To catch time by the tail, let the badger go! Look at him go, with his nails clacking away across the floor!*

"Look at him! He's got a little penis!" The little girl is pointing to his favorite display, in the Hall of Human Evolution.

She looks at Jason, then back at the display. She sees the resemblance. More than a few children have looked back and forth between him and the man in the display; one little boy even pointed out shyly, "He looks like you." And he does. Short and somewhat squat-muscled, with wide prominent cheekbones and a flat nose, a chin tapering down to a pointed cleft that lends a slightly comical, elfin look. When the boy made the remark, Jason's heart started fibrillating. Shame dilated his pores and made him prickle with sweat. Increasingly, though, he nods down at the kids, grinning, as though inviting another spoken comparison.

The little girl's mother looks down, embarrassed, and hustles her away. She is still protesting, "But he has a little penis! I saw it!"

Every time he looks at the display, he remembers something he saw on TV at Stacey's place one time. It was one of those shows where you get to travel around town with the cops. They pulled up to a 7-Eleven, where there was a crowd of people standing around a car. The cops parted the crowd and found themselves looking down at a guy who was sitting naked in his car, smiling dreamily. Beside the open car door, on the ground, was a neat pile of his clothing.

"What're you doing, son?"

(No answer.)

"Why're you naked, sir?"

"I'm not naked."

"Yes you *are.*"

"Naked? I don't think so."

"Pull up your drawers, sir."

And they took him away. But his body was gorgeous, perfected. He made everybody else look wrong, in their clothes.

Although the Stone Age Lifestyles display is his favorite, there's plenty to interest him in the Hall of Aboriginal Peoples. Taking out a pen, he copies a placard into his lab book:

> *By submitting to the desert's harsh environment rather than trying to dominate it, the Kalahari Bushmen survive where others would certainly perish. . . . Nomadic ways Blah blah blah. . . . The simple, even austere material aspects of the Bushmen's lives may seem at odds with the richness of their dream world.*

He has a book about Bushmen somewhere that he likes to flip through. Practically the only thing he can remember from school is something he wrote down in an anthropology class, a Bushman saying: *Why should we plant when there are so many mogongo nuts in the world?* There's no end to the question, when you think about it.

Other questions are not as interesting. He finally has to disconnect the phone, which won't stop with its *What are you doing down there? Why aren't you in school? Blah blah PLANS? Blah blah CAREER? Are you just going to throw everything we've given you into the blah blah blah?* He can't stand those dry voices. When he needs to call Stacey, he just plugs it back in. The clarity of the air without the anxiety of those rings is intoxicating.

"Why are you still here? Didn't I see you this morning?" It's Dr. Foster, ransacking the place, looking for some printout of Zoe's.

"What?" asks Jason, looking up from a tree shrew.

"Aren't you part-time?"

"Well, sort of. But I, uh, need to be here." Zoe has said if he wants to, it's fine by her, as long as he understands that the grant only covers twenty paid hours a week. Foster looks at him strangely, and Jason guesses *he's* not into matted hair either. He can't think of what to say under those eyes, and hears himself start to babble. "Hey, you know there's a nursery rhyme about you? I always used to love that one. You know, Doctor Foster went to Gloucester in a shower of rain / He stepped in a puddle right up to his middle and never went there again." Foster doesn't even try to smile. "Foster, you know like your name." What the hell did he say *that* for? Why? Why? He should just have his tongue cut out.

"Oh, yes. Well. Ha. I hadn't heard that." Foster goes on rummaging and upsets a stack of cardboards. "Damn it. This bloody . . . Look, will you please ask Zoe to give me a call tomorrow? I can't find anything in this mess." After he's gone, Jason snaps a bone in his agitation and finally gives up and leaves.

On his way home from the museum, in the alcove of an antique shop on Palace Street, he sees Kook Mary gumming a soft peach. The alcove is her home. Slurping the pulp off her fingers, she looks intent, blissful. He can see how good it tastes to her; he can almost taste it with her. It tastes like god to her. It's the unexpectedness that makes it so blessed, he realizes. Every day, the wonder: *What's going to give itself to me?* Like those Buddhist monks, carrying nothing but a begging bowl.

A few days later he sees her again, trundling along with briny snorts, talking at some man who nods at everything she says. On a whim—*why not?*—he follows them five blocks down to the Shop-Rite. They go around back, to the edge of the loading bay, where there are open boxes of food. After they leave, he looks. Fruit that's only a little scarred, or bruised, but can't be sold because it's not perfect. Still soft bread, bundled in bags. Vegetables. Even yogurt, waiting to be put into the Dumpster. There's another man there now, muttering as he sorts, "Perfectly good cucumbers. Don't like to waste perfectly good cucumbers. Good sandwiches. Don't like the crusts personally, so I just cut them off."

Just the sight of it makes him hungry, and he has to stop himself from taking much more than he can carry.

Stacey just stands in shocked amazement, looking around. She doesn't like coming to his place; she hasn't been here in months, in fact. His bed sags into a trough in the middle, which drives her crazy, so he's always gone to her place. But the rude stares of her roommates are starting to really aggravate him, and he has finally prevailed upon her to come over to his place. *He's really freaky,* he heard Karen say in the kitchen last week. He can only imagine what else those tubers are saying about him behind his back. *Loser. Creep.* But could they stand the clean room for even ten seconds? Five?

"JJ, what the hell is going on? Where's all your stuff?"

"Uh, I pawned a couple of . . ."

"But why did you need . . . are you on drugs?" But he hasn't had money for that in a while; the only time he gets high is when they share joints at her house.

"No, just paring down. All those things, they were really wearing me out."

At first he sold some of his belongings because he had to. The job at the lab barely covers his rent, and a second job is out of the question; there's no time, and besides, what would he do? Some crazy retail bullshit, where they'd make him cut his hair, or a telemarketing job or playing security guard? So the TV went first; he hated its radioactive flicker anyway. If it wasn't something exploding, it was golf courses and trudging refugees, animated toilet brushes singing songs that rattled in his head endlessly. He couldn't make any sense of it anymore. The stereo was no great loss, he always forgot to turn it on. Ditto the computer. And the momentum took hold of him; once he started, he couldn't believe how much useless shit he owned: clothes and shelves and lamps, chairs and CD racks, no end of clutter. Who needs a table when it's more comfortable on the floor? With each piece that was subtracted, he liked his room more, until now he's down to some books, clothes, his blanket, and camping stuff, his. Things are looking very Zen.

Stacey is still staring, her steps echoing through the room.

"I thought you'd like how clean it is," he tries.

"Well, I guess. It's just a little radical. No, I guess I like it. But all your stuff . . ."

On the day of the rare Daniel Lemur specimen, he walks into Maurice's Diner, ravenous. The place is busy, rustling with hard metal noises, snorting laughter. When he slides into the banquette, he pushes away the uncleared plate, and stops. Somebody has hardly touched their dinner. Don't they know they won't get dessert if they don't? He shoves a finger in the yellow sauce. Kind of jammy, tasting of pineapples and something else, something sharper. Another dip: horseradish! What an idea! And then he figures, *Why not?* It's almost whole. An almost whole pork chop. He sets about busily sawing the thing. Gray, with its whorled rounds of sinews, all stacked together, what a marvel muscles are. And delicious! Wow, he'd never in a million years have ordered that, and here it turns out to be the house specialty. By the time the waitress comes, he's done.

It's so easy. The town is riddled with people eating out, all the time. The fat tourists, the contented residents, all of them pleased to be offered gigantic portions that they can leave half of. He can sit, sipping water, wait for the right moment, and then just get up and cross the floor, saying, "I'll take that out of your way for you, sir," and bring it back to his own table. The first time, everything goes as smooth as clockwork, but the second and third he is spotted, and bolts when the manager starts lumbering toward him. Both times fear plugs his throat; his heart yammers furiously. But both times, he's thinking of the next time, as he bolts out the door. The urge is an itch he can't stop scratching.

He is eating rice and some slightly past-date hot dogs he found behind the Shop-Rite that are just a few days older than the date stamped on them. Sitting cross-legged on the floor, he holds a fork arrested in midair. And it seems that he's grasping a slender wrist bone that ends in a claw. Poor cut-off thing, what body would it imply? How can he not know? The fork looks forlorn; poor claw, it has no beak to feed. He paws the rice with this new extension of his hand, and the grains slide through its digits like little grubs. There's something pathetic about it.

What the hell is cutlery for anyway? He has hands, doesn't he?

He's asked nicely, he doesn't see that it's an unreasonable request. To smell her. The real her, without the fog of shampoo, soap, deodorant, hair gel, perfume. She's the one who's always going on about patriarchy this and that, society and its constrictions on women. The first few times, she laughed, and finally she says scornfully, "Look, *you* stink, not me. You smell like a dog that's been rooting through garbage, okay? It's embarrassing." Does he really? He sniffs and sniffs and can't smell anything objectionable.

A few days later they are out at a diner, the one that serves up gigantic omelets dripping with cheese. She's going on and on about how *in*teresting some stupid professor at school is, yadda yadda, and behind her voice he sees the lemur he put into the clean room this afternoon. Suddenly, he realizes she has stopped.

"Jesus fucking Christ that's vile." Her voice is low and angry.

"What?" He studies her delicate gold nose ring.

"This is exactly what I'm talking about. You. Doing *that*." He has been chewing absently on some fries left on a plate. Why did he do that? In front of her! Idiot. Idiot! But why, on the other hand, does she give a damn?

"They're fine. Perfectly clean."

"That's so gross! It's scavenging."

At this he perks up. "You know, Schroeder says—"

"I don't give a good goddamn about what Schroeder says. Miss? Miss? Would you please take these off our table?"

So he apologizes, thinking abjectly about the vanishing possibility of sex. And sure enough, when they get back to her place, she starts in about her paper, how she has to finish it for Tuesday, etc., etc., and good night. Just to really mix the message, she kisses him long and slow, feeling his "scavenging" tongue with hers. Her hand travels down to give him a squeeze.

"I'm sorry I barked. Don't forget the party next Friday. Don't forget, don't make any plans." As if he *makes* plans.

He wanders aimlessly, the vision of her pale, flaccid body tormenting him; at home he beats off to the sight of the two of them rolling around in the woods, screwing up, down, sideways.

While he's defleshing a tree shrew, Schroeder comes bounding over, brimming.

"You want to go on a field trip in a couple of days?"

"Where?"

"Out to the zoo. They've got a javelina out there and I'm going out to butcher it. You can be staff photographer. Foster's got some bee in his bonnet about some guy's paper he says is wrong." Schroeder's told him about this before, about Foster's contentious position on Meso-American hunter-gatherer culture. They've been waiting, in fact, for an appropriate specimen to come their way so they can perform the experiment, using Schroeder's own tools.

"It'll be an adventure. Thursday, six A.M., outside the west door. I'll drive you."

"Be there or be square."

"*I'm* the one who's supposed to say that, not you!"

"Oh, yeah." Why does he always get these things wrong?

When Thursday comes, Jason is so worried about sleeping too late that he doesn't sleep at all; when Schroeder and Dr. Foster pull up in front of the museum, he's been waiting for hours. Schroeder gabbles on about javelinas very similar to the one they're going to cut up today, that have been found at sites in Clovis, wherever that is.

When they get there, they're given an empty pen, and the dead, swaddled javelina is brought out. It looks like a black, runty pig. Jason obediently snaps pictures of it and of the tool lying on a white sheet. Foster directs, and Schroeder cuts. It's hard going, especially with just a stone ax, because the hide is so tough. It's fascinating how much harder it is when the animal hasn't been frozen, thawed, and cooked to loosen the flesh. Schroeder goes on and on about the skill it takes. It takes most of the day, separating the hide from muscle and fat, and eventually Jason and Schroeder spell each other, cutting according to Foster's instructions. Jason keeps seeing how he'll put the remains in the clean room.

He can't explain why he does it, but late in the day, after all the exertion, six hours of sawing through sinew, he starts feeling strange.

He just wants to see. He plunges his arm into the skin flaps that had once contained the javelina's hind leg, as though it's a sleeve. "Javelina jackets for everyone!"

"Jason," Schroeder says warningly, but it's too late.

"Put that down for Chrissake!" Foster barks. "What the hell do you think you're doing?" and in that moment, Jason has a whiff of terror. He tries to tell him he was only messing around, but Foster just looks at him. As though he's a bush pig.

So it's no surprise when it comes, really.

He is sitting in a park off Alameda, letting the sun burn his brain to wooziness, in a paste of misery. In two weeks the lab job will be gone, the thin dribble of money will stop. "I'm really sorry, Jason, but there's no more money in the grant, I've stretched it as far as I can," Zoe tells him.

"Oh no, don't worry, I've got oh, about a million things."

"Are you going to go back to school, JJ?"

School? The thought of that frantic anxiety makes his stomach flutter: he remembers flipping through books too fast to read them, falling asleep in the library and missing tests. What does that have to do with anything?

On the bench beside the fountain in the central square, his legs tingle in the sun, taking in its energy directly, through the skin, filling him. In a few days, he'll be shut out for good. It was that fucker Foster. The light floss of snow that fell last night is melting, huge mossy patches are gnawing outward on the pavement. His skin crawls, itching and ready to split. He dozes in the warmth, but wakes with tooth-rattling chills. Agonizing aches run through him, he's a lock-jointed cockroach caught out in the cold. If he doesn't move soon, he'll definitely get sick. Finally, gritting his teeth, he jumps up, does ten jumping jacks, throws himself down to do a couple of push-ups, and sits down again, panting. Sure, he could be in the army. The exertion makes him want to sing aloud, to jump on the bench and perch there like a bird.

A passing office gaggle looks at him quizzically. He smiles, somewhat malevolently, a caped marauder about to swoop down on them. A black patch to his left makes him whirl toward an older man who has stopped to watch him. Why does the skinny old cockroach give a damn what he does? The old man continues to wait, expectant. His blue eyes pop out like feelers from the wrinkled pouches around his eyes. An audience. How can Jason disappoint them? He nods, coughs, adjusts his book as though ready to begin a long sermon. His arm scoops the book aloft, like a preacher with his Bible, and he begins to read from the book he's carrying, at the Fire Dance section: "How the dancers found the power to go on ever faster and faster, hour after hour, seemed beyond explanation or belief." He's enjoying this, sensing people listening. They're getting it, he can feel it. "Long before the end they seemed to pass over into a dimension of reality far out of reach of my understanding." But now someone is laughing greasily, rudely making him lose his place. Now his feeling of irrational happiness is vanishing. What is he doing? He tries to keep going, as the lines start sliding: ". . . and to a moment . . . and to a moment and a place which belonged only . . . technically to the desert in which we were all gathered . . . Then suddenly they halved the circle-dancing with their bare . . . feet . . ." The words don't make sense to him and his audience, if it was an audience, is dispersing. Looking up, he sees eyes. Their buttons glitter like eyes on their coats. All those eyes, these people look like monsters. That one woman, over there under the arcade, looks like a swollen caterpillar standing upright, regarding the world from the five eyes on her belly. Her white, pouchy face is like a baboon's bottom, sitting up there on top. And then she snaps back, to a regular middle-aged woman, looking lots like his mother in her fur, coming toward him with concern. He shudders, and walks away. The lecturer has concluded his speech. Someone, one of the street kids who hang around the plaza, claps him on the back.

"Nice reading man. Powerful stuff."

"Uh, thanks."

"What's the book?"

"*The Lost World of the Kalahari*." Jason holds it up.

"Yeah? I'm really interested in anthropology. Got a butt?"

For several seconds Jason can't get what he's talking about. Butt as in—? "Uh, no."

This guy has hundreds of safety pins in his jacket; it flashes like chain mail as he goes off to ask for cigarettes. Jason wouldn't mind talking to him, but he can't think of anything to say. He's still nervous after that woman in the coat, and besides, the guy's already returned to his group. His clan seals like a capsule around him.

Every day, the anguish and terror of knowing he won't be able to come here anymore have kept him in a kind of stupor, but when the day finally comes, it's almost a relief. On the last day at the lab, he peels the hare perfectly, and, not wanting to throw it away, stashes the hide in his knapsack. In the clean room, he fingers each of the specimens, the soft backs of a few patient gnawing bugs. In his last entry in the lab book, he writes, *Why should we plant when there are so many mogongo nuts in the world?* and decorates it with doodles to give to Zoe, then decides to keep it and take it home anyway. All of the animals are listed there.

He doesn't want to go out for beer, wants it to end right here, so Zoe kisses him sweetly, and tells him to call anytime. Ozzie manages to detach himself from some rock he's scratching to tell him gruffly to go back to school, "or you'll end up an underling like me." But it's Schroeder's gift that wins the prize. One of his Acheulian ax creations. Jason can't stop touching it, feeling its frigid power. He blows steam clouds onto it again and again, as though it's a mirror for wiping, until a thin rime of frost makes it absolutely perfect.

The last goddamn thing in the world he wants is to see people he knows from school at Stacey's party, but she cajoles, threatens. *Come on, come on, it'll be fun, nobody's going to* . . . . He waits as long as he can, wading through the crowd that's mostly her friends anyway, thank God. He sees Stacey, gabbling happily in the packed kitchen, and slopes out into the living room. Someone passes him a thick reefer, and he drags deep, again and again. It's truly excellent weed, the guy who's brought it is holding forth on the bud size and flavor, which he claims to get sent up specially. The music is making the floorboards throb and tingle through his shoes.

He finds things go more smoothly if he's in motion, if he keeps moving around, looking like he's headed for someone he's recognized, then changing direction and doing it again. Out on the grass, people are spread around in clumps, swaying and jiggling in the cold, vaguely in time to the music.

He's reached that really good high, touching the hem of something, and he finds himself talking to some guy who has a theory about Socrates and some poet. Loose tongued, he hears himself spouting pretty intelligent-sounding stuff for a change, watching a couple of girls dancing, a few more, until there's a whole crowd swaying to the pouring music. Hell, even *he's* moving, and in a rush of adrenaline he gets an idea, and tries to start things in a circle. It's amazingly easy to get it going, just push a shoulder here, grab a hand there. They're just like him, they want what he does, and he starts stamping, stamping and grinning and encouraging until everybody's doing it, laughing, and Jason realizes the one essential thing that's missing.

With almost unbelievable spryness, he gathers newspapers off the porch, some boards that have been there forever, somebody's lighter. When he dumps it in the center, a cheer goes up—for *him*. The fire blooms immediately, and for a time past counting it's incredible, all those shoulders shaking, and blue-jeaned thighs scissoring against the flames, knees gleaming like bones through torn denim, everybody's into it, hooting their own incoherent chants, they are in him and he in them, and the music thumps on and on in the wild firelight.

By the time the fire truck comes it's out, but Stacey and her roommates are incensed, they won't shut up, the three of them, *If the tree had caught* yadda yadda *What the hell were you thinking, why didn't you stop them?*

The next day, he wakes on her couch to a rich charred smell. Outside, on the front lawn, the back of a half-burned chair rears like a black harp from a small charcoal heap. He remembers how good it was, the rapture is still lingering even as Stacey emerges smudge-eyed and bleary, breathes orchestrally several times and tells him they have to talk.

In the restaurant, he stifles the urge to pluck a soggy piece of toast from amid the half-filled glasses of the clearing station.

"Jay. It's not working out." He can hardly understand her in the clatter and the throbbing queasiness that's engulfing him. The words roll around like stones. *Order priorities differences working out.* It had to come to this. It's a relief, actually. He's so far away from her he can hardly see her. He watches the gluttonous lickings of a fly in an open packet of jelly on the table.

He dips a finger into the jelly absently. She pounces.

"That's exactly what I'm fucking talking about! It's gross! That's disgusting, you don't go around fucking putting your fucking fingers into somebody else's fucking jam!"

"But it's good," he says. Roll of eyes. She pushes away her plate of eggs. "I feel sick."

"Are you going to eat those eggs?"

"Jesus. Whatever." After a long pause, watching him eat, she asks quietly, "We've really had some good times, right, JJ?"

He appears too busy eating to hear. "JJ, listen to me, I need some closure on this. You agree this just isn't working out."

"Mmmmmm. Mmmmmm hmmmm."

"Do you want your car back?"

"Huh?"

"Do you want it back? Your car? I mean since we're breaking up I'd . . ."

"Car?"

"Your car, JJ. I mean when you said I could have it. I mean you don't need . . ."

"Oh, no. It's yours. I wouldn't know what to do with it."

"JJ, why don't you think about going home? You could work for your dad for a while."

"Oh, I don't think so."

"But, JJ, they . . ." She starts again. "You can't live on nothing. If you're not taking money from your parents, you've got to get a job. To make money. Money, remember? You do a job, they give you money, you get to eat."

"But what is money?" She used to laugh about how neither of them had a clue about it.

She suddenly becomes angry. Her pale gold nose ring quivers. "Stop with the passive aggressive bullshit."

"Passive"? "Aggressive"? The words are nuggets of some other language. "Bullshit" brings up a picture of a hardened pile with bits of straw visible.

"JJ, I want this to be friendly. I want some closure here and you're just being obtuse and difficult so I feel fucking sorry for you and we get to go home together. Forget it. It's over. Done. Money is what you need. Everyone does. Job plus money equals food on the table."

"But what if it didn't?"

"I can't be having this argument. If you want the car, you can have it back anytime. Look, JJ, you need some help."

For days, he lies in bed like a wrapped caterpillar until he can't stand it any longer, and then goes out into the street, his mind skittering with resolutions to do something, to go on an expedition. Chewing slowly on what he finds, an almost full bag of corn chips, a half bottle of fruit juice, he slouches along the streets. Sometimes, he decides to visit somebody he knows, or knew when he was in school, but he gets lost, confused by the apartments that all look the same, the menace of the streets puts him in a fog, and he always loses his nerve. What would he say, anyway? His fingers prickle; he can't stop seeing scenes from the museum, the clean room, strange visions of Foster and Zoe, the displays. He itches to go back just one more time, but the thought of Zoe's face, pinched with hurt and embarrassment when he asked her if he could just stay on at the museum for no pay, keeps him from going back. He's even picked up classified sections of newspapers lying around, but when he gets there the job is always gone; the managers look past him shiftily.

When it finally hits, the idea cracks through his fog like splitting rock. He wakes knowing he was dreaming about the arch. It was on a camping trip, the last one he took with Dave the Rave before they both went off to college. They were camped on a little island, hardly more than a massive boulder, in the middle of a lake. The humped stone sloped down steeply to the water, and about halfway down to the water, he'd stopped, mesmerized. The clouds and the steeply treed hillside of the opposite shore were perfectly reflected in the water; you couldn't tell where the tree bottoms stopped and their reflections began. From where he stood, he was looking down from a great height into another world, where an arch of trees soared down toward a darkly clouded sky. He'd stared at it for an hour. An unsuspected world, right below the usual one.

Why didn't he think of it before? Why shouldn't he? Hasn't he lived for weeks at a time on canoe trips? In fact, now that he thinks about it, he realizes that the main happiness of his life has been crashing through the forest with a canoe on his head, preferably barefoot. Shitting in the woods, feeling the leaves beneath him. Ramming his tent peg home with a rock, just thinking about it makes his hand itch. He knows perfectly well how to survive, he doesn't need anything but himself. This is definitely a sensible plan. Until he figures things out. This is going to be an adventure. This is the first thing that's made some sense in a while. Oh, not to creep home late anymore past his landlady's windows because he's a month behind on the rent! It'll be an adventure.

He drags down his pack from the shelf.

He wonders if he might see the guy that was interested in anthropology, maybe join up and have a discussion, so he decides to go first to the foundations. He's never been there, but he knows where it is, in the Grant Hill section of town; a series of concrete foundations that were abandoned, and have become a hangout of sorts. But there are only a couple of middle-aged people passing a wine jug. Thick rinds of beer cans, wrappers, rotting blankets, and the dry ends of weeds are scattered in vague lines all over the place.

"Camping out?"

"You mind?"

"It's all yours. Make yourself at home."

The one in the cracked nylon overcoat says, "When I'm camping, I always like to pick a nice section of town."

One of them is on his way to Phoenix, or some place called Alabaster, looking for his wife, or his ex-wife, and the woman huddling in the quilt keeps sending him dirty looks.

"My mother's a minister. She'd fucking die if she saw me out here. I like to live nice."

Overcoat confides, "She's Pentecostal. Those folks'll fuck you up but good," to which she reacts by trying to land a punch.

Another guy goes on about how much he made in either repossessing or reprocessing something, and Overcoat threatens to deck him if he starts up with those lies again.

He pokes Jason. "You look like a smart kid, tell him he's full of shit . . ."

For a long time, it's good, about Springsteen's best concerts and really friendly people who've helped them out. And then somehow they're all trying to get him to drink. He tries to tell them he has an allergy to alcohol, that he'll wake up in a hospital, but that only angers Overcoat, who is having trouble making the words come out in the right order.

Thrusting the bottle in his face, "Catch something . . . afraid of that? 'Cause if I pissed before . . . 'Cause if you think I pissed in this piss . . ."

Jason can envision himself torn and bleeding in about three minutes. He reels away, back up the hill. Rocks trip him up, and he finally stumbles into the blades of an agave, cutting his hand open. The blood drips and drips until he finally has to open his pack and wind a shirt around it. He can hear them, far below. Tremendously tired, he realizes he won't even try to put up the tent tonight, and he sits shivering for hours, his sleeping bag draped around him, clutching his ax with his good hand.

Before dawn, in the blue hour of morning, he climbs a short bluff, and looks out over the tangles of rectangles and roofs. Something is moving, glints that resolve into light being reflected from the wings of thousands of birds. They're all over the city, swooping on their errands, pouring upward, wheeling. For moments on end he sees the world from their angle, swooping down on the dark, sharp edges. For these moments, he knows if he leans out, offering his chest to the wind currents, they'll hold him up. But before he can make a move the certainty is gone. All day he finds himself looking up, feeling the wind with his hands.

Walking west, he finally reaches the place he has in mind, a nature trail that starts in a park and winds parallel to a dry creek bed, and then rises through a series of hills to end at another park. Stacey and he have hiked here before, but the terrain feels different at night, and he stumbles continually. In the moonlight, the caliche gravel glows radioactive; on the ridge above, houses blink yellowly through the trees. There are others roaming around in here, maybe predators, but the spot he chooses is well protected, a shallow level space far up the hill, halfway between the trail and the houses above.

The ground is rocky, but bedded with a thick layer of dead leaves. He picks up the big sticks; brushes the ground even with his boots. As he pulls up a big stone, it offers a pleasing resistance, a whisper of suction. When he pulls the tent out of its sack, he can smell the northern forest in the sap stains all over it; he used it every summer at camp. A few dead mosquitoes shake off it as he unfolds it into a long square. The thin metal stakes go in easily; he places rocks on their buried heads so they won't pull out. A taut square. When he pulls up the center pole, the tent rises with a sigh. Inside in the little room of bright green light, he's home. Nomad motel. Perfect.

The night sounds are different here, drier. At home it was the creaking of pines, soft leaves lipping the wind, but here it's harsher, crackles and papery rustle. And he can still hear the cars, but he'll certainly get used to it. His heart almost explodes with panic when he hears shrill laughter. And then it settles down to quiet. Happy, he takes out the half Twinkie he saved, probing gently with his finger, savoring.

Sinking down into sleep, safe in his new shell, he can't stop thinking about Fred Emerson, his speech-impeded high school biology teacher intoning: *Thee hewmit cwab takes the shells of othew animals. As it scuttles fwom its outgwown shell to find a new one, it is the most vulnewable cweatuwe in the sea.* He used to do an imitation that had them rolling in the aisles.

In the morning, he buries the tent, which is too heavy to carry around all day. For the hungry explorer's breakfast, a quick forage behind the Shop-Rite yields some grapefruit and a cellophane package of hot cross buns, cooked only two days ago. Leisurely, he walks all the way back to the main square, humming. Tourists are milling around, taking snapshots, and none of them have any idea. They seem as cowed and frightened as rabbits to him. On a table outside one of the cafés on the square, he takes a quick splash of coffee, still almost lukewarm, though unfortunately without sugar. He's done it. He's gone.

Through a whole cycle of the moon, he lives in the same place, re-creating his homestead with joy each night, until the day he returns in the evening to find his tent gone. He digs in the spot where he left it, marked with a stone on the hillside near the fig trees. His hands paw the loose earth wildly. He lurches up, letting out yelps a little like a dog's low moaning, "Ow owww owwwwwwwwww." He digs deeper. Maybe he put it in farther than he thought but the picture of how it was, hardly covered, is vivid behind his eyes: the green nylon gleamed through the rocky soil and dry leaves, totally visible. He looks around, struck suddenly by a thought—maybe it wasn't *this* rock. In fact he's almost certain it was *that* one. This makes the moaning softer. On his knees, he digs the cold earth furiously; dirt flies onto his sweating face. Deeper, deeper, howling. The enormity of his stupidity and incompetence spreads like hot oil inside. Another hole, and another, it seems to him that all he needs to do in this world is dig a little deeper. His hands are thick red throbbing paws, blood welling up underneath some of the nails. There are sobs now, too, that he cannot stop. He will have to go up the hill and talk to those people, who will take one look at him and call the . . . No, he won't do that. A picture comes to him, of himself from above, kneeling like a prisoner, weeping in the forest, in the dark, for it is now full dark. And then it occurs to him that this is fine. Less to carry, less to worry about. It's going to be fine. After all, he still has his tarp and sleeping bag, doesn't he? It'll frost tonight, but that sucker's warm to, what does it say? Minus fifty! He pictures the poor bastard who had to test this thing, out in the arctic snow: *Hey fellas, let me in, it's no good at fifty-five below!*

He doesn't want to stay at his old campsite, spoiled now, so he scrambles down the hill, which was too hemmed in for his liking anyway. He needs to get away from this claustrophobic place, to walk off his puddled rage. A high place, with a view, he knows just the one. He can choose his spots, any one he likes. It isn't that far away, a couple of miles maybe, he can be there before the moon gets even halfway up the sky. He's happy now, walking quickly to warm himself up, though from time to time he thinks of his tent, sitting secretly somewhere. Did he miss it? The thought has him stopping dead in the middle of the street a couple of times. Maybe he should go back. But no. It was gone. And then he thinks of the fucker who took it; it singes his brain with rage to think somebody would be that low. He'd kill the fucker, twist his neck like a chicken's with his bare hands, press his bloody nails into his neck until the blood spurted out. Clenching fists, he checks the moon from time to time, moving quickly and purposefully northeast, walking straight down the middle of streets in this peaceful neighborhood, where the poor frightened people are already bedded down tight, and only a few solitary kids peer out from their beds at the same moon that's following him like a fat melon-headed baby. The thought makes him skip a little down the calm light-glazed streets.

He gets lost twice looking for it, shambling up and down hills, bumping into high chain-link fences around property. And he finally gives up, and plunks down exhausted on a little hill just outside a fence. The dry forest behind him settles its skirts for the night, and he sits for hours, watching the spatters of light, strange fruit that glows in the darkness. The red eyes of cars follow each other on a patch of road he can glimpse below the house.

He finds he can't get enough of walking, and his foot soles are getting tough as rubber. While he was in school he mainly shuttled between his dorm and the university, making forays into town to go to clubs or restaurants. Now the city gradually reveals itself to him as a complicated, tumorous fruit. At the center, near the museum, is the hard ancient nut of a village, with its main plaza, its cathedrals and museums and carefully rustic adobe shops and restaurants. Around that, a thick rind of neighborhoods, narrow streets of traditional adobe houses, with their pale white and terra-cotta walls. Farther out, strip malls and apartment complexes and buildings. On the mountain, great houses sit on swaths of piñon-forested land. Adobe and glass fantasies breast the wind, looking out and down at the valley. And far, far below, on the opposite end of the city, the flat plain of desert bulges out with new growths.

The smell of rank vegetable decay draws him through the cold, down the hill. It's frost-blighted vegetables, in someone's garden. Some rich woman playing Mother Bountiful has left most of the crop out to rot. The whole thing may only have been for display anyway. He pictures her, a woman like his mother saying, "That over there is the corn, and the snap peas, and the tomato plants, and of course the peppers! I'm so happy when I'm out there, with my hands just filthy and grubby." The cucumbers, lying like turgid green penises amid the withered foliage, are toast. The corn is dried, but he thinks he can roast it later, in the fire. And the peppers are in fine shape, since their stems lift them off the ground. Their sharp peppery crunch brings tears to his eyes.

*   *   *

In the evenings, downtown, there are often pizzas behind the Domino's on San Gabriel. Boxed, sometimes still warm, the ones they put wrong condiments on, or didn't deliver in time. He finds he can easily do with one meal a day, supplemented by a few scraps here and there. He likes the clear, empty feeling that comes over him as he sinks down slower and slower. He can look at a tree until he feels its roots poking through blackness, spreading invisibly beneath him.

He is convinced that on this diet he is beginning to fill out, to grow muscles where muscles have not been before. The sour anxious stomach that has plagued him for the last year begins, nearly miraculously, to clear up. Possibly from the pizzas, he even notices a tiny, spongy layer of fat developing around his middle. Bushmen think a belly's handsome, a sign of well-being.

There's so much extra out there that there's always choice. When the pangs really start, when his legs start to feel twitchy and weak, he knows that it's time to start toward it. After the lunch crowd has left, they let in the shambling army that collects in the alley. He gets to recognizing regulars; bloated, they sit around in the plaza, braiding hemp and threading beads into necklaces, or gamboling with their dogs. Sometimes, he even joins a hack circle, kicking at the small pebble-filled sack, trying to keep it in the air. Veronica calls herself an "ecoterrorist" and has a plan to sew up the hole in the ozone layer. Kris spouts Trotsky to anyone who'll listen. But Jason finds he can't talk to them for long; he's lost the trick of filling the air constantly with words. He craves silence, the high hillsides and wind. A dog would be fine though; he thinks he might get one, when Veronica's big shepherd has her puppies. He practices not understanding people speaking around him, making billboards into hieroglyphics. Separating the characters, and convincing himself they can only be looked at from right to left, they start to look like Babylonian pretty soon. 37' H C. S W E N. There's nothing to it after a while.

He is walking aimlessly in the orange hour, when the sun makes all the adobe walls of the city glow as flesh. Adobe walls of flesh surround him, separating him from all warmth in the world. Bone-chilled, his chattering teeth rattle his whole frame, and the icy sweat drips over his brow. The walls will be warm. He just needs to wait till the right moment. Where he touches it, it will redden around his hand and leave the outline of a handprint, like the white ghosts of hands printed on the caves of Australian aborigines. The contented rosiness of that womanly wall-flesh begins to excite him, as something forbidden to touch, like the tender swell of a girl's belly.

He's drawn farther and farther down the adobe canyon, until he sees something hanging from a box on the curb of an apartment complex. In the ashy, moted light, a blackened stump protrudes from a garbage bin, a footless leg. He sees a flashed vision of a leg in fire, swelling like a sausage splitting its casing. Nearing, he sees the split, a long gash down the leg; he senses a tiny whiff of the clean room on the piny air. He nears carefully, a soft-footed ape, reaching out to touch the woven nylon bonded to rubber. And he lifts up the skin, which is completely intact except for the long tear down the right calf. It's blue-black, with a zipper and yellow stripes down the arms, on the sides of the legs.

It fits on easily over his jeans and T-shirt. A new black rubber scalp for his head, framing his face. Finally he feels warmer, indescribably light. A new skin, the toughest yet.

The walls of the Dumpster are mottled steel, inescapably beautiful. Inside silence padded by sheaves of paper and boxes, he can savor the illusion that there is nothing outside. His nose picks out the layers of smell: dusty mold, ripe bananas, something as salty as dried fish. Collages of images, discards and scraps, occur to him without particular connection to one another. Hot and slippery inside his new skin-suit, he has the impression that he is fermenting, that his heat is making the Dumpster glow subtly from outside.

He cannot recall how long he has been walking, alternately freezing and sweating. There is nowhere to go to get out of the gelid rain, its needles sharp on his face. Pausing, pushing aside wrappers and puddled Styrofoam cups in an open bin, he withdraws a perfectly intact potato sitting in a foil pan. The potato is soggy, squelching a little with each bite, and the rain patters pleasingly on the aluminum pan. Chewing, feeling the damp mealy thing go down, he experiences an intense joy, realizes that the water in the potato is the same as the rain falling onto him, the same water he is chewing down and drinking. He cannot even tell where he ends and the pavement under his feet begins. The mouths of garbage cans, all lined up on the street, look beautiful and open, as though they are singing. For a moment they *are* mouths singing a song of joy and bewilderment. He lopes from one to the other, pokes into one and snatches a can and hurls it high, watching the quick spray of cola. He runs on and on, which makes him feel that he is being pursued, and as he glances backward, the mouths of the garbage cans acquire a plaintive, hungry aspect. Careening around a corner, he nearly knocks over a man who looks like a mushroom under his umbrella. He keeps running, dragging hoarse scouring breaths, until he can finally stop, doubled over and heaving, on a street with no cans on it.

He can't understand what they're calling to him, these three men at the picnic table. The sounds are puddled under his new and improved scalp. Gesturing, pointing. They look so strange in their unprotected skins, so soft and flabby, anything might poke through them. And suddenly he's laughing hard, which upsets them. One of them pushes his shoulder, so he pushes back, friendly as a dog. Another push, and then the splintering pain in his leg. The wind smells afraid, so he tries to run, but the branches overhead are tangling up his feet. It's one punch, then another, a sharp blow behind his knees. A boulder crashes into his stomach, and for time past counting he gawps helplessly for air with vise-held lungs, anticipating another blow that doesn't come. Surfacing briefly, he hears the crunching sounds of their retreat. He hears a voice moaning hoarsely without words, which he remembers is his, and then he's alone in a reddish darkness, bedded tight among the dry stems and stones. His face is composed, serene, as he sinks deeper and deeper, until he rests motionless, curled up and small as a bean (and he remembers how he used to curl up sometimes in the playground, trying to impress the girls, saying, "Look! I'm a human bean!" and they'd all go off shrieking). Up again and walking on into the forest, he sees his friend approaching through the trees, feet padding easily over the sharp stones, which Jason marvels at briefly, and then they fight like brothers, intensely, grappling like strong bears, swatting spindly branches, thwacking into tree trunks. When they're tired, panting a little, they walk through the forest, listening to their footfalls. And then Jason shows him an open patch where they can pick blackberries, like he used to do at the cottage in summers. The berries are guzzly and sweet, and he watches his hands stain purple. Farther on, in a field of high grasses, they come upon a deer lying dead, flies crawling over its eyes. They have to brandish sticks to keep off other animals, there's a fire now, and gulls flapping overhead. He shows Jason how to skin the deer with his Acheulian ax, and they live barefoot forever.

Tenaya Rahel Darlington
Indiana University

RELEVANT GIRL

Everything before this is irrelevant: one day Gum, a small-time lawyer, comes home from the office early, changes into his jeans, sets off down the street with his hands in his pockets, and begins to follow a woman. She is young, in her early twenties. He is in his thirties, has been married for several years. The girl, in her own way, is irrelevant. Who she is or what her name is, they're irrelevant facts. Still, she is in every way relevant to all the successive events in his life despite the fact that their interaction is minimal—lasts not even ten seconds. She is attractive, from behind anyway, and has long dark hair that waves down her back, shining like a pelt, almost to the waist of her khaki pants. A black bag is strapped to her back, and in one hand she carries both her umbrella and what looks like a brown velvet suit coat, perhaps a man's, perhaps her own. Gum does not know, though he is curious.

It is important to point out that Gum has not sought her out in any way. He has not chosen to follow her over other women. He does not even realize he is following her until he is. They seem to be heading in the same direction, though he has no particular destination in mind. He has simply come home early from work and, finding his wife to be out of the house, has gone out for a walk. He cannot remember the last time he just strolled. In fact, he cannot remember the last time he really indulged himself or took time to go off alone, unless he includes the occasional drink after work. He sometimes sits at the bar and shoots the breeze with the bartender over a Jack and Coke. Sometimes there is an old-timer slouched over an ashtray or another businessman with whom Gum talks. Then they joke around and exchange occasional glances with the waitresses.

When Gum thinks back on the girl he followed home on this particular day, he will wonder what made him continue down the walk after her in his crisp white sneakers. He will wonder what came over him. He will not be able to remember his thought process at all, and he will even question the reality of the situation, despite the fact that it will change him for good. He will, from time to time, see other women like her, women who resemble her from behind, and it will make him bend down and tie his shoe or dodge into a store for a gumball.

The woman does not remind him of his wife, whose name is Belle. The woman does not remind him of any of his clients or of any former girlfriends or even women he has thought about in secret. She is just a woman ambling down the street. She stops to check her bag for something. He stops to wind his watch. When she crosses the road, he keeps up his pace so that soon he is only feet away from her. He sees that she is carrying something square in her back pocket, perhaps a thin wad of bills, perhaps a love letter. He can see the edge of her neck where it meets the collar of her blouse. He can see a bracelet with blue stones around her left wrist. She is wearing sensible shoes, the kind in which one can easily run.

After a few minutes, he can tell that she senses him. She looks slightly to the side without turning all the way around to check his position in relation to her. She speeds up a little, then slows down to let him pass, but he does not. He is not doing anything out of the ordinary: he is walking down the street. They have just passed the grocery store where all the people with food stamps go. To his left is a row of four houses, all of them two stories with porches upon which there are swings and pots of bedraggled, brown leaves—the remnants of summer flowers. It is a neighborhood not much unlike the one where he and his wife live. It's broad daylight. Anyone looking out a window can see them. Cars pass in various colored blurs on a busy street ahead of them. It's four in the afternoon.

Perhaps he did not expect her to be so surprised, though he still cannot remember if she called out, if she gasped, if she yanked his hand away. He does not remember the minute before nor the minute after, though he remembers her face, her hair caught in the edge of her mouth. He remembers her moving quickly away, her gait unrhythmic and haphazard as she half walked, half ran to the house on the corner. She had gone up the steps and through the door. No, she had literally flown up those steps, casting only a quick glance his way through the shrubbery.

He had stood there, still hearing his own voice, though he could not recollect hers or recall now if she had even spoken. When he looked down, his hands were open to the air, as if holding something—the moment gone, yet heavy in its past existence.

At dinner, Gum tells his wife about a woman with long blond hair who came to see him about a case she was interested in taking to small claims court.

"I hope you didn't take it," his wife says, serving herself small potatoes. "The more of those little cases you take on, the more you get mired in minor scuffles."

Gum nods and nods. They've been through this before. He's had a rough start in Belchertown.

"This is a different sort of case," Gum says, and his wife can see that he is visibly shaken, so she listens with her special cheetah ears that are capable of hearing the most minute sounds.

Here's what happened: a woman, a young woman, a young attractive woman is minding her own business and walking down the street when a man begins to follow her.

"What does the man look like?" his wife breaks in, setting down both her fork and knife. "Maybe I've seen him. I was out all day."

Here's what he looks like: he has a crew cut or maybe it's just a very short cut. He's of medium build. Slightly muscular, not wiry. Definitely not wiry. He's wearing a dark shirt, jeans, sneakers.

"How old was he?" Mrs. Gum asks, chewing slowly, craning over her plate to catch every word.

"Thirties, mid-thirties, late thirties," says Gum, giving a shrug.

"That doesn't tell you anything at all," his wife says with concern, putting an index finger to her temple. "That could be anyone."

Gum nods and stirs his peas around on his plate. Then he continues, his voice low. His wife's neck stretches across the table like a giraffe's. Gum feels himself getting smaller, less articulate. How can he explain what really went on?

"He did that in broad daylight?" his wife asks, astonished. "What a strange thing to do."

Gum nods. Yes. It is very strange. He can still feel where he touched her. He is holding a spoon in that same hand. He has a dark napkin tucked down into his collar, covering his chest where he can still feel the indentation of her bag as he came up behind her.

After dinner, Gum and his wife watch television and drink port out of small, bulbous glasses on their new sofa. There is nothing on, nothing they like—which is almost nothing. His wife stands up, straightens her skirt, and says, "Why don't we watch a movie?" She holds up a black case, something she rented from the library. "As long as you don't mind watching *Barefoot in the Park* again," she says. His wife is a huge fan of Robert Redford, to the point that Gum sometimes gets jealous. In the scene where Redford runs around in the rain, feeling desperate and shattered, Gum's wife always cries into the arm of the sofa, ruining the upholstery with her mascara.

There will be no Redford and Fonda tonight. The tapes must have accidentally been switched, for what comes on is a documentary about the zebra. "In this case," his wife says, "we better pour ourselves more port." And she goes into the kitchen and returns with a tall glass.

Outside their tiny house the wind knocks the branches of the bushes against the windows, but Gum is immune. He is watching the zebras with fascination and awe. A baby zebra is being born. It stands almost instantly, bending then straightening its pool cue legs. Now the crucial moment, says the narrator. The female zebra must circle her young so that she can memorize her mother's stripes. If the foal sees another pattern, even out of the corner of her eye—if another zebra comes up unexpectedly behind them, for instance— the foal will be lost. She will never be able to recognize her mother's pattern, and she will eventually get separated from the herd and die.

Gum sits entranced, his thumb pushing against his front teeth, a habit from childhood. Sight is a kind of memorization, he thinks.

The eye spots something and holds on to the imprint somehow. A single vision can change the route of our existence, can help or hinder our survival in the world. There are some visual experiences that we forget right away, but others remain with us until death. Sights have shelf lives, Gum thinks. For instance, Gum cannot remember what he wore last Friday, yet he can remember perfectly every pair of pajamas he has ever owned, especially the ones he wore as a child. He can also remember all of his mother's different bathrobes: the silky pink one; the furry red one; the aqua blue one with the white zipper up the front; the quilted white one. And on and on. He thinks of his mother circling his bassinet in her different robes, his eyes fixed on her, memorizing just where the pockets were, the eyelet lace. Why do we remember the strange things we remember? What about the things we forget? Do we choose to forget them, or do they begin to decay on a shelf far back in one's mind, turning into a puddle?

Gum thinks about the girl he followed down the sidewalk. He can remember everything about her, at least almost everything. Parts of her have begun to fade, like her face. He does not remember the color of her eyes, for example—if her nose was large or small. What does she recall? What will she remember for the rest of her life? Will she be able to forget what happened on the walk? Will she choose to forget it or will it be forgotten for her? And if she remembers all through time, think of that! She will carry his face with her forever. The notion terrifies Gum. In the head of an unnamed, unknown woman, his visage might reappear numerous times in the course of her lifetime. Even as he grows old and she grows old, she will remember his face exactly as it was on October 21, 1996.

Gum turns to his wife. A herd of zebras is racing across her eyes.

"If a man came up to you," he says, swishing around a circle of port in the bottom of his glass, "and did what I described over dinner, would you ever forget it?"

His wife turns to him and blinks.

"What you described," she says, stopping for a gulp of port, "is something no woman could forget."

The credits roll until the screen goes fuzzy. Gum's wife has fallen asleep, her head on his thigh. She is probably drunkenly dreaming of zebras, their lines rippling and blurring. He lays a hand on her brown curls and finishes his drink, watching the fuzzy screen, which after a while begins to look like busy fabric. It moves so fast, it almost stands still. The mind plays tricks on you; the eye is rarely a lie detector.

The storm outside knocks over some lines, and the lights go out. Gum cannot see a thing. He lifts his wife's head, lays it back down on the couch, makes his way to the kitchen, pushes aside a chair, opens the far drawer, reaches in, feels the candles in with the knives, and lights one immediately with his Zippo. He stands there with the candle, looking at his path of travel through the living room and dining room and kitchen, unsure why he even bothered to find a light. He can remember where everything is in the dark. So he blows out the candle. Its burning smell lingers in the air for a second, then he sets the candle on the counter. He stands there in the dark, unable to see anything, and the event of the afternoon begins to replay itself in his mind, only backward.

The girl walks backward down some steps that lead away from a house. She walks hurriedly backward in her shoes, swinging her arms backward, her hair blowing forward in the breeze. She is visibly shaken, but backward. Likewise, he walks backward. They face each other, several feet apart. He says something, but backward so that it is nonsensical, and she gasps backward so that it sounds like a sigh. Her face breaks into a smile, which is a frown backward, and then his hands have grabbed her, they are reaching, they are just beginning to reach around and touch her, he has just begun to think about it, he is coming up behind her, he is walking home backward, he is taking his hands out of his pockets, taking his shoes off, taking his jeans off. He is standing in front of the mirror, not looking at himself.

Gum replays the scene over and over, forward and backward. He begins to see more and more of her face each time she spins around—that horrible, aghast look after being violated. He wants to take off his hands. He wants desperately to take off his hands, to run them through the dishwasher. The lights are still out. The tub is ice cold. He is thankful that he cannot see his face in the mirror, the same face that will come up behind her in her sleep, haunt her forever. *Had he thought, he never would have, no one wants to, no one means to, no one, certainly not him.* Here he is watching a zebra movie with his wife. Here he is squirting some Pert into his hand. Maybe the girl uses Pert. Everyone uses Pert. He's not that kind of man.

* * *

This goes on for days and weeks. The irrelevant girl is always near, her face aghast, frozen to the back of his mind. He can hear the shriek she sent up. Right in broad daylight, what was he thinking? And so out of character. He wonders if his father, his gentle dentist father, ever took a woman by such violent surprise. Surely, it's not something in his genes.

Gum grows nervous. Gum grows pale. He has trouble sleeping and trouble getting out of bed.

"Touch me," his wife says in the dark, running a hand along his thigh.

"I can't," Gum says. "Not with these hands."

His wife rolls over with an irritated sigh. "That's all you keep talking about," she says. "You and your hands."

Gum lies awake. He has to. He's not sure what he might do next. He has been wearing thick, wool gloves to work. In the morning, he sprinkles some Comet from the bathroom into each of the fingers so that his hands are gritty and grow raw. He shuffles papers, and when anyone asks, he tells them he is sensitive to photocopies.

When an attractive woman walks by, he imagines she is a zebra—made up only of lines. He doesn't let his gaze rest anywhere too long. He doesn't want to suddenly do anything crazy or let a woman's visage stick around in his vision too long. It's bad. It's very, very bad. His wife tells him he needs to see someone. And he does. He does need to see someone.

"But I don't want to *see* anyone," he tells his wife. "I don't want to see period. I wish humans would evolve without eyes. I wish we all just looked like a bunch of shapes."

"Whatever do you mean?" his wife asks.

"I wish all people were triangles or squares. Maybe there would be some slight variation—along the hypotenuse. But then we would get into arguments over who was pointier. Forget it," says Gum, going back to his work.

"Are you having trouble seeing?" His wife bends low and looks at him through his glasses. She touches the edge of his frames with her thumb and forefinger. Then she squints and looks deeply into his eyes.

"Who's that?" she asks, craning her neck into his face.

Gum looks at her lips, which form a diamond, her triangular nose, her trapezoidal eyebrows.

"Mr. Gum," she says slowly. "There's a woman in your eyes."

Gum leans back in his chair and takes off his wire-rimmed glasses, rubbing his eyes with his knuckles. "It's your reflection," he says. "Anytime you look into someone else's eyes, you're going to see your own face."

Mrs. Gum sits down on his lap in the dining-room chair and takes his chin in her hand. Gum struggles for a moment and then relinquishes his retinas to her gaze. Mrs. Gum has small gray eyes like a pelican that can detect fish underwater half a mile down.

"The woman in your eyes," she says, "is facing away."

In his ski goggles and wool gloves, Gum goes to his office every morning and meets with the few clients he has, mainly unsatisfied husbands and wives filing for divorces. It is fall. All the leaves are tinted black.

"Getting ready to go to Aspen, I see," one client comments. "Which resort do you and the missus prefer?"

"Are you trying to look like Roy Orbison?" someone jokes. "I hear he always wore those shades because he was cross-eyed."

An older woman comes in crying. "You've got the right idea," she says. "I could never do your job without having to wear shades. Sometimes I cannot bear looking at the world either." With that, she draws out a pair of Ray-Bans and puts them on for the rest of her visit.

Mrs. Gum never makes another reference to the girl in Gum's eyes. Gum himself has not looked in the mirror since. Even worse than being haunted by the girl is to be haunted by himself.

"I'm marked," he says to himself, sitting in his car one evening in an empty parking garage. "It's like having a yellow star or a pink triangle. It's like having stripes all over me in the midst of a lion's den." He rubs his gloved hands against the lightweight fabric of his pants. Then he weeps. He thinks of a line from a Leonard Cohen poem he memorized in law school: *They could only drone the prayer, They could not set it down.*

That's how it is, Gum thinks—like a prayer he could not set down.

Not only can he not set it down, he can't keep his memory from retrieving the same information over and over. Even when he closes his eyes, she is there with her small mouth open, her eyes almond-shaped and greenish brown, staring horrified at him, staring at him: Gum. At night, the incident plays on a dark reel at the base of his brain, like the famous Zapruder film. Where exactly had he grabbed her? He remembers the feeling of her breast, stiff like a stack of coffee filters in her bra. How long had it lasted? How soon had she turned? Had he grabbed her hips? Had he kissed her? Had he unsnapped her khaki pants?

The recollections don't stop in real time. They go on, becoming more elaborate and fantastic until he can no longer separate what might have happened from what really occurred. Where does memory bisect truth? Where does the bad dream intervene? He no longer knows.

Gum pushes his wool knuckles up under his ski goggles and wipes at his eyes. Then he leans over and opens the glove compartment where he keeps his Dictaphone. He rarely uses it. There is an empty tape in there, ready to go.

"This is to set the record straight," Gum rasps. "Here's what happened." The recorder is voice-activated, which is good. It allows Gum to lean his head back against the headrest, get comfortable, close his eyes.

"Let me preface by saying that I am an honest and well-meaning man," Gum begins, settling his shades on his nose. "I am the son of a dentist from Dayton, Ohio. I am not a religious man, except for Easter and Christmas, upon which I present myself before the United Methodist Church. I have a liberal arts education, graduated Phi Beta Kappa and magna cum laude." Gum clicks the stop button and rewinds the tape so he can begin again.

"Let me preface by saying that I am not a pervert. I will admit to having fantasies about older women all through college, to entering a sex booth in Munich whereupon I watched fifteen minutes of graphic intercourse between partners in latex suits for five marks. I will also admit to several one-night stands in my youth, which, for lack of better judgment, I consider to be my fault. I was breast-fed and sheltered, and as a child never witnessed any sexually aggressive behavior other than a bull mounting a heifer."

Gum tosses the Dictaphone onto the passenger seat. What is he doing? What does any of this matter? He isn't before a judge and jury. He is sitting in his Honda Accord.

"*I have no money, I murdered the pharmacist*," Gum says aloud. That is from a Cohen poem called "I Have Two Bars of Soap," which Gum's college roommate had laminated to the tile in the shower. By the end of their senior year, the water had made its way under the plastic and turned the whole page pink with mold, but he could still read the words. Gum never thought they made much sense, but he liked the idea of poetry serving up a joke on perceptions.

Gum drives home to his wife. It is after dark. He feels he has a new attitude about life now, after his hour or so of meditation on the parking ramp. He is not going to let himself think about the girl. People allow stuff like this to take over their whole lives. A bad decision turns them sour on life. He has repented enough. He has been thinking about it for weeks now, atoning for it in small ways, like with the wool gloves and the Comet. He has rubbed his palms raw.

"Screw the girl," he says to himself, putting on his blinker. "Screw the girl. Just forget about her."

He nods to himself. "Yes!" he says. "The girl is over and done with. She's dead, done, down the drain. Ha!" Gum sends a fist up into the air.

Inside the house, Gum's wife is waiting for him at the door. She is wearing a dark red robe he has never seen her in before.

"Do you like it?" she asks, helping him with his jacket. From the kitchen, he can smell dinner—a roast in the oven. His wife hands him a glass of wine, and he takes it and sips it, walking over to the couch in his gloves and scarf and shades.

"Take off those glasses. I feel like I have an impostor in the house," his wife says, lighting a candle on the table.

Gum kicks up his feet and laughs. "That's why this is a special occasion," Gum says, turning to look at her. "I am the new Gum. I am the unabridged and uncut version. This is my new look."

His wife smiles at him from the kitchen doorway where she is stirring something in a pot. "What is your new name?"

Gum thinks for a second. "It is—Gum backward."

"Mug?" his wife asks.

Gum jerks his head back. "Is that what our last name spells?"

"Of course," his wife says. "Don't tell me you've never noticed."

"How long have you known?" Gum asks, sitting forward on the couch, as if she has just disclosed something terrible about her health.

"It's the first thing I thought of when you introduced yourself to me," his wife says, turning off the kitchen light and entering with the roast. "I thought, I am about to fall in love with a man whose name is both a noun and a verb, forward and backward."

His wife smooths her robe under her thighs as she sits down at the table. The lights are off, one candle burning, Mozart slipping from one reel to another on the old tape deck.

"I can't believe this," Gum says, joining her. "Backward, I am Mug."

"Take off your shades," his wife says, extending her monkeylike arm. She lifts them off for him and blows out the candle, so that the room is completely dark.

Gum puts his fingers to his temples. Mug—it's in his genes and in his name. He is destined to violate. Now it makes sense, though it makes no sense at all. At least it lends a farfetched explanation as to why he simply walked down the street one day and attacked an innocent woman: it had nothing to do with who he thought he was but who he was destined to be. He'd always thought of himself as a respectable and respectful human being, but clearly he was not. That was his forward self. His backward self, the deep region of Gum, had its own set of demands.

"I have no control," Gum announces.

"Should I turn on a light?" His wife's chair moves.

"No, not the light," Gum says. "I didn't mean what I just said. Everything is much better perceived in the dark."

His wife laughs her wine-filled laugh. "Would you like to perceive these carrots?" she says like a grackle.

Gum can feel the heat of the bowl. He takes it and begins to pile his plate full of warm food. It's dark. He wants to take his gloves off. He wants to eat with his hands, eat the little carrots one at a time and suck the butter from between his fingers. It's been weeks since he's taken off the gloves except in the shower. His hands feel alive when the air hits them, when he holds them over his steaming plate. He cleans them on the tablecloth, feeling like a sneaky rabbit, and plunges them into a mound of mashed potatoes.

"Great dinner," Gum says. "This was a terrific idea." He can hear his wife pouring wine as he pushes handfuls of food into his mouth, feeling gravy run down his chin and drip down his front. He delights in the mess he is making in the dark, where his wife cannot see. I am Mug, he thinks.

"I am going to turn the music up a little," his wife says. "I love this movement."

"Sure," Mug says, laying a thin slice of roast across his face like an all-beef mask. "Do anything you want to. I haven't enjoyed myself this much in weeks."

Then she is at his throat, not trying to strangle him, but to hug him, though later he is not sure. First he feels her fingernails, then her arms coming up from behind. The slab of roast on his face alarms her as she bends down to kiss him. She gasps and he tries to grab her so he can explain, but she pushes him away.

There is a short scuffle on the floor, then the lights go on. He is standing there with gravy spots all over his white shirt, dressing in his hair. There is meat on the floor. She is standing by the wall, her shoulders rising as she gulps for air. One arm is around her stomach. She stares at him across the room, and there is the aghast face. There is her disbelief. Her eyes are memorizing him, taping this vision.

"What is going on?" she whispers.

He can see her eyes moving quickly over the table with its white tablecloth, burgundy napkins, platters full of food, vase of pink carnations. She is memorizing, reviewing, remembering. This is how she will describe it to her friends.

She pulls her robe closed about her neck and glares at him, horrified. "Look at you. You've turned into a maniac. Just who do you think you are?"

Gum stands with his hands at his sides, surveying the supper from the other side of the room. He does not want to forget any of it. No, he wants to make sure he has it right this time. In his mind, he will go over and over this scene again and again, and he wants to keep everything straight, so it doesn't begin to take over, metamorphose in his mind.

Then she is gone. In her new red robe she is gone, leaving everything just so, the front door open in her wake, in her haste to escape. His car is out of the driveway before he can even get to a window. He sees the two rear lights cut down the street like eyes.

A man named Gum or Mug is walking down the street in a pair of jeans and a dark jacket. His hands are stuffed in the pockets of his jeans. The air is crisp and there is no one outside. He is a man whom cars pass, whom people glance at without taking notice. Who expects a single man walking down the street at night with his hands in his pockets to be meditating on violence? Has he attacked someone before? Has he just tried to strangle his wife? We don't ask these sorts of questions unless we have had some prior encounter with fate, in which case we are a little leery of Gum—his potential to be Mug. Is this man walking forward or backward? Are his perceptions scrambled? Is he vile or evil, live and let live? Has he lived the devil? A simple word like desire spells die, rise, seed, sired, and red sir. Thread is death with an *r*, and pear spells reap and rape. Threat is also tear, heart, and rat. Everyone knows about God.

At the steps of the relevant girl's house, Gum fumbles with his hands, trying to decide how to make his entry. What if she answers the door? She will (a) recognize him, or (b) not recognize him. If (b), then she may (a) slam the door in his face, (b) lunge for his adam's apple, or (c) reproach him verbally. His only logical choice is to (a) introduce himself and apologize right away unless she does (b). Hopefully, she will (d) do none of the above. She will (e) either not be there, or (f) refuse to come to the door altogether. If she (c)'s him, he will try to explain what he has not been able to explain to anyone else, not even himself.

He will say, Miss, I don't know if you remember me or not, but months ago now, I came up behind you and grabbed you as you were walking home. After that, I don't remember what truthfully happened. I hardly remember the moment it occurred or the moments before it occurred, but since that moment, I have lived with your face in my face. I have not been able to lead a normal life. I have not been able to sleep or eat normally, to touch my wife, to fulfill the duties of my job, to exist as what I call myself: Gum. I can assure you that what I did was not out of some malicious intent, that it can only be explained by some unconscious ill-humor, some fateful side of my personality that slid past me between blinks. I have not come to your door to ask your forgiveness, only to acknowledge what happened, to get a second glimpse of your face as a human being.

She is in every window behind the curtains. She is coming up behind him on the walk. She is lurking in the dark shrubbery and has been waiting all these months for him to come looking for her. The house is dark, but there is a glow behind the drapes upstairs as if someone might have lit a candle.

Gum shifts restlessly around on the porch after he has rung the bell. He looks around at the things on the porch: a couch, a child's rocker with the padding ripped out, a strand of Christmas lights, several coffee cups full of cigarette butts, a yellow towel, a bunch of plastic flowers branching from a single plastic stem, a bike lock, and some cardboard boxes folded and propped behind a chair. Gum goes over to a wooden support beam where there are two mailboxes. Under a piece of clear tape, written on a piece of white paper, are the last names of the inhabitants: Cormican, Daniels, Maurer, and Moll. He wonders which last name belongs to the relevant girl. He wonders why there are two mailboxes to begin with.

It takes a second ring to bring footsteps to the door. By this time, Gum has broken out in a cold sweat. In the next moment, Gum thinks, my whole life will change again. Maybe I will end up on the lawn with a broken nose, but at least I will be acknowledged for who I am.

It is not the relevant girl who answers the door, but another woman. She stands behind the screen with her hand on the latch. Gum can barely make out her short brown hair, her glasses behind the mesh. There is a pen behind her ear. One hand is in her pocket.

"I'm looking for someone," Gum says. "Is there a woman who lives here with waist-length, dark hair?" He indicates the length by touching his own hips with either hand.

"She doesn't live here anymore," the woman says. Gum notes a faint accent in her voice.

"Do you know where I could find her?"

"What's this about?" The woman comes a little closer to the door, still holding on to the handle from the inside. The screen is torn. He could reach right in. But he's not that kind of man. Still, the woman looks at him skeptically. He is not wearing his shades, and he wonders if the woman can see the relevant girl in his eyes.

Gum takes his hands out of his pockets and rubs them together to keep warm. He knows that if he doesn't say something convincing, the door will close. He will never find out where the girl has gone. He will never see her again. In person.

"This is about Leonard," Gum tells her, tilting his head to the side, squinting beneath the porch light.

"Leonard?"

"Yeah, that's right," Gum says, trying to give his voice the air of importance. "This is about a man named Leonard Cohen. Do you know where I might be able to reach the former tenant?"

It's obvious the woman in the doorway has never heard of Leonard Cohen. She is Irish, and even if she weren't, it isn't likely that even many Americans would recognize the name Leonard Cohen even though he is a celebrated songwriter, folksinger, novelist, and poet. One of those guys who has it all.

"Look, I'm a lawyer here in town," Gum says, holding up his palms like maps explaining everything.

The woman opens the door a little farther, more trusting now. "I wish I could help you out. All I know is that her family's from Iowa, but she didn't say where she was going."

"Thanks," Gum says. "Sorry to bother." The woman nods and Gum heads down the steps back into the darkness.

Two days later, Gum gets a call at his office. He is there cleaning out his desk, taking his name off the door: GUM. From the inside, the letters spell MUG. How could he have sat at his desk for so long and missed it? He has spent the past two nights alone, sitting at his wife's vanity, staring at himself in the mirror. The girl was still there, standing with her back to him, her backpack on, the umbrella and the brown coat in her right hand. He could even make out the gleaming bracelet on her arm, tiny though it was, this little dollhouse version of her. It was because of her. It was because of himself, his selves. He was starting to talk to himself about himself in third person: What has Gum done? How long must Gum remember in order to stop remembering?

A voice on the phone says, "Now you're done for. I found your tape."

"What tape?"

"The cassette tape in the car. What's this about the pharmacist?"

Gum is puzzled. "What pharmacist?"

"The one you murdered. And what's this about the girl, screwing the girl?" His wife's voice is icy, and she is overenunciating.

"I don't know what you're talking about," Gum says, dumping the contents of his pencil drawer into a box.

"It's a good thing you're a divorce lawyer, Gum, because that's what I want."

"Listen," Gum says, trying to keep himself from reeling.

"I can't believe this," his wife suddenly breaks into a sob. "And to think that night at dinner—I just don't understand how you could do this to me, to anyone."

Gum is at a loss. "It's not what you think." He tries to make his voice sound soft, but it is shaking.

"And that girl I saw in your eyes a few weeks ago—I suspected it, but I never would have imagined that you, of all people."

"Sweetheart," Gum says. "Darling, dearest."

"Just who do you think I am anyway?" she asks, angrily.

"You're you of course," Gum says.

"What about you?" his wife sniffs. "Who do you think you really are?"

The Zen master Shunryu Suzuki once said that "When we express our true nature, we are human beings. When we do not, we do not know what we are." Gum had read this from a book called *Zen Mind, Beginner's Mind,* which he had once found in his seat on a plane. He had memorized it. He had also memorized the seat number, which was 36B, because he considered the book to be a sign, and from time to time, when he requested that seat on other flights, he found other things—someone's bifocals in a leather case, a child's drawing of some horses.

Gum, when he had existed in his true Gum nature, not as Mug or modern Gum, had often believed in signs. He believed in stop signs and signs that warned him of avalanches. He also believed in omens. The girl was an omen, the girl was more than an omen. He has begun to believe that maybe she was sent to test him or maybe to save him somehow, if not to expose him: his true nature to himself. Does he have a will? He is not sure. And so when he finds himself on the road in his wife's Beretta, driving aimlessly with his backseat full of divorce files, he lets a higher force lead him.

The future has caved in on Gum. The past has caved in on the future. The past rewinds itself and plays itself back. Some events do that. They haunt us. They walk around us and around us with their striped flanks so that we can do nothing but trace a pattern of destiny, right or wrong.

Gum listens to the sound his wheels make, humming through the light layer of snow that is beginning to line the paved road. He is outside of town, winding through a maze of fields. Anything can happen. He has on his gloves and his shades. He's wearing his wife's hosiery under his slacks. He thinks about driving to the other side of the continent and going by the name of Blank. Right now, he is Numb. He is not sure of his destination, if there is one. Maybe he will keep searching for the girl. With one eye on the road and one eye on the mirror, he feels like he is driving both forward and backward. Maybe that's all he will ever do. Maybe that's all any of us are capable of after we realize we don't know who we are. We run over ourselves back and forth in the dark, trying to figure out if we've hit something or if what is dear has run off into the trees.

Greg Changnon
San Francisco State University

HOW THE NURSE FEELS

I play the Nurse but she's a mystery to me. The week before the show opens, we rehearse in full dress and even the costume—this burlap nun getup with hood and collar—doesn't help me. Juliet is easy: ruled by her parents but led by her heart. But the Nurse is a different story. She's really a nanny but Juliet's almost fourteen, only a year younger than me, so they can't call her that anymore. So they call her the Nurse. I wonder why she cares that much about the Capulets. The Nurse is a paid employee; why get so involved? I ask our drama coach this question and Mr. Swick says to me with a squinty, exaggerated theater stare, "Think motivation." I don't want to tell him that this isn't helping. Mr. Swick holds his glasses in his fist and waves them at me like some kind of magic wand. "Dig deep, Tess," he says. "Look at everything." That doesn't help, either.

As the Nurse, I have eighty-eight lines, appear in eleven of twenty-four scenes, and, unfortunately, I have no costume changes. From what I know, most of Shakespeare's women don't. The Nurse has sixty-three lines less than Clytemnestra but that's okay because on any given day, I'd trade sixty-three lines (no monologues, though) not to have to wear a bed sheet pinned together under my armpit. Or those beach sandals spray-painted brown. After a few rehearsals as the Nurse, I was even glad to be out of the skin of Linda Loman, who I played in the fall show. She had a ton of lines but most of them were just simple questions trying to get her deadbeat husband to open up. After Mrs. Loman, I know what hell it is to be a housewife.

It's Tuesday, the day of our final dress rehearsal; it's been snowing for three days, and this morning they canceled school for the rest of the week. On Thursday night, we're set to open. January in Winnetka is supposed to be snowy but not like this, not with eight-foot drifts and flying clumps of ice and winds that freeze the wetness inside your nose. This is completely arctic. Because of no school, Mr. Swick has set up a phone tree so the cast can keep on top of weather information. Trudy Painter, who's a dismal Juliet, is assigned to call in the morning to tell me if Mr. Swick has found a way for us to rehearse and I turn around and call Tiger De Soto, whom I barely know.

When I tell him we won't rehearse today unless the snowplows get out, Tiger waits for a long couple of seconds and says, "That's rough." I imagine I can feel his breath in my ear, coming through the phone.

"So, anyway," I say, not knowing how to end the thought.

He finishes it for me. "I should keep going over my scene, right?"

"Yeah, you don't want to forget your lines."

Tiger is the Apothecary. He's only in one scene at the end of the play, which is all he could probably manage. I hear he's stoned most of the school day and the only reason he's in drama club is that it's a condition of his school probation. The principal must think he'll shape up in a straighter crowd. During most rehearsals Tiger just sits in the back of the theater and holds his guitar, rubbing a finger up and down the glassy strings. Last week, during wardrobe fittings, he saw me in my costume, all that brown fabric hiding what I don't like people to see, and he said to me, "That's sinful." I gave him the glare I'm famous for but all he did was stand there looking at me like no other high school guy. Then his mouth turned up into a strange, lazy smile that made me feel like I didn't need to hide anything. "I can't even see you," he said and I got a twist in my stomach that has yet to work itself out.

Over the phone, I can hear Tiger playing his guitar. I picture him in his bedroom and I don't want to hang up. I say, "You must hate doing this."

"Hate doing what?"

"Being forced into theater."

"I wasn't forced. This is the third time I tried out. First two I got dinged." Tiger laughs. "Would've liked a better part, though."

I imagine him smiling, his lips opening, that one yellow tooth of his peeking through. There's four miles of hard-packed snow between us but I've never felt so close. I can see him pulling at the guitar strings while he squeezes the phone between his chin and shoulder. He lets his little garden of whiskers grow wild and I hear them scratching the receiver. I'm almost sure he doesn't comb his hair at home, that white hair of his without a single strand of brown. He keeps his bedroom dark, filled up with the warm odor of his sweat. He hangs a bandanna over the only lamp. My ear on the phone feels hot now. It's almost better that I've never been inside that bedroom.

"You want to go over your lines?" I ask, winding the curly phone cord tight around my thumb. The finger is red and puffy but I can't let it go. It feels too right.

"My lines? Which ones?"

"Any of them, I guess."

"All right. I'm not looking, okay? Here goes. 'Who calls so loud?' That's the first line."

"Sounds like you got it." One line down, three to go. This phone call's going fast.

"The next line is this: 'Such mortal drugs I have. But—' "

"I bet you won't be forgetting that line," I say and chuckle, but Tiger doesn't say a word. I can hear the crackle of silence over the line.

"Whatever," he says.

"Well, you know, considering."

"Considering what?"

"I don't know, whatever."

The guitar on Tiger's side goes crazy. One chord after another. I listen and wonder who else in all this snow is sitting on the phone listening to a guy play music. I hope I'm the only one. I can feel the conversation ending so I ask, "Hey, where'd you get the name Tiger?"

"When I was a baby."

"Yeah?"

"I screamed a lot." Then he mumbles something and hangs up. The four miles of snow between us fill up again. He must have thought I'd inched over the thin line between complete indifference and horrible obsession. He had to end the call. I hope there's some kind of news tomorrow, so I can take advantage of Mr. Swick's phone tree again.

But there is no news. By Wednesday, the snow lightens up. School may open on Monday. Until then, we can't rehearse. Instead of suffering alone, me and Kimberly Pope lie around my basement going through theater withdrawal. We listen to Kimberly's homemade Edith Piaf tape, "La vie en rose" recorded back-to-back on both sides. I adore Kimberly. She has the right mixture of bitchiness and homeliness to sell Lady Capulet. Together, we wonder when we'll ever get back on stage.

Kimberly has brought clove cigarettes but we can't smoke because my dad is already back from plowing snow out of the church parking lot. I asked him if we could put on the play there, right on the altar of Saint Gregory's, but he wanted to read the play first and I took that as a bad sign. Ever since I played Big Mama in *Cat on a Hot Tin Roof,* he's been a bit suspicious of high school drama. Instead of running lines, we just lie on the basement floor, sniffing the unlit clove tobacco, commiserating with the Sparrow.

Kimberly stands, hugging the cement pole in the middle of my basement. "Do you think Trudy Painter dyes her hair? Last year, when she was Maggie in *Tin Roof,* I swear it was redder."

"That bitch," I say, groaning. This groan feels good. It's drawn out and takes all my breath. I can use it sometime, maybe in Act IV of *R & J.*

Edith sings and I let her voice surround my body. That voice is about a million years old. It sounds like it's seen it all. If it was up to me, I wouldn't have called her the Sparrow.

"Remember last year?" Kimberly says and then I smile, dreaming of the time we were cocaptains of the speech team and told Trudy Painter she wasn't good enough for the squad. In the category of dramatic monologue, I was district champion. I went to state but didn't make the finals. I did Martha's speech from Act III of *Virginia Woolf,* the one where Martha breaks down and lets it slip that her son is only a twisted fantasy. Well, she doesn't quite admit it—she's loon-crazy, her marriage hanging on by one drunken thread—but it's a great speech and I really tore it up. The rules said no costumes, but before my turn in front of those three frowning judges I used the ladies' room to tease out my hair into midstage Liz Taylor and got into my mother's old cardigan sweater with the cigarette burn over the heart. Those state judges never cracked a smile. They scowled and made notes on their clipboards, giving me a ten, I know, in articulation. I never got below a ten in articulation. I saw the score sheets. It was in emotional verity that they screwed me. One judge at state wrote in the comments box that I seemed to be too rehearsed, my emotions planned rather than felt. Right, like a sophomore girl from the suburbs of Chicago has ever felt what Martha feels. Like a high school student can ever have the hell-on-earth experience that Martha has. High school is dull, the judges know that. What do they want me to play, that skinny little virgin Emily from Grover's Corners?

Just after Edith finishes another round of "La vie," my dad comes down in his church shoes, Hush Puppies that squeak when he walks up to the lectern, and orders me to turn down the music. Mother has a migraine—the window of the fabric store she owns has blown out in the snowstorm and ruined her Christmas sell-back stock.

Dad stands near the bottom of the basement steps waiting for us to talk back. He's a man who seems perpetually frightened, but of what I'm not sure. "Did you hear about Richard De Soto?" he asks.

"Tiger?" I move closer to the stairway.

Dad backs up a step. "His parents came by to see me today. He's disappeared."

"Cool," Kimberly whispers from behind me.

The left side of Dad's mouth quivers and pulls itself back. This tic is usually saved for the two days surrounding the church's monthly budget meeting. Edith trails off and the music stops. All that comes out of the speakers is the buzz of blank tape running across the tape heads.

"Did he run away?" Kimberly asks and I think that no, he didn't run away. To run away sounds so preteen. He didn't run away. He got the hell out of here.

"Richard's parents told me he was in the play. Do either of you know anything about this?" My dad takes another step back, preparing himself for the worst.

Kimberly pushes in on her closed eyes with her fingers. A think-ing-hard gesture. "He was depressed. I don't know, Reverend Powell, maybe he didn't want to graduate." She's too far away for me to elbow.

My dad has one hand in a fist. The tiny end of a silver cross sticks out between his thumb and index finger. "His parents think some-thing went wrong at school."

"Life," Kimberly says. "Life's gone wrong."

"Keep it to the stage, Miss Pope." My dad stares at us, looking like he's trying to see some sort of terrifying truth we're hiding inside. But he doesn't get it.

The truth is, if Tiger De Soto had the guts to sell marijuana at school, then he had enough guts to take off and start over. I try to imagine a life where there is no high school. Both my parents think that after college I'll come back and take over Mother's fabric store, but they have no idea. If I could leave now, if I could forget about those dusty linoleum halls, those shoe-box dioramas of the Pilgrims that line the walls of Mrs. Seeger's American history class, I would do it in a flash, just like Tiger De Soto. I want to live in New York City, in a basement apartment in the Village. I want to worry about rent and the smelly man who sits on my doorstep. I want to have three lovers at three different theater spaces, one suicidal and the other two Caribbean. Instead, I have to sleep in a pink satin bedroom designed by my mother and, during supper, give feedback on my father's sermons that have titles like: Is Family Love Passé?, The Power of "I Respect You," or Jesus Says, "Come Every Sunday." I imagine one Sunday I will hop up to the lectern and do Martha in front of every-one. Dad will read George's lines: "Martha, you drunken sot. You've ruined my lousy life." We'll do the "fuck the hostess" scene. That would give the congregation something to sing about.

"What do you know, Tess?" My dad scowls, catching me gazing into my dreams. "You seem like you're hiding something."

I shake my head. I know that I've called Tiger once in my entire life and that I could recite the conversation word for word.

"Tess, if you do—"

"I don't, okay?" Tiger screamed when he was a baby. Maybe he wanted to make a break for it even way back then.

"The De Sotos have called the police," my dad says, testing our reactions. I wonder if and when the cops will think about checking phone records. "If you could have been in my office and seen them, Richard's parents, you would know how worried they are. With the snowstorm and the temperature and the roads and all the rest of it."

"Dad, listen, just say a prayer or something."

"Tess," he says, eyes narrowing.

"I don't know where he is."

My dad climbs up to the top of the stairs, murmuring to himself. I've noticed church people can vanish inside themselves faster than the rest of us. At the top of the stairs, my dad, still talking to himself, flicks off the lights and Kimberly and me are left standing in the dark.

Because there isn't any school for the rest of the week, Mr. Swick drives around with snow chains, visiting the cast. He has a kid in Florida and lives in a studio in Buffalo Grove, so he's the kind of person who'd rather be at work. He comes over on Thursday afternoon and we run lines at my kitchen table. He has temporarily postponed the play one week and wants to keep us fresh. My mother stands in the kitchen nearby and looks at Mr. Swick like he's a lunatic, risking his life crisscrossing the icy town just to read Shakespeare with his students. I want to ask him if he knows anything about Tiger, but I'm afraid he and my mother will fly to conclusions.

"So, Mr. Swick, when are you going to do *Cats*?"

"Mother, please."

"What? I love *Cats*. At least it's something that won't remind me every performance that fourteen-year-olds have sex."

"I'm the Nurse, mother. I wear a habit. And cats have sex, too."

My mother tosses her hand in the air and leans against the kitchen island to watch me perform.

"Let's take Act IV, Scene V," Mr. Swick suggests, one hand around a coffee cup that says SHELLEY'S FABRIC FIESTA. "From the top, right when the Nurse discovers Juliet knocked out from the Friar's potion."

I close my eyes and go through the blocking in my head. "Alas," I recite. "Alas! Help, help! My lady's dead!/O weraday that ever I was born!" But my heart isn't in it. This is my mother's country kitchen and a gingerbread house left over from Christmas still sits in the center of the table. This is miles away from anything crucial.

"What's wrong?" Mr. Swick asks. "You need a line cue?"

"Sorry. I'm just wondering how to feel in this scene."

Mr. Swick closes his script, takes his glasses off and points them at me. His motivation pose again.

"Let's talk about motivation," he says. "What does Shakespeare tell us about the Nurse?"

"Nothing."

"Think, Tess."

"What?"

"Well, how does she feel about Juliet?"

"She loves her like her own?"

"I like that," my mother says, barging her way back into my life.

"And why does she love her so much?" Mr. Swick asks.

"Does it say in the script?"

"No. This is where you help Shakespeare. Tell me, what does Juliet mean to the Nurse?"

"I can't think," I say, shutting my eyes, trying to dream the woman up. "We know she had a daughter once. A girl named Susan who died. And that girl was exactly Juliet's age."

"Keep going, Tess."

"And so maybe now, whenever she sees Juliet, she thinks of Susan. Everything she felt for one, she now feels for the other. Sometimes, when love shakes up her mind, she really believes that Juliet is Susan."

"That's wonderful," my mother says and takes a loud sip of her tea. What does she know? She's never even read Shakespeare. She couldn't tell a quatrain from a dirty limerick.

"Remember that." Mr. Swick puts his glasses back on and goes to his script. "Remember how it feels to love Juliet so intensely, so much more than anybody knows you do."

I sit for a dramatic pause, trying to get into this.

"Madeleine?" my mother asks, holding out her tray of fancy cookies.

I push away my script. "There isn't going to be any play. There's too much snow. Who cares about high school Shakespeare?" I imagine taking the bus to New York with Tiger, making plans under a blanket in the last row of the bus, watching all the people stumbling back to the toilet. I daydream about getting a job waitressing in a Greek diner off Broadway while Tiger washes dishes. Ushering in alley theaters where the actors go nude and moan about the government. Taking classes with a Swedish woman with a thick braid and a bum leg who says to me, "You're as good as they get."

My mother pours more coffee for Mr. Swick. She's put a sticker on the side of her coffeepot: "Danger: Hot Beverage." She raises her eyebrows and asks, "Mind if I try a role on for size?"

"Yeah, Mom, you can lie down on the floor and play dead Juliet."

She swirls what's left in the pot and rolls her eyes. "It's that old cabin fever."

I can't help but blurt out, "And everybody wonders why Tiger De Soto took off." I immediately regret saying it. I know Mother will read volumes into this one stupid sentence. She'll start putting her clampers on me, wondering what I'm really thinking. Neither of them, not Mr. Swick or my mother, not even my dad with his direct phone line to Jesus, know what it's like to be in high school five days out of every seven. What it's like to have your whole world contained in the ten-block radius of the church, school, home, and the fabric store. This, I know, is why I act. I have to feel what it's like in somebody else's skin.

By Monday morning, the storm is over and the roads get plowed. Driving back to school with Kimberly in the Popes' station wagon, I can't help but love all this snow. It's like we're flying through Siberia. I'm Lara, in Dr. Zhivago's sleigh. I don't ever want the temperature to go up, the snow to fade away, all this ice to melt. Kimberly sits in the front seat, ignoring her older brother, who's back from a culinary academy and chauffeuring us to and from school. Kimberly says he flunked out, and I'm sure because of it he stands naked in front of mirrors at night and thinks about food. He looks the type.

Kimberly spins the AM radio dial and announces, "I swear, real music is an endangered species." Bursts of static pop out of the car speakers. I hear the single word "missing" from behind a chord of music, and through the window, for just a second, I see Tiger out there. He's standing at the side of the road, watching the cars go by. He's standing still, hands behind his back, not wearing a hat, but then it's only a mailbox perched on top of a pole. Tiger's hair is a cap of frozen snow reflecting the sunlight.

After school, Mr. Swick calls the first all-cast rehearsal since the snow week. It's been six days since Tiger disappeared. Mr. Swick decides that we can just leave the Apothecary scene out and give Romeo a line in the next scene that would explain where he got the poison. No one complains about it. We all think that's pretty much the story with Shakespeare: you can take out any scene and nobody will really notice. As long as it isn't one of my scenes. The cast and crew sit in the theater seats while Mr. Swick gives us a pep talk and then Mr. and Mrs. De Soto come out from backstage. Everybody stops talking. Mrs. De Soto wears a plaid skirt and black stockings, which look clumped above both knees. She has her hair pulled back into a ponytail. Her husband holds her around the waist and never looks up at us. They both wear open raincoats. It looks like they've gotten the season wrong.

Kimberly leans over to me and whispers, "Now that's what I call an entrance."

Mr. Swick introduces them and Mrs. De Soto steps forward. "We've tried everything and we know most of you aren't friends but—" She stops and turns to look into her husband's face, but he's looking down. She bends a bit to see into his eyes, but he turns away, to the side. He's breaking one of the big rules of theater. You have to cheat out toward the house at least a quarter turn so that the audience can see your face. He's disappearing into the back of the stage.

Mrs. De Soto's hands are moving fast, the fingers stretching out stiff then collapsing back into fists. "We've run out of leads," she says and then repeats herself louder so she's sure we can hear. I can't look anywhere but at Mrs. De Soto's sagging stockings peeking out below the bottom flap of her raincoat.

"Please," Mr. De Soto says, "he's a diabetic." He shrugs and walks off the stage. Diabetic, that doesn't sound right to me. Maybe his parents are just saying it to shock us into something heroic. Mrs. De Soto watches him go, then stumbles over to Mr. Swick. She talks to him with her hand hiding her mouth. Mr. Swick squeezes her shoulder before she turns to us one last time. Mrs. De Soto is standing in the exact spot where I stand in Scene V when the Nurse discovers Juliet dead.

After she leaves, Mr. Swick doesn't say anything. He flips through the pages of his master script but he can't talk. He rubs his thumb at the bottom of his eye and just sits there. Kimberly, sitting next to me, says, "Fuck," so softly I can barely hear it. Mr. Swick looks up into the stage lights, squinting. I see, in my head, Mr. and Mrs. De Soto back on the stage in their rain gear, holding each other. Mrs. De Soto's stockings and the spit her husband kept wiping from his chin. That is a moment I should memorize. *Remember,* I tell myself, *remember.*

The night before we open, I go crazy over how much I don't know about Tiger. The play will have come and gone and nobody will have even missed him. The snow is melting and taking Tiger along with it. In a strange way, I want more snow so the play will be postponed again. We should wait for him.

I know that sometime earlier today my mom met with Mrs. De Soto. My dad suggested she call his mom up and offer some comfort. Tonight my father's at church leading a class for parolees who have found Jesus and my mother's in her office, fiddling with her fabric. From the doorway, I can see her sitting in the light of a single lamp, sewing something by hand.

"Mother?"

"Tess," she says, slipping off her bifocals.

"How's Mrs. De Soto?"

"Not good." She leaves her needle pointing straight up, waiting for the next stitch.

"What's the last thing they know?" I ask. "About Tiger."

"Tuesday morning, he told them he was going out to shovel the driveway. And that's the last they saw of him." She plunges the needle into the dark fabric over her lap and keeps it there. That doesn't seem right to me, the shoveling snow business. I can't imagine Tiger doing things like that. What would he care about the driveway? He lied to them.

"Did you know him?" my mother asks and I'm not quite sure how to answer. Through the window I can see the light from the full moon reflect off the snowdrift pushed up against the house. I know there are plants under there, all kinds of green plants my mother and I planted together one summer.

Before I can think, I'm lying too. "He's in New York. He had to get out of here or he'd go crazy. He took the bus to be an actor in New York."

"An actor? My gosh." She takes a breath and says in a phony

voice, " 'All the world's a stage, and all the men and women merely players.' "

"What's that? Psalm 101?"

"It's *As You Like It*. Shakespeare. You read it when you get a chance."

Now she must be making things up.

"You tell your father about Tiger and New York. That could help."

I want to ask her if she believes you can be absolutely certain of someone without really knowing them, but the air has become too heavy with lies. My throat tightens and I can't get out a syllable.

"Look here," she says, holding up the fabric she's working on. "I've lined your costume with cotton cloth so the burlap won't rub your skin raw. If it's too heavy, I can take it out."

I think of that garden of ours outside under all that snow and remember it's been five years since we worked on it.

Minutes before opening curtain, Mr. and Mrs. De Soto come back to the theater. It's chilling the way they keep showing up. Dressed in our costumes, we stand in the wings and stare at them on the stage while they make their appeal to the audience. "Anyone with information," Mr. De Soto says. "Calls can be anonymous," Mrs. De Soto says. I suspect they're repeating exactly what the police told them to say. Both of them seem overrehearsed. But I can't take my eyes off Mrs. De Soto's hands. She holds them up to her stomach and her fingers wiggle on her belly like hooked fish. It's as if she's trying to keep all that she is afraid of pushed down to the ends of her limbs. Her voice is calm, but her hands are wild.

A sense of gloom settles over the performance. We're all thinking about destroyed parents instead of star-crossed lovers. Kimberly forgets a line cue during the ball scene and asks Potpan, the servant boy, for Aqua Velva instead of an aqua vitae. In Act II, Scene V, when the Nurse brings secret news to Juliet about Romeo, my memory spins away and I grab at anything. I pick up some of my lines from my last scene, when the Nurse thinks Juliet's dead. Trudy Painter stares at me; she's definitely not looking dead at this point. She may not be an actress, but she's a lifesaver and she pulls me back into the scene. The damage is done, though; for the rest of the show, I'm Tess Powell, never the Nurse. In the last scene where Juliet and Romeo both die, the Styrofoam tomb door won't open and I stand with Joshie Cohen, who plays Mercutio and is already dead, our fingers crossed hoping that that freshman who plays Paris can shake the door loose. It ends up that he can't so everybody in the finale—practically half the cast—has to jump off a riser into the tomb instead of walking through the door. After curtain, Mr. Swick tells us we've never been better.

In American history the next day, I get a note from the office that Mr. Swick wants to see me. My mother must have told my father what I said about Tiger and he told Mr. Swick, who probably told them I don't even know Tiger. Maybe Mr. Swick is mad at me because I broke character during the show last night. When I get to his office, I find him standing up, facing one wall. He has pictures all over of our high school hits. Joshie Cohen as Willy Loman is up there. And so is that cherry tree that gets cut down at the end of *The Cherry Orchard*. Every time I'm in here, I'm reminded that I am not up there, not in any of the pictures. You have to die onstage in order to have a spot on Mr. Swick's wall.

Mr. Swick knows I'm standing here, but he doesn't turn around.

"I know I flopped last night, Mr. Swick. And you're right, it's all because of motivation. I didn't really have any. But now I do. I thought about the Nurse overnight and what she feels and I figured out that she does love Juliet just like she's her mother." Mr. Swick doesn't respond. He just reaches out and straightens a picture of Job's whole family from last year's production of *J. B.* "When Juliet was a baby, all she did was cry. She screamed all the time and the Nurse had little nicknames for her, but really she was always afraid that something was wrong, that something awful was going to happen to Juliet just like it happened to Susan. So she gets this habit of shaking her hands all the time. She holds them but they twitch, they can't stop twitching. She may act zany the whole play, but that's a front. It's a mask. That sense of humor is covering up all her fear. Don't you see?"

Mr. Swick turns around but he's not happy about my breakthrough. It's probably too late. I can't change anything now. I'll have to save it for another show.

"Tiger De Soto's been found," Mr. Swick says and his voice sounds off, too flat and dry. "His body, right outside his house."

I have to sit down but I miss the seat of the chair. I end up sitting on the armrest, the metal biting through denim into skin.

"I didn't want you all to hear it from somebody else. I didn't want to make a scene. I thought this way was best." He places his hands on the top of his desk and drops his weight into his arms. "Apparently, he went out to shovel. He was walking around his house and fell in a window well."

"Is he all right?"

"He suffocated." Mr. Swick moves to another picture, pushing one corner up out of balance. All the pictures are crooked. Off by inches. Everything was straight once. Now he's gone and straightened them all crooked.

"We won't have a performance tonight, Tess. But tomorrow night we'll close with one more show."

For the rest of the day I look around at faces, trying to decide who knows and who doesn't. I hear that Tiger fell upside down, that he choked and vomited, that when the snow melted, his mother found him from inside pushed up against the basement window.

After school, I sit by myself in the last row of the dark theater. To get my mind off things, I try to think how I'll play my last scene now. Act IV, Scene V. Trudy's laid out in the prop bed, the covers up to her blank face. She's holding her breath, trying to look knocked out. But she takes tiny gasps that shake the sheets. My lines come into my head. "Most lamentable day, most woeful day/That ever ever I did yet behold!" Onstage, I see myself looking up to what I imagine is God, but all I can make out is the stage lights aimed right for my eyes. All I see is that blaze of whiteness and I think of snow, eight feet of snow. I remember the empty color of Mrs. De Soto's skin, more white than white. And the blond of Tiger's hair, without a single strand of brown. Juliet is lying before me and I see all this and I think, now, right now, I am the Nurse.

Athena Paradissis
Concordia University

CLEAN

I scrub, dust, vacuum, and do laundry every day. Sean doesn't understand this latest craze of mine. That's what he calls it, "latest craze." It began almost three months ago when he drove Princess Daphne and me home from the hospital. Let Sean call it what he wants. I know only this: if I stop cleaning, even for one day, the house will go to hell.

"Honey," he says from where he sits at the kitchen table, designing the canopy crib he plans to build for Princess Daphne. "The place is clean. It can't get any cleaner."

I hate his calling me honey when we've never been anything more than friends. Don't call me that, I've told him, but he just shrugs and says I'm reading too much into things.

"What if a social worker was to unexpectedly come in and find the house this way? What then? I'll tell you what then," I say when it's become obvious he doesn't intend to answer. "What then is they take Princess Daphne away. I bet you never once considered that."

"Social worker?" His pencil stops. He looks at me in what he would call a patient way, but there is condescension in his eyes.

What to answer? The social worker appeared the same day I gave birth to Princess Daphne. Now I see her every time I set out to clean house or change a diaper. No sooner do I begin when the doorbell rings. I answer and this woman, whose name I know to be Mrs. Snyder, barges in.

Mrs. Snyder is tall with broad shoulders and a hefty build. Mrs. Snyder strides toward my kitchen. Mrs. Snyder opens the cabinet door underneath the sink. Mrs. Snyder shakes my garbage bag, expecting the clink clink clink, but I haven't touched a drop in eleven weeks, not since Princess Daphne was born. Mrs. Snyder asks me where Princess Daphne is, only she doesn't say Princess, and I tell her I left Princess Daphne in her basket when I went to answer the door. Mrs. Snyder runs her short, stubby finger across the counter. Daphne is all the proof we need, she says, raising her dust-speckled finger to eye level.

"Sarah?"

"The grease won't come off, Sean."

"They don't see her until Friday. It bothers me." His pencil scribbles on paper. "It bothers me to know you're just sitting here waiting," he finally says, his eyes on his design.

I continue to scrub the kitchen floor, behind the stove. My knees hurt from kneeling for so long. So does my arm with the back and forth motion, every muscle strained in my effort to rid my floor of this grease. By *they*, Sean means the hospital's team of specialists. I press down harder on the rag. My waiting bothers him, he says, when he knows damn well there's nothing else I can do.

"Maybe I should spend my time ballroom dancing. Would that, perhaps, bother you less?"

"What's done is done," he says, his tone casual, like he's talking about the weather.

"Meaning?"

"Meaning nothing." And what can I possibly respond? It'd be easier if he'd just come out and say what I know he's thinking, something like, Thanks to you, Princess Daphne may be brain damaged, because then, at least, it would give me the chance to fight back.

But Sean isn't straight about anything anymore. Instead, he holds Princess Daphne, aims his narrowed eyes at me, and says, It's okay, Princess, no one's going to hurt you now. Any idiot can tell it's me he's talking about. Fuck you, I think, though I don't say it because he'd probably look at me like I was being defensive, if not completely paranoid.

"I think she's going to like this crib," he says.

"I'm sure she will. It sounds like the kind you'd find in a maga-zine."

"I love her. I only want the best for her."

"So do I, Sean."

"Well of course you do, she's your daughter."

I glance at him, not sure if he's being sincere or sarcastic, but maybe that's got more to do with me than him. Somehow, it's almost inconceivable to think of myself as somebody's mother. It seems too farfetched, like a story you just know is a lie because, really, how could such a thing have happened. It's impossible, I tell myself. Impossible. Fifty times a day I repeat this word. Sometimes, I wake up at night and think, perhaps, that I've dreamed up her existence. Then I look on the floor beside my bed and there she is, asleep in her basket, and it's like looking at a miracle because how did this other being come from me?

I stare at her for hours when she's asleep, awed by her tininess, her helplessness, her innocence. When she's awake, I can hardly believe how she lets me hold, feed, and clothe her, her complete trust in me as incredible as it is intimidating. It makes me back away, her trust a constant reminder that it took the doctors eighteen minutes to raise her heartbeat from twenty to one hundred. They kept her in inten-sive care for close to five days and I didn't need anyone to tell me that this would never have happened had I, her mother, taken seriously my responsibility toward her.

After they took her away, one of the doctors came into the deliv-ery room holding a pad and a pen. The baby is underweight and undersize, he said. Do you drink? he said. Do you do drugs? For Chrissake, I told him, I just had a baby. I tried to raise myself from where I lay on the bed. Sean, who was there, didn't offer to help. He remained by the window overlooking the hospital parking lot, his narrowed brown eyes examining me, and all I could think of was how big he looked. There's a reason why they're asking, he said, and something about his voice, or words, brought Mrs. Snyder alive in my head.

"Sarah? You okay?"

I scrub and pretend I don't notice him looking at me. I'm lucky to have him, I tell myself, and Princess Daphne adores him. She's only eleven weeks old, but I can tell—and this, *this* shows—that despite the doctor's warnings she is capable of reaction. And Sean adores her. I overheard him once. Say Dada, he said while changing her diaper. Come on, Princess, say Dada.

Sean telling Princess Daphne to call him Dada made me feel sorry for him. It made me feel sorry for me and Princess Daphne as well, because here we were, man, woman, child, the components for a family, only we weren't anything like a family. Not even Princess Daphne and I, the bond between mother and child not as natural and uncomplicated as everyone would have me assume. I remember when I first told Sean I was pregnant. Four months and I'd just found out, my period never too regular. Whose is it? he'd said.

I don't know.

You don't know?

How to answer and not make it any uglier? I got down on my knees, held his large hands in mine, and promised myself I'd try to love him as more than a friend because he's a decent man. For one month I came home straight from work, and cooked healthy, and invited Sean for dinner, and twice we ate by candlelight. But when Sean leaned over to kiss me one night, it was more than I could stand, and the next night I was out again, gulping down shots of absurdly named drinks. One thing about drinking buddies, they keep you from dwelling on the fact that you're thirty-five and all you've got to show for it is a dead-end job. It keeps you from thinking about the improbability of today ever changing.

"Sarah?"

"Please," I tell him. "I need to clean."

We sit in Sean's car, heading toward a gigantic hardware store located outside the city. Princess Daphne is snuggled safely in her car seat. On the seat beside her is Sean's design for what he's come to call the Princess Daphne Canopy Crib. We stop at a busy intersection, behind a car. The driver of the car, a woman, reaches over to the passenger side. She straightens herself and raises what looks like a flask to her mouth. Sean's fist smashes his horn.

I jump and think, *Mrs. Snyder.* "Goddamn bitch," he yells. "What's she waiting for?"

"Maybe she's waiting for you to get a girlfriend," I tell him.

He glares at me and the person behind us honks and I thank God Princess Daphne didn't wake up. Then I panic because doesn't she hear all this commotion?

Sean starts forward. His big hands grip the wheel, his thick knuckles red, the little brown hairs on his knuckles like ugly, sickly shrubs. I stare at the gray stretch of highway and think about how much I sometimes hate Sean. And for no reason, for no reason at all—Sean, a man who's never been anything but very kind to me. I once saw this movie where a woman demanded a divorce from her doting husband. Because every time I see your face, I feel like punching it, she said, and I knew exactly what she meant.

In my meaner moments, I wonder why Sean is still around. I figure helping me must make him feel like some sort of magnanimous saint. I told this to the lady who owns the repair shop down the street and she said it made sense, even if she didn't know who Sean was. I went home after that and then I started to feel guilty. You're an ungrateful bitch, I thought, saying such things about someone who spends his every free moment helping you. He and his brother own their own business, a small computer company with a staff of three, which enables him to leave for a few hours whenever he wants to. Every day he does more and more for Princess Daphne, changing her, playing with her, bathing her, gently rocking her to sleep.

I, on the other hand, find myself holding her less and less, especially with the hospital appointment quickly approaching. I do a mental countdown and the closer we get, the more I worry something will be wrong. She senses my anxiety. She fidgets in my arms, she cries, and instead of holding her tight so she knows she's safe, all I can do is to say, there, there, while I look her over with a clinical detachment I didn't think I possessed. Do her facial features look okay? Is she much smaller than other babies her age? Does she respond when I clap my hands? Does she respond when I suddenly turn off the light, then turn it back on?

I glance at Sean, but he stares straight ahead. Inside the hardware store, all we discuss is what kind of wood to buy. Sean suggests oak, and I tell him, Sure.

Sean places Princess Daphne's car seat across one of the store's shopping carts and a few people stop to ooh and ah. I'm relieved at this, deliriously, almost embarrassingly so, and it suddenly hits me how completely I would break were anyone to look at Princess Daphne with scorn or pity. It makes me think back to a neighbor of mine whose son was born with severe heart problems. His eyes were crossed and he was painfully skinny and very tiny and every time she'd see another mother with her normal, healthy child, she'd feel this need to explain. And I remember how we always made it a point to be extra nice to her son, Michael, telling her he was special and, oh God, what a smile, each of us secretly grateful he wasn't ours.

"Boy or girl?" they ask.

"Princess," Sean says, a large smile on his broad face. I smile as well, happy to be with him and Princess Daphne. "Princess," he says again. He looks at me, his narrowed eyes like those I see on Mrs. Snyder and right away, it kills whatever was hopeful inside me.

"Oak," he's now saying. "I don't think we can go wrong with oak."

"I'll tell you what. What if I meet up with you and Princess Daphne in a while. I want to look around."

"What about the crib?"

"You're the one who's building it, not me."

"Suit yourself." He shrugs and directs the shopping cart toward the carpentry section.

Sean once asked me what kind of person I was. This when we were first getting to know each other. I told him I was a kitchen and bathroom kind of person because those were the places I found most comforting. I didn't mean my kitchen or bathroom, but the kitchens and bathrooms I see in decorating magazines, nice warm spic-and-span kitchens with their cozy suggestion of family and friends, and the bathrooms, always with the kind of tubs that insist on abandon.

They have these kitchens and bathrooms here, lined one after the other along the aisles of the home renovation section. Entire displays are set up like walk-in theater sets. There's a country-pine kitchen, its walls painted a pale, pale yellow that complements the perfectly pressed red-and-white checkered curtains decorating the fake window over the sparkling sink. The counters are uncluttered, the chrome fridge .catches my reflection, the built-in oven self-cleans. Inside the cabinets, new plates are perfectly aligned.

Functional kitchens! read the banners on the walls.

Function is how the doctors refer to Princess Daphne's brain.

Functional kitchens. Functional bathrooms. Bathrooms with sparkling Jacuzzis and free-standing elegant sinks in shimmering colors like burgundy, green, and electric blue. My bathroom at home is anemic, the paint on the ceiling peeling, two tiles on the floor missing, the inside of the bathtub rusted. All the scrubbing in the world doesn't change my bathroom, and the bright yellow towel set I bought after Princess Daphne was born only accentuates what's wrong instead of making the bathroom a cheerier place as I had hoped.

Maybe I should work on the bathroom when I get home. I think about what Mrs. Snyder would say if she were to see my bathroom. I think about how there are too many damn people here, dragging their shrieking brats behind them, opening cupboards and touching walls, leaving fingerprints everywhere.

It doesn't take long to find the home care section, its rows and rows of cleaning products promising to rid my bathtub of rust, my floor of grease, my walls of the kind of yellow that comes with age. "Watch it!" a woman's voice warns too late as we collide. We drop what we are holding. Me, my cleaning products and sponges. She, a small jar of paint. The jar breaks and a red pool spreads across the floor. I try to stop it with my boot, but the paint sneaks underneath my boot. It wraps itself around my boot. It continues beyond my boot. "Your fault," the woman says, before scurrying away.

"Hey," I yell after her. "Hey, you've made a mess."

The woman looks over her shoulder and gives me the finger. She disappears around the corner. I get down on my knees, peel the paper foil from the top of my Old Dutch cleanser, and pour Old Dutch onto the pool of paint. The Old Dutch absorbs the paint. Paint and Old Dutch become sickly pinkish red clumps, like clumps of vomit. I tear open one of my sponge packages and begin to scrub, and then I scrub some more, but my sponge only spreads the pinkish red across the floor. Pinkish red gets onto my hands, underneath my nails. This man, wearing the store's uniform, appears and tells me it's his job to clean and am I all right?

I search for an answer to his question and finally tell him I've just had a baby. He tells me I don't have to pay for what I've opened; he'll take care of it, he says.

"I've just had a baby," I tell him again.

"A new mother," he says. "Well, new mommy, allow me to help you up."

"Me? Are you talking to me?"

He looks at me, worried. "Who else would I be talking to?"

Sean turns down this aisle and maneuvers his shopping cart toward us. He sees me, of course. He sees the young man help me up. Keeping one hand on Princess Daphne's car seat, he quickens his pace.

"Jesus Christ!" he says. "What the—"

The young man lets go of my arm. "Your wife—" he begins.

Sean laughs at this. "She's a new mother," he says, his narrowed eyes looking at me. "She's the mommy of this beautiful princess. Right, Sarah?"

"I just had a baby. Is that what you mean?"

The young man shifts. Sean smiles and slaps him on the back. He digs into his pocket and pulls out one of the chocolate cigars he bought when Princess Daphne was born. It's wrapped in pink foil with a sticker that reads "It's a girl!" glued on one of its sides. He must be holding it too tightly because his big hand breaks it in two. He laughs, says he doesn't know what's wrong with him, and pulls out another.

"Bite the tip," he says. "Best cigar you'll ever have."

The young man laughs an uncertain kind of laugh, like he's not sure whether or not Sean is joking.

I scrub. Princess Daphne sleeps in her basket, which Sean has placed near the kitchen door. Sean sits on one of the kitchen chairs, his concentration focused on the scene he's chiseling for the crib's last corner post. He's got a T-shirt on that's a little tight around his waist. Sean's a big man. Six feet four inches and two hundred and fifty pounds.

Sean's hand carefully works his chisel around the corner post. He's carved a series of nursery rhymes on the other three corner posts, like Little Bo-Peep and Humpty-Dumpty. It's amazing how his big hands can carve such intricate and minute details, Humpty-Dumpty sitting on the wall, Humpty-Dumpty taking a fall, the falling down Humpty-Dumpty's tiny eyes wide, wide open, his miniature mouth a perfect utterance of surprise.

"Done." Sean lets go his tool and wipes his brow with the back of his hand. He holds the corner post a little away and carefully inspects his work.

"Do you want to see?" he says. "It's Little Miss Muffet, and up here it's the Three Little Pigs and the wolf who huffed and puffed." His thick long finger points out the different scenes.

"It's beautiful, Sean. It's the most beautiful thing I've ever seen."

He takes my hand and uses my finger to trace the wolf. I don't like him holding on to me like that. I gently try to free my hand, but his grip tightens.

"It's really beautiful." I tug my hand, which loosens his grip and causes the corner post to fall. His fingers wrap around my wrist. Princess Daphne begins to cry. I glance toward her basket, where she struggles to get loose from the blanket Sean's swaddled her in. She looks like a burrito, all wrapped up like that.

"Let me go."

He does and I almost lose my balance from the force of my pull. He pushes past me toward Princess Daphne. He picks her up and holds her very close, rubbing his big cheek against the side of her tiny face. It infuriates me to see him do this. It should be me who's holding her, me who's comforting her. He begins to waltz with her while singing his corny Princess Daphne song and I almost hate how quickly this makes her stop crying.

I get down on my knees and dig my nails into the rag, so they can help scrape the grease off of the floor. The skin on my hand is rough and dry. My knees, I noticed yesterday, are the same way, and they hurt every time I bend.

"What are you doing?"

"Cleaning."

"Now?" he says. "You have to do this now? If you let me put the stove back, no one will even know the grease is there."

"I'll know. You'll know. Mrs. Snyder will know."

"Mrs. Snyder?"

"The social worker. The one who's going to take Princess Daphne away."

"You stop that, Sarah."

"She's going to come one day. She's going to ring the doorbell and demand I let her in. Maybe she's already here."

He stands behind me, his large frame casting a shadow on the spot I try to clean. I get up and, carefully, so that no part of me touches any part of him, squeeze past him. I stand behind him where I can see Princess Daphne's face over his shoulder. Her trusting brown eyes, her small upturned nose, her beautiful puckered mouth, everything so seemingly perfect it hurts to believe there could be anything wrong with her.

"Hello, sweetheart." I raise my finger so it's level with her nose. I slowly move my finger to the left, then the right.

"Stop that," he says, turning to face me. He cradles Princess Daphne in one arm and coochie-coochies her. Then he looks at me. "You did this." His neck has turned red and his arms have begun to tremble and I know that this is what Mrs. Snyder will say. This is how Mrs. Snyder will look at me. "Two years, Sarah. Two years before they know the extent of the damage."

I listen to him talk. I watch his mouth move. I watch his narrowed eyes examine me. "Remember how you kept making me coffee?" I tell him and his mouth stops moving. "Remember? I'd call you and you'd race over and make me coffee so I could make it to work. Remember?"

He backs away a few steps.

"I forgot, Sean, I forgot how you kept coming over and making me coffee."

He looks at Princess Daphne who's fallen asleep on his shoulder. He walks her over to her basket and, kneeling down, carefully lays her on her side. I hold my breath, expecting her to wake up screaming at any second, but she doesn't.

"You know what I remember, Sean? I remember how you never asked me what was going on. Not once. You just kept making me coffee."

Sean remains on his knees and begins to sing his Princess Daphne song, only this time he sings very softly.

"Sean? Sean, did you hear what I said?"

"Stop singing," I tell him.

"You bastard," I tell him, my voice bathwater calm. "Look at me."

He slowly heaves himself up. He turns around and I can see his face falling apart. I can actually see his face falling apart. "Please," he manages to say.

"Coffee. You kept making me coffee."

I raise the liquid cleanser as if it's a glass I'm using to propose a toast. Why I do this, and what he thinks I mean by it, I don't know. He lunges forward. I lose my grip on the container and what's inside spills on both of us.

"Sarah," he says. He leans his head against my shoulder and I let him do this. "Sarah," he says between his sobs.

Sean comes over early this morning. I open the door and stand aside to let him pass.

"Where's my Princess?" he says.

"In her room." I ask him if he'd like some coffee and he says yes, if I'm not too busy cleaning. I tell him I've pushed the stove back, grease or no grease. He doesn't look at me directly, but I can tell he's surprised about the stove. He shifts and shoves his hands in his pockets. Like me, he is worried about the hospital appointment this afternoon.

"I'll just go see her." He disappears into her room and his voice booms out a cheery "Princess!" I remain where I am by the front door, waiting. I listen to him pick Princess Daphne up, I listen to Princess Daphne gurgle, I listen to his voice softly say, "Who did this, Princess?"

"I'll wait for you in the kitchen," I tell him, though I don't move from where I am.

"Princess Daphne's crib," he says, appearing at the doorway leading to Princess Daphne's room, Princess Daphne in his arms. "Who put it together?"

"I did. I followed your blueprint."

"When?"

"Last night. After you left."

He stares at me, his brown eyes not so narrow anymore. "Looks like you did a good job," he says, disappearing once again into the bedroom. Curious, I position myself by the bedroom door.

"What are you smiling at?" He looks up from where he lays Princess Daphne down in her crib.

"Nothing," I tell him, though really it's me I'm smiling at. And the crib. And Princess Daphne. I spent most of the night putting the crib together, Princess Daphne in the room with me, lying in her basket, me explaining to her my every move. See, I'd tell her, we screw this together with this, and then we . . . The thing is, Princess Daphne seemed to be paying attention to everything I said, and I didn't think once to clap my hands or turn off the light, then quickly turn it back on. I just enjoyed my time with her, even told her a few jokes, and I promised I'd stick by her no matter what. She fell asleep toward midnight and it felt good to be putting her crib together with her in the same room. It felt good that I was doing something for her, and she was doing something for me, and somehow I felt we both understood this.

After I finished putting the crib together, I carefully picked her up and put her in it. She fussed, but only for a moment or two, her eyes tightly shut, her beautiful mouth slightly open. I got a blanket and slept on the floor, next to her crib, listening to her snore.

Sean gets on his knees and examines the various screws. A part of me is angered at this. I should ask him something, like, Do you think me completely incompetent? But another part of me wants to show him—and Mrs. Snyder—up. I know they won't find anything wrong with the crib. I checked it myself a hundred times and I'd never have let Princess Daphne sleep in it if I thought there was even one screw slightly loose.

"Sarah," he says, and I can see he's impressed, but also, maybe, a little afraid because I've done this on my own, without him. I try to think of something I can say, something true and kind.

"It's a beautiful crib." I look at the crib and it really is the kind I'd expect to find in one of those decorating magazines I love so much. Sean chose oak, which he stained a deep, deep burgundy. The crib's frame is simple, only the eight-foot-high corner posts are ornate. I tell him how I plan to sew the canopy for the crib. I tell him how I plan to sew a bumper pad and quilt to match the canopy. "Something in off-white," I tell him. "So it doesn't distract from the crib."

Princess Daphne gurgles and waves her little arms up and down. A minute later, she begins to playfully kick her feet, her hands instinctively trying to reach out for them. I laugh as I approach her crib and lean over it, gently pinching one of her toes. This makes her gurgle louder and her hand manages to grab on to my finger and for a moment, I picture myself standing on this stone veranda I once saw in a magazine called *Beautiful Homes*. I'm standing on this veranda overlooking this incredible garden, a swing set to the right of the rosebushes. I'm wearing a long silk dress and Princess Daphne is about five or six and she's swinging and humming a song, something she learned from a man we used to know from a time in our lives when things were much less certain.

Colleen Conn Dunkle

University of Central Florida

BREATHE IN BREATHE OUT

Steve's ex-wife, Donna, was in love with a podiatrist. He heard it from their fourteen-year-old daughter, Kelly, and he had to believe it.

"She's really smitten, Dad."

"Smitten?"

"Yeah," Kelly said. "You know, like she really likes him."

"I know what smitten means, Kell."

They sat on a curb in the downtown business section of the city, munching on bananas and drinking a low sodium, high glucose-fructose orange drink from paper cups. They were waiting for results of the 5K race they'd just run; they often ran races together on weekends. Steve finished at 19:19 and thought he might have placed in his age group. He was forty-one.

"So where'd she meet this guy?" he asked.

"She went to him, you know, for her feet."

Steve thought about Donna's feet and couldn't recall any problems there. Didn't he always buy her a new pair of cross-trainers every Christmas? Didn't they fit? He had known she wasn't really appreciative of the shoe gifts the last few years of their marriage because more than one pair still sat snug in its box, unlaced, with spotless soles. "Isn't that illegal or something?" he asked Kelly. "Dating people you treat professionally?"

Kelly swallowed the last piece of her banana and without standing tossed the peel into a nearby trash can, a perfect shot. "Nothing but net," she said and then shrugged. "How would I know?" she asked. "He didn't call her until after, though."

"After what?"

"After he did her feet."

"What's wrong with her feet, anyway?"

"Well," Kelly said, "nothing, now."

Tents had been set up near the finish line with complimentary fruit and PowerBars, yogurt and drinks. They walked over and Kelly picked up a cup of blueberry yogurt and someone handed her a small, plastic spoon. A shoe salesman sold running shoes from a van that he had backed up onto the lawn. "Sure, they're more expensive," Steve heard the salesman say to a nearby runner, "but this cushioning is so much better than E.V.A. construction. State of the art in shoe design. Here, try it on. Your feet will love it. Try it." Steve could taste salt on his lips. His pulse rate had slowed, but he was still dripping sweat. He asked Kelly if she was cold. She shook her head and told him she was fine.

"So," he said, "tell me what you think of this foot man."

"Foot man? Oh, Dad." Kelly rolled her eyes in a way that had become quite common for her lately. The look of total exasperation, the I-can't-take-you-anywhere look that girls her age seemed to flash so often. Steve wondered if daughters practiced such looks in the mirror. "I like him," she said. "He's nice and Mom's crazy about him. He makes her laugh."

"Laugh, huh? A funny guy?" Steve couldn't remember the last time he'd made Donna laugh. "I guess you'd have to be funny if you spent your days clipping toenails and buffing bunions, eh?"

"I don't know, Dad. I think there's more to it than that."

"What more? It's not like he's a real doctor or anything."

"I think he is. I saw him one time wearing one of those operation outfits, you know, a doctor shirt. Looked official." She put her finger in the yogurt and rolled it along the sides of the cup. Her finger came out purple and creamy, then went into her mouth. She smacked her lips. "And," she added, "he has initials after his name: D.P.M."

"Big deal," said Steve.

He remembered reading somewhere that children of divorced parents forever wished they could somehow get their parents back together. He wondered if Kelly felt this way. She seemed okay with this new guy. "Crazy about him, eh? So what is his name?"

"Dr. Faber. Oakley Faber," she said.

They stayed until all the race results were in. Steve placed fifth in his age group. No cigar. Kelly came in first with a 20:07 for the fourteen- to eighteen-year-olds. She won an authentic-looking marbleized plaque that read "1st Place 14–18/ Run for the Arts," and a one-hour long-distance calling card. She gave the card to Steve.

The walk back to the car was slow. Steve opened the door for Kelly and then sat in the driver's seat and took off his shoes and socks. He rubbed his feet with a towel from the backseat. Bones in his toes cracked. "Tell me more about this friend of your mother's," he said. "I'm all ears."

"I think thou doest profess too much," Kelly said.

Steve shook his head. "That saying doesn't apply here. I just want to know more about this guy. Anyway, it's protest."

"So, like what do you want to know? I don't know much. What would I know? I don't even know what a bunion is."

"Tall? Short? Fat? Medium, what? Come on, spill it. Why haven't I seen this guy?"

"I don't know. I can't tell. I guess he's medium. Maybe. He might be short. Well, no." She put her hand, salute-style, a few inches above her head. "Kind of," she said. She told Steve that they went out a lot. "He takes Mom all over the place."

"Oh yeah?"

Steve thought how little he'd seen Donna the past couple of months. She was usually there when he came for Kelly, waved hello or good-bye to him, whichever, or had some newsy tidbit about mutual friends to share with him, some eye contact, some recognition, a smile. But not so lately. This boyfriend thing explained it.

It was still early and traffic was light. Steve rolled down his window. Humidity was low. He watched Kelly pull the tie from her hair, and dark curls fell around her shoulders. Her bangs were stuck to her forehead, and her cheeks were still flushed from the run. He knew that his daughter resembled him most with her dark hair and eyes, and her long, thin legs that at this stage made her look gangly and awkward. Gangly maybe, but awkward she wasn't. She had won other races before today's; this wasn't her first, and Steve was proud of her. Kelly liked running, and she was good at it, but basketball was her favorite and best sport. She had learned to beat Steve one-on-one even before her growing spurt. She liked it when the net was clean and intact, so Steve always kept a spare at the house. "So, what's this guy's game?" he asked now. "What does he play?"

"Play?"

"Yeah. You know, sport."

"Oh." Kelly pulled the end of her T-shirt out and wiped her face. "Golf, I think," she said. "Sometimes. Not much. I don't know."

"Golf? Golf's not a game. It's a ride in a cart. It's landscaping and little flags. Golf." Steve laughed. "Huh. How do you get your heart to work with a game of golf?"

He pulled up in front of the house, his house once, and put the car in park. He looked for an extra car and wondered if one had been parked in the back by the garage when he had come for Kelly at six-thirty this morning. He didn't think so. Kelly asked if he could take her to practice that week and he said, "Sure. Call me." He asked if they were on for the race the following Saturday, and she reminded him of her basketball game that morning. She played for a local all-girls team. "The game starts at ten. Mom will get me there. Don't be late."

"Got it," he said, and leaned over the seat to kiss her cheek. When Kelly got out of the car and turned to go into the house, he called, "Hey, Kell."

She turned around. "Yeah?"

"What kind of name is Oakley?"

She leaned inside the passenger window. "I don't know what kind of name it is," she said. "His, I guess."

Steve had started running shortly before the separation two years earlier. It was his sport, his game, and he liked the freedom of it. There was no equipment, no teammates, no playing field needed. Steve liked the individualness of the sport and how it was all up to him: pace, stride, foot placement, muscle control, heart rate, pumping, breathing, coming down, coming down again, waiting for those endorphins to kick in. Waiting. Sometimes they never kicked in. Maybe he had farther to go before he could experience what everyone talked about. Steve tried to run at least thirty miles a week. Shoes, of course, were very important.

The day he left Donna had been a weekday, a great day for running, he remembered, because he had gone a full six miles that morning. He told Donna simply, "I think it's time, don't you?" Then he went into the bedroom and packed a small bag. He told her he'd come for more of his things later. Donna stood by with her arms folded and cried silently, but she didn't wail or scream or threaten. "I'll always love you," he said to her when he left, but later he would wonder why he had felt the need to say that just then. He'd left because there was nothing there between them to grasp, or to hold. They never talked of anything other than Kelly, never touched; it had been months since they'd made love. They never argued either. Steve had waited for the anger, the passion, something to boil over, to show between them, but nothing ever did.

It was months after the amicable divorce was final that Steve began to worry about the ease with which it had all happened. During the proceedings everything was fair, divisions were equal, resentment was kept in check. After all, Kelly and her well-being were at the center of everything; let's be adults about this, he remembered saying. But it was at unexpected places and times, long after the divorce, that things about Donna and their relationship would suddenly occur to him. When his hairstylist had shaken her head and told him that gray hair was always coarser and less manageable than hair with color, he thought how Donna had told him more than once that he was just a kid at heart, in spirit, how she could never keep up with him. She was getting tired. Older. "You're too much excitement for me," she'd said. Alone in an elevator another day, feeling energetic, having run that morning toward the east and a spectacular sunrise, Steve had thought about Donna saying that scuba diving made her feel claustrophobic. "Claustrophobic?" Steve asked, surprised. "How can open water, miles of blue, crystal-clear water, make you feel claustrophobic?" "I don't know," Donna said. "It scares me." And once at work, while feeding his computer actuarial data, his wrists had begun to ache, and he thought about Donna breaking her arm on a ski trip they took to North Carolina. Not her leg or ankle like other skiers, but her forearm. It happened when she tried to stop herself and grabbed hold of a passing tree branch. The branch held fast, but her arm bone snapped. She told him, "Never again, I'm through with all this physical stuff, all this excitement. You can keep it." The last year of their marriage Steve had gone skiing alone and had slept well wrapped in an arctic sleeping bag at a "Closed for the Season" campground on the Tennessee border.

Steve hadn't changed. He still had a thirty-two-inch waist and wore a size-eleven shoe. He still played roller hockey one night a week (he was the oldest player in the league), racquetball at the Y during lunch (everyone there was his age or older), and then there was his running.

Tonight he ran slower and at a steady pace. It was dark, more risky, and the bugs were unusually bad. Most times he didn't run the evening after a race, but tonight he felt restless, antsy, and he wanted to get out. He headed toward their house; it was less than two miles away. He was close by for Kelly's sake, for his sake.

The house was a small two-story with a big garage (built years after the house, Steve knew) at the back of the yard. The garage door was closed, but it was easy for Steve to run back there and look through the small rectangular window to see Donna's car inside. Music blared from the house. Steve stood on the porch, still running in place. He pounded and knocked until finally the music stopped and Kelly's footsteps could be heard in the hall. The door swung open.

"Hey, Dad," she said.

"Don't just open the door, Kelly. You didn't even ask, 'Who's there?'" He came inside and closed the door behind him.

"But, it's you," she said.

"Yeah, but you didn't know that. How could you know that?" They'd had this discussion before. "Never mind," he said. They walked together into the kitchen and Steve wiped his face on a dish towel hanging on the side of the cabinet. He opened the refrigerator and took out a pitcher of cold water and poured himself a glass. He listened for Donna somewhere in the house. He peeked into the utility room next to the kitchen. "Where's your mother?" he asked.

"They're out," Kelly said.

"Foot man?"

Kelly nodded. "They went to a movie."

He swallowed the last of his water with a loud gulp. "Isn't it kind of late? And has your mother been leaving you here alone all the time?" he asked. "At night like this?" He went to the window above the sink and looked out. He pulled aside the curtains, stretched his neck, and looked down the driveway.

"It's only seven-thirty, Dad. I'm fourteen. Geez." Steve didn't have to turn around to know that Kelly had just done the eye thing. "They'll be home early. Then we're going to grab something to eat. Maybe you should hang out for a while."

"What? Oh, no. I've got to get going." He turned and headed for the front door. Kelly followed. "I'd thought I'd go by Sports World in the morning," he said. "Big shoe sale this week. Just thought you might want to come along."

"Sale, eh?" Kelly smiled. "Sure. Come get me." He kissed her cheek, then reminded her to lock the door. "Immediately," he said. He wasn't yet down the porch steps when he turned around and tried to catch her before she locked him out. "Kelly! Wait," he called, but he ended up having to knock on the door again. "I was thinking," he said when she opened the door, "why don't you just come home with me now? We'll rent a couple of movies, pop some corn, you know. We haven't done that in a while. It'll be nice. Leave your mom a note."

"Ah, sounds great. But we kind of made plans already. Dr. Faber is taking us to that new pizza-and-pie place that just opened," she said. "You know the place."

Steve nodded. "Oh yeah, yeah. Sounds like a plan. Well, you have a good time. We'll do it another night, I guess. No problem."

He backed off the porch, turned, and ran slowly across the grass. He wasn't fifty yards away when he heard Kelly shout, "You know how Mom is about apple pie!"

Steve didn't stop or turn around. He raised an arm in the air—too dark and too far away for Kelly to see, he realized—quickened his pace and said aloud, "Apple pie? She loves it."

Steve was up early. He swallowed a handful of vitamins (male/high potency), drank a half cup of coffee, and ran his usual 4.6 miles in 31:02, a good time for him.

He showered, read the sports page, and soon was back on their front porch, knocking again. When Donna opened the door, she was still in her bathrobe. It looked new. Her hair was uncombed and hanging in her eyes, a cup of coffee in her hand. Steve couldn't remember when she had looked more attractive.

"Hey, Steve," she said. "Come in." She pulled bangs out of her eyes. "What brings you here so early?"

Something smelled good. Steve couldn't tell if it was just that homey kitchen smell, or if it was Donna, something she had on, or maybe just her clean smell. He told her the plans. He mentioned how it really wasn't so early, and was Kelly still asleep, where was she anyway?

"They went to get bagels," Donna answered. "They'll be home soon. Can I pour you a cup of coffee?"

"They?"

Donna smiled. "I guess you haven't met. Today is as good a time as any. I've been seeing someone. His name is Oak and—"

Steve shook his head and held up a hand. "I know all about your new beau," he said. "Spare me the details. But it's only nine-thirty in the morning. What's he doing here so early?"

Steve waved his watch in front of her face. Donna smiled again and Steve couldn't tell if she blushed or if the color in her face had been there all along and he was just now noticing it. "Oh, I get it," he said. "He spent the night. Jesus, Donna. In front of Kelly? What are you thinking? What's wrong with you?" He raised both arms. "Huh?"

She took a sip from her cup. "Don't get so excited. It's not like I did anything in front of Kelly. She's fourteen, almost fifteen. She knows what happens when two people—"

"But guys spending the night? It's not right. Not right at all."

"It's not guys," Donna said, remaining calm. "It's one guy."

"I don't care. I don't like it."

Steve knew that there hadn't been any men since the divorce. He'd heard from a mutual acquaintance that Donna had dated an old friend from school once or twice but nothing had come of it. But now this foot doctor. "I don't like it," he said again. He poured himself a cup of coffee and headed out to the front porch. "I'll wait outside." He let the door slam.

The porch steps were still wet with morning moisture, but Steve didn't seem to notice as he sat there waiting and looking out toward the street. He didn't know which way to look.

He blinked and looked again when he saw a silver Volvo turn into the driveway. Kelly was behind the wheel and the boyfriend sat in the passenger seat. The car came to an uneven stop, jerked and bounced, but finally braked just inches behind his own car parked there. He was off the porch in seconds.

"What the hell's going on?" Steve asked. He moved to the driver's side of the car and yanked on the door handle, but it didn't open. "Kelly! What are you doing? Open up." He tapped on the window.

"Oh, hi, Daddy," Kelly said when she opened the car door. She was beaming. "Did you see me? Did you see me driving the car? Pretty cool, eh?"

"Not cool, Kelly. Get out of there." Steve looked over the roof of the car and saw the boyfriend shut the passenger door. He was smiling a big friendly smile. He walked over to Steve. "Hi. You must be Kelly's dad. She's told me so much about you." The man extended his hand. "I'm Oakley Faber," he said.

"What the hell's going on here?" Steve asked. "She can't drive. She's only fourteen." Faber withdrew his hand. "It was just from the stop sign a few houses down," he said. "She did real well." He looked from Kelly to Steve and back to Kelly. He held up a small bakery-style bag he was carrying and said to her, "I'll see you inside." He turned to go and then stopped. "Hey," he said to Steve. "It was nice meeting you." Steve watched him walk up the porch steps and through the front door.

He turned to Kelly. "You can't drive," he said to her. He shook his head.

"I think I can," she said. "I went real slow. And Oak was right there with—"

"I don't care. And it's Oak now? Oak?"

"Well, that's what he said I should call him. It's no big deal, Dad. Mom lets me move the car up and down the driveway all the time. I'll be fifteen in two months. Driver's ed starts, you know."

Steve didn't tell Kelly that the day after he turned fifteen, he and a couple of his buddies pushed his mother's Chevrolet out the driveway and down the street before he started the engine and drove off. It wasn't his first time behind the wheel. He drove to the A&W, bought a round of root beers, then drove all the way down Jefferson Street to Burko's batting cages, where he parked right up front so everyone could see him. The three of them got out and leaned on the car until it was time to head back. His mother had never even missed the car.

"Okay," he said to Kelly. "Okay. But let me teach you. I want to make sure you learn the right way. Deal?" He held out his hand.

"The right way? I guess," she said. She shook his hand. "But it was cool. It was fun." Steve put his arm around her shoulder and pulled her close. "But, Kell," he said. "It was a Volvo. How could it have been fun?"

"It was safe," she said. "Oak says Volvos are good cars. Sturdy. And safe."

Steve was late for Kelly's game. The 5K race he'd run had started at eight A.M., but today he'd broken nineteen minutes, had posted an 18:58, his personal goal, so he'd hung around after to hear all the race results. He came in second in his age group and won a deluxe pair of running socks. He put them on right there at the finish line, in front of all the other runners. They fit his feet perfectly, now felt good inside his shoes.

He hadn't gone home to shower or change but had gone right to the game. When he got there it was already a minute and a half into the third quarter. Kelly's team was ahead 43–28. He stood on the sidelines and looked for Kelly. She was on the bench and hadn't seen him come in. He didn't worry about Kelly being upset with him for being late; he was anxious to tell her his race time.

He scanned the bleachers for Donna and saw her sitting a few rows up, right next to the boyfriend. When she saw him, she smiled cheerfully and waved him up. He took the bleacher steps two rows at a time and slid in next to her.

"Steve. I'd like you to meet Oakley Faber," she said. She sat between the two men. Faber held out his hand. "We've already met," he said. "Good to see you again."

"Oh, yeah. Me too." Steve took his hand and squeezed. "Hope I haven't missed much," he said. He noticed Faber's shoes right off.

"Well, look at the score," Donna said. "Kelly's MVP of this game, let me tell you."

Steve tried to focus on the game. He figured his morning victory was making him feel charged, because he was having trouble paying attention. He kept sizing Faber up from the corner of his eye. The guy wasn't really short, but stocky. Built like a spark plug. A wrestler maybe, Steve guessed, years ago. He had an obvious paunch and round shoulders, and Steve felt uneasy thinking about him and Donna together. But the shoes. Hard-soled shoes to a basketball game? Nobody wore street shoes to a game. Maybe I should take this guy aside and remind him that we're in a gymnasium, Steve thought. This is basketball for Chrissake, a national sport. Geez.

Kelly was back in the game. She was the tallest girl on the court and she moved with a fluid grace and coordination that the other players seemed to lack. Her teammates passed her the ball; plays were designed around her. Fourteen seconds off the bench she scored a three-pointer, a beautiful shot from two feet behind the line, and everyone, including Faber, stood up and cheered.

Then it happened. Kelly brought the ball down, passed it, broke away, and for an instant was open right under the basket. The ball came to her and she jumped. Another player, arms and hands out of control, jumped too. Kelly fell to the floor. Her hands went up to her face.

Steve was down the bleachers and out on the floor before the refs even blew the whistle. Kelly was holding her eye. Steve saw blood dripping down her fingers, onto her jersey. It ran down the side of her face. "Kelly! Oh, God. Kelly." He pushed aside a player and knelt in front of her. He eased her hand away from her face and saw blood oozing from a cut on her forehead. The blood was thick and red and smeared on her face and Steve couldn't see just how long or how deep the cut was. It looked bad to him. "Your eye, Kelly. Honey, please open your eye. Let me see." She opened her eyes and looked at the blood on her hands. "Oh my God!" she cried. "Oh, Daddy!" Steve felt sick to his stomach. He heard someone behind him ask for a towel. He heard a girl wail.

"I didn't mean it! I'm sorry. Oh, no." Then the girl started to sob loudly and Steve turned to look. The player was staring at her hand, staring at her ring smeared with blood. Steve stood up and charged toward the young girl. "A ring? You were wearing a ring? What's the matter with you?" Steve shouted at her. She sobbed harder and backed away. "Huh? What's the matter with you?" He heard Kelly say, "I think," and he saw her coach bend over her. Someone wiped drops of blood from the floor. He took two steps toward the coach. "What kind of coach are you?" he said. He raised his arms. "Don't you teach these girls anything? They can't wear jewelry in a game! What kind of coaching is this?"

The coach didn't answer, didn't even turn around. Steve bent over. He poked a finger into the coach's shoulder. "What kind of coach are you?" he said again. "Didn't you see that ring?" He looked at Kelly and the blood on her face. He felt his own blood pulse behind his ears, his heart pound. He didn't know what to do. He stood up and raised his arm again, but before he could strike out or grab anything, he felt someone seize his wrist. His arm locked and he turned to see Faber standing there, his grip tight around his arm.

"Steve," Faber said. "Calm down." He looked directly into Steve's face. He didn't blink and his grip didn't lessen.

"Hey!" Steve said. He tried to pull away, but Faber didn't let go. "She's hurt. She's my kid. She's my daughter."

"I know," said Faber. "But it was an accident. You need to calm down."

Steve felt the muscles in his arm twitch; his fists clenched. Somewhere back in his throat muscles tightened, and he tried to take a deep breath. Over his shoulder he heard Kelly cry, "I don't know. It's in my eyes. Get it off." Steve relaxed his fists and quit struggling.

Faber let go of Steve's arm and said evenly, "Here's what I want you to do." He held out a clean towel. He bent over Kelly and said, "It looks superficial. Here, Steve. Hold the towel tight against her forehead."

He took Steve's hand and placed it on the towel. "You have to apply pressure," he said. He put his face closer to Kelly and told her she would be all right. "Try to relax, Kelly," he said. "It looks worse than it is." Then he said to Steve, almost a whisper, "There's always a lot of blood from this part of the face. Don't worry."

Faber turned to Donna, who was kneeling beside Kelly. She had been there all along, Steve realized, holding Kelly in her arms. Blood was on her sleeve and some had dripped onto her jeans. Faber put his hand on Donna's shoulder. "You going to be okay?" he asked.

When Donna nodded, Faber stood up. He spread his arms and took a step backward, pushing away the players and coaches there, watching. "I think she's going to be okay, everybody. We just need a little room. Please." He looked down at Steve. "I'll go get my car. Can you carry her out?"

Steve nodded. He could do that. He lifted Kelly and she started to cry. "It's okay, hon," he said. "Just hold on."

The emergency room was crowded. Faber had dropped them off at the entrance and then left to park the car. Steve carried Kelly in and explained the accident to a nurse. "We need to see a doctor," he said. "Right away." The nurse lifted the towel from Kelly's forehead, took a quick look, and told them to have a seat. She wrote Kelly's name on a clipboard, a long list of patients. She handed them a clean towel. "How long?" Steve asked. "How long will we need to wait? We can't wait long." The nurse politely told him that they would see to Kelly as soon as they could and would he please, please just take a seat? Steve didn't like her attitude.

He set Kelly down in a comfortable-looking chair next to Donna. There wasn't another chair for him, so he stood next to Kelly's, hovering. He wished that she were small enough, or he were big enough, that he could gather her onto his lap and hold her there. He stood and stroked the top of her head. Donna kept her arm around Kelly's shoulder and she leaned into her mother. Steve looked at his watch.

Faber came in and asked if everything was okay. He asked if they'd checked in and then, looking around, said it looked like a long wait. Donna put her hand out and Faber took it. "Let me see what I can do," he said. He went over to the nurse at the desk. He talked low, but Steve could hear him politely ask about a Dr. Halsey, and was he on duty today? "Could I speak to him, please?" He said something to her that Steve didn't hear, and then he said his name. "Tell him it's Oak Faber. He'll see me." The nurse went behind closed doors; Faber followed.

Less than five minutes later they called for Kelly. Faber came back through the doors and told them that Dr. Halsey would take care of them. He suggested to Donna that she go around the corner and fill out all the necessary paperwork. He told Steve to go with Kelly.

"She's going to need you to hold her hand," he said to Steve.

"They're going to have to give her a few stitches." He reached past Steve and touched Kelly's sleeve. "You'll be all right in there," he told her. "You're in good hands."

Kelly took the towel from her forehead. Blood had dried along her hairline and in her eyebrow. The cut ran down her forehead, a straight line two inches long, just missing the eye. She handed the towel to Steve.

Then Kelly turned her face up to Faber as if she had been doing this for years. He kissed her cheek and Steve saw how his mouth barely touched her skin. "I'll wait out here for you," he said.

It turned out they were neighbors. Faber had lived next door to Dr. Halsey for nearly five years and had spent every Fourth of July and Labor Day over at his house for barbecues. Steve learned all this as Dr. Halsey skillfully put ten tiny almost unseen stitches in Kelly's face. Steve was thankful for all the chatter because he felt himself getting lightheaded and nervous when they started in. He held Kelly's hand tightly, stroked her arm, and told her more than once that the stitches were perfect and certainly wouldn't leave a scar.

When Donna came in, someone said that one of them would have to leave, only one parent allowed. "I'll wait out there," Steve said. He was glad to go back to the waiting room. He bought two cups of coffee and walked over to Faber.

"Thanks," Faber said, accepting the coffee. "Is she okay?"

"She'll be fine. They're just finishing up." Steve sat down. "Listen," he started. "About the way I acted back there at the gym. When I saw all that blood, well, I just lost it."

Faber nodded and smiled. "Any father would have acted the same way," he said. He leaned back in his chair and sipped his coffee. "Anyone would," he said quietly.

The waiting room was still crowded. An older man sat in the corner, alone, and coughed into a handkerchief. A small child toddled around a woman's chair, began to whimper, and then crawled into her lap. Steve picked up a magazine and tried to concentrate. He read a short article about how the human heart can increase its power, can grow, with healthy habits and regular exercise. The heart gets stronger, more toned, the article said, and grows just enough to increase its load. The growth was a good thing, a natural thing; it helped.

Steve finished his coffee and tossed the cup into a nearby wastebasket. He looked down at Faber's shoes. He noticed now that they weren't ordinary shoes. They were dark but not black, and the leather had a matte finish, not shiny, so it looked like it was molded to the foot, and molded to the soles. The soles were thin and flexible looking; stitching couldn't be seen anywhere. They were slip-ons.

"Nice shoes," Steve said.

"Oh, you like these? They're great shoes." Faber folded his foot over his knee to get a better look. "They're sturdy, comfortable shoes. Reliable, if shoes can be. I've had them for years." He went on to tell Steve how he'd had them custom made, and how the shoemaker kept a mold of his foot on file. Now he could just pick up the phone and order. "They're a little more expensive, sure. But, worth it. Shoes are important."

"Right," said Steve. "I couldn't agree more."

They talked more about shoes, feet, bones of the foot, socks. Steve showed Faber his prize socks. "Nice," Faber said. They talked about running and walking and soaking the feet. Faber gave Steve a business card. "Call me," he said.

Donna and Kelly both looked tired when they came out. Faber stood and asked if they were okay. Steve stood and kissed Kelly's bandaged face. "Does it hurt much?" he asked. He watched as Donna easily put her arm around Faber and said something to him under her breath. He wondered what it was she said. Faber pulled her into his arms and held her there. Steve heard Donna say, "Oak."

Steve felt good for her, happy.

"Well," Faber said then. "I'd like to take these lovely ladies out for something to eat. Are you up to it, Kelly? You feel like it?"

Kelly said she thought she could eat something; she felt okay. When Faber asked Steve to join them he said, "No thanks. Some other time, maybe." He said good-bye to Kelly, asked again if she was going to be all right, and told her he would call her later. "I love you, honey," he said, and he hugged her close.

He held out his hand to Faber. "Thanks," Steve said. Faber smiled, took Steve's hand and shook it. "No problem," he said. Then Steve put his hand gently on Donna's shoulder. He smiled at her and said quietly, "It might take me some time, but I'll get there." He leaned forward and kissed her cheek good-bye. He felt her whisper, "I know."

He walked out into the afternoon sunlight and roughly estimated how far it was back to his car, still parked at the gym. Probably just over three miles, he figured. He knelt down and retied his shoes, checked his socks and pulled them tight. He pushed the timer on his watch. Steve thought about how he would have to set another goal; nineteen minutes was history. He started running in the right direction. There was a lot of traffic, but he didn't mind. He ran his usual steady pace, heels coming down, coming down, nearly painless, heart drumming against his ribcage, growing, breathe in, breathe out, arms tight against the body, heels coming down, legs do the work, feet do the work, do the work, do the work. The heart does all the work.

Melanie Little
University of British Columbia

APNEA

1. Theme Park Odysseys

Welcome to the Zumba Flume.
You must be at least this tall to ride this ride.
Keep arms and legs inside your car at all times.
Pregnant women and persons with heart conditions should not ride this ride.
   "Dad, do you—"
   "Bah."
Secure all loose articles.
You may get wet.

Navigate the Cassandra cluckings of the signs and you're in.

This one's my father's choice: he likes the rides that go straight up and down—the greater the climb, the steeper the plunge, the better. The ones that go around and around crimp his innards into painful, slippery knots. This is, he says, a male/female thing. Even the names of the spinning ones are effeminate, somehow: too sibilant, I suppose, too ornately Oriental. The Sol Loco, the Sea of Sorrows, the Swings of Siam: all spinny. Even Shiva's Fury, which for him conjures up images of Smurf-hued boy-gods with hairless chests and nests of wriggling, seductive arms. He favors the linear, no-nonsense rise and fall of the Wildebeast, the Dragonfyre, the Mighty Canadian Minebuster. I do too: I just go on the twirly-girly ones to keep my mother company.

The kids in the lines do a lot of sneering. They're from Toronto and—you can tell—I'm not. The dressy red sandals that seemed so inoffensive two hours north of here now make me want to click my heels together and disappear. But my father's serene, goggly-eyed surveillance buoys me up. He acts like everything is as good as we could possibly wish. He affects it so well, this untroubled omniscience, this cool panoptic gaze: always has. He makes you want to believe.

He doesn't guess that my mother polices the one-way glass for him, keeps it clean, attacks the smirches with her skirts while he's napping. The same way we both monitor his breathing, even in our sleep; listen to the comforting rumble through the papery walls, keep ready to rush in and fill him up with oxygenated air the second it stops.

The moment he likes best is the pause before the plunge, the hanging in the air, suspended, thumbing our noses at gravity, water, the crowds below. I'm nervous, I hold my breath, and I count out his heartbeats in my brain. The final sign, now, admonishing the obvious: *Do not stand up.*

We do get wet. We exit past the waiting queue with shy, sodden smiles. The American behind us is yelling: the water's soaked right through his trousers, and the twenties among his Wonderland Funbucks have all been bled to look like ones.

2. Forbidden Things

In my personal mythology, my father is the god of doorways. His stories are played out across the endless thresholds of his entrances and exits. Slamming out a door during breakfast; sneaking out a different one in the middle of the night. Reappearing at the screen door with a bouquet of flowers picked from the town garden; being pulled in by the hair by my mother from where he lay shaking on the concrete steps.

But I don't remember his goings away as much I do his comings back, a failure either of will or imagination that my mother, I know, regards as a fatal misdirection of loyalties.

The first time my father came back, my mother barred the door of their room. He's been an exile ever since, relegated to the airless spare bedroom because, they say, of his snoring. I endure agonies of embarrassment every time an overnight friend imposes herself on us and my dad has to sleep in the basement with the cat litter. On these occasions, I set my alarm for 6 A.M. so that I can wake him up with my foot stomps in the kitchen overhead. The idea is to avoid the unthinkable spectacle of my dad trudging up the basement stairs in his underwear while our guest sits at her breakfast.

His first heart attack is during one of these underground times. Nobody hears the breathing stop, the resulting silent implosion of the heart. What saves him is a nightmare, rousing him in time to drive to the hospital without waking us, the pain radiating steadily up through his steering arm like a fiery compass. He can't relax his grip because he's a new driver, still unsure of his touch.

Shortly after his release from the hospital he decides to take me to the end of the earth, which is what he says Gaspé means in English. "Like you'd know," I snort, heady from my high marks in French. But he just smiles. "Actually, it's a Micmac word. And don't worry. You can interpret for me out there."

"What about work?" I ask him.

"What about it?"

He makes me wait until we've hit the highway before he lets me call my mother.

"Just make sure he doesn't fall off the end of it," she says, when we're somewhere east of Kingston.

"What?" I say, because a truck is screaming by.

"Off the end of the earth," she answers.

Through three provinces he never takes his hands off the wheel: he's a ham actor's parody of what driving is like.

"Why don't you let me drive?" I ask him.

"I'm a good driver. Get off my back."

"I didn't say you weren't—it's just too much for one person, that's all. The normal thing to do is share."

My father stares at the highway unfolding in front of us for a long time. It's puddled with mirages, murky black lakes that disappear right before you get to them. When he speaks, it's to the lakes.

"When I was about ten years old, my father brought home a car."

"What kind of car?" I ask, thinking this is the sort of question he's looking for.

He just shakes his head no, keeps talking to the lakes. "We were the only Frenchmen in the whole county to have one."

He pauses for a minute to concentrate on driving while a guy in a Porsche roars past us, slick and low to the ground. When it's out of sight, he continues, as if he's been waiting for an odious gossip to leave the room.

"When I thought my father was asleep, I snuck outside to the car. It was locked, but I was small enough to crawl in the open window."

I know he wants to close his eyes and remember this, so I do it for him. I can feel the smooth caress of the leather seat, still warm from the day's sunshine. The wheel, a perfect circle tingling under his small grip, an emblem of the world opening up around him.

"The keys were still there, in the ignition. He must have forgotten; he wasn't used to owning anything, I guess. Maybe he remembered just as he was about to fall asleep; maybe that's what made him come back out. Whatever it was, I was just reaching out to touch those keys when he grabbed me by the neck. He took my hand and he opened the glove compartment. Those little doors were heavy buggers back then, not like the plastic toy in this thing that falls open at every second stop sign. Felt like an iron vault when he slammed my fingers it. 'Hold them steady,' he said. Nobody ever disobeyed my father. There was always something worse he could do."

I can't think of what to say.

"He kept slamming my fingers in it, over and over. He told me to hold them steady and think about the car. Think only about the car. 'This will cure you,' he told me. 'This will cure you of wanting things before your time. That aren't yours to have.'"

I look at the disappearing lakes. Is this supposed to tell me why he wouldn't drive for so long, or is it simply the reason I can't drive right this minute? He shakes his head again, as if I'd asked out loud.

"From that day forward, I never spoke another word of French."

A transport truck appears in the mirrors, growling up slowly behind us, stopping the longest flow of words I've ever heard from him.

That night in the motel, though, he says: "It was the only thing I had to get back at him with. The only thing he couldn't take away from me himself."

We find a road that takes us right to the water's edge. We want to scrub our grimy hides clean with salt. We comb the coast of the Gaspésie for a decent beach, but the shoreline is confettied with the shiitake mushroom bodies of jellyfish. They look like squashed hearts, flattened but still beating, raw veins throbbing through the translucent skin. Finally, he snorkels in spite of them; he's itching to try out the mask I gave him as a present at the start of our trip. What he doesn't know is that I found it by the Lake Ontario shoreline, washed up, unclaimed. I try not to ponder the fate of its previous owner as I chart his progress, watch the small white tube ride the murky tide. It looks as if the water's smoking a stubby cigarette, which makes me laugh since that's another thing you're never supposed to do around my father's heart.

"Nah," he says afterward, when I ask him if he's seen anything disgusting. But I can tell he's only trying to protect me, to spare me from dark visions of electric eels and sea snakes cozying up to the salt-candied knots the water makes in my hair.

The silence he makes wakes me out of a soggy dream and I'm startled by the sight of my father on the cot in the corner, sleeping with his snorkeling mask still on. But then my eyes adjust, and I see the white fabric cradling his forehead and chin. So this is what I saw earlier, not quite under his bed, what in the quick lightning of my averted gaze I'd taken to be a pair of discarded Jockey shorts. There are things about your dad, I'd thought, you just don't want to see.

This is the first room we've shared (money's starting to get low), so it's the first time I've heard—not heard—him sleep with this new machine, this apnea apparatus. It's supposed to avoid what happened before, when his breathing stopped in his sleep and his heart seized up in empathy or fear. But it erases his snoring, too, and I'm spooked by the absence of his usual nasal roar. I wait, propped on my elbows, for some sign of life. Finally a voice, as if from far away, gargling underwater. Doll, it says. Go back to sleep. He speaks it into the mask, and the machine bubbles angrily at this small surfacing, this tiny rebellion against its regulating air. It sounds like a caldron on the boil, ready to swallow him whole.

Yes, my father calls me "Doll." Though from him, I actually sort of like it. Anyone else would be dead.

Because of the machine, he doesn't need very much sleep. He used to wake up an average of sixty times a night from his stopped breathing, which left him, allowing five minutes for drifting back off each time, about three hours of sleep a night. He got used to it. Now that the machine lets him sleep right through, after three hours, he's awake. He's raring, he says, to go.

Where to? I ask. Just out. He goes out every night of our trip together. Drives around, he says. To practice. He generally leaves after he thinks I'm asleep, and rolls back in around four. I try to picture him prowling around these strange roads, smiling at the floodlit churches bigger than the towns themselves, peering at the hieroglyphic warnings of the language he's never tried to remember. It just doesn't seem very *him*.

One night, Dad and I go out to a French Canadian country bar. Actually, he goes, and I sneak in after. I want to know what's up. In Percé, it's perfect: we get a deal on a suite, so we each have our own room. I climb out my window when he thinks I'm asleep and I stow myself in the back of the van. He seems to take longer tonight, but finally he ambles out of the motel, hikes up his rugger pants, and climbs in.

I stay out in the parking lot for a long while. DANCING EN LIGNE TOUTES LES SOIRÉES admits the sign. Oh, God: this is only slightly better than the worst I'd feared. And Jell-O wrestling cannot necessarily be ruled out yet.

But there is only a smattering of couples ambling around the dance floor. There's a live band, probably because there aren't enough recorded country songs in French to fill an entire SOIRÉE. I'm sidling up to the bar in time to a very loose translation of Kenny Rogers when I spot my dad over in the corner. He doesn't see me, doesn't seem to see anything: he's pumping loonies into a machine that's marked, hysterically, LOTTO VIDEO LOTTO WIN WIN WIN.

There are a couple of empty glasses around him already, one half full of a liquid I hope I recognize.

I turn to the bartender. "*Avez-vous du* root beer?" I ask her. This is my father's permissible poison.

She gives me a really strange look, which I'm pretty sure includes a glance over in my dad's direction. "Yeah." She's not impressed. A few gum smacks, a few beats. "One?"

I shake my head now as if *she's* the one who's crazy. I order a Long Island, in English, with diet Coke. I feel guilty for doubting him, but I'm satisfied. About that, at least.

But after a couple of hours, he hasn't moved and I'm out of money. I go back to the van and pass out under the blankets. When I feel us moving again, I open my eyes and I can see daylight filtering in through the weave in the wool.

"Don't you want to go and see the place you grew up in?" I ask him.

"We did see it. We passed right through it. About three days ago. There was nothing there," he says.

"You mean the house had been torn down? Where was it, along the coast?"

He shakes his head repeatedly, three separate sets of no.

"It wasn't just the house. It was everything. There was nothing there."

3. Apnea

Five-twenty A.M., our last morning in Percé. We haul our motel room chairs across the highway to watch the sun rise over the ancient, gargantuan rock. But it seems to get stuck at the eponymous hole, it hovers there, not quite sure it wants to get up just yet. "Dad," I say, because his head has rolled back on his shoulders, his body growling through the furtive, larcenous jungle of machineless sleep. The rock winks over its illuminated eye; the sky flushes a purple, streaky blush. "Dad," I say again. He's going to miss it. The deep crevices in the rock and the puckered skin of his eyelids dance an arrhythmic pas de deux, flicker in and out of focus, light flashing and receding in the Janus-minded tease of a narcoleptic dream.

It's up. He's missed it. I stand and stretch, ready myself for the long drive back into the world. "Dad," I say.

I don't mean to be, but I'm shouting.

I sit back down and close my eyes. I still see him but it's a different image. A week earlier, stuck out of the top of our van, shouting, "*Bonne Fête*" in someone else's voice. He said *fête* like "fight," which made me cringe. We'd turned a corner one morning, the morning of the *Fête de L'Acadie*, and found ourselves shipwrecked right in the middle of a noise-making parade, a pot-and-pan approximation of wild carnival riot. He'd thrust his shoulders up through the popped sunroof, telling me to grab the wheel, eager to belie the cold foreignness of our sober blue van and Ontario plates. Get down, shut up, put your arms in, do not stand up! I'd wanted to yell, but I was laughing too hard.

I'd watched, entranced, as the features of the Acadians leached into his through his gaping, gorgeous, unfamiliar grin. But then I noticed a plastic pail from some casino pulled upside down over his head like a jester's crown.

"Where did you get that?" I asked, later.

"Get what?"

"Never mind."

He breathes beside me, ignoring my calls. Breathes as deeply, with as much abandon, as if he were in love with the air itself.

His pants have been thrown on in such haste they're inside out. Stuck to the insides of the pockets are the gummy remainders of scratch-and-lose blackjack tickets, like the fused corpses of the candied mints I always stick in my pockets after meals in restaurants. I edge closer but I guess they've been through the washing machine: it's impossible to tell whether he's won or lost. All that's left is a clotted mess, a jagged rainbow of torn and melted color.

I get out of the shower and open the door a crack to let the steam pour out. I wait until the ghosts have almost evaporated from the mirror and then I lift my right eye up to it, contact lens poised on the index finger of my right hand.

"Shut the door, I'm changing," he yells.

The lens goes in and in the sudden surge of vision I see him kneeling beside the bed, already dressed. A newspaper and what must be lottery tickets are spread out all over it; looking quickly at the other bed, I see that one is full of tickets too. I try to find my dad's face but before my eye can reach it, the door slams shut.

Two hours later, we're sitting in the van, everything loaded in. We're ready to go back.

"How much are you down?" I ask him.

No response but twitch of facial nerve. I press on. "I mean, should I be walking around with knee pads on, or what?"

He slams out of the van. Another day's delay.

Halfway back to Montréal, the casino in Charlevoix: "Just one hour," he says. "I promise." We were supposed to use this day to try out the roller coaster at La Ronde. But now that I know about it—that this is what he does—it's like he has this whole new freedom, a freedom I've given him. So what can I say?

It's like an airport inside, all glass and mirrors, people standing with their backs to one another, stagnant din. I watch him for a while, the way he can communicate with the dealers without words. I've never seen him do anything so well before. I've never liked him less.

"Here," he says, handing me a plastic pail full of quarters. It's a banishment, as if he's told me to go play in the sandbox.

I wander over to the bar and ask the guy for the stiffest drink he knows. I expect him to laugh at me, or to pretend he can't speak English. I'm only seventeen. But to my surprise, he pushes it at me, something neon and nameless, along with a grand, loopy smile. I sit at a table with my bin of quarters secured between my legs and I put my head down into the cradle of my arms, away from the smoke, the bells, the glare, the garish, garish waste of our lives.

I dream of a slick, muscle-bound Pan rising up to greet me from an ocean of reeds. He has a great goatee, and I like his sound. But Dad takes one look at him and says, "Don't trust a single thing that guy tells you."

When I come up, shaking seaweed from my hair, the bartender looks different. In fact, he might be different. In further fact, all of the faces at the tables look other than they did before, as if they've been shuffled. I find a clock and—goddamn him—we've been here for over three hours. I wander around, poke my face into the stiff, suited backs at the roulette tables. Not there. I plop myself at a machine near the entrance and wait, decide I may as well play my quarters out. The more expensive machines need special tokens, but the twenty-five-cent ones are for old ladies and neophytes, they don't even flatter us by requiring a translation. So I feed the quarters in directly, and the machine eats them without so much as a burp. One after the other, an automated chant. I'm almost at the bottom of the pail. Then my touch lands on something that feels like a mistake. Larger, look: blue-and-red plastic. A five-hundred-dollar chip. A thin elastic band tripled around it.

I turn it over. In its center is a small square piece of paper, pulled slightly to one side by the grip of the elastic.

BUS FARE. DON'T DRINK IT ALL. LOVE ALWAYS. D.

He must be the only father on earth who would sign "D" for Dad. Still, I appreciate his attempt to let me feel mysterious. In keeping with the absurd romanticism of the gesture, I don't cash in the chip, pocketing it instead in case I'm ever back this way.

But I feel cheated. I'd always wondered how he'd go; I'd been rewriting and rehearsing it in my imagination for ages. Would he rocket off the side of a waterslide, would his heart stop at the top of the Death Drop, would his breathing seize up in the middle of a frightening, a beautiful, a dirty dream? Perhaps he'd be attacked by rabid dogs or teenagers, Satan worshipers, or barroom thugs. I had pictured myself in all of these different scenarios, saving him. I didn't know, I never dreamed, that he'd write me out of the script.

Those evenings at Wonderland, we'd always been the last ones out of the park. We knew my mother would be waiting to drive us home, headlights fuming through the exhaust of the emptying lot, she refusing to turn off the engine, to admit defeat. We knew what sort of trip back we were making for ourselves, but we just couldn't leave. That last half hour was our favorite time: most people had gone home and we would run right off the rides, hop the fence, then right back up the path and on again, over and over, without the wait. For some reason they'd never allow us to just stay and ride again without running that circuit, even though no one else was waiting. But we were still grateful every time we got back up there and the thing was still running. Giddy with pleasure at having cheated closure again, that one last time.

I start walking toward the highway. Slowly. Breathe in, breathe out. It's not as if there's anywhere I have to be. We told my mother we didn't know when we'd be back. *Dad,* I say. This time, it comes out a whisper. My voice drowns in the sound of the water, still beating its eternal return, retreat, return in my ears.

Christopher A. Pasetto
University of Pittsburgh

WAITING FOR A CRASH

My parents sat in the living room, watching the Olympics on TV, waiting for the bomb to go off. On the road, it's called rubbernecking—when people slow down as they pass an accident. Mom said that folks do it to see if they can lend a hand. But Dad insisted that they want to get a good look at a dead body. He would never rubberneck on the road; TV was an altogether different animal. Dad watched every program like most people watch auto racing: waiting for a crash. Usually he taped stuff and made me watch it later on. "These are lessons on how life works," he would tell me. As the Olympics approached, the newspeople talked about the possibility of a terrorist attack. And wouldn't you know it, the day before the opening ceremonies a cassette got stuck in the video player (Dad's priceless tape of that politician shooting himself in the head). The machine whined, growled, and died. So, determined to make the best of a bad situation, Dad glued himself to the set. He would call to me every once in a while. "Clay," he would shout, "something's going to happen. I can feel it." Maybe under other circumstances, I would have gone downstairs to watch. But I was waiting, too. That night, the National UFO Reporting Center Web site went nuts. The reports choked the phone lines; my computer fought to keep up as I downloaded everything to my hard drive. It was the night I found out about the alien ship.

Millard County, UT—18 June 1996—Many witnesses, including members of the local police force, observe an intense
green-orange "fireball" moving first west and then turning,
heading downward in a northerly direction, crashing in the
Sevier Desert.

By morning my shoulders were cramped and my eyeballs grated
against my lids: I felt deformed. As I walked downstairs to get breakfast, fatigue hit me at head level. I sat there at the table and ate cold
cereal slowly. I watched the sugars from each flake diffuse into the
milk. Dad sat across from me and dug his fingers into an apple. Mom
moved at her morning pace, walking everywhere at once. She
stopped and touched her belly, already swelling, and said to no one in
particular, "Alexandra."

"No," said Dad. "Too large. She'd be pressured to grow into it."

"Esther," offered Mom.

"The name of a senior citizen. Eighty years old on the day she's
born."

"Joyce."

Dad turned in his chair to look at her. "Are you insane?" he asked.
"Do you want to sentence your daughter to serve as a minor office
functionary to every ass-pinching executive boob in the United
States?"

"There are a lot of writers named Joyce," Mom protested. "She
could grow up to be a writer."

"No one reads a Joyce," Dad said in disgust, as he looked over at
me. He looked closely. "Something wrong?" he asked.

"Hm?" said Mom. She'd already gone back to touching her belly,
poking it like a melon to feel its firmness.

"I'm talking to Clay," Dad said.

I told them both "I'm fine," but my voice was lousy with the lie.
Mom just nodded. Dad eyed me suspiciously, but said nothing else.
Off to the side, where Mom couldn't see, he made a thumbs-down
gesture at me.

I felt sick on the bus, of course. I leaned against the window and
kept my eyes pasted to the road. The winter's salts still stained the
asphalt white in places, like smudges of chalked names. The snow

had fallen deep that year in Ithaca, slanting southward out of Canada. So deep that the snow days kept us in school till late June. Students cursed the winter all year long. I cursed silently, head aching, and the bus hit all the bumps.

A month before, I couldn't have given a damn about UFOs. Computer games were the singularity of my adolescence before then. A black hole that let nothing escape. There were moments when I wondered if I would ever pull free. Somehow I did, every so often, to eat, sleep, attend school. So life was computer games, and the occasional porno site on the World Wide Web. I was fifteen years old.

Somewhere in between the Bone Storm Frequently Asked Questions and the Top Ten Tits of the Day, I followed a link into the world of UFOs and EBEs and many other acronyms. Http://www.sti/m-parades.entrance.html; Miguel Parades for short. His page was a soapbox and slide show presented in a sleek, animated gallery. Above the doorway entrance, a unique piece of advice changed daily:

ALIEN HYBRIDS—OR MEN IN BLACK—ALL WEAR DARK SUNGLASSES BECAUSE THEIR MUTANT EYES ARE IMMEDIATELY RECOGNIZABLE TO ORDINARY HUMANS. IF SOMEONE IN DARK SUN-GLASSES OFFERS YOU A RIDE, DO NOT GO WITH HIM!

The interface allowed you to click on various document icons—all leading to Parades's finger-pointing rants on life, liberty, and the pursuit of E.T. The ufological photo museum really put the hook in me. There's one picture of an alien (your typical gray boy: short, hairless, big head, narrow body, my father naked) shaking hands with President John F. Kennedy in the Oval Office. In another photo, an alien leads Elvis up a waffle-steel ramp into an iridescently glowing spaceship. The two of them hold hands as the smaller fellow takes an aging, bloated King to a brighter world. Parades had other photographs of ships in midflight, portraits of shaken astronauts, close-ups of alien autopsies. This being my first encounter with UFO culture, who could blame me for losing sleep, falling into that particular rabbit hole? What fifteen-year-old boy would have resisted the allure, when the first hit was that potent, rang so loud, and touched all the bases?

Besides, school was just a walk-through at that point in the year. No one wanted to be there. I safely nodded off in every class but one. Information Theory. Our final projects were due soon and I hadn't even started mine yet. So talking to the teacher at the end of class seemed a good reason for me to stay awake. But there was another. There was a girl.

Tamichi Hurt, Tammy for short. She sat next to me. I don't think she was Asian, but she had long black hair like fine wires. She let it hang in bundles that would just eat up light. One of the few juniors in class, she had a year on me. Taller than me, too. She didn't talk much. But when she talked, smart and quick, it put you off. Sometimes, after Tammy made a comment, I'd try to catch her eye. She had a way of tilting her head down and looking up at you, looking at you with those dark brown eyes. With absolutely no red veins in the corners of them, innocent eyes like cartoons, hooded and maddening. I never could match her gaze for long. But my gaze was still pulled toward her, drifting there almost magnetically.

I contemplated all of this as I sat on the toilet before class, cramps clenching my stomach into a painful fist. This was my visceral reaction to Tamichi Hurt, knowing I'd see her soon. There was no reasoning past it; I shit every day before Info Theory.

When I got there, she'd already assumed her characteristic hunch at the desk next to mine. I saw a pen between our desks and picked it up. I put it on Tammy's desk. "You dropped this."

She glanced at it, at me with the eyes. "It's not mine," she said. But she left it there and foolishly I stared at it throughout class.

On my way to the front of the room, I brushed by Tammy. Miss February Quenard watched me approach, waited. On the first day of class, her appearance had made us all groan. Frankly, she was dumpy and schoolmarmish. An unwieldy black woman with silver hair and hexagonal-rim glasses. In reality, Miss February (as she preferred to be addressed) turned out to be both formal and friendly. "Mr. Griggs," she greeted me. She lifted her glasses over her face and peered closely.

As I prepared to speak, I looked down at her desk. She had a little sign that said IGNORANCE IS POTENTIAL KNOWLEDGE.

I said, "I have a question about information."

"What a coincidence, Mr. Griggs." She smiled; her lips shined.

"You told us that if things are made clearer, it's good. It's information."

Miss February nodded vigorously.

I nodded also. My books started to slip out of my hands, exhaustion was killing off my nerves. "What if the more I gather, the more confusing it seems?"

"Then it's not information."

"What is it?"

"It's bullshit," she said, shrugging at her own casual profanity. "But there may be information buried inside. Do not get bogged down in what could have happened but didn't. You only have until next Wednesday, Mr. Griggs."

I continued to nod. The books started to fall.

"Is that all?" Miss February asked. "You should really feel free to ask these questions in front of the class."

I gathered my things and retreated from the room, jittery and shambling. She watched me bow out the door gracelessly, possibly wondering if I was on drugs.

I dreamed my way through the rest of the day and finally returned home. In my room, I looked briefly at the bed. Then I rebooted the computer. New postings flickered into existence on my monitor screen. Reports of reports.

> USAir 894: We just passed traffic on the left wing, uh, about 2000 to 3000 feet above us. It, uh. Um. What the hell traffic was it?
>
> FAA: That was not our traffic, USAir.

Mom knocked on the door and I was in bed, panicked for a second as I wondered how I got there. At some point, I must have leaned toward it a little, and the pillow reached to meet me halfway. "I'm coming," I said. I gulped the contents of my mouth, which tasted like glue.

She ushered me downstairs, where Dad waited. He said, "Your mother and I have reached a point of decision." They made me sit on the couch between the two of them, right on the spot that sank to the springs. From either side they looked down on me like Egyptian sentinels, and put me on the short end of a good talking to. I spent too much time inside with that damn computer, they said. It wasn't healthy: Dad was gracious enough to point out the rings around my eyes, my sallow skin, poor posture, and general boniness. And I didn't have any friends. "Isn't there anyone in school?" Mom worried. Why didn't I have kids come over to the house? Staring at my feet, I bore generous amounts of these and like things on the top of my head. And though my parents' words stung me, it was familiar water, a recurring theme of our talks—that and televised disasters.

As a short-term solution, Dad sent me on a quest, something to get me out of the house. I would hand-deliver a package to a writer who lived at the other end of our neighborhood. "He's sort of in hiding," Dad said.

I held the package, a sheaf of pages wrapped in brown paper, solemnly before me and calculated the distance and time of the walk. "What is it?"

"Wouldn't you like to know?"

Giving Dad a look, Mom said to me, "It's your father's book."

I made a motion of weighing it. "Why not just mail it?" I asked.

"I told you, he's in hiding. He's got a thing about the mail."

"A thing?"

"I don't understand," Mom interjected. "He doesn't trust the US postal system?"

I told Dad, "Just call him up and tell him you're sending something."

"He doesn't answer the phone."

"So, I don't know, fax it or something."

"Doesn't he trust the phone company?" Mom asked.

"Look," Dad said to her, over my head, "you're not getting the point. It was your idea to get Clay out more."

"Why don't you drive me over there?" I suggested.

"You need the walk. The air."

"We can roll down the car windows."

"Clay," he said, and the last word had been spoken. I struggled and climbed up out of the hole in the couch. Head hanging low, feet dragging, I laid the Trail of Tears act on pretty thick.

Mom said to Dad, "Robert, I hope you're not sending Clay to the house of a crazy person."

Dad just yelled after me. "You be damn careful with that manuscript, Clay."

At that point in my life, Dad's behavior toward me seemed neither strange nor threatening. He taught classes on English Victorian literature at Cornell, and somehow this meant that in everything he would expect the worst. Clearly he obsessed over the idea of being at the head of a twisted Gothic household. A Heathcliff of Ithaca. Dad took the Oedipus story way too seriously; I was, in my father's mind, his mortal enemy. When I was four years old, he tucked me into bed one night and explained the way life works: I would kill him, or he would kill me.

For some reason, I never took him very seriously. He comes across as something of a joker—a shriveled, glaring Jerry Lewis. I think that I disappointed him by not living up to his tragic expectations. I tried to keep his hopes up, though. When Dad asked me to pee in a plastic bag, I did. He mailed it off for drug tests. The negative results must have broken his heart.

I held his package tight to my stomach like a compress, and I walked. The hills bulged to meet my steps. Bleached neighborhoods and old houses with steep roofs leaned one into another. I wondered what Millard County looked like, if places were basically the same everywhere. I mentally reviewed the reports. Literally hundreds of inexpert witnesses testified as to what shape in the night sky streaked where at so-and-so rate of speed, and why Mr. and Mrs. Kirkwood just happened to have a video camera mounted on a tripod in their bedroom in the middle of the night. I pecked at those stories in my mind until my brain could digest no more contradictions. Dusk had come upon the town and I hadn't slept in days. By the time I reached the writer's house, mental and physical exhaustion were Sumo-sized: two fat men crushing me between their powerful bellies.

The house of George Lindberg the Writer was tall and off-white, roofed by numerous gables facing in all directions. I took the steps to the front door and rang the doorbell. My legs started to itch as I stood still; I sweated into my T-shirt, into my shoes. The sound of slow footfalls inside the house, then light poured through the opening door and spread like a smile.

And Tamichi Hurt gaped at me, puzzled.

She wore a long baseball jersey and, though I couldn't tell until later, invisibly short shorts. Tammy glistened, beautiful, and her hair hung in tangles. I froze, of course. For the first time, I stared directly at her face for quite a while. Her wide forehead, her long nose pointing like a blunt arrow toward her mouth, her cheeks and ears. Her brown eyes blinking.

"Hey," Tammy said in the most offhand way, "you're in my information class. You've got a funny name."

"I'm Clay Griggs." My voice sounded too high, childish, Muppet speak. The corners of her mouth hooked upward in an indifferent way. I decided to fib, a little. "I, um, forgot your name."

She told me; it was worth lying to hear her say it. "Do you live around here?" she asked. "Do you need that book on yellow journalism? When I took it out of the library, I figured you'd come looking."

My head puffed obscenely, like a helium balloon. The fact that Tammy had noticed me and remembered that our topics were similar, plus that she thought of me outside of school. Well, she didn't remember my name but I could rightfully claim the elevated status of "you." I could feel the balloon effect carry me upward, stretching out my neck and spine. "No," I said, "I'm here to see Mr. Lindberg. Is this the right house?"

Tammy frowned full on. She glanced behind her, into the golden brown recesses of the foyer, lit by electric candles the color of buttered toast. The door started to swing closed. For a second I thought maybe that was it. Good-bye, dorky kid. But then she came back, all business. "Who are you looking for again? What's this about?"

I took a breath. "I'm here for Mr. Lindberg. Professor Griggs is my dad. He wanted me to bring him this." I made a movement with my father's package, and came off looking like I was masturbating a rectangular organ with both hands.

"Oh," Tammy said. She walked inside and waved me in behind her. When I started walking again I had all sorts of extra joints to manage.

"Hey, Dad," she yelled up the curving stairs. "There are some papers here for you from Professor Griggs!" She bounded up two steps and perched there, extended. I lost a heartbeat as her shirt rose—then I saw the shorts.

A voice returned to us, and it seemed to bounce off many walls, distant and low and traveling out of a maze. "Is he here?"

"No."

"Don't let that bastard in this house!" shouted the esteemed Mr. Lindberg.

"He's not here, Dad," Tammy replied patiently.

"Well, how do you know it's from him, then? This didn't come in the mail."

"His son is here."

"For the love of God, don't let him in the house!"

The itching in my legs turned all the way up. Bugs bled into my guts. Tammy didn't look back at me. She pitched a yell upward. "He's already in the house."

Hurried rustling sounds, stamping through the ceiling. "I'm coming down in one second. I'm getting my gun."

"Dad," Tammy shouted playfully, like it was a game between them. I hoped so for my sake.

A short pause. "Tell him to come back in late February," the shout dwindled to a speaking voice. "Tell him I'm not home. I've passed on. And then burn those papers."

"Okay," Tammy answered him. She faced me and drew close, and she rolled her eyes in exasperation. But it was a forced roll, meant to explain what was perfectly clear to her. "Don't worry," Tammy told me as she looked at me under her lashes, whispering, "Late February is our code. I'll give it to him later on." I felt her breath on my face, incensed air off the wings of angels.

"Thanks," I said. And then I felt foolish. There was nothing left but to leave; I'd outlasted my purpose. So I improvised, as a good fool should. "While I'm here, I wouldn't mind looking at that book. If it's okay."

Tammy shrugged; the thin shirt rasped against her shoulders. "Sure." She walked down the hall a few steps, stopped, looked back at me, puzzled again. "Come on, Clay Griggs." My name, sculpted upon her lips. My stomach tightened up.

"This is a, um, big house," I chirped behind her, just like an idiot. "Do you have any brothers or sisters?"

She coughed. I think it was supposed to be a laugh, but I was nervous and the explosive sound made me jump. "I have hundreds," she told me, "with names like Monroe Vinici, Sharon Altergott, Bobby Joe Glenn, Baron 'Stitches' Williams." I was trying to convince myself that it was okay to be attracted to a crazy person, when she explained, "They're all made up. I'm made up, too. I'm one of my father's characters."

It took me a second. "He named you after a character that he wrote?"

"Yeah," she said. Then, like I was entirely stupid, "My last name is different than his."

"Right. I didn't want to say anything before. I just figured, well, you know."

"Divorce? Nah." She stopped and turned toward me, and smiled. As if divorce seemed funny to her. She stopped at a white door. It seemed out of place next to all the wood grains and subtle yellows. She turned the knob.

"Where are we?" I asked her.

Tammy tossed her hair and said, "Home."

I do not suppose I was much different from many inexperienced boys throughout time who have fantasized about the private living quarters of the other sex as a space of intense sexual mystery. I imagined a Cleopatric place of cushions heaped like soft jewels and air clotted with occult spice. And I saw that place, in a way. Tammy led me to a room where piles of pillows touched the ceiling, inordinate quantities of pillows. Some of the pillows were stuffed animals. A Mediterranean scent encircled me; Tammy had a microwave in the corner and she withdrew a cup of ramen noodles from its shrouded recesses.

"Want some?" she asked.

I nodded, starving for the smell. She heated another for herself. The food warmed and untied something in me. I felt unbelievably comfortable, more comfortable than I'd ever been with anyone else. It was her treating me as an equal in a Styrofoam-packed handshake. We forgot about the book. Tammy and I sat cross-legged on amorphous padding and talked. She laughed at my description of Miss Quenard; her laugh sounded like another cough. She told me a story about a nasty accident she had had riding her bike. Cheerful, Tammy showed me the shining red scars on her knees.

"What's it like," I asked her, "living with your dad?"

"It's okay, I guess. You have to get past the weirdness." She pulled her hair up in a tight tail. "Mostly I hang out with my mom," she said. "She's pretty down-to-earth. She showed me how to masturbate."

I choked on my food. Tammy put her hand on my arm and apologized.

"Oh, I'm sorry! Sometimes I forget that I'm talking to people."

It seemed a strange thing to say. But I was getting my wind back and I said, "That's okay. I have the same problem." Her legs bare and bony; I stared. "Does he ever go out?"

"Who?"

"Your dad."

"Sometimes," she said. "Sometimes, when he's just released a new book, he'll go out in disguise. A homeless person, a blind man, even a woman once." Tammy rolled her eyes, this time in earnest. "As if people are really looking for him."

She laughed. Small, hacking spasms at first, then uncontrollably. I caught the disease. Seeing her smile made me want to get infected. My own laugh sounded like a real one played backward. "Ah ah ah." We laughed together. I asked her, "So no one's looking for him?"

"I don't know," Tammy said, and she stopped laughing. "At least, I've never been approached or anything. Now you've got me thinking that my life is creepier than it really is." She mauled a stuffed white bear or dog. Brightening quickly, she said, "Maybe that wouldn't be so bad. I love *The X-Files*. Do you watch it?"

What could I say? Once I had sampled the all-night buffet of the UFO-aware underground, fiction (and science fiction) had nothing to offer me. Maybe that was my dad's influence—all those forced hours of *Cops* ruined me for L. Ron Hubbard and *The X-Files*. I saw myself as one of the few real people walking and breathing, Mr. Rogers in the Land of Make-Believe. Kid stuff, I thought.

But instead of saying all that, I swallowed hard. The truth was a lump going the wrong way. Mechanically, I said, "I love *The X-Files*," voice cracking.

"Hey," Tammy started, loud and sudden, "you should come with me to the university library on Saturday."

"I should?"

"My dad always has me pick up books for him. Research for his latest novel. You'll like some of the freaky stuff he has me pull out."

The thoughts of a split second: Did the invitation entail some kind of "date"? Was Tammy implying that I went in for "freaky" or, worse, that I was freaky? I said, "Sounds great." And I worried, Where am I going to get Cliff's Notes for *The X-Files* before Saturday?

I got home late, much later than I had expected. Numbly, I powered on my computer and watched it silently allocate memory blocks. Lord knew how much network activity I had missed out on, but then there was Tamichi Hurt. I fingered the keys to match the word in my head: PERFECT. Could lived days be saved to disk? I wondered. An anxiety struck me—that it would all be lost if I didn't back it up twice—and I immediately recognized that my parents were right in one thing, at least. I'd been spending too much time with the computer.

With the image of Tammy Hurt still burned into my tired retinas, I allotted myself ten minutes. It would only take that long to check the Web. Then big sleep, I promised myself. I connected to the host and patched into the National UFO Reporting Center's Web site. Total exhaustion dulled the shock, as I found absolutely nothing. No new reports. The newsgroups had gone back to bickering, the usual threads like "Earn Fast $$$ Working at Home" and "All Niggers Must Die" and my favorite, "A Quick Annihilation Is Too Good for Humans, A Horrible Fatal Illness from Outer Space Is Only Fair." I searched for records of the old reports to see where they ended—but, as if the incident in Millard County had never existed, the computer mocked me with a blank stare. Dried up. Blacked out. Nothing. Even Miguel Parades's page was under construction. Bands of safety yellow tape crossed his doorway, and beyond, the animated GIF homologues of hard-hat laborers bobbed back and forth. Only a note above the door remained:

MY THEORIES CAN ALL BE CONFIRMED IN A GOVERNMENT INTERNET DATABASE WHICH CAN BE FOUND AT RANDOM ADDRESSES.

I slept, finally, fitfully. I woke at intervals tangled in python coils of my sheets, brought to consciousness by the sound of my own voice. My father may have entered the room at some point, or I dreamed his silhouette in the doorway.

In the morning, I took a large piece of poster board from under my bed and created a detailed flow chart in the style of Miss February, complete with crooked boxes. I tried to link up all of the different Millard County reports, but too many holes riddled the picture, too many contradictions. I filled the gaps with question marks. The questions outnumbered the facts, and the facts were fighting with one another. By the time I went downstairs for breakfast, my poster appeared to be a perfect diagram of a massacre.

The day passed like an interminable series of salesmen—even simple tasks such as showering and eating seemed a distraction. I envied the life of George Lindberg, tucked away behind the protective measures of his own Daedalian labyrinth. School annoyed me only so much as I was asked to apply my mind to things. Walking from room to room, fumbling with combination locks, the ultimate expenditure of answering questions in class. "Clay, what is contained in the purloined letter?" "Clay, what is the logarithm of equiprobable events?" "Clay, how are you today?"

This last was Tammy. I answered as eagerly and attentively as I could, but that may have been only a friendly mumble and a sparse nod. If I had thought about it more, I would've been surprised that she said anything to me. Outside of school, speaking to someone a grade lower than yourself carries no risk. But within the building people notice, they talk. Tammy didn't seem to care. At some point I realized that Tammy was no more popular than I; she was beautiful and intelligent, quirky and alone. And I was alone, too.

Where was my head, so far removed from even the alluring, bowel-wrenching Miss Hurt? I reviewed the facts that I'd collected already regarding Millard County. I considered the reasons for the communication blackout, of course. But foremost in my mind was a more personal kind of anxiety. To cross the line from passive watcher of the network data stream to a source, a hand in the water, meant going over to the other side. I had regarded my until-then limited and passive participation in the Internet as "still safe." But the publicization of one's ideas via computer network seemed like a tattoo that read simply: WEIRDO. Still, after poring and brooding and folding this problem over and over, I found that I couldn't extract myself. The loose slaughter of computer games had ceased to thrill me. Naked women twisted into pretzel shapes made me go soft. I considered the possibility of an inconclusive, sterilized summer at home. And then I put my fingers on the keyboard and tapped.

I sent out a tame little note asking for anyone with further information on Millard County to please e-mail it to: c-griggs@pub.ithaca3.edu. I posted the note on alt.ufo.conspiracy and other like-minded newsgroups and electronic bulletin boards. The deed done, my hands trembling, I slept well for the first time in days.

The following morning, a Saturday, I awoke to the sound of Mom and Dad playing their cat-and-mouse name game downstairs.

"Dolores," Mom said.

"It means 'pains.'"

"Annette?"

"I used to date an Annette. She broke my heart."

"Gwendolyn? Francesca? Christine?"

Dad cried, "Please! My tender ears!"

"I don't understand," I heard my mother complain. "You got to pick Clay's name. I want to name our daughter."

"Oh, come on. Clay doesn't count."

I loafed in my room until midday and played with my diagram poster. I imagined that the question marks were American Indians, and I penned feathery headdresses on them, gave each a war-paint face. The text boxes were members of a wagon train. I sketched wheels on them. I filled the air with arrows.

Initial responses to my note were disappointing, to say the least. Foremost among them was the message from Hill Air Force Base, claiming that a test craft launched from its strip had crashed in the southern desert on the night of June 18. Clearly, the note said, it was all a huge misunderstanding.

The other messages ranged from openly abusive to strangely chilling. An older man from a town to the north of Ithaca said he was also interested in the Millard County incident, and wondered if we could get together in a secluded place and compare notes. The High Priestess of the Church of the Real assured me that in Millard County, as everywhere else, "Everything is in its place." A man who called himself Frank Stranges claimed to have been abducted by aliens on the night of June 18—no mention of how a crashed ship had taken him to the far reaches of the star system—and over a hundred times previously. "All Class 4 abductions," he assured me, "with at least one Class 5, where I recalled a past life." I stopped reading at the point where Stranges began to describe the process of his own impregnation.

In the afternoon I met Tammy at the university library and she waved as I approached. Beautiful from a distance, too. Her black hair tied back, wearing denim shorts and a plain white T-shirt, an army knapsack. Tammy's smile seemed as open and friendly as humanly possible. She winked to add to the effect.

"Hi, Clay," Tammy said. She said my name with such ease and familiarity. Then she handed me a piece of paper. "Here's our list for the day."

I only glanced at it before she walked off, leaving me to follow after the shadowed backs of her knees. We descended through stairwells, where Tammy had to duck her head. Doors slammed behind us. The fluorescents trembled between light and dark states. By their indecisive glow, on the move, I stared ahead and walked in the wake of Tammy's smell: a perfumed soap, light sweat, something in hair care.

"You've been here before," I panted, trying to keep up with her.

"Every week," Tammy replied over her shoulder. "I don't even need to use the computer catalog anymore."

She turned sharply and began touching darkened book spines, as if she was feeling for the names.

"Help me look," she said.

I glanced helplessly at the shelves, then at the list she'd given me. "What for?"

"The title is either *Plastic Reconstructive Surgery* or *Reconstructive Plastic Surgery.*"

I got down on my knees and searched the low shelves while she scanned the high ones. I didn't help much, but our bodies occasionally rubbed together in the dusk.

Tammy asked me, "What's your dad like?"

It threw me off guard. First of all, because I had forgotten that we were picking up books for her father. Second, because no one had ever really asked me a direct question about my dad like that. I didn't know where to begin.

"He thinks I'm going to kill him," I told her. "He says it's all a son can aspire to."

"Weird," said Tammy. I wanted to stand up and hug her for putting my dad in place with one word. I loved her for it. There in the nether levels of Cornell's library, I must have glowed. "Are you looking?" she asked me.

"Yes."

Tammy placed her hand on my back and stretched above me. Her stomach touched my cheek. When Tammy came down, I was to be the proud bearer of *Plastic and Reconstructive Surgery*. We moved on as before: Tammy whisking smoothly forward and me sputtering behind like a kite that won't fly. We passed through uncountable stacks, floors, rooms, corridors, stairwells, with Tammy heaping books into my arms as we traveled. I bore the load and ran to keep up—I thought if I lost her I might be lost forever. Every time I believed I knew where we were, Tammy touched a button and quiet engines shuttled a section of shelves sideways for us.

When we'd gone through the list, Tammy found a table and I dumped the books down noisily. But there was more. Mr. Lindberg's list had topics assigned to each book—once we found the volumes, Tammy (and I by extension) had to mark pertinent sections with slips of yellow paper.

"It's not hard," she assured me. "Besides, he doesn't use half of this stuff. Sometimes I think that he just does this to make me learn." Tammy shook her head and frowned.

"What? What's wrong?"

"I don't know. I've spent so much time with books, I feel like I've missed out on something. I feel like I've always been an adult. It's how my parents always treated me."

I reached a hand out toward her and put it flat on the table between us. "That doesn't seem so bad," I said.

She shrugged and tried to smile, but the frown wouldn't let go of her face. From then on, we kept our heads down low. I turned pages. I placed paper squares at random. There were pictures of faces in various stages of mutilation: open, sutured, unfortunate. Tammy Hurt within arm's length. I harbored lustful thoughts and fidgeted like an obedient dog waiting for the command to speak, with no one around to give it. What would I say to Tammy? Occasionally I glanced up at the direct top of her head, seeing where her wonderful hair had been woven into her skin. She read intensely and actively, moving her shoulders with the words. The lush tail of her hair swung from side to side.

Before I knew it, we headed out the door, into the failing light. Still I had nothing. There were no words. I stopped and handed her the heavy satchel of books. I screamed at myself: Say something, Clay!

"I'd better get going," Tammy said. She looked into the sky, at the murderous-looking clouds that tumbled together. The curve of her throat gave me a familiar stomach cramp.

"My mom's coming to get me," I said, too eager. "Do you need a ride?"

"I have my bike," she answered.

"Oh."

"I'll give you a call. Or I'll see you Monday."

That's it, I told myself. I blew it. "Yeah. I had fun."

Tammy smiled and turned away. I turned also, and then there was a touch upon my arm. Tammy. She handed me something and said, "My dad told me to give you this." It was a piece of paper with a name on it. D R VAN STAVEREN. "It's someone he worked with a while ago, when he wrote his science-fiction novel. Dad says the guy is a 'reverse engineer' and you'll know what that means."

"Wow," I mumbled. "Thanks, Tammy."

"Sure." She started off again.

"Tammy," I called after her, "did we talk about UFO stuff the other day?"

"I guess," she said. "You said you're doing your Info project on a UFO story on the Internet, right? And you said you were in a bind."

"Right. I forgot. Thanks again."

"See you." I watched her pedal from street light to street light, and felt a vague stirring in my heart that I thought was love but later came to recognize as paranoia.

As soon as I got home, I connected to the Internet and found that my small initiative had stirred up something. Some postings scattered throughout the newsgroups claimed that c-griggs was a government agent, attempting to snare some poor soul clutching desperately at his or her official secrets. Some repeated the information I already had; they mentioned the Air Force story of the experimental craft. I received a note that said that "alien abduction is a deeply uncon-scious form of white guilt as people are kidnapped by advanced 'races' and presumably made into slaves." Then there were inexplicable others, such as that of dmv21@aol.com.

REJOICE IN THE ENTROPY OF 0 = 21 minus itself. 21 because it is the sum of three 7s the number of apocalypse seals and because it is 1 subtracted from the number of letters in (United States Government). i face the inevitability of gradualness in holding 21 years of age and do not think i will live to see 22 (LOVE sum on your telephone dial) for fear of UNDE-TECTABLE EXTERMINATION. i have been unwittingly targeted by glowing gray jellyfish orbs malign on and before 6.18.96 and used also randomly as a NONPLANETARY TEST subject under persecution of radio cyborgation/nuclear alienation experimentation and disposal since 2 january 1984, against my will, consent and physical safety, myself used as a radio zombie with wipe on hormones and laser beam. this situation has prevented me of flourishment of life, LOVE, accumulation of wealth, a residence of my own being forced to live with my grandfather and wash the sores on his backside every morning. Donate money or even a manual typewriter to me for your only hope for a future: (BEAR ALL THINGS, BELIEVE ALL THINGS, HOPE ALL THINGS, BEWARE ALL THINGS.)

Notes like this only encouraged me to search for an Internet address to match the name Tammy's father had given me. D R Van Staveren. Dr. Van Staveren? I tried several different permutations of the name and came up with a good number of e-mail addresses. They all received a note similar to the one I had posted on the general Internet groups: looking for more information on the Millard County incident of 18 June 1996, can you help? And I added, Referred by Lindberg.

At the dinner table, I asked my dad, "What's a reverse engineer?"

"Why?" he said. "Where did you hear about it? From whom?"

"At the library today."

He narrowed his eyes. Mom went to get herself another helping of her five-inch-thick lasagna—and I thought Dad was going to give me the thumbs-down again. "I guess," he said quietly, "it's the opposite of a person who puts things together." When Mom came back, Dad touched her shoulder while she eased into a chair.

Mom said, viciously, "Phoebe."

The next morning, my electronic mailbox had a note from D. R. Van Staveren—which originated at the address: jan@mrbeans.charlotte.au.

My name is Maj. David R. Van Staveren and I am writign to you from a hi-tech coffee shop in San Francisco. I have kept a small piece of the Roswell "balloon" debris isnce I was there in the summer of 1947. I was a Blue Team recovery agent/reverse engineer at over 50 ohter bases including Hill near Millard County just days ago. You mention Lindberg and I hope that you are not an "author." Understand htat you face a difficult provlem Mr. Griggs. Mapping external qualities of the event to arrive at its internal motivation—which must remain necessarilty "alien." In this we are alike and my urge is to be frank withyou. I will tell you first of all to forget everything you learned from those lying SETI bastards. We arrived at the Salt Lake Desert site and saw the remains of a craft which appeared ot have been around 44 feet in diameter. Pure magnesium fragmnts with hieroglyphic markings were scattered over a ¾ mile area. The main body of it was embedded in teh sand and canted at an angle. I was there to determine the trajectory and velocitty of the ship. There were 2–12 badly burned "humanoids." I would like to tell you more but I am currently writing a children's book on the subject of alien abductio s and my publisher insists that I retain some "material" for the book tour.

The back of my neck tingled as I read, and reread, Van Staveren's message. I had been given a thing both fine and valuable, like a rare coin in the change slot of a vending machine. Elated, I saved the message to disk and printed out a hard copy. Then I looked it over again.

What had he told me? What had I learned? The bare facts only hinted at other, more fundamental parts of the story that I desperately needed to know. I began to make a list of questions for a second note to Van Staveren, hoping that I'd be able to contact him again. The list continued to build in my sleep, questions for the information angel, dreams of enlightenment.

Five minutes into my Info Theory class on Monday, the school-wide intercom delivered a pained wail of feedback, followed by a definite squelch, and then Vice Principal DeVries called me down to the office. Miss February let her glasses slide down her nose and looked at me. Tammy looked at me, too. Something made me afraid, my hands shook as I gathered my books. Tammy handed me something on a piece of paper: it was her phone number.

I passed through the swinging door to the office, and immediately the tension was there. It had a taste. The dentist's rubber-jacketed fingers working in your mouth.

From the end of a dim corridor, Vice Principal DeVries called, "This way, Mr. Griggs." He made a curt gesture, wagging his thick fingers. I never thought I would walk the length of that medieval hallway, the light fading into another time, a remote world. DeVries gazed imperiously down at me and held the door to his office open. With his massive jaw—I could see it hanging on the wall in a future museum, an exhibition of human atrocities—he motioned for me to go inside.

I entered. The vice principal didn't follow. He closed the door behind me. From the inside, I saw his figure in the frosted glass. I watched as it disappeared.

Wet breathing sounds in the room with me. Nightmares.

Turning, I took in the vice principal's office. Thin sheets of sunlight pierced the blinds, drew lines on the bookshelves, the desk, and hard-looking red leather chairs. A man wearing a black suit perched in one of these chairs. The bright stripes fell across his side like lashes. He had dark glasses on his face and a cane rested across his thighs. A massive German shepherd sat between the man's feet with its ears at attention. Loops of golden drool swung from the dog's tongue and black gums, spattering the worn carpeting.

"First of all," the man said, head inclined toward a spot on the ceiling, "I'd like to apologize for the interruption of your school day. Nothing more important than a boy's education."

I didn't say anything. Instead, I observed him quietly. His hair formed gray waves over the grid in his brow. His nose was thin, his lips thin. He was a model of perfect posture in the chair and he smiled over my head.

"You are Clay Griggs," he said.

It was one of those things people say that is not a question but a statement, so there's no clear way to answer.

"My name is Alan Smithy," he continued, easygoing and confident. "I am an agent of the Federal Bureau of Investigation. Do you know what that is?"

I nodded, then I said, "Yes." My voice was hoarse. The dog regarded me crookedly when I spoke.

Smithy said, "Why don't you have a seat, Griggs?"

The counsel of Miguel Parades came to mind readily: do not get in the car. I gingerly set myself in one of the chairs—as if forceful, abrupt movements would set off a bomb. The seat was uncomfortable, almost violent under my bony pelvis. Subject to a process of slow bruising, I squirmed.

"A piece of broken glass is still glass. It has its own place and completeness," Smithy said to me. "Why is that not enough? Why do we need to see the whole window?" I didn't know if I was supposed to answer these questions. "Oh, we try to," he went on, "but instead the pieces open up into a much more compelling truth, a beauty apart from oneself, fluttering into the unknown. But people aren't satisfied with that, they have to pin it all down."

He sighed, and the dog sniffed up at him.

"There's no appreciation of ambiguity anymore. No love of stories. I blame movies, and the steady increase in television news. What do you think?"

"I'm, um, sorry Mr. Smithy," I stammered, "but I don't understand."

Smithy cleared his throat and his head moved, like he was scanning for me. "Griggs," he leaned forward and spoke to something a little to my left, "there's enough confusion growing up without having to worry about UFOs."

A hard, loose feeling settled over me. I sat still and took the punishment of the chair. Maybe it was fear, but I became calm beyond calm. "I didn't know that getting UFO information off the Internet was illegal."

"No," Smithy said. He talked fast, officially. "But our Internet watchdogs report that you have been in contact with a known terror-ist, D R Van Staveren, alias David Staveren, alias D. Arthur Crocker, alias Charles Kalish, alias Christine Mquinn, alias Jeremiah or Ben-jamin Neon." A deep breath to finish his thought. "This could con-stitute criminal computer activity."

The words sat there between us for a second. The dog huffed and slobbered, dripping noises.

"You brought a dog into the school," I noticed aloud.

"Emir goes where I go. I am blind."

I had nothing to say to this.

"Don't you believe me?" Smithy asked. He tilted his head and I could see my own reflection in his dark glasses. My body appeared miniature and curved, a fun-house effect.

"Could you take off your glasses and show me your eyes, Mr. Smithy?"

"You don't believe me."

"I'd like to see your eyes," I repeated, incredibly brazen.

"My eyes," he faltered. His face turned red. "My eyes were burned out a long time ago, in the line of duty. I'm still a little self-conscious about the scars; they're quite horrible, I'm told. Why don't you just kick me in the shin?"

I looked at Emir, the dog, its gruesome teeth. "No thanks."

"Go ahead," he encouraged. "I'm helpless."

He wasn't kidding, and I felt a deep pity for him. A government agent waiting patiently on street corners, the dog looking left and right for a gap in traffic. "I'll take your word for it. Are you going to arrest me?"

"No," Smithy said. "Just warn you. Van Staveren is a dangerous man. He used to work overseas for our government, spreading pro-paganda."

I felt cold. "What if I don't listen to you?"

Smithy made his mouth grim, tight. He enunciated each word flawlessly. "You could remain in the tenth grade indefinitely."

I tried to keep a straight face, but then again, he was blind. I smiled and then so did Agent Smithy, a flashing smile on his face opening up toward a sharp laugh.

"'What if,' Griggs? Come on." Happily, he thumped his open

palm against Emir's side. "What would you say if I told you that D R Van Staveren and Miguel Parades are the same man?"

A loose string on my shirtsleeve caught my attention. "What would I say?" I murmured.

"I mean, this is an evil game," said Smithy. "It's going to mess you up, Griggs. I say that as a man, not a government mouthpiece."

I pulled gently at the string. Something ripped. My UFO awareness insisted that this "warning" constituted some pretty unusual misdirection on the part of the government to conceal a monstrous conspiracy. Reason, small-voiced and nasal, told me otherwise. I asked Agent Smithy, "What if Van Staveren is still working for our government? What if he is spreading lies just to cover up a deeper truth?"

Smithy nodded, slowly. "I have considered it," he said, "but if that's true, all the more reason to warn you, because then he's got some vast machinery standing behind him, waiting to sweep up the tracks no matter who gets hurt in the process. Even the lies have to be covered up. They must be, you see. Otherwise, no one will believe them."

"Are you an arm of that, um, machinery?" I asked him. "Do you know whether you're covering up a lie or the truth?"

He bowed his head, smiled sadly. I pitied him again. "I've decided that it doesn't matter." Smithy touched his glasses briefly.

"Is your real name Alan Smithy?"

He laughed again, curt and high. "I like you, Griggs. But you're too smart for your own damn good. Live your life, discover girls, look up at the stars at night and be happy."

After some time, I understood that I'd just been dismissed. I wanted to shake his hand or ask what it felt like, being blind. I wanted to ask him if he carried a gun. But I moved to leave the room instead. "Mr. Smithy, could you do me a favor?"

"Yes?"

"Could you call my dad at work and tell him what you told me about my 'criminal computer activities'?" It would mean a lot to him, I added silently.

Whatever Smithy thought of the request, he kept it to himself. Silently, he nodded, and the dog glared at me as I left the room.

Night. I tried to access my account, but couldn't get in. I tried six-teen times, and then poked through all the hardware. After I tried calling my Internet provider, the phone rang and someone picked it up downstairs. Mom came running and knocked on my door.

"Clay," she sang, breathless. "It's for you. It's a girl."

"Did you get her name?" I asked.

"Yes," Mom said, elated, "and it's beautiful."

I picked up the phone. "Tammy?"

"Uh, hi," she said.

"This is Clay."

"I know. What happened in school today?" She sounded off, somehow.

"Oh, um, it wasn't much. Office stuff. You know, paperwork." I pictured her in her room crouched atop a pyramid of cushions as she held the phone, wearing the T-shirt and short-shorts ensemble, her hair tossed away from the side she listened with. I asked intuitively, "What's wrong?"

"Nothing."

We stayed quiet on either side of the line, then I said, "Tammy, I need a favor."

"What?"

"I wouldn't ask if I didn't think it was important—"

"Just say it, Clayton." No one ever called me Clayton. It's an ane-mic, conspicuous name. Tammy said it, and suddenly it was blood-rich. I wanted her to call me Clayton forever, to fill me with heroic bulk and tone.

"Can I borrow your e-mail account and password?" I asked. Before she could answer, I told her why. I sketched out the Millard County story and my research, everything up to Agent Smithy. In short, I babbled. At some point I figured that maybe I wasn't making much sense. So I looked at my information map, tacked to the wall above my computer desk, for details. I saw it. My mouth went dead.

"Hello?" hissed the phone. "Clay?"

My chart was in the exact same position as I'd left it days ago. I glanced away and stared at it again to be sure of what I saw. There were no more Indians. Chills gripped my shoulders and shook me, my vertebrae chattering like teeth. Someone had filled in the empty boxes on my chart and drawn the corresponding lines between. All the information was there. My entire project had been completed. They'd even gotten my handwriting down perfectly.

"Tammy," I droned, "I have to go."

She hesitated only for a second, then gave me her account number and password. Somehow Tammy sensed a danger—perhaps she could taste it, too, even over the phone lines. She said, "Clayton. Be careful."

I nodded. Of course, she couldn't see me. "Yes." I hung up the phone. I looked at my empty hands, the baby-pink skin of my palms and the intricate cross-strands of soft wrinkles within wrinkles. I wandered aimlessly around my bedroom, now a foreign country, the footprint of a stranger. The clothes in the drawers all seemed in order. Stacks of old comic books still filled the closet, the space under the bed. None of my floppy disks were missing. Only the chart. I couldn't remember when I had looked at it last. When did they complete my chart? Why did they complete my chart?

Because I was supposed to be very, very afraid.

Because the spots they filled in would lead me off the right track.

Because it was all truth, and it didn't matter that I knew. I was a distinct nothing. A potato chip.

I hoped that Van Staveren would have something for me. If nothing else, he could confirm or deny the puzzle pieces given to me by an unseen Them. I resumed my spot in front of the computer, feeling warlike. I dialed in through Tammy's account and attempted to locate Van Staveren again. Messages to jan@mrbeans.charlotte.au all bounced back. I posted another note to frequented electronic bulletin boards dealing with aliens and UFOs: Van Staveren I am in trouble. Need directions to Millard County.

In the middle of typing, I was interrupted. Someone requested to "talk" with me in real-time over the net. A Kim Strickland—but I was using Tammy's account. This Kim Strickland could have been a friend of hers. I agreed to the connection and the first thing I did was explain to this person that I was borrowing Tammy's account with her consent. I didn't need any more suspicion of "criminal computer activities"; I told Kim Strickland my name.

"I know who oyou are clay Griggs."

The text errors seemed a sure sign. "Van Staveren?" I typed.

"Yes," Van Staveren wrote back, "I am a 'womnan' todya. I see that you ahve become a womant oo. Good. I feel more comrfort-abletalking to nother woman."

"How did you find me? Did you get my message?"

"I am writing to you from n office suply store computer classrrom with Internet hooku9ops. There is no tmuch tim. 'Thay' are wachign me."

For a frantic second, I feared that I would soon receive Van Staveren's death message, his misshapen, Shakespearean last breath. "Who is watching you? Is it Alan Smithy?"

"Nno," he replied. "Its' the man who teaches the classs weare supossed to be elarnging spreadshtetes. I think smy disguise must be slippgin. Its these damn 'berasts'. did you talk to A. S.?"

"Yes. He told me that you're evil. He said that you're playing a game with me."

The screen erupted into small bursts of random letters—I could only guess that Van Staveren was punching at the keyboard with his fists. Abruptly, sentences formed. "Youore beig ndisinfoerrmd!that sonfoa bich SMiythee." A pause, then he tried the word again, letter by letter. "d I s iin for m d." Van Staveren tried long strings of letters that seemed overly dramatic, but I suppose he was deliberately hold-ing down each key with one finger, to get the word right. He con-cluded with a long line of exclamation marks.

"Van staveren," I typed, hesitant, "is somthing wrong?"

"Yess. yes somethging is wrong.. As a nabductee'specimen' I hav maade mylesf uselees. Ii force myself to ead choclae te coffeee ciga-resetett sugaer alc9ohol drugs in order toe keep my bosdy impuyre-with toxins. ineverr thought tehey wold poisin me."

It took some effort to hit the letters correctly—whatever Van Staveren's difficulty, it seemed contagious. "Who poisoned you, Van Staveren?" I wrote, concerned. "What's happening?"

"Soeme kind of palsi," he replied, "ithink I've ben explosed to a neruotoxin wich attack langeuage centsers of hte 'brain.' Hearsd of it befro at Aera 52. virus wth Aliene origans of coures."

I sweated; I trembled; I spoke aloud. "What . . . I don't . . ." I urgently began to tap out a message, "Van Staveren you need—"

"Notttime," he cut in, "Youg can excape clya grggigs. geta awayh form yours 'home' RRUNN AW YA. evven now2 eyouoa er elavign inrofmnation traiaals whishc marrrk yerou wfwehjerrvern ggso."

"What? I don't understand. Please try to make sense."

"OKK." The words came up slow; I saw each character as a series of finely detailed brush strokes. "The black box CIA computer 'satan' lissten. ww.ungoliant.rg—ORG that'ss' Rmember conneery lazienby moore adn too a lesssr extednt dal5tone wll cee youi htruioowuidhgh."

I copied down the disfigured Web address on a small slip of paper. Uselessly, I typed "Van Staveren."

His message continued in a garbled mix of letters and numbers as the typographical illness took complete hold. None of it made any sense, and it didn't stop. Endless trains of stray characters galloped down the screen. I wished, horribly, that someone would shoot him. Van Staveren's final line held no dignity, no clues to my own fate.

"sW#$as90 uq q[230"

Then he must have disconnected. I made myself visualize Van Staveren's last words carved in marble, yellow flowers planted underneath them.

I kept staring at the computer screen until my stomach rumbled, angrily. It took me a moment to stand. I didn't think. I didn't know what to think anymore. Everything spiraled, and I allowed myself to lose momentum. Like when you try to peel off a sticker and it only comes away in shreds, and you pull away another piece and blood begins to well up. Everything is true; nothing makes sense.

On the night before the last day of school, I checked out Miguel Parades's page one last time. Above the door, it said, "D R VAN STAVEREN IS AN ALIEN HYBRID!" Frustrated, I tried to pin down the Web address that Van Staveren had given me. I mixed up the words and bounced off of countless File Not Found messages until a window finally came up.

PASSWORD:

Something possessed me and I could not account for it. Like walking or breathing or speaking, my answer came out of a knowledge so deep it's invisible. I hit the keys that I knew were correct. Van Staveren had said: Connery, Lazenby, Moore, Dalton. There was no question in my mind. First try, I hit it right on the head: BOND JAMES BOND.

"Welcome to the Black Box, Mr. Bond."

I asked, "Who are you?"

"I am SULTAN. I am an intelligent information system. You may ask me any question."

Millard County, I thought, Van Staveren, Alan Smithy. UFOs. My fingers hovered over the keyboard and the cursor blinked at me. It was the eye of a machine that also observed, with infinite patience, human behavior. Hundreds of questions filed through my head, bronze and painted. My Indians took on bodies, I pictured them. The feathers in their hair bobbed as they walked, and animal skins hung across their shoulders. They addressed me with their silence. With the sense that my actions had been preprogrammed, I typed, "What is the best way to attract a woman?"

SULTAN hesitated at the other end of our link. Then It answered me. The answer went on for pages and pages, lovingly detailed, instructive, profound.

The phone rang as soon as I disconnected, and I picked it up, expecting Smithy. "Hello?"

"Clay," Tammy said. "I've been trying to get through for half an hour."

"Sorry. I was hooked up to the Web."

"Aren't you watching *The X-Files*?"

"Jeez. I, um, lost track of time. Why?"

"Just turn it on," she said. I noticed her voice shaking. "Call me right after."

I went downstairs and no one was around. I turned on the TV in the living room. Just in time. On the screen, two FBI agents were searching for information regarding a UFO crash just southwest of Salt Lake City, Utah. They talked to a boy who looked about fourteen years old, who'd gathered some reports off the Internet, just before everyone clammed up. The name of the boy in the show was Chris.

The FBI duo spoke with the boy in his bedroom. On the wall, above the computer, he had my flow chart. The original, complete with wagons and Indians.

I thought of Tamichi Hurt, named after a fictional character. Like dmv21@bvp.com, I faced the prospect of my own Undetectable Extermination—the kind that denies you an existence outside of TV and fiction.

Later, still dazed, I heard the doorbell ring. Seconds afterward, Dad knocked on my door.

"There's, um, a girl here, Clay," he said, mumbling through the crack. "She wants to talk to you."

I went out into the hall and saw Dad, cradling the pages of his manuscript like an orphan returned. "You got it back," I said.

"What do you think of the name Tamichi?" Dad asked me.

I smiled at him. "Mom will never go for it. Where's Tammy?"

He grinned, nervous. His pupils were immense. I imagined this man teaching me to masturbate. "She's downstairs." As I walked away, he spoke three words, "Criminal computer activity." He sounded happy.

From the top of the stairs, I saw Tammy standing in our foyer, waiting. She wore a large pair of athletic shorts and a Cornell rugby, speckled with black mud. Her hair was pulled back except for the occasional stray. As she took deep, controlled breaths, she massaged the muscles of her thighs roughly, like she wanted to shake them loose from the bones. I watched her chest swell, her hands move over the skin of her legs. Her head turned upward to smile at me.

"You didn't call me back," Tammy accused, a little wounded.

"Oh man," I said, wiping my hands across my face, "I'm sorry. I'm such a putz. You rode your bike over here?"

She nodded.

Then she stared at me, shaking. Tammy wanted me to say something. I didn't want to talk about *The X-Files* so I asked her, "Did your dad like the book?"

"No," she said. "Yes. I don't know. Do you want to go for a walk?"

"Sure."

I laced up my sneakers and we went out the back door, into the trees. The first movement of night sounds encircled us with a rich symphony, crickets and trees and cars humming in the distance. We walked on hard ground without speaking.

"I don't know what to say," Tammy said finally. I realized that she was uncomfortable, struggling. Her steps and voice always seemed so perfectly effortless, it was hard to tell otherwise. But her feet snagged on roots, and she reached out and touched each tree she passed as if she were a blind person. She spoke softly, "I'm sorry."

"Why should you be sorry?"

"I don't know."

"That's the third time you've said that now."

Tammy brushed her fingers over pale birch bark. "If there really were aliens," Tammy said, "what would they look like?"

"What do you mean?"

"Would they look like us? Would they have eyes, faces, hands? Skin, teeth, bones?"

I stooped to clear the dirt off an old, cracked tire. "I don't know."

"Got you," Tammy said. Her look of worry shifted and she laughed in her throaty way. I had to giggle, though I tried to hold it back.

"Ignorance is potential knowledge," I managed to say. Tammy gave me a shove and I fell over, curled up on the ground, laughing backward, relieved. She carried on loudly, her cackles echoing through the forest. When we both stopped, I looked up at the interlaced branches. Between the dark lines and the feathery masses of leaves, I saw fragments of twilight sky and it was enough, Agent Smithy. I heard Tammy moving off and rose to follow.

A few steps ahead of me, she said, "I guess what I mean is, we're so fascinated by the things we know nothing about. We're attracted to them."

I asked her, "What do you think of all these things that are happening?"

Tammy made a slight noise. "I think that you're getting yourself into some kind of trouble. When you didn't call me back, I got scared." She turned to me. "Do you really believe in this alien stuff?"

Her eyes held me like headlights, stopped me dead. I wanted to adjust my underwear, but didn't. I said, "I'm not in any trouble, so don't worry."

"Right." She rolled her eyes and wheeled away, taking long strides onward.

"This way," I told her, indicating a space to our left.

"You know where we're going?"

I arched an eyebrow at her and deepened my voice, doing my impression of an all-powerful computer. "I know everything." She tried to push me again but I skipped out of reach.

Beyond the edge of the trees, we stood on an elevated bank that overlooked a small pond. The reflected image of the sky rolled slowly on its surface.

"Right here," I told Tammy, "I used to go fishing with my grand-father."

She faced me, her cheeks and forehead bright in the darkness.

"He died," I went on, "in a hospital bed, over a long period of time. In my clearest memories of him, he's threading the hook on the line for me, because I've already cut myself twice. He's impaling the worm on the hook. He's wearing his favorite hat and sitting on a fold-ing chair with me at his feet, learning about solitude and patience. When I cry, he cries with me until I start to laugh. He has beer on his breath." I wept streams of tears, while Tammy watched and listened. I wiped snot on my hands and kept talking. "Mom wouldn't let me go to his funeral because I was too young. Instead of saying good-bye to him, I watched three hours of the worst fucking cartoons ever."

Tammy's eyes were wet now, too. I couldn't bear it anymore so I walked toward the pond. I picked up a rock and cranked my arm back, filled with passion and uselessness. The surface of the water was perfect cellophane. It gathered the few stars that came out. I could feel Tammy watching me. I put the rock down.

For a while, neither of us said anything. The sky dimmed slowly, painlessly. Frogs gargled but we didn't see them. On a wooded hill-side in the distance, tiny porch lights winked at us through the trees, sparkling in parallax. Tammy stayed somewhere behind me, sniffing quietly.

I looked up at the heavens. Nothing moved, nothing mattered but the two of us. I said, "I guess I just want to be in a better place. Some-where I feel like I fit in. I want someone to drop down out of the sky and take me there. A place that's so great it's impossible—or very unlikely."

Tammy came up to stand next to me. She also looked up and put her hands out, palms facing upward, as if feeling for rain. "You can wait for something impossible all of your life, Clayton," she said slowly, "or you can do it yourself."

Like she'd just given herself a cue, Tammy walked around in front of me. I rubbed at my eyes to get her face into focus. She smiled briefly. Tammy tilted her head and I saw flecks in her eyes, pene-trated by a weird sliver of moon. I noted again the complete absence of red in them—my stomach lurched once, then resigned itself to the future. She leaned down and her nose went next to mine. I felt her eyelashes on my cheek and was afraid.

Forgetting the lessons of television, I kept my eyes open while Tammy kissed me. They must have made neat white shapes in the dark as I stared, horribly transfixed. Naked terror made me tremble, threatened to cut the power to my knees. Tammy felt my body shudder and fed on it, demanded that I hang from the point where our faces joined. If she'd tilted her head back, my feet would have left the ground. Something vague in me wanted to pull away from her.

Tammy's mouth pressed harder, probing. I could feel the bone structure under her gums. She drew a short breath and it came out of me. I was fifteen years old and I had seen immaculately rendered images of mass murder. I'd seen photos of an alien's head split in half for dissection purposes. I'd seen pictures of a woman fucking a dog. I told myself, "Tammy is kissing me. I am kissing Tammy." And I closed my eyes. Everything disappeared.

A sudden brushing warmth told me that her body had moved closer. The skin of her thigh touched mine, both bare. Her hair tickled my shoulder and all at once I noticed so many smells, like a layer cake that went down forever. Spice of her hair spray, her skin perfume, my own saltwater tears, our light sweat, the grass, the pond nearby, the cool night air and sweet spongy earth. "We are kissing," I observed. I just stood there, and ached without breath. I wanted to find her fingers with mine, wanted to press my palm against her narrow chest and grip the small of her back to pull her hips toward me. With her tongue, lightly, playfully, Tammy took the saliva from my lips.

Reality—25 June 1996—"We kiss." The kiss lasted all night. It lasted all summer, through seasons heaped in leaves, snow, flowers, insects. It lasted through three college degrees, one and a half marriages, five children, twenty-two birthdays. Through my troubled drinking years, my successes as a creative historian, my brief and near-disastrous employment with the United States government. The kiss took me into the floating, bodiless now—that point like the crane-elevated camera's eye that so easily persuades you of its nonpresence, its ability to move quickly from place to place at will, in order to capture the best possible angle of the crash. In the spirit of that world-spanning kiss and that camera, I am writing to you from the main branch of the New York Public Library. I am writing to you from a terminal in a shopping mall in Wisconsin, inside a toy store for advanced children. I am writing to you from a deep underground military base. I am writing to you from an invisible satellite, high above the earth.

Aimee LaBrie
DePaul University

VISITATION

It is the last night of my sister's visit and I am determined to get her drunk. Her visit has been a complete waste of my life and I can tell she is getting to the point where she feels she must ask me something poignant about my life. There's a hesitancy about her, as if she were saying ahem every time she looks at me. She probably wants to have late-night sisterly talks in our nighties, to sift through our cherished childhood remembrances until the sun peers sweetly through my miniblinds. But when I look at her, no sudden understanding arrives. I don't think, Gee, I love my sister. Isn't life wonderful? Instead, I've spent the entire week mumbling, Jesus Christ, please give me the strength not to pinch Anne blue when she bites the inside of her cheeks, which she does all day long. It's one of the many nervous habits of hers that I'd forgotten.

We were supposed to go out to the Gingerman Tavern but Anne has developed a stomachache, caused I'm sure by the fact that she can't stand to be outside. She doesn't like the leather-jacketed men loitering on the street corners and yelling Hey, where you going? or the broken bottles, potato chip packets, and cigarette butts lining the curbs, or any of the chaos of the city where I live.

What I hate is how Anne walks down the street with her shoulders around her ears and how she ducks like a puppy about to be beaten when anyone raises their voice or if it looks like someone's going to get shot on TV or if an old man is walking down the street with a limp.

I am tired of how she has to do everything a certain way in order to feel safe, like washing her hands with a special soap or measuring the pasta in a glass cup before pouring it into the pot.

And how slow she is. It takes her forty-five minutes to shower, and believe me, she is not doing what it is that would take me that long, not my sister who calls sex making love and once confessed to me she could have an orgasm by thinking about her boyfriend asking her to marry him.

Her exactness and care make me feel like I'm being too loud. I feel my arms moving in their sockets, and it seems I have turned into an ogre lurching around the room, ready to knock a china shepherdess off the mantel with an unthinking flick of my wrist.

I make dinner on the stove, throwing spaghetti into a black pot like I do almost every night when I'm alone. I know I should cook some spectacular final meal, but fuck it.

Anne floats into the kitchen and opens the refrigerator door in a way that makes you think she's afraid of the refrigerator's sensitivity to being opened abruptly. If you have any lettuce, I could make a salad, she says.

I lean in next to her, our shoulders nearly touching. We peer at the empty refrigerator. Anne smells like vanilla extract.

If you can make a salad out of old grapes and yogurt. I turn back to the pasta, stirring it with a wooden spoon.

It was just an idea, she sighs, still staring into the refrigerator, as though she could come up with something brilliant to make out of margarine and ice cubes. Have you got any bread?

Do you see any in there?

No.

Then my guess is I probably don't have any.

You know what Anne is like? She's like one of those perfect girls you see in fifth-grade black-and-white health films from the 1950s, the kind who wash their hands after meals and wear ironed white blouses with gold buttons marching in neat rows up the front. The kind who don't slam doors and always say please and thank you and wipe their mouths with napkins. The kind who carry their books tied in leather straps that they swing over their shoulders when walking down the sidewalk with their boyfriends Biff and Skippy who have just made Junior Varsity football and won't that be great because they are also cheerleaders and in the Junior League. She was born in the wrong time and seems to know it, which is probably why she hates the city and doesn't understand the way things go here.

For one thing, you do not take your time writing a traveler's check at the grocery store. You don't take fifteen minutes to fish out your ID and write the difference in your little leather book. You don't count out change in the middle of the bus. You cannot expect people to be polite to you when they've got other things on their minds.

I trick Anne into drinking by giving her a large shot of Kahlúa disguised in warm milk. I tell her it will soothe her stomach. Kahlúa is sweet and the drunk you get is a slow, spinning feeling like when you twist the chains on a swing round and round and then let them unravel, so the world spins and everything gets out of focus and wonderful.

I serve the drinks in big plastic cups with our last supper. Our last supper, if represented on one of those velvet paintings you buy at garage sales, would be Anne as Jesus, looking at the sky, eager to get away, but wearing a benevolent expression, hands outstretched. I would be Judas. On the table would be my final offering of green beans and spaghetti. The other eleven apostles would be various people in our family shown outlined in dashes, nearly invisible but still present.

Anne picks at her green beans. I turn on the TV and take a sip of my glass to prove it isn't poison. I say, Anne, how's your stomach? Anne takes a small sip and sets the glass back on the table. She says, I should probably pack tonight. She smooths her hands over her skirt and touches a thread unraveling at the hem, but she doesn't yank it off, which annoys me. Yeah, maybe you should pack. We only have— I count on my fingers—seventeen hours until you have to leave. She looks at me to see if I am being mean and sees I am and decides not to say anything.

Anne came right after I told her about my conversations with Mom. I don't remember Mom very well, but one night, while I was throwing my covers around, I felt a weight on the edge of my bed, and looked up to see my mother, wearing her white nurse's uniform with the tricornered white hat and smoking a Kool. I don't believe in ghosts, but there she was. I decided to take advantage of it while I could. What were Anne and I like when we were babies? I asked her. She said, Oh, well, you were a perfect baby and so beautiful I thought you had fallen from the sky. She paused, her head tilted back. She had brown hair like Annie's. She looked exactly like the Kodak picture I have of her, the one where she is standing in front of Grandpa's pickup, wearing a white dress with a cabbage-sized corsage pinned on the bodice. On the back of the photo, it says, Donna. Going to the dance. 1952. I imagine she had many dances on weightless feet with tall, handsome, straight-shouldered young soldiers.

What was Annie like? I asked my mother that night. She said, Oh, Anne, well. She wasn't a very good baby, no, not at all. She had colic.

Now Anne finishes her drink. Do you want another one? She says, Yes, I'll get it. I follow her into the kitchen. She pulls out the bottle of Kahlúa I've hidden underneath the sink and splashes a cupful in the glass. Cheers, she says, holding the glass up to me.

When I called, Anne answered after the second ring. Hearing her voice, even knowing she lives elsewhere now, I couldn't help picturing her sitting at Grandpa's kitchen table, hunched over a crossword, eating popcorn out of the big white tub we used to use Saturday night during *Creature Feature*.

Before *Creature Feature* I always ran to brush my teeth and put on my white nightie so that while the show was on I could sit crosslegged in front of the TV while Anne braided my hair, pulling gently at the tangles that were sprayed with No More Tears, and didn't you want to be that girl on the front of the bottle with the long blond hair, how could anything ever be wrong with her life? I purred at the feel of the brush across my head, getting sleepy, but I kept my eyes open because if I fell asleep, it would be over and I would wake in bed, one leg hanging cool off the edge, the house deathly quiet. A chill would ripple across my skin like a fever breaking from believing everyone was never going to wake up and I'd be trapped in the purple shadows with the moon outside the window as the only light, left to wander through the world with the crickets as company.

Anne has a boyfriend now. They live together in a perfect little house I've never seen. I imagine it sometimes when I'm trying to fall asleep. I picture a cottage nestled somewhere in the woods, safe, full of *Better Homes and Gardens* knickknacks and do-it-yourself projects, fresh flowers in jars on wooden tables. I imagine what it would be like to visit, but I always picture myself as the wicked witch, slinking down the path in a black-hooded gown, knocking on the door with a shiny red apple in my hand, ready to catch Anne unawares.

There's a fairy tale Mom used to read us when we were little about two sisters, one good and one bad. When the good one speaks, pearls, diamonds, and sapphires spill from her lips. When the other one opens her mouth, snakes, toads, and spiders gush.

When I was packing to move away, Anne kept taking everything out of my suitcase. She'd say, Oh, look how wrinkled this is! and run for the iron. She'd smooth the hot face of the iron back and forth over some polyester blend, but she'd never put anything back. Finally I grabbed the clothes she'd piled in neat stacks and jammed them into the suitcase. There is just no nice way to leave when someone doesn't want you to go.

Now I sit on the bed while Anne moves between the dresser and her suitcase, carefully folding everything and assigning it a space in the bottom of the bag.

You didn't put anything in my laundry basket, did you?

She shakes her head.

I watch her pack. What about your shampoo? Don't forget your shampoo.

You can keep it. There's not much left.

No, I don't want it. I don't use that stuff. I go into the bathroom and get her bottle. I look in the mirror, checking my eyes, my face, seeing nothing different. I go back into the room and hand her the shampoo.

Thanks, she says, throwing it on top of her clothes.

I sit on the bed again. We'll take a cab to the airport this time. The train takes too long.

I thought you said that would cost over twenty dollars.

Yeah, but don't worry about it. I'll pay for it.

I don't mind taking the train.

It's no big deal.

No, the train is fine.

Yeah, it's fine. That's why every time we get on you look like you're about to die.

Anne zips her bag shut with a sound like the end of something.

I say, Do you mind getting this off the bed? I'd like to go to sleep.

She yanks the suitcase off the bed and lays it on the floor on its side, like a fallen deer.

The day I called Anne I'd been sitting at the coffee shop, smoking a cigarette after my shift when I saw these two little girls come whirling into the parking lot. It was a Saturday, around four. The parking lot outside of the restaurant is smooth; it doesn't make your teeth chatter in your head when you roll over it. Both girls had the same snow-white sugar hair down to their waists and matching purple skates. The older one could spin and skate backward, but the younger one couldn't. She held on to the wall, Bambi legs wobbling. I watched her watch her sister. Her sister was an angel, spinning and turning with her hands over her head and her skirt flaring. She made it look so easy.

I like the cowboy truck drivers who come to the coffee shop where I waitress wearing wrinkled flannel shirts and John Deere hats pushed back on their heads. I like their tired eyes that stare at endless roads, back and forth across the same highways. Sometimes, the truckers fall in love with you. I keep pouring coffee. Some mornings, it feels like we're in a wartime operation and I am Florence Nightingale in pink polyester keeping that hot coffee coming, let's go boys, and they are nothing but grateful for my constant attention and remembering what they want.

Anne is washing her face with Camay, her hair pulled back with a headband. I sit on the toilet, watching her. Anne taught me how to put on lipstick, do your mouth like this, her hand on my chin, holding it still, brushing the lipstick across my gaping mouth. Her breath fanned cool across my face in a peppermint breeze. We held our breath together for a minute as she finished. There, now blot, never mind it, there's toilet paper on your lips, look, look in the mirror. Anne is who I see in the mirror, her eyes opaque like the polished green surface of a fairy-tale lake.

I don't want Anne to leave. It's not so much that I'll miss her, it's that I don't want to find her half-moon sliver of Camay in the shower, or her hair in my brush. I don't want to watch the violets she bought die in the lemonade pitcher. Her fingerprints are everywhere and I don't want to spot them some morning while I'm eating Cheerios. I would like her to vanish in the night, so I could get to the business of forgetting.

I say, So, do I remind you of Mom at all?

Anne looks at me. You've got her hair. Except she used to wear it short. Short like this, to her shoulders. And you've got her shoulders. Both of you have man's shoulders.

No, I don't.

Yes, you do. Anne splashes water across her face. I wait for her to tell me something else.

Sheldon Robert Walcher
Pennsylvania State University

DURIAN

From Hua Lamphong Station in Bangkok to George Town, Malaysia, across the rain-swollen Strait of Malacca to Sumatra they rush, hoping to outdistance the storms. But the monsoons just keep coming. Rain such as they never knew back in England, warm and thick and heady, like the sweet juice of the rambutan hanging in spiked red clusters in the trees along the Parapat highway.

"I don't feel well," Kitterage complains, leaning her head against the worn seat as the old bus shimmies over another set of ruts in the road. Her green eyes are bloodshot and the natural paleness of her face has taken on a ruddiness Malcolm doesn't trust.

"It was that fish soup last night, I'm telling you."

These past few weeks haven't gone as he planned. The ceaseless rain, for one; Kitterage's listlessness for another. The sense Malcolm gets that he's dragging her everywhere, despite months spent this past winter sitting on the floor of their one-bedroom flat in Brixton, poring over guidebooks he brought home from the bookstore he managed. Now just three weeks into their trip, the only interest Kitterage seems to show is eating out at the public stalls at night.

Granted, there's something enticingly *exotic* about the streets of most Malay and Indonesian towns after sundown, so unlike the rows of staid brick houses in South Bank. The way the cars clear out at dusk to be replaced by clusters of small tables beneath patched awnings; the rows of beef and chicken satay roasting over charcoal pots along the sidewalks; the fevered drone of Chinese and Indian hawkers rattling off the night's menu while chopping vegetables for soup. Scenes worthy of the Kipling and Conrad novels he'd read so avidly as a boy, no doubt, but not without mangy dogs urinating in alleys, flies circling over the tables, trails of countless microbes lying on cup rims, worming over chopsticks, along the lips of soup bowls, and across stained countertops.

No, on the authority of Sam Veterson's *Guide to India and Southeast Asia,* Malcolm makes a strict point of eating only what has been cooked either in a hotel, or at one of the hundreds of restaurants listed in the book's index. He avoids raw vegetables and almost all fruit and is careful to check the seals on bottles of water before drinking them.

"You may have giardiasis," he says, leaning over to feel Kitterage's face for fever. "Or amebic dysentery."

Kitterage rolls her eyes and sighs. "I'm just tired of sitting here."

The driver slips into low gear and the bus creaks through the final stretch of bamboo groves before breaking onto the open grass of the summit. For a moment they seem almost to stop; spread out beyond the terraced fields of tea lies the lake, its great blue surface glittering in the rare afternoon sun. It's so clear and calm the twisted clouds seem to hesitate before it, kneeling to touch their dark reflections before being swept over the far-off ridges. Inside the bus there is a similar hesitation, broken only moments later by a collective tearing as Velcro is pulled apart to get into camera bags.

Kitterage lowers the window and leans out. "Isn't it all so beautiful?"

Malcolm nods, then looks down to find the place he's marked in the thick book cradled on his lap. *Lake Toba: The deepest volcanic, freshwater lake in southeast Asia.*

The deck boys stow their backpacks as they clamber aboard the ferry that will take them out to the island. The air-conditioned cabin below is packed—most of the tourists from the bus cramming in together beside villagers carrying baskets of clothes and food on their heads—and Malcolm and Kit make their way to the topmost deck with ten or so other people. The afternoon rain has begun to fall, but much gentler than they've seen it before, and in the slight shower the lake seems still and quiet. A pair of European honeymooners from the bus, dressed in matching batik shirts, snuggle on the lone wooden bench. Their talking is soft and low, and Malcolm imagines he can almost make out what they're saying above the lapping of water and the now steady thrum of propellers. He looks to Kit, but she moves forward to the front railing instead. Malcolm finds a dry spot beneath the worn canopy and takes his book out.

"It says the Toba Batak are the only remaining Christians in all Sumatra." Malcolm pauses, smiling at the prospect of sleeping through a morning without amplified prayer calls. Mosques with loudspeakers seemed a wonderfully strange clash of cultures in Malaysia, but have grown simply annoying in the weeks they've been in Indonesia. "And that they bury their dead in those little white tombs up on the ridges there. See Kit? They look like condominiums." Kit leans out over the side, trying to see if any fish dart within the clear ripple of the boat's wake.

Behind her the man murmurs something to his new wife, takes one last drag from his cigarette, and flicks it in a perfect arc off into the water. A moment later she does the same and, laughing, they kiss and descend inside. "Did you see that?" Kit asks, turning suddenly to the spot where they were just sitting, but hesitating when she realizes a pair of Americans are looking at her.

"Yes," Malcolm nods in agreement, "how utterly vulgar and *Italian*."

Kit flashes a nervous smile as the other couple laughs, and though Malcolm didn't mean it to be particularly funny, he turns to look at them. He's always been a poor judge of age, but from the thinning gray hair and the slight bulge beneath his blue T-shirt, Malcolm guesses the man to be in his forties. The woman, on the other hand, can't be more than eighteen or nineteen. Her blond hair is tied in back with a blue bandanna, and she has the shiny glow in the face and sparkling eyes American girls always seem to get when they travel. Both wear shorts and sandals, and have those sunglasses hanging from bright nylon straps around their necks that so clearly distinguish Americans from their much quieter Canadian cousins.

"Where you two headed?" the woman asks Kitterage a moment later, the act of communal mockery having somewhat broken the ice.

"I'm not really sure, to be honest," Kitterage begins, dropping down on the recently vacated wooden bench, then nodding back over to Malcolm. "My fiancé handles most of the itinerary on this venture."

The woman laughs, exposing a set of dazzlingly white teeth. "Yeah, Doug's the same way. I only get consulted when we're hopelessly lost or something." She crinkles her face over at him.

"Hey," Doug complains, holding his hands up in feigned defense, "I don't get lost. I just have a roundabout way of getting to places."

Kit clears her throat and Malcolm realizes he's missed something because they've all turned to look at him. "Yes, well, we've made reservations at the Bukit Pusuk Hotel."

Doug smiles broadly and nods. "Nice place."

Malcolm is surprised. "You know it?"

"Oh yeah, I stayed right by there a couple of years ago," he says with the off-hand assurance Malcolm dislikes about Americans. "The Pusuk is a little too rich for our blood though, right, Tania-baby?"

Tania shrugs. "Anything you say. You know I'd sleep in a ditch as long as they served fried bananas and had a blender." Kitterage snorts a laugh at this, and they all start laughing in turn.

When the ferry has docked beside the hotel's pier, they are greeted on the landing by a group of half-naked boys in brown sarongs, who immediately take Kit and Malcolm's bags.

Tania doesn't seem to have any bags, and Doug quickly slings his olive green duffel over his shoulder before another boy can seize it. "I've got it, thanks."

There is a moment of confusion as they all stand around on the rain-speckled lawn.

"Well, maybe we'll see you two later," Tania says as she and Doug are finally led up the hill by one of the boys.

"Sure." Kit waves back as their bags are carried in the opposite direction. "See you."

Their cottage lies sheltered by a stand of bamboo and has its own veranda overlooking the quiet inlet. After weeks of dirty sheets and room doors with broken locks, Kitterage tries to keep herself composed as they are shown the mosquito net, the control for the ceiling fan, the bathroom with its hot and cold running water. After the boys have left she flings herself on the large bed and laughs in a way Malcolm hasn't heard in months. Not since his aunt passed away and they both first learned of the inheritance.

It wasn't a fortune, but sizable enough to start Malcolm thinking about quitting his job and traveling for a year. Kit's father had scolded him for being unreasonable, saying the two ought to finally think seriously about getting married and investing the money in a house, but Malcolm wouldn't hear it. His aunt Mary had been a woman of literary bent and imagination who'd spent her whole life trapped in the smugness of Edinburgh tea parties; she would have wanted him to use the money on something as reckless and *impractical* as a trip. Still, Kit's family kept at it in that stodgy Northampton-shire way of theirs until Malcolm, who was by nature rather quiet and reserved in most things, shocked everybody with the vehemence of his resolve: he went out and purchased two round-the-world tickets. Kit quietly acquiesced.

"Malcolm," Kit says almost breathlessly, tossing a pillow across the room, "this place is wonderful. We can stay here for a while, can't we?"

"Yes," Malcolm says, warmed with the pride of having chosen it. "As long as you'd like."

Aside from a Japanese couple whom they see occasionally, Malcolm and Kitterage have the hotel to themselves. This far south the rains are still light and confined to only an hour or so every afternoon, so they take their meals on the roof of the lodge. At breakfast they watch the village men row their fishing boats out while women scrub laundry in the rocky shallows. Afterward, Kitterage takes walks along the shore, while Malcolm spends the mornings sitting out on their veranda, trying to write.

At home he often thought about the stories he might tell if only his work gave him more time, but sitting now beneath swaying palm fronds, the chit-chattering play of monkeys somewhere behind him, Malcolm's mind becomes as still and quiet as the lake before him. He ends up composing letters to old college friends he'll never send, and watches as Kit sketches the shy village girls bathing in the teal shallows, carefully holding their thin sarongs close to their bodies so as not to reveal too much of themselves.

Lunch is announced by the sputtering engines of the town ferry passing, the ferryman shouting, "Pa-ra-pat! Pa-ra-pat! Para-pat! Para-pat! Para-pat!" like an echo of himself, and they go up to the lodge and eat *nasi goreng* and listen to football scores on the BBC World Service. They talk about where they will go when the rains begin again in earnest, or about nothing at all. At dinner they watch dusk fall from the dining room, sunset clouds ablaze; the dark silhouettes of the fishing boats returning; and the faint streams of wood smoke drifting up from unseen houses.

At night their lovemaking is as clumsy as it's been since they wandered into that Bangkok sex bar by mistake, the grotesque and contorted writhing of the teenage girls onstage still haunting their thoughts, making them burn with secret desire and shame they cannot understand, let alone confess.

In this way one day slides into the next, and the one after that.

Next to the cluster of souvenir stands a few hundred yards down the road there is a tiny secondhand bookshop, and one morning as he's scouring through shelves of cheap romances, looking for anything that might last him more than an afternoon, Malcolm happens upon Tania. She is sitting cross-legged on the ground in one corner, absorbed in reading—of all things—a worn copy of James's *The Wings of the Dove*. Her hair is down and she's wearing glasses, and she's got such a fierce look of concentration on her face that for a moment he doesn't quite recognize her. Yet just as he's about to turn away she seems to catch the movement in the corner of her eye and looks up.

"Oh, hey Malcolm! Have you been standing there long?"

It strikes him as an odd question, but no stranger than finding her kneeling in the dirt in the middle of Sumatra, reading the most laborious writer in the English language for pleasure. Before he has a chance to come up with a good response, though, she stands and puts the book back on the shelf. "James not your type?" he finds himself asking instead.

"Not really, " she says, patting the dust from her tan legs. "I find him a pretentious, sexless bore." She turns back to the shelves, but then hesitates a moment and turns back. "Except for maybe *Daisy Miller*, which was just incredible," and she smiles.

The day is already hot, the sky a brilliant blue through the slatted windows above them, but inside the building is dark and stuffy and becoming uncomfortable.

"So, where's Kit?" Tania asks, picking up a book missing its cover and leafing through it.

Kitterage rose early that morning to go on a tour organized by the hotel to one of the nearby craft villages, and as Malcolm explains this to Tania, she grins.

"Was the tour heading to Pangururan, to see the silver workers?"

"Yes, I think so."

Tania's sudden laugh surprises him, but it turns out that Doug has left that morning on the same trip. "You know, if we're not careful," Tania teases a bit later, "we might just have an elopement on our hands."

Malcolm grins and they both turn back to the shelves. For a long time the conversation just sits there between them, a stalled thing.

"You want to go have some lunch?" he finds himself asking a few moments later, and to his surprise, she nods eagerly. As they walk toward the door, she draws close beside him, and glancing down he sees her slip a faded copy of Hesse's *The Journey to the East* under her shirt. Passing the cashier, she looks up at Malcolm and winks.

He'd actually given up on seeing the Americans again, which was just as well, for in all the years he'd lived in London he'd never met an American he actually liked, though in truth his opinions were based less on direct experience than midrange observation of the college students who descended on the city in swarms every summer. They'd stumble into the store, seemingly drunk at all hours of the day and night, looking for maps of the Underground, or loudly insisting on directions to Kensington Gardens or Buckingham Palace, completely ignoring the queues of paying customers in need of assistance. In short, he'd found them boorish and stupid. But walking now toward town on a broken path edged by rows of hibiscus and wild fern, listening to Tania talk about the months she's spent traveling through India and Nepal, Malcolm is no longer so sure. She seems so uninhibited and natural, so completely alive, that he feels more like a cardboard cutout of a man standing next to her than a living being. Even her theft, which most certainly would have enraged him back home, not the least of which because it would have been his store she was stealing from, seems fresh and amusing under the cool shade of bamboo. Kitterage never showed any interest in talking about books, much less in stealing them.

"Most Americans are pigs when they travel," Tania admits as they sit down in a small restaurant overlooking the pier. "Fortunately there aren't that many of us in Asia."

"Well, you're no worse than the French, really," he counters, trying to be funny, but she just stares back at him blankly.

"So, you don't like the Italians," she says, leaning back in her chair after the waiter has taken their order, "the Americans or the French. Tell me then, Malcolm, who do you like?"

Maybe it's the tatty copy of Hesse's book lying on the table between them. Or maybe it's because they have just ordered beer, and with the lake spread out before them, it seems like nothing he could say would fill up all that light, airy space. But he tells her about the summers he spent as a kid, fishing with his uncle on Loch Lomond, or across the Clyde, near his grandparents' house in Paisley. About moving to Manchester as a teenager, and what growing up in England was like. She nods sympathetically, and he recounts the trip he took to Ireland, to see Joyce's old house. Encouraged, he lies and tells her about going to Montparnasse in Paris to visit Hemingway's and Fitzgerald's old haunts. At this she has no reaction, so he gives her his impressions of Florence, a city he'd inexplicably hated while there, but had grown fond of later, after reading a book about a man and woman who fall in love after meeting just once, on the steps of the Stazione Santa Maria Novella. She smiles and he tells her he's always wanted to be a writer.

"Ah, so I'm in the presence of an artist," she chuckles, but not cruelly, and looking into her blue eyes, the sun dipping low toward the arc of shimmering water behind her, he realizes how silly he must sound, and begins laughing too.

Kitterage comes back from the tour late that night, and through a dinner of assorted fish and fried rice, they talk abstractly about their respective days. Yes, she saw Doug on the tour. They sat next to each other on the bus, in fact. The jewelry was beautiful, but too expensive. No, she didn't buy anything. Yes, he ran into Tania at the bookstore. Indeed, they had lunched together. No, he hadn't slept with her.

They both laugh nervously at the joke.

Lying in the dark later, listening to the hum of insect life through the rattan wall, they can feel the weight of each other's body on the mattress, though they don't touch. The ceiling fan above turns almost silently.

Doug and Tania drop by their hotel the next afternoon and ask them if they want go into the village for supper. Though it is a warm evening, Kitterage changes into a blouse she bought at the street market in Medan. Malcolm thinks about wearing a tie, then looks at Doug standing on their veranda in khaki shorts and a Heineken T-shirt, and decides to forget it. They take the same road Malcolm and Tania strolled back along the day before, and as they round the same curve by the shore where Malcolm had resisted the sudden impulse to kiss her, Doug decides he and Tania need cigarettes.

Off to one side there is a small tobacco stand. Behind the counter, a little girl and her mother sit holding hands. The woman looks about Kitterage's age, mid-twenties, and her dark forearms are covered with brass bangles. Her daughter is eight or nine and wears a bright blue embroidered handkerchief on her head. She smiles when she notices Kitterage looking at her and nudges her mother, wrapping a thin arm around her waist. The woman looks at Kitterage, then over to Malcolm and Tania, then at Doug, then back to Kitterage, then whispers something to her daughter. They both giggle, exposing teeth and gums stained reddish black by the habit of betel-nut chewing. Kitterage grins back and reaches to unzip her bag, but hesitates.

"You want to take a picture?" Doug asks over his shoulder.

"Yes, but I'm too embarrassed."

"Nonsense," Tania laughs, moving to stand beside her. "All you have to do is ask them."

"But how? I don't speak a word of Indonesian."

Doug takes out his own camera. "Okay, here are the only three words of Bahasa you'll ever need to know."

He kneels down until he can look directly into their faces. "*Horas!*" He feigns holding and looking through a camera with his free hand, then makes a clicking sound with his mouth and pretends to hit the shutter with his index finger. "*Terima kasih?*"

Mother and daughter look confused at first, but after he repeats the gesture a couple more times they finally laugh and nod.

"See, no problem!" he says, this time focusing the real thing and snapping off a picture. The girl jumps up and down and claps, and so he takes another one.

Within minutes a throng of other people on the road have gathered beside the shopkeeper and her daughter, posing to have their pictures taken. Kitterage gets out the camera Malcolm bought her and starts taking photographs as well, and all of a sudden one of the boys who's come up from swimming in the nearby lake decides to push his friend into the water, and soon it seems everyone is laughing and screaming and throwing water at one another.

Malcolm takes a few steps back to better appreciate the pandemonium that is breaking out, nearly stumbling over a tree stump.

Somehow they wind up at the most expensive restaurant in town, and end up eating little and drinking too much. Doug regales them with impossible stories from his stint in the navy. At one point Malcolm feels a stretched-out leg run up his thigh, and ends up playing footsie with its owner half the night, though he can't be sure if it's Kitterage or Tania. When the bill comes, there's some confusion that ends in them all laughing hysterically and ordering another round of drinks. The new total comes, and after a good show of it, Doug graciously relents and lets Malcolm pay.

Malcolm has no idea how they managed to get back to their hotel, but he and Kitterage are awakened early the next morning by creaking on the veranda.

"Hey, are you guys up yet?" It's Tania, wearing only a light brown summer dress, and as she stands in the open doorway, midmorning light filtering around her into the dark room, Malcolm can see every line and curve of her body through the thin material. She meets his nervous smile with a little shake of the head and a smile of her own. "Doug and I have a surprise for you."

Following Tania and Kitterage up to the lodge, Tania's thongs slapping against the still damp concrete next to Kit's measured step, Malcolm is suddenly overcome with nausea and must step off into the bushes to throw up. He finds them all a few minutes later, waiting at the table closest to the road. Doug is talking to the boy from the village with the long dreadlocks who comes around nearly every afternoon trying to sell marijuana, but as soon as he sees the state Malcolm is in he orders a round of coffees and some toast.

"So, what's the surprise you were talking about?" Kit asks after Malcolm has been returned to some state of composure. Tania and Doug look at each other and smile again, then Doug rummages in his shirt pocket and puts a small key on the table in front of Malcolm.

"I hope you can ride a scooter better than you handle your hangovers, friend, or we're in trouble."

Kit flashes Malcolm a nervous smile and he shrugs back.

"There's this incredible waterfall we've heard about," Tania says, putting one hand on Kit's shoulder. "It's supposed to be absolutely gorgeous."

Kit looks at Malcolm again, but when he doesn't say anything, Doug leans forward. "Come on, man. An adventure into the heart of deepest, darkest Sumatra!" Then he glances over at Tania and Kit, and lowers his voice conspiratorially. "It'll give you something to write about."

Malcolm hasn't ridden a scooter since university, and while Tania goes back to the room with Kit to fetch some things, he has another cup of coffee, then takes some practice laps around the courtyard to get his feel and confidence back. Still, he's a bit nervous when Kitterage gets on behind and puts both hands around his waist. "Are you sure you're all right?" she asks, leaning forward to look at him.

"Of course."

Beyond the few treks he's made down the road to the village these last few days, Malcolm hasn't ventured much beyond their hotel, and he is surprised now at how open the landscape becomes once they get away from the coast. Doug and Tania ride ahead, gunning it once they clear the last curve through a stand of palm trees and get on the open highway. Malcolm opens up as well, enjoying it when Kitterage latches on more tightly.

Rice fields alternate with groves of banana and sugarcane, and every few hundred yards they pass groups of tan boys herding water buffalo that are reluctant and sleepy in the afternoon heat. It is hard to make out anything else too clearly, though, what with the wind and the condition of the road. Doug slows down enough for Malcolm to catch up, and they ride in tandem, Tania leaning out with her camera.

"Smile!" she yells over the engine whine, and the flash goes off. Kitterage yells something back that Malcolm can't make out and Tania leans forward.

Up the road there's a market of some sort, and Doug starts to pull over. Malcolm does too, but then hesitates. With the sun on his face, and feeling the sudden freedom of independent mobility after weeks of traveling on motor coaches, he is tempted to gun the engine full throttle and keep going. Kitterage tugs at his shirt and he hits the brakes instead, wheels locking, and they start to skid. Coming off the pavement and into the soft gravel of the shoulder, the back of the bike slides out, and he's sure they'll go over. He can feel the sudden rush of warm air against his cheek as Kitterage gasps and leans against the impending impact, but he shifts his own weight to compensate at the last moment and they skid to a stop just beyond the thatched entrance.

"Whoa, partner, that was some stunt!" Doug calls from behind, clapping in appreciation. Malcolm doesn't respond, just sits on the bike a few moments, shaking with adrenaline.

"Are you okay?" he asks after a while, leaning back in Kitterage's arms. He is surprised and grateful for her laughter.

"Remind me not to get on one of these things with you again, all right?" She gets off, pulls her skirt back into place, and walks over to Tania, who greets her with a little hug. They disappear into the dark of the shop. Doug saunters over, digging two beers from his knapsack. "You could probably use one of these about now."

Malcolm hesitates in taking the offered bottle.

"Best thing for a hangover," Doug adds, holding out the opener as well. "Besides, Dutch courage, and all that."

"I had everything under control, you know."

Doug holds his own beer up in tribute. "Hey, you handled it beautifully, especially when Kit started to panic and threw off your balance." He takes a deep swig. "A lot of guys would have lost it then."

They stand there a while, by the side of an unmarked road in the growing heat of a tropical morning, drinking warm beer and listening to the dull thudding of wooden cowbells echo across the rice paddies.

"You planning to head down to Bukittinggi after this?" Doug asks after a time, pushing his sunglasses to the top of his head and peering directly into Malcolm's face.

"We've thought about it." Malcolm nods back.

"Well," he says, glancing over his shoulder to either side, then leaning forward, "here's something you don't want to miss." Doug proceeds to tell him about the water buffalo fights they hold in the province every other month. It seems villages from all over Sumatra send their prize bulls to compete, but instead of facing a human opponent, two bulls are placed in pens next to a sow in heat until they've been worked into a sexual rage, then they are thrown into the ring together. "I mean, by the time these animals square off, they're ready to kill from the lust. You can see it in their eyes." Doug takes another swig of beer, then explains that while most bouts end with one bull scaring the other off, if both bulls score enough hits early on and get the smell of each other's blood, they'll fight to the death.

"Agh, I saw this match so bad even the Sumatran gamblers around me couldn't keep watching. Still, it was something to see." Doug takes a step closer, about to launch into a blow-by-blow description when Kitterage and Tania suddenly emerge carrying a large plastic bag between them.

"Well, ladies, what have you got there?" Malcolm asks, glad for the interruption. The two look at each other and smile.

"A durian," Tania announces in triumph, lifting the great green globe partially out of the bag.

"The queen of fruit, or something like that," Kitterage adds quickly.

Malcolm has never actually seen one, but Veterson's has a lot to say on the subject of these unappetizing things. *Durian: A foul-smelling fruit with thick spikes, shaped somewhat like an avocado, but hard and the size of man's head. Considered so noxious that countries like Singapore have banned them from all forms of public transportation. Popular wisdom in Malaysia contends that if you drink whiskey while eating a durian on a hot day, your stomach will explode.*

"They're supposed to be powerful aphrodisiacs," Tania says.

"And highly addictive," Doug adds, wagging his eyebrows at each of them in turn. "As much as you may hate it, once you've tried a durian, you'll crave it for the rest of your life."

Kitterage looks at both Doug and Tania doubtfully, then at Malcolm, who feels the slight pangs of nausea returning. "Rubbish."

"Okay, man," Doug laughs, "but six months from now, when you're back in England, searching every market you can think of for durian, don't say we didn't warn you!"

Malcolm turns and walks back to the scooter. Across the road a group of Batak children sit on a small rise, watching him. He gives them a little halfhearted wave and they giggle, then he mounts the bike, waiting for Kitterage to follow. He is startled by a much lighter touch on his shoulder.

"There's been a slight change in plans," Tania says, tilting her head slightly to one side as she speaks. "I'm riding with you now, if that's all right?" Malcolm looks back to see Kitterage getting on the other scooter behind Doug. She waves and Doug starts the engine. Malcolm looks back at Tania. "Don't worry," she whispers. "I don't think they can get too far away with us riding behind them." Then she smiles, one side of her mouth curling slightly higher than the other. Malcolm has absolutely no idea what he's supposed to say to this, so he just nods. Tania gives Doug the thumbs-up, and he and Kit peel onto the pavement and quickly disappear in a cloud of dust.

Tania laughs and pats Malcolm on the shoulder. "There's that British mettle I've heard so much about!" But her face darkens a moment later. "We have one serious problem, though."

"What's that?"

"How to carry this," she says, lifting the durian out of its bag.

They try riding with it resting on Tania's lap, nestled between her stomach and his back, but with the spikes it's too painful. They try tying it down on the back fender, but it's too precarious. They end up hanging it in front, looping the handles of the bag over the handlebars. It makes steering a bit awkward, but if Malcolm keeps under twenty-five miles an hour, they manage all right.

"So, are you doing okay?" Tania asks once they're back on the road. She keeps one hand on his hip and the other curled across his chest, just above his navel. She leans forward so she can hear his answers, and he feels her chest flatten against his back.

"Yes, but I can't remember a damn thing about last night. Can you?" He can't so much hear as feel the vibration of her laugh emanating up from her diaphragm.

"Not really!"

They ride on for a time in silence, the road getting rougher as it winds through hills of tropical fern and palms. Malcolm gives the bike more gas and carefully leans into a turn. Tania's pushing closer to him, trying to follow his movements exactly.

"So I wanted to ask you before, how did you two meet? You and Kitterage, I mean," Tania asks when they are back on a straight section of highway.

It's Malcolm's turn to laugh. What can he say about this? How can he tell her that he's always been awkward and shy with women? That like his courses in college, or his job at the bookstore, his engagement to Kitterage is just something that fell into place with a kind of quiet inevitability that never seemed to allow for the question of how or why. Like an object finally coming to rest at the base of a hill. Like rain falling during the monsoon. "Her brother and I were good friends in university."

Tania presses her mouth close to his ear, her breath warm and moist on his cheek. "Such a lovely girl, too!" and she nibbles the lobe.

He laughs nervously, gassing the engine.

"Can you pull over, Malcolm? I've got to pee." They're halfway through another set of curves, and the road has become crowded and dark with overhanging vines. The durian is swinging back and forth like a mad pendulum, and his arms are beginning to tire from trying to keep the wheel stable. As soon as the road opens up a little he stops.

Tania hops off, walking behind a small clump of trees nearby, and between the thin trunks Malcolm can see her pull up her thin dress and squat down. He turns and strolls over to a little grass-covered hill on the other side of the road. He had no idea they'd come so far into the mountains, for spread out far below is the lake, its surface mottled dark blue and gray beneath a canopy of heavy clouds moving from over the ridges to the north. Tania comes over a minute later and sits down. She has her sunglasses on, and when she stretches out on her back all he can see is his own image, marshaled in the round frames. He sits down beside her.

"I wonder when it'll start raining again."

"Mmm," she says. "Sooner or later."

Malcolm leans back on the grass as well and closes his eyes. Tania moves a little closer and he imagines he can feel the static electricity of her skin intersect that of his own. She smells sweet, like coconut oil.

"So what about you and Doug?" Malcolm begins, not sure exactly what he's asking. "I mean, how did you two meet?"

Tania's laugh is loud and sudden, like a bark. "We picked each other up in some bar outside of Chiang Mai about six months ago, and we've just sort of bummed around together since."

"Chiang Mai?"

"In northern Thailand. Near the Burmese border."

"Oh."

She puts her hands back and pushes herself into a sitting position, then leans over and suddenly kisses him. Then they just sit like that for a while, on the side of the road, Malcolm's head resting near her waist, their breath coming and going. Malcolm believes she may be the most beautiful woman he's ever seen. Tania finally leans over and kisses him again, but when he tries to sit up and hold her, she pushes him back down gently.

"You're not really comfortable with this whole arrangement, are you?" she asks seriously, and for the first time Malcolm thinks of Kit and Doug off somewhere, doing God knows what. He imagines Doug putting his thick arm around Kit's waist and his pulse quickens.

"No, not really," he says, trying to sit up once more.

"Good," she says, pushing him back down again.

When they finally pull up next to the other scooter and park, Doug and Kitterage are nowhere to be seen, and Malcolm quickly unties the durian and slides his arm through the plastic handles of the bag. The fruit is starting to smell, sticky juice dripping from one corner where the skin of the durian has cracked open from repeatedly banging against the handlebars. Malcolm doesn't care. He's much more interested in discovering what Doug and Kit are up to.

Tania leads the way, and he watches the muscles in her calves work as she negotiates the steep slope. The sound of water grows louder, becoming a mad rushing as they circle an enormous outgrowth of ferns and stand at the base of the falls. "Hey there!" Doug yells from somewhere up above, but his voice is hollow and distant, almost completely swallowed by the flood of sound. "No, over here!" He calls again, and looking up to the left this time, Tania and Malcolm spot them standing on a little outcropping of rocks about thirty feet up, waving. Tania waves back and Doug dives headfirst into the center of the pool, where the water is a dark green almost to the point of black. He doesn't come up for the longest time, and Malcolm wonders whether to jump in after him when Doug suddenly surfaces right in front of them with a splash.

"Wow, this water's cold."

Doug gets out and picks up a towel lying on a nearby boulder, leaning over to kiss Tania, and Malcolm sees that what he mistook for flab on the ferry the other day is in fact all muscle. Doug turns to look up at Kitterage, revealing the spiraling coil of a brilliant purple snake tattoo winding up his back, trailing across one shoulder, ending in a diamond-shaped head on his pectoral muscle, a thin, forked tongue encircling his right nipple. He cups his broad hands around his mouth.

"Come on, Kit! Don't think about it too much, you'll be fine! Just aim for the center!"

Kitterage slowly pumps her arms methodically by her side, leaning over the edge, but even from where he stands, Malcolm can see her knees shaking.

"You can do it, Kit! Come on!" Tania joins in, clapping her hands. "Come on down here and let's try this durian!" Kitterage smiles and nods, but just keeps swinging her arms.

Malcolm is struck by how crazy this is, trying to push an obviously frightened woman into jumping when her own good sense tells her not to. "Kit, you needn't jump if you don't feel up to it!" he yells.

Both Doug and Tania turn to look at him in surprise, and Malcolm is about to say something more when there is a sudden high whoop and they all turn back in time to see Kitterage stumble forward, head down and feet kicking out in a clumsy dive.

Malcolm knows instantly that she will hit the water wrong, her body rotating out of position and without the forward momentum to get her to the center of the pool. He steps forward, letting the durian drop, and there is a sickening snap as the fruit cracks against the ground. Kitterage's body folds over on itself, picking up speed, and she hits the water on her back with a violent splash. When she comes to the surface, none of them can tell if she's laughing or crying.

"You scared me half to death," Malcolm complains as he tosses the splintered durian back into the plastic bag, relieved that she's all right but unable to look her straight in the face.

Kitterage's voice trembles with excitement and her body is flushed with an exhilaration Malcolm has never seen in her before. "I scared myself half to death as well."

Doug and Tania are all smiles. "You did a super job, Kit. We're proud of you."

After they've gathered up their clothes and bags, Doug leads them up a narrow path behind a wall of rock and eventually out onto the flat top of a giant boulder. It's much quieter here, and sitting close to the edge Malcolm can see why. The river is calm and swift just before it drops off into the falls below.

Tania and Kit spread out a blanket they thought to bring from the lodge, and with the aid of Doug's knife, pry the fruit the rest of the way open and divide it into four roughly equal segments. Inside the pulpy flesh of the durian is yellowish white and peppered with tiny seeds. It smells both nutty and sharply sweet. An overly ripe smell, Malcolm thinks, like something rotten. Doug and Tania begin eating, the fruit's juice, white and heavy like milk, rolling down their hands. Kit nibbles her piece and makes a face, then sets the fruit down. She picks it up again, and licks it, closing her eyes and frowning. Malcolm takes a tentative bite. It's sickeningly bitter and sweet at the same time, and he has to fight the impulse to gag, but as he sets the fruit back on the bag his taste buds are tingling.

"Like I said, an acquired taste," Doug says, wiping his mouth on his towel. "It acquires you!"

"That's right," Tania laughs, "we're all infected now."

Kit breaks out a bottle of water and each takes a deep drink in turn. They all sit still, listening to the sounds of the river, suddenly sleepy in the afternoon heat. Malcolm reaches out to grab Kit's hand, but just at that moment she leans back and closes her eyes. Doug gives Tania a kiss.

"Did you have a good time, baby?" he asks, and she smiles and nods and kisses him again. "Good," he says, then glances over at Malcolm.

Malcolm isn't sure what to make of it. From the time he mounted the scooter back at the village, he's been lost, as if all of their gestures—Doug's and Tania's and Kit's, even his own—are words spoken in a very foreign tongue he perhaps once knew but now only vaguely remembers. Doug stands and takes his shirt off again suddenly. "Time for another dip. Malcolm, why don't you join me."

It's a command, not a question, and Malcolm hesitates.

"You guys go off and do manly men-type stuff, I'll stay here and mind the fort," Tania says, nodding when Malcolm looks at her as if to say, *You'll be all right.*

He stands and Doug motions for him to follow.

Instead of leading him back down the path, Doug takes Malcolm up another set of trails winding through bamboo, and they emerge a few minutes later at the base of a much taller waterfall. The pool is narrow and very dark, bounded on the far side by a cliff face notched with a series of thin ledges. "How about a dive?"

Doug points at a tree about halfway up that juts out over the pool. Malcolm guesses it's a good fifty feet high. "You've got to be joking."

Doug shakes his head. "No, it's not bad. Look," Doug says, pointing at the black center of the pool, "the water here is really deep. You'll be okay."

They climb down to the pool and throw their towels over a spiked plant Malcolm's never seen before near the water's edge. Doug follows a ragged little path around toward the other side, but stops about halfway and turns back. "Come on, Malcolm. Don't be a pussy."

What appeared as solid rock is in fact shale, and scrambling higher and higher up the cliff face, they send a steady stream of clay chips and dust raining down into the water below. At one point Malcolm glances down, but fights the impulse to do so again. He keeps his eyes focused on the edge of the tattoo running across Doug's tanned back instead. Soon enough they reach the top.

The tree's trunk is thick, and though barkless, is rough enough to stand on without the danger of slipping. Looking out toward the horizon, they can see parts of the highway they took to get here weaving in and out of the forest and down the mountain. Malcolm almost imagines he can see the hill where he and Tania stopped just an hour before, and beyond that, the rice fields sweeping down to the coast, but perhaps it is just approaching storm clouds.

"It's hard to believe," Doug begins. "It took thousands of years, but they've managed to pave roads all the way into the heart of the rain forest so guys like you and me could fool around on them. That's progress for you!"

They stand for a while in silence, as if casually admiring the waves down at the beach rather than being perched on the edge of a great height. The sun still hangs high in the sky, but has lost its morning brilliance, and filtered through the canopy of leaves overhead it casts a mellow glow over everything. "Still," Doug continues, "I suppose it's a testament to the fact that even the most civilized fellow has a bit of a savage inside him. Wouldn't you say, Malcolm? Don't you have the heart of a wild thing beating inside you?"

Doug's eyes are wide and suggestive, and Malcolm is suddenly overcome with irritation. "The Sumatrans aren't savages, you know," he blurts out, but he knows even while saying it that he's missed the point.

"Yes, yes," Doug says, chuckling. "You're quite right." He takes a quick look over the side, then smiles at Malcolm again. His face is odd, though, like he wants to say something else but fights back the desire. "Well, in case I don't make it," Doug begins again, stretching out one meaty hand to shake Malcolm's thin one, "it was nice knowing you." Doug spins around and without another word walks to the end of the tree and steps off.

The trunk and roots block most of what's below from view, and it seems like forever before Malcolm hears the splash, then Doug's thin hoot of triumph from below. There's more splashing, then another deep silence before Doug calls out, "Whenever you're ready, Malcolm!"

Malcolm steps onto the trunk and walks slowly toward the edge. Despite its girth, Malcolm can feel the whole thing bounce and shimmy slightly with each step, and when he reaches the end he must take a few breaths before he can look down. The pool seems impossibly small from up here, but he can clearly see his towel and their footprints on the muddy bank below. There's no sign of Doug, though, and there's a sudden shift in the pit of his stomach.

Sweat begins to fall from him, every pore of his skin like a dam on full release. Malcolm can feel it dripping off his arms, down his back and belly, rolling down his thighs until he's sure he can feel it pooling beneath his feet, and for the first time he can actually smell himself—the metallic odor of fear mixed with the pungency of the alcohol and sex; the aching sweetness of the durian. He thinks of Tania's soft lips against his own, of Doug's thick hands. Of the unexpected changes in Kit. Then standing at the edge of this high cliff, he suddenly realizes exactly what's been going on. Why they've made this long trek into the mountains. He launches himself into empty space.

The water is much colder than Malcolm expects, sending a shudder through him, dark and to the bone, as if the center of his body were suddenly resonating with something deep in the core of the mossy rocks and mud of the bottom.

"Doug! Tania! Where are you guys?" he calls out when he reaches the muddy bank, but there's no answer. "Kit? Kit? Are you there?" He tries again, and this time he hears a tiny call back.

"Malcolm? Where are you?"

He pulls himself out of the pool, shaking and panting, and rushes toward the path.

"Malcolm?" Kit cries again, her voice growing louder as he scrambles back through the brush toward the base of the falls. "Doug? Tania?"

"Kit?"

"Malcolm, I went over there to watch for you, and . . ." He emerges from the bushes just in time to catch the realization passing across Kit's face, a sickening look that confirms what he somehow already knows. "Our money . . . the passports . . . our tickets . . . "

He is tempted to keep running, to let the incline of the hill and his momentum carry him farther in pursuit, but the sight of Kitterage standing on the hotel blanket draws him up. It seems like some twisted joke, almost too bizarre to imagine. The empty water bottle, their clothes littered about the small clearing, Kitterage wide-eyed and staring in disbelief. But far away, indeed so small he's half sure he's imagining it, but no, there it is again, Malcolm can hear the drone of the two scooters barreling off in the distance. He looks down and lying there before him are the half-eaten remains of the durian.

There's nothing for them to do but walk down the mountain, Malcolm realizes some time later. If they start now, they might make it back to the lodge before dark. Perhaps even before the now inevitable storm breaks. Without Veterson's guide it will be difficult, but Malcolm is sure that once they're on the highway he can find the way. Or maybe they can cut across the rice fields to the coast. From there they can contact the authorities, although he has no idea what the police can do for them. Still, the thing is to start walking. Yet when Malcolm looks at Kit again, at her red hair falling down in wet tangles across her shoulders, her mouth slowly opening and closing as if searching for the words to some silent prayer, he must sit down.

He listens to the soft hush of leaves swaying against leaves, to water moving over worn stone, the darkening jungle wrapping itself tightly around their small clearing, the sound of their own breaths, coming and going. Malcolm grabs a piece of the durian sitting next to him. The fruit glistens with moisture and the smell is unbelievable, but he hungrily takes a bite, then another and another, letting the juice flow freely down his face and neck, letting the taste and whatever else might come wash over him.

Andrew J. McCann

Temple University

ZENITH

One sandpaper hand squeaks against Styrofoam as the other raises a Chesterfield pinched between thumb and finger toward a graying, bristly face. Second coffee, third cigarette. Their vapors spiral upward, a double helix in the dim factory bay, striking a yellow girder high in the corrugated ceiling, before slipping into final darkness. The windows were painted fifty years earlier against possible attack from the *Luftwaffe*. Instead, destruction would come years later through the plodding calculations of corporate accountants. Eddie Painter stands with cigarette and coffee, thinking of that incremental devastation, the acres of broken macadam where once within his lifetime the buildings stood shoulder to shoulder, heaving with life. Now the factory is a quiet place at the heart of Zenith, New York, its empty stretches dotted with brick buildings and a few ripples of parked cars.

The factory bay is silent but for the unheard cicada hum of electricity. Eddie hunches over a blueprint for a ring scrapped on third shift. The last waves of first-shift workers gather by the coffee machine at the end of the aisle, waiting for the clock to force them to their workstations. He knows the third shift is already queued by the time clock now, waiting to punch out, waiting for the clock to kick over the last remaining minutes and release them. That clock is everything to them; their weeks are measured by its mechanical *ka-*

chunk, their bank accounts filled by it. He has hated that lineup for thirty years, hated their eagerness for time's passage, their lingering in the locker room and padding of coffee breaks to cheat the clock. Each minute stolen is a victory for them, the creative act of getting over.

He squints at the blueprints, eyes narrowing as he drags on the cigarette. A stubby pencil serves as a calculator, marking fractions in the margins of the paper, its gold letters glittering in the semidark: ELECTRIC CITY PUTT-PUTT. He estimates feeds and speeds, calculating the time necessary to cut the raw metal to polished tolerance. Behind him, the Giddings & Lewis manual turret lathe rises from a dented chip catcher, bristling cutting tools and steel blocks, her hoses a woven tangle of arteries pumping coolant, cutting oil, and grease. The G&L has been Eddie's home for twenty-five years, and only his callused and deft touch on her worn gears can coax a three-foot-diameter metal ring, with its intricate keyholes and slots, from an engineer's paper design. It is the same touch that had brought pianos back to singing life after the ravages of fire, water, or simple neglect. The touch that had pulled customers from up and down the East Coast, and kept his garage workshop busy on weekends, and in the hours after the factory. But that had ended eight years earlier in a conspiracy of environmental regulatory paperwork, worker's compensation insurance, and the availability of cheap, new pianos.

The frustration of reworking a ring screwed up by someone else dilutes Eddie's concentration and his mind wanders to the previous night, to the questions Suzy had asked under the haze of the nightly news, as they sat eating stir-fry in the kitchen that had been boardroom, accounting department, and production control in the years their business thrived.

"Are they going to offer early retirement again this year, Eddie?"

She had been talking about plans to travel to the following Saturday's marching band competition at Oneonta State—whether to sleep in the van or get a motel room—so her sudden question about retirement confused him.

"I don't know, Suz. I haven't heard anything."

He didn't take his eyes off the NBC News report on the Federal Reserve's upcoming meeting to discuss interest rates.

"Do you think they will? It's been three years in a row, hasn't it?"

"Yeah, I guess. But they can't force me out. I've got too many years. They'd have to close half the plant to get me. And if they'd do that, they'd offer early retirement. Once I hit fifty-five, I'm safe no matter what happens. What made you think of that? Did you hear something?"

"No, I haven't heard anyone talking. But . . ."

He sensed her effort, her difficulty at continuing, but the subject had no immediacy for him and he resisted encouraging her.

"Well, did you ever think of volunteering to retire? You can go at fifty-five, right? That's only three weeks from now."

The news cut to commercial, and Eddie turned to face Suzy, saw her eyebrows angle, pinching a wrinkle of skin above the bridge of her nose. Her worried face. The face that he had learned to watch for when piano restorations ran through weekends, or factory workdays blurred into one another, exhausting his ability to think. It was the face that pronounced some uncomfortable truth.

"Why are you bringing this up all of a sudden? What does it matter to you, anyway?"

He didn't mean the words cruelly, but he saw them cut her, saw them fold her brow into shadows. He knew his suspicion had forced the words. Retirement preoccupied him, as it preoccupied all of the men at the factory, and had for twenty years. But sixty-two was soon enough. He had seen men waste away working around the house, putting in patios, flower beds, and additions that they would never use, would only show off. The old-timers called them "honey-do" retirements—honey do this, honey do that. Suzy had never been like that, but he had faith in their ability to drive each other nuts somehow. And then there were the hobbyists. They would corner you at the hardware store on a Saturday and take twenty minutes to tell you about their new boat, or golf club—some new widget to complain and brag about. Eddie didn't know which fate was worse.

"It matters to me, Eddie, because I see you angry all the time. Angry at that Gary, and the men you work with. You don't even like Stanwicj anymore. It's a bitter anger, Eddie. That's what bothers me. So I wondered if you would have the opportunity to leave if you wanted. That's all."

"Gary's a poisonous prick. End of story. You want me to like a guy who works for two hours and spends the rest of the day bitching about the crooks in the front office?"

A beer commercial blasted out of the TV and Eddie got up to turn down the volume. He pulled a cigarette from a pack on the countertop and offered one to Suzy. She took it and waited for him to pass the lighter.

"There have always been men like him down there, and it never bothered you like it does now."

"Maybe they're getting worse. The less they do, the more they screw up. Then Stanwicj comes crying to me to fix things. Poor guy, he doesn't know if he's a foreman, a team leader, or some bastardized combination of the two. They keep sending him to classes on how to *coach* us for Chrissake. How do you coach a guy like Gary? You throw him off the damned team, that's how you coach him. It'd make all the rest of us feel better, I know that."

"It might make *you* feel better, but don't most of the men like him?"

"Do they like him, or are they afraid of him? His gang will get in at the next election, no doubt. Then things will really get hot with management. I just wish he'd leave me alone to work."

Eddie felt that Suzy's desired conversation had gone offtrack. He struggled consciously to bring it back, still not understanding why she had brought up the subject.

"Why do you want to talk about retirement, anyway? I don't think about it actually happening."

"Eddie, maybe you should. Maybe you should think about getting on with your life and let the factory go."

"What do you mean getting on with my life? What do I have to get on with? You'd think we were hustling for the grave the way you talk. You want we should get in the van and drive around the country? Join all the other useless old people gloating over their ten percent discount at Denny's? What's the point to that? At least now I'm building something."

"What are you building, Eddie? You're working for a company that doesn't give a hoot about you or Gary or Stanwicj, never mind the damned rings. They'd be happier making them in Taiwan. You aren't needed there, and worse, you aren't happy anymore. I don't want to turn our life into mornings reading the paper and watching the talk shows, then afternoons working on the house. We can *do* something, Eddie."

She paused, then continued. "John could use you at the repair shop, for instance. I could do the books and help Mary with the baby."

"I ain't living through my son. He's got to learn and fight on his own. If he asked, I'd go. But he ain't asking, and it'd be meddling to offer." Eddie stamped his cigarette into the sink and walked out the screen door, for once letting it bang behind him.

Suzy's voice cried down the steps, "You've got to think about it, Eddie. It's going to happen."

Even as he walked into the cold spring air he recognized her tone, and knew it to be a voice that had saved their business before. But this time she was wrong. He had seven years to think about retirement. Seven years of good work and good money before he went out—and then at the right age.

Eddie sat in the garage workshop until the lights in the house went out. Suzy would know where he was and know to leave him alone. His eyes traveled over the wood lathes, the table saw, noticing the dust lining the edges of drawers. He suddenly resented their handles, neatly labeled and fastened with samples of sandpaper cut to an exact shape. They served no purpose now.

In the far corner of the garage, John's go-cart lay under a drop sheet. He had meant to give it away years ago, but the hundreds of hours of work they had invested together stopped him. They hadn't raced it in ten years, but Eddie kept it lubricated and ran it twice a year. Those were the rare times he actually worked in the garage now; nothing brought him to the woodworking tools anymore. He had tried making furniture, even birdhouses, but it wasn't the same as a living business. He was more likely to bring the newspaper out to the workshop on a Sunday to enjoy the quiet and the lingering smell of varnish. He got a rag from a drawer and, breathing the work smell of lacquer, he dusted the equipment, work tops, and edges, letting Suzy's questions fade with the motion of his arm.

Now at his workstation in the factory, her questions seem even farther away, and Eddie thinks only of the rework ring and the incompetence that created it.

The noise in the bay grows as operators man workstations and start drive motors. Eddie loads a raw metal ring onto the G&L, tightens the hold-down bolts with a socket wrench, and takes refuge in the work and in the anger. The ring will take him five hours to machine. Five hours of redundant effort, of rework hours spent on a job that the night operator ruined through laziness, ruined because it was too hard to take three minutes with pencil and paper to check the design. It was much easier to throw the ring on the machine and push Go. Much easier to stand for four hours chatting, reading the newspaper, smoking, and watching the clock while the computer worked. Easier still to pull the ring off the machine without checking it, without caring, to leave for the washroom an hour before the end of shift, letting the day man worry about the mistakes. Eddie knows there will be no consequence for that action, and he starts from scratch in order to get the job back in Stanwicj's schedule, running the old manual machine that punishes mistakes immediately.

The man-door across the aisle from Eddie's G&L opens, throwing a parallelogram of light onto the oily brick floor, and Gary Van Vrank—burly and bearded—enters. Eddie glances at the clock mounted over the door, and then back at Gary. His eyes are rocks plunged into the chubby face. They peer over bifocals, confident.

"I've still got two minutes to punch in, Painter. You just keep your nose to the grindstone like a good boy and let me worry about the time."

Before Eddie can respond, Paul Stanwicj calls out as he squeezes between the machines behind the G&L, his clipboard swinging with early energy.

"Morning, Eddie. You got PERCO there?"

The hard jaw turns, eyes narrowing as when a wolf judges the herd, seeing the old, the infirm, letting Gary escape down the aisle.

"Yup. Your boy on third shift really fucked it up. Hard to believe you can cut a ring so out of round with a push-button machine."

"I think he got the calculations wrong. Or the print wasn't clear. I know they've been having trouble with that lathe, too."

"So you bring it over here to a decrepit old man running a

decrepit old machine? Why doesn't Campagni do it on the CNC? It'll take me hours with the feed rate I can run."

"Well, Campagni can't fix it. You know you're our point man. No one else can do the delicate work."

"So you've got an idiot on third shift machining eggs, and a guinea on first shift who can't do more than push a button—what kind of business you running here, Stanwicj? I'll be all morning fixing this mess."

"You think it'll take all morning?"

Eddie, letting the question hang, turns back to the table to tighten the clamps that hold the ring in place. He calls over his shoulder, "Easy. Why? You and the team going to create some more rework for me?"

Eddie's voice is even, matter-of-fact. There are no surprises because it is their usual discussion, repeated on a weekly basis. Eddie knows Stanwicj's only method for getting production out of the men is to coax and mollify each in his own peculiar way.

"Hopefully not. PERCO's the last rush job. Actually Don wants you to go to a meeting."

"You're really trying to get on my good side, aren't you?" Eddie leans around the side of the machine, reaching for a chromed handle that he pulls gently. The cutting tool moves to within a half inch of the glinting steel ring.

"Yeah, I invent this stuff just to torture you and get my best man off the line. It's the new VP's meeting —they want a *representative* sample of workers."

"Why don't you send the Eggmaker? He could entertain the new veep with his magical math skills. Management could use a guy like him. He'd make their quarterly results come up blooming, no matter what."

"Come on, Eddie. Don wants you to go 'cause you're fair and you won't get wound up over some stupid little thing. You know how most of these guys will whine about a tooling problem or how the boss didn't listen to their great idea in 1987. Will you go?"

"Where is it? The Big House?"

"No, the Training Center."

"Shit. You want I should go home and change?"

"No, they're casual up there now. You'll be fine. Just keep those jeans clean if you can. And smoke a couple of cigarettes before you go. No smoking up there, you know."

"What time?"

"Eleven-thirty. And Don said you can go home whenever it ends. The meeting includes lunch."

"That's mighty big of him, since I was here working before my shift even started. What happens if it runs past three?"

"Just tell me tomorrow and I'll change your time card."

Eddie's foot slides to the right, eyes fixed on the intersection of tool and metal, to push a lever that starts the table spinning. His right hand turns a chromed wheel, the action identical to a WWII submariner or antiaircraft gunner, until perfect silvery commas peel off the ring and tinkle into the chip catcher surrounding the table. Stanwicj, dismissed but content, turns to continue on his rounds.

At eleven o'clock Eddie lifts the ring off the machine, loads it onto a hydraulic lift, and toes it to final inspection. No one is there, although lunch isn't until noon, and he has to find Stanwicj to make sure the ring is inspected, boxed, and shipped. Then he returns to his workstation and shovels metal chips into a bin and sweeps the area. He washes in the locker room, scrubbing up to his elbows with gritty soap, rinsing lemon scent into the round stone sink.

As he drives to the Training Center, he alternates bites from the PB and J sandwich that Suzy made that morning with drags on a cigarette. He follows a private road through the rolling, groomed campus surrounding the facility. The building rises in flying buttresses and mirrored glass, a combination that simultaneously reaches for and captures the sky, reflecting its blue-and-white brilliance in gray facsimile. He passes the arc of reserved parking spaces in front of the building's double doors and enters the visitors' lot, driving past rows of cars to find a place. He leaves the van, Suzy's floral curtains shining out of the windows, between a German sedan and an American pickup truck, noticing with a wry smile their matching gray leather interiors.

Double doors lead to a circular room with a single desk puddled in reds and blues from a skylight set high above the doors.

"May I help you?"

The receptionist is not surprised to see a common man. Equal opportunity training, Eddie thinks.

"I'm Eddie Painter. I came for a meeting with the VP."

"Certainly, Mr. Painter. Straight down the hall, first door on the right."

"Thank you, miss."

He enters an anteroom, empty except for a table laden with cold cuts, bread, muffins, juice, and brownies. A stainless steel coffee server sits steaming, surrounded by unbroken pyramids of cups and saucers that imply Eddie is the first to arrive.

With a cup of black coffee in hand, he walks through another set of double doors into a room whose size surprises him. He assumed the meeting would be large; this room can fit maybe twenty people. He takes a chair on the far side of the U-shaped table, remembering the building of the Training Center eight years earlier. That year they had knocked down seven buildings in the plant. By the time they got around to the Training Center, people had stopped watching; even the old-timers avoided the demolitions.

Alone, without work, his mind wanders to his son's Connecticut auto repair shop, little more than a well-equipped garage. John had worked in the piano shop as a kid, gradually moving from errand boy to rougher, to an experienced hand whose workmanship challenged Eddie's own. Eddie thought if they had learned anything from the restoration business, it was the impossibility of making money through individual craft; a business had to make money through the labor of others. But John was trying, performing detailed work for leasers who would trade their cars within a year. It would be an insult to volunteer help. It was a dumb idea, but what else might he and Suzy do? Eddie liked to travel in the van, but their trips—mostly to see band competitions—couldn't be the focus of his life. Work was Eddie's love made visible and he was smart enough to know it.

Voices jolt him from these considerations. Eddie looks up to see five or six men, all in jeans and work boots, salad plates loaded with sandwiches and brownies, enter the room. Another group enters, and it is clear that only the leaders of the meeting are missing. The men fill all the seats around the table. Four empty chairs sit against the front wall, two on either side of a projector screen. It is eleven-forty, and Eddie thinks of the stack of rings in front of his machine and the money it takes to pay him to sit in the conference room. Then the doors open and the empty seats file in. Two are union:

Buddy Tines, Local 298 president, and Tony Bianchi, secretary and treasurer. Eddie voted for them both at the last election because they sought to work with management instead of running militant. He has never seen the other two.

The young one is slender and tall, over six foot easily. His companion is grayer, with eyes that lock on to the few personalities in the room, picking out charisma like a black light on phosphorescent paint. Stanwicj was right, Eddie thinks, they're both casual. However, the sweaters they wear—embroidered coats-of-arms of crossed golf clubs and blossoming trees—look expensive as suits. The young one speaks first.

"Not many of you know me yet. My name is Mark Pressfield and I have just started here in Zenith as VP of production. This is Dennis Barston, my human resources executive. I'd like to welcome you to the first of a series of roundtable discussions between senior management and the folks on the front lines. I don't believe this has been done in Zenith before, so your patience and support are appreciated. But before we get started I'd like Buddy to talk for a minute and then do some introductions. Buddy—"

Buddy thanks Pressfield and talks briefly for five minutes about the great challenges the business faces and how union/management cooperation will be critical to their survival.

Pressfield outlines his plan to get their cost structure back in line; he likes to call it "High Involvement." He tells them that they can't afford to lose one great idea, that they need every brain pulling in one direction—toward productivity, quality, and customer service. Then he asks for questions.

The room is quiet. Peripheral visions stretch to their maximum—checking reactions, watching for the first break. Barston suggests Pressfield give them some examples of how "H. I." will work. Pressfield monologues for ten minutes: examples of work teams and productivity leaps at other factories—devoted, happy customers, solid profits, secure futures. The union contract is a constant, silent, backdrop to Pressfield's speech. Nothing he says breaks the rules, but his vision of consolidated job classifications and quality teams is borderline blasphemy in a factory where move men and crane runners, not management, pace production. Buddy and Tony sit with crossed arms and feet, scanning the room. Pressfield stops, the glow of passion fresh on his face, obviously hoping for conversion, expecting acknowledgment.

"Yeah, I got a question, Mr. Pressfield."

Eddie knows the questions that will be asked. They will be small embarrassments for management, small accusations that matter little. He has sat through these meetings before and knows the dance.

Pressfield's chipmunk energy focuses on the questioner.

"Sure, go ahead, Bob."

Jesus, Eddie thinks, he's memorized all our names.

"I'd like to know how we'll make all these great improvements when I can't even get tools for my machine. I mean, I sit idle at least two hours a day waiting for the setup man to get to my machine and change tools and lay out the job."

Eddie wonders why he doesn't do it himself.

"Well, that's a good example," replies Mark. "Many factories eliminate setup men and have operators lay out the machine themselves. Imagine the productivity hit if we did that here."

Barston and the two union leaders are behind Pressfield and he cannot see their reactions. The group in front looks mystified, like cavemen having the wheel explained to them for the first time. Eddie feels a difference, a sense that the meeting is breaking from the program-of-the-month club. Behind Pressfield, the implications are equally clear and the three men struggle for a way to interrupt gracefully. Barston, the seasoned politic, beats his blue-collar equivalents to it. In a voice so low the men lean forward to hear, he addresses Pressfield.

"Mark, you know that would entail careful consideration by the union and a major rewrite of the contract. While those are exactly the issues we want to consider, we don't want to give folks the impression that we're jumping the gun."

Buddy finds his voice: "Yeah, Bob, we don't want to give you the facetious impression that those kinds of events would be foregone conclusions. But we do got to make progress in areas like this. A better question for the current moment in time is why you're waiting two hours a day for setup. Maybe Mr. Pressfield can look into that for you over the next week or so."

Pressfield turns, gesturing subconsciously, working consensus.

"Absolutely, Buddy. I'll have a word with the manager of Bob's area tomorrow."

Eddie knows that a good foreman would have asked Bob if, when he is ready for a setup, he notifies anyone or just sits for an hour or two reading the newspaper. But Eddie knows the deal, knows the managers are little more than number crunchers and mouthpieces.

Pressfield answers more questions with energy and the insight of ignorance. On almost every one Barston backs him up, then spins the answer to satisfy the flexing forearms of the union leaders, effectively sucking meaning from the answer. Human resources has always seemed like the CIA to Eddie—omnipresent, vast, but without identifiable duties. Eddie realizes Barston could have ended up running either, could be sitting next to a president instead of a business executive. He wonders if Barston would get away with his tactics in front of reporters.

They must have really picked the crowd, Eddie thinks, to avoid any hardcases. There are enough holes in Pressfield's commonsense talk of consolidation and streamlining to walk a five-hundred-person picket line through. Eddie sees some shifty eyes in those who don't speak, no doubt recording Buddy and Tony's collusion for relay to the hard-line opposition party. It doesn't matter to Eddie because it doesn't affect him, but then Pressfield turns his attention to Eddie.

"Eddie, you haven't said anything. How do you think H. I. will go across in Building 62?"

He looks up, startled, like a daydreamer called on by the teacher.

"I don't think it much matters."

"To you, or to Building 62?"

"To either."

Eddie sees Barston start, recognizing an opinion he hadn't cataloged or foreseen.

"But it's got to matter if we're going to save this business in a brutally competitive marketplace. How can you say it doesn't matter?"

"It doesn't matter to me because it won't work. It won't matter to the rest of them because they'll do the same thing they do every day, regardless."

The union leaders look uncomfortable but not surprised. Eddie's answer is the expected, negative voice. No one in the room knows his usual, positive role in public and they do not hear the danger.

Eyes roll in boredom at the extension of the meeting. Pressfield is the only one who takes Eddie's words seriously.

"I don't believe that. Everyone wants to do a good job, to feel pride in what they do. It's my job to remove the barriers to that end, and to do it in a cost-effective manner."

Eddie wonders what barriers keep his teammates from returning to their workstations at the proper time, from working eight hours in a day.

"That's a nice way to think of folks, but it isn't the way this plant works. I can't speak for other places."

He pauses, looks down. Pressfield steps forward, and asks him to continue. Eddie feels the sincerity behind the encouragement, a real desire to understand, and pushes forward.

"No one here cares about saving the business; we know there's no saving, just postponement. Most only care about saving their retirement. I've got less than a month to fifty-five. You'll be laying off more people soon, and the worst that will happen is I go out with an early retirement. The young blood, the ones who would care, you wiped out by reductions based on seniority. Any idea of saving the business collapsed when you knocked down the foundry and eliminated the apprentice program."

A couple of heads nod around the table. Buddy and Tony appear interested for the first time. Pressfield is only puzzled, and Eddie wonders if he is surprised at the opinion, or simply that an argument has been offered instead of the tail-wagging approval or mindless refusal of normal meetings.

"I know this plant has been through some rough times, but I don't understand your attitude. I know you guys in sixty-two are putting out some great work, even with the challenges you face. I've seen the numbers."

"You've seen the numbers? What do you compare them to?"

Eddie senses the room awakening, the men around the table stirring as they realize the departure from normal word games. Consequences rise in his mind. But for the first time in years he is speaking truthfully and with passion to someone with the power to do something. The danger in ignoring the chain of command is insignificant in the onslaught of joy, the thought of a factory working to do the best job possible.

Pressfield replies, "The numbers are all compared to last year—your team is up twelve percent, which, while not good enough, is a solid improvement. So you can't say you aren't trying."

"Try comparing it to fifteen years ago. I guarantee we're down fifty percent."

These are arguments Eddie has with Stanwicj on a weekly basis. They have been just words in those conversations, but now they carry power and balance his thirty years in the factory on a pivot point. He is tired of thinking only about his work, worrying only about retirement. He is tired of young managers without history, without a desire to understand history, and he presses forward.

"Look, it doesn't matter. You run the business how you think, make a name for yourself in the two years you're on the job, and enjoy a promotion to another division. It's been done before and will be done again. Just don't expect us to do handstands for your new program when the commonsense solutions that any real business owner would pursue are ignored."

They are words saved up over years of learning to expect less from others than himself. Thirty years of sweeping cigarette butts, dropped by his teammates, off the floor. Of fixing careless work. Of listening to the taunts of "company man."

He looks down at his hands resting on the tabletop and ignores the now openly hostile stares of the working men. Barston seems to bounce on his seat, desperate to get into the debate. But Pressfield doesn't turn, doesn't seek help, and the HR manager cannot usurp the spotlight from his boss.

Buddy speaks first, in the union voice of appeasement. He is calm and unsurprised. "Come on, Eddie, we can't get down on the place. We've got to keep moving forward, got to keep our attitudes up so that the company knows this is a good place to invest, a good place to keep doing business."

Pressfield, ignoring the attempt to discharge tension, replies in a voice tight with anger. "It really comes down to whether you want to roll over and die, or fight. Whether you're going to have a winning attitude, not just for the company and the stock you undoubtedly own, but for yourself."

Eddie sees the words as a knee-jerk reaction and knows he has misjudged the young man. There is nothing but retribution and anger in his tone. But Pressfield is not finished.

"If, Mr. Painter, you are happy with defeat, happy with shoddy work, and unconcerned for the customers who depend on us, I question what value you consider yourself to the company, and, more importantly, to yourself. These are exactly the problems that need fixing in Zenith. Are there any other questions or comments?"

Pressfield scans the group, now blanked by raw emotion, and turns to the three men behind him. Barston does not look happy. There is nothing more to say and Pressfield continues, "Great, thanks for spending the time with us this afternoon. Look for me on the floor; I'll be out and about quite a bit, expecting more honest feedback and looking for the best cup of coffee in the plant."

This gets a chuckle and the men stretch and begin to stand. Buddy and Tony are up, poised to work the crowd and distance themselves from management while taking credit for organizing the dialogue.

Eddie's stored words have escaped, but they are flat, and for the first time he worries. He worries about the middle managers—Stanwicj and Big Don—who can lose their jobs at a whim, about the guys trying to do a decent day's work who will get caught in a war conducted by a management incapable of anything but punishment. Uncertainty grows, and Eddie wonders if betrayal is usually more dramatic, more conscious. But he cannot leave without finishing the job. From the end of the table, still seated with hands resting palm down on the swirling wood grain, Eddie speaks finally from anger and a sudden, strange equality.

"I'm only going to continue because you seem like an earnest young man intent on doing a good job. I'm not going to challenge the opinion you hold. You're an educated man, all I know is what I've lived and seen. But if you really want to learn how this place operates, look into a few things. Find out why, as I sit here drinking coffee, my machine sits idle because no one else is qualified to run it. Find out how many of your class twenty-five machinists can do basic math, can read a blueprint accurately. Ask why our straight-eight workday is really five hours long for most; why the union has safety monitors on your payroll, supposedly running your machines who are in meetings all day every day and never do any real work. When you finish with that, go looking in the nooks and crannies, behind stacks of palettes, for the card tables, hot plates, and televisions that entertain *your* workforce at *your* expense. Keep an eye out for mattresses too, especially on third shift. If your conclusion is to kick the shit out of your foremen, think again. All they can do is beg us to work; they can't bear responsibility for a business that is flushing itself down the toilet because no one will have an honest conversation and do a fair day's work. That's all. I've said too much. But you seem like someone that should hear it."

Eddie nods at the three older men behind Pressfield and looks back down at his hands. There is no response, although a few men sit down at the renewed discussion and look confused as to whether the meeting is over. Their eyes turn to the front of the room as Pressfield speaks in an even, corporate voice.

"Thanks for your input, Mr. Painter. We always seek an honest dialogue in our meetings. I'm sure you've given us all a lot to think about."

Then he leads Barston, Buddy, and Tony out of the room and the workers follow, leaving Eddie, jittery with receding adrenaline, in a room of slopped-over coffee cups and crumpled paper napkins. He imagines explaining all of this to Suzy, sees himself walking into his building with his words marked on him like some Old Testament curse and realizes there is no joy in the truth. There hasn't been for many years, and he wonders when they gambled it away, and what they thought they would gain.

Eddie picks up a raw ring of steel, clamps it to the machining table, and begins to rough out his next job. His birthday safety net hangs on him like pieces of gold as he waits for the repercussions, barely curious, only wondering how much damage he has done to others, his own immediate future empty like the unimagined retirement seven years away.

Stanwicj comes up the aisle, head scanning, on the hunt for someone. He speaks, faster and higher than usual, as he walks toward Eddie.

"Jesus, I don't know what happened in that meeting, but Don just got off the phone with Pressfield and he's royally steamed. You've got to get in there right away, Eddie."

Eddie nods and walks down the aisle toward the office. At least there has been no waiting, he thinks. It is Don—like Stanwicj, once a machinist, once a foreman, now the manager of a hundred and fifty hourly workers—who will suffer for what Eddie has begun to categorize as an indulgence. Pressfield can't hurt Eddie, can't really hurt the union or any of the workers but he can hurt the managers who dance between the company's production quotas and the men's demand for overtime.

The quiet of the office is abrupt. It is a narrow room, running a desk and a half wide for twenty feet before opening into a square that holds an old photocopier and matching fax machine. Production Support used to occupy the desks, equally spaced under fluorescent lights that are bright to Eddie's eyes. Now the desks support dust and the odd remains of a machine shop in crisis. Crumpled computer printouts and phones, too many phones, lie haphazardly on steel shelves, leading the eye in a connect-the-dot mess to the end of the corridor and Don's office. As Eddie walks toward it, the door behind him opens and Don's voice booms out.

"You created a real commotion up there today, Eddie. Damnedest thing I've seen in a while. Were you getting bored? You could've told me and we'd have arranged something."

Eddie stands aside to let Don's round bulk pass.

"Come on down to my office and let's chat a while, huh?"

Don shambles down the narrow aisle between desks and wall, his neck, shoulders, and upper arms arcing in an immense half circle. Eddie follows and sits in the guest chair as Don closes the door to his office.

"How you doing, Eddie? Been to any of your marching band championships recently?" He pauses, not expecting an answer.

"You know this factory can't run like one of your bands. You can't expect it to. This ain't some music score that we can keep practicing until we get it right; it's life. You should know better than to paint a VP into a corner, especially in front of a whole room full of other people. Christ, Eddie, Pressfield had me on the phone for twenty minutes wanting to know about men sleeping on the job and whether his workers can add two and two. You know how much it costs the company to pay for twenty minutes of his time? You've really got them all wound up. You pissed off at something?"

"No. Same old around here."

"Yeah, but it ain't a bad same old is it? Look, I know it's frustrating being in your position. Imagine how I feel dealing with some of these guys on the floor. All we can do is make each day a little better. You got to think that way or you'll go crazy. Now Pressfield's going to have all the managers in on weekends and nights doing bed checks. You know the effect that'll have—I'll have work slowdowns and mysterious quality problems that Pressfield won't understand. I'm dealing with you straight up here, Eddie, because I know you're a good guy, but I got a building to run and the less notice we get from the big boys, the better off we all are. Now I've got Pressfield crawling up my ass with a flashlight. He'll be coming through here next week on a tour and I want you to think about what you'll say when he talks to you. You got anything you want to add?"

"No."

"All right then. Don't be taking this the wrong way, Eddie; you're the best damn machinist I got and I like you a whole lot on top of that. If you'd heard the screaming fit I got from Pressfield, you'd know how reasonable I'm being about this. Another manager'd put you on third shift pushing a broom. So damn it, if there's anything you want to say in the future, try running it by me first, okay?"

There is nothing to add. Eddie is relieved, surprised at Pressfield's and Don's reaction. The old managers, back when confrontation was an art form, would have shot first and never asked questions. The phone rings and Don picks it up, spinning in the captain's chair until two-thirds of his back is toward Eddie. Don swivels back to face Eddie with his hand over the receiver and, in a just-remembering tone, says, "Hey, Eddie, I got to take this call, but keep your head down, huh? I imagine some of the boys are pissed off. Don't say anything else to rile them, okay? Thanks for stopping in."

Eddie half nods, realizing Don is already focused on the telephone call, his shining head bobbing fluidly, and he gets up to leave. He hears Don's calm, reassuring voice as he walks out: "Yeah, I'll have those numbers over to Mr. Pressfield's office tomorrow morning at seven. But you've got to understand, ten years ago the product mix was different: the rings were all the same and we could make them faster. Maybe I can explain when I come over."

Eddie walks up C aisle, toward his G&L, past men watching

machines spin. He knows they could be setting up the next job while the machine works, but instead they choose to stand, read, smoke.

Two rings, complete but for some necessary cleanup, lie askew at his workstation, metal against metal. He squats to examine them, tracing their curve with his cigarette thumb. The edges are pitted and dinged in homogeneous, circular shapes, some deep enough, he knows, to deny repair. He glances around and sees the hammer leaning against the side of the G&L. A quality control tag is tied to its handle and he leans over to read it. The side with different categories for quality problems has two boxes checked: "Out of Tolerance" and "Operator Error." On the blank side of the tag "Benedict's Hammer" is written in a precise hand. He stands, holding the hammer lightly in his hand and with a smooth motion throws it into the chip Dumpster. They didn't wait long to retaliate, and the childish act seems insignificant compared to what he has done to Don, Stanwicj, and all the other white-collar lieutenants.

Then he sees the hoses and connectors to the G&L. Or at least their torch-cut, blackened entrails hanging in haggard submission to the violence done. He whirls, realization battling disbelief, to open the main compartment of the tool chest. Inside, the organized shelves remain, their contents of socket wrenches, tape measures, masking tape all present. Then he reaches for the top drawer where a folder holds the photograph of John winning his first go-cart race, the management award received in 1982, and a letter addressed specifically to him from Florida Power Corp., among notebooks, pens, clipped articles, and cartoons. But he sees none of these items as the drawer slides open on its ball-bearing runners; grease fills the drawer like mud. He plunges a hand into the viscous muck and pulls out the manila folder, scrapes the sludge off the top, and opens it to find the grease has permeated the thin paper and stained the photographs and clippings an even brown. Eddie slumps back onto the stool and lights a cigarette he doesn't taste. When he has smoked it to a nub, he goes looking for Stanwicj. The relief at Don's goodwill is gone, its existence forgotten in the furious revenge of his teammates and brothers. The terrible logic, the self-destructive mentality, overwhelms and he has to get out of the cloying, coolant air, away from the grime-soaked block flooring, and under an open sky.

At the loading dock he finds Stanwicj, tells him he is going home sick, that two rings are scrapped and will have to be started from scratch because of his error. Any one of those facts would have shocked Stanwicj, but the combination leaves him nodding in confusion.

Walking back to the remains of the Giddings & Lewis, his head down, he hears his name called.

"Hey, Painter."

It is Gary's voice.

"Can I have a word with you? It looks like you're ahead of schedule today. I saw two rings already roughed at your workstation. You must be trying to make your team look bad."

He smiles as he speaks, a good-natured grin cracking across a bearded face under the tilted, bifocal gaze. Eddie sees the smile as proud confession, the real face of the factory.

"Those rings are scrap and I'm going home sick. Why don't you rough them out? Maybe by tomorrow afternoon you'll have them done. I don't have time to talk."

Eddie knows he is finished at the factory, is beginning to think he has been finished for years, and he tries to sidestep Gary. His head fills with a weekly schedule dominated by car washes and trips to the market. Everything a man should dream about—security, free time, and a pension—only makes him ill. Another cigarette, another drag into lungs hardened by the years of abuse. How long will he last before the lungs betray him? The final betrayal, he thinks.

"Oh, you can make time for me, can't you?" Gary continues to smile and reaches out, like a man giving a pat on the back, for Eddie's elbow, gripping it with strong fingers, steering Eddie into an alcove behind final inspection. His smile falls, stripping the muscles until only his eyes remain tight and hard in a slack, jowly face draped from the ears. He wears Gap jeans, a pocket T-shirt, and L.L. Bean moccasins. Eddie gives up on getting away and listens. He deserves to listen, he thinks.

"We go back . . . well, shit, I remember the strike of sixty-six. You and I were out there full of piss and blood. Remember how we all kept our hands in our pockets for the benefit of the TV cameras, but had nails pounded through our shoes? Those fucking managers never did figure out what happened to their cars as they drove through the crowd. Those were the days all right. Look, I ain't going to talk down to you, Eddie. You're a smart guy, everyone knows it. But you can't go throwing the brotherhood in like this. We won't allow it. You got a history with this place. We're family and we won't suffer traitors."

Eddie looks away, toward the man-door at the end of the aisle.

"Look at me, Painter. Everyone fucks up once in a while, but you better be our number-one boy from here on out. I heard somebody already messed up your workstation. I know you didn't scrap those rings. I'll find out who and make sure they wise up, as long as you show us you made a mistake. We've all fought too long for what we have to let anyone rock the boat. Unions built this country, gave every working man the rights he enjoys today, and you got to respect that."

He gives Eddie's elbow a little shake before letting go.

"We sold out, Gary, we sold the next generation for the right to be lazy. The guys taking the work out of this factory, doing it cheaper and better, are apprentices that we trained and then laid off because of seniority when the cutbacks came. And now all we care about is retiring to live off thirty-two-thousand-dollar-a-year pensions."

"Okay, Eddie, you can make five rings to my four. Big deal. Figure out what's really bothering you. It ain't the next generation, they'll do all right. I got a kid in northern California making eighty grand a year programming—that's today's blue-collar job, not running an oversize weed whacker. Think about it, Eddie."

The locker room is empty and Eddie washes in the stone sink without interruption. He prolongs the scrub to avoid checking his locker. But it is unscathed and he gets his coat and keys and walks down the aisle and out the man-door at the back of the building. The sky is a high, hard blue and cloudless over the open flats of the factory. Behind the parking lot, the top of Building 321, the Big House, is visible. Eddie weaves through the cars, relieved to be away from the oily smell of the machine shop, to have avoided talking to anyone else.

He always parks the long wheelbase van at the far end of the lot. Even from a distance something looks wrong. The van slumps forward on the ground and as he nears he spots the gashes in the front tires—not just punctured, but shredded.

He keeps walking, past the van and onto the gray expanse of tarmac that separates buildings and lines of cars. He will call Suzy from the front gate; her car doesn't have a security sticker to get into the plant anyway. The damage to the van has not shocked him; it seems somehow appropriate that he walk away from the building, as he used to walk when tens of thousands worked each shift and buildings still covered the acres.

Eddie is alone between buildings, small in the expanse. He lights a match, watching the sulfur flare and settle to a slow burn, then ignites the cigarette to a smolder with caved-in cheeks and half-shut eyes. Beyond the factory, beyond the train trestles that cobweb from the plant, all built before 1910 when Zenith proudly proclaimed itself the City That Lit and Hauled the World, there is growth and new struggle. He thinks of Suzy, her thoughtful tone so often right through the years, and then of John's auto garage. The cigarette hangs burning in his hand, forgotten, as he trudges toward the front gate, wreaths of smoke curling, disappearing, but marking his slow progress. He thinks consciously of consequences, wondering if two pairs of hands, working together, might not stand a chance in the world beyond Zenith.

Nelinia Cabiles

University of Alabama, Tuscaloosa

WAITING FOR THE *KALA*

My father makes a living by being invisible. He stands knee-deep in shallow water and waits for the *kala* to come.

He knows this place, the leeward side of Kaena Point, where a necklace of coral reef barely reveals itself even in low tide, *ulua* and *uhu* jabbing nervously, hiding in underwater warrens, feeding on *limu* and witless sea life.

If you know how to wait, something will always happen, my father tells me. He is teaching me how to fish with a net this summer.

"The wind will change his mind and hold his breath for a little bit," he says, "or maybe the sun will shine so strong you remember where to look." My father peers into the sea, a blue so unforgiving you feel bereft of grace, a blue that leaves you wondering just how deep the color travels in the water. "Keep still and wait. Only this you have to do. Are you hearing me, Felipe?"

My father's English is crooked and full of holes; he substitutes indiscriminately the sound of p's for f's and v's for b's. His net is slung over his shoulder and uncoils itself loosely in his hand. He squints slightly. His fingers curl and tighten and relax around the thick waist of the net. I can tell he is getting ready.

He crouches lower and threads through the water without a sound. Then with the sweet grace of a manta ray descending, he

303

casts the net, a clean arc, a spray of knotted nylon thread billowing like an enormous, edgeless sail over the water.

"I'm needing your help now, Felipe!" The water has become a dark, roiling wave, furious with *kala*. In a smooth sweep, he begins pulling in the net, hand over shoulder, hand over shoulder, bending over the water as if he were giving blessings. "Bring to me please the floater!" he yells.

I jog clumsily out of the water, my tatami shoes like leeches on my feet, and grab the floater from our Jeep, which is parked a few yards away. Fashioned out of a galvanized steel washing tub and squeezed into a tire's inner tube, the floater spars and weaves as my father tosses *kala* into it. I stand a few yards behind him and hold a drape of net, feeling unsure of what to do next.

"Watch the tail, son. Your eyes—keep open. Follow the *kala*. You move like that: quick, quick."

I bend over a *kala* and carefully untangle it from the net. The *kala* is designed like a bayonet with a small flat razor at the swish of the tail. In timid hands, a *kala* can slash its way back to the water. This *kala* startles and thrashes, snapping its head. Its fight to return to the ocean catches me off guard, and so I falter, and the *kala* slips into the water, leaving the sting of its struggle, like shame, on my fingers. I feel foolish, my hands empty.

"The middle," my father says, eyes fixed on his line of net. "Hold the *kala* in the middle. Easy, easy now; is not so good to hold too tight. You hold, how you say, *soft*, but make small your hands. No give the *kala* too much room."

I work alongside my father, prying the fish loose, then tossing it in the floater, occasionally glancing up at him to follow his lead as we circle the *kala*. My father's knotty arms are like rope, his motions fluid. He knows how to move in the water, shifting his weight with the oncoming waves, never going too deep to lose his balance.

When we have pulled in the last of the *kala*, the floater is like a deadweight, defeated, heavy with fish. We drag it to our Jeep, delighted with the haul.

"We have the mother lode! There must be a hundred fish here, Dad!" The *kala* teem like a charm of bewildered children.

"We get good luck today, yes?" He grins.

He gathers the nets, ties them into a square knot, and places them behind the driver's seat, making room for the octopus and crabs we caught earlier. He picks up his sunglasses and our cooler and stows them near the floater.

From the dirt road, you cannot see this side of Kaena Point, where a dense bramble of kiawe bushes, stretching for five or more miles, obscures access. The kiawe's thorny branches are strewn with strands of pale orange *wana,* the island flower, like a Hawaiian chant unraveling, in fragments sonorous and wild. The color of the *wana* has always looked out of place in the lush green yawn of kiawe and coconut leaves. It makes an unruly lei, its tendrils resisting composition. Its scent is light even when it is crushed between the fingers. The rootless *wana* reminds me of my mother: restless, drawn to open spaces. The *wana* clings to seagrass, to kiawe, to dry coconut husks left on the road, to whatever catches it when the wind stirs.

My father has promised to show me all of his fishing haunts this summer, places like Kaena, which he and my mother discovered during his courtship of her. So far, he has shown me where the *limu* sprawls like idle, reckless chatter, and where a lone sea turtle, as if exiled, makes his home in a forgotten cove of black sand, and where, underwater, the moray eels spy in shadowy grottoes.

My father tells me my mother has forgotten these secret places. She used to know, he says. She used to fish with him when they were first married. But that was before fishing became my father's livelihood. *Is not so much fun to fish when you need to fish,* my mother says.

Over the years, my mother has cultivated a grudge against fishing, against our living on Lanai, strangled by its small-town charms, by its enclave of gossipy islanders, related to each other by blood or marriage or scandal. *We will move to Oahu,* she declared a few years ago. *Oahu have good shopping; we can buy big house with big yard. Lanai only has junk kind company house—Dole company,* she snorted, *yard chi'isai, same kind people all over.* But my father reminded her that Lanai has the best fishing. *No better job than fishing,* he said, placing his hand on her arm. *Lanai so small, chi'isai,* she countered, snapping her head back and jerking herself free from his hands. *I see every place already.*

She appealed to my father to work at her brother's bakery, pushing him toward something solid and unshifting. *You work in the bakery, so you no smell anymore like one stink octopus.*

But my father resisted by fishing with a kind of vengeance one spring, catching enough fish during the season's running of *halalu* along the Naha coast to buy her a shiny black Buick and a sofa so heavy it took my father and two of his brothers to lift it into our house. It huddles now in the corner, its back stiff against the wall.

For a while, my mother was pacified by her new car and sofa, and slowly, she seemed to surrender the bakery idea and her dream to move to Oahu, and in the resolute way my father understands my mother and what it means to love her, my father learned to make fishing separate from his life with her, washing away, as she asked, all traces of the ocean and sand and fish from the Jeep, from his feet, his hands, from him, when he comes home at night.

My father and I sit on the sand. My arms are tired and feel loose in their joints.

"You a big help today, Felipe." His smile is soft, a tenderness I have seen when he is gazing at my mother. It is shy, this smile, and my mother, who has no use for shyness, will often fidget in response and remind him of the wheezing refrigerator or cranky oven—things that require a necessary distance.

My mother has not always been so disapproving. When I was much younger she used to name parts of my face and call them hers. She would hold me close and say, *Eyes are mine, your nose, my nose—the same, all mine. And Dad?* I would ask. *How about Dad? No,* she'd laugh, nodding, *your hands, hai, okay, but most of you is me,* and she'd give me an upside-down kiss on my forehead, her black hair falling over my face, and though I pretended to want to peer out from her thick net of hair, squirming the way I did as she hugged me, I liked the scent of *awapuhi* in her hair and the way light could barely enter into that crawlspace she made for me: her shoulders curving around me, her face slender. She'd press her hands on both sides of my face and laugh, *Now you look like one manini.* She tossed her laugh into the air, and I remember loving the sound of that, its weightlessness. She once told me I was her favorite child.

My mother now says she was mistaken—I'm beginning to resemble my father more and more each day, she tells me. She looks sad when she says this, as though I've slyly been keeping a secret from her.

My father pulls off his tatami shoes and rubs away a thin isthmus of salt on his cheek.

"You fish with me every Saturday. Always we leave early like today," says my father.

"Okay," I say.

I want to hug him. My mother was right: I can see my hands look just like his, knuckles large, ridges bony between the fingers, a generous breadth of open palm.

We lug the floater to the back of Sam Choy's Fish Market. It is so heavy that I feel irritable. Mr. Choy, a small, nervous man, greets my father with a cagey exuberance.

"Plenty fish, Mr. Aquino!" Mr. Choy says. His smile is bright and loopy, but does not quite reach his lidless eyes.

My father nods.

"Yes, big *kala*," Mr. Choy murmurs, inspecting our fish. He handles a *kala* carefully, as though it were a baby who hadn't yet learned to hold up its head. "You go to Kaimanu Beach?"

My father says nothing.

"You the only one get good luck. Seto and Harvey come up empty today."

My father is quiet. He looks intently at Mr. Choy.

"I give you one dollar a fish," Mr. Choy proclaims, making the words sound important.

My father's eyes narrow briefly as if he is trying to keep Mr. Choy in focus.

"Let's go, Felipe," my father says.

I reach for the floater's rope handles.

"Wait, wait, Mr. Aquino," Mr. Choy says, stepping in front of us. He finds his smile.

Because it is so unwieldy we set the floater down.

"You drive hard bargain," he says. "I give you a dollar and a half a fish."

"Felipe," my father says, motioning for me to grab hold of the floater.

"*Kala* is big fish," Mr. Choy says. "My customers like smaller fish. Tasty, you know, the small fish." He circles us, vaguely challenging, his gaze falling to the floater.

"*Kala* is good fish," my father says evenly, his eyes never leaving Mr. Choy's face.

"Yes, yes. I'm not meaning disrespect, Mr. Aquino. Of course, ha ha ha," Mr. Choy laughs, without mirth, and slaps my father on the back, a hearty sound like applause.

"But is hard to sell so much fish," continues Mr. Choy, serious again. He gives my father a sidelong glance, waiting. He places his hands behind his back as he walks.

My father waits until Mr. Choy stops his pacing before he speaks.

"Sorry to trouble you, Mr. Choy. We will go to Tamashiro's. He likes *kala*."

"Okay, okay, okay," Mr. Choy says quickly. "I give you two dollars a fish." He puts two fingers up, as if we were deaf.

"Three dollars," my father says.

"Three dollars? Is too much!" Mr. Choy protests, his voice suddenly shrill.

"Three dollars," my father repeats, "and I throw in three eels."

"You have eels?" Mr. Choy's eyes are shining. "You really get good luck today, Mr. Aquino." He claps his hands together to close the deal. "Okay, three dollars a fish and three eels."

"Good," my father says.

"Mr. Choy is one greedy sonofabitch," I mutter to my father as we drive home.

"Most people are greedy, Felipe," my father says softly. "They wanting always more, always more. So you must know already what you no can give away."

I consider this for a second, thinking that he must have misunderstood me. "What I mean, Dad, is that you could have easily gotten five dollars a fish."

"We get good price on our fish," my father says.

"But you could have gotten a better price, I bet. He was ready to—"

"What I say about greedy, Felipe? Are you not hearing me?"

"Sorry," I say, chastened. My father knows what fish is worth. But I feel strangely empty anyway, as though my father has been duped, even though the price, at the time, seemed perfectly fair and reasonable.

"How'd you know the *kala* would be at Kaena today?" I ask, changing the subject.

"I know how to watch. I know how to wait," he answers.

My father's language is sparse and tied to fishing. I have learned to infer meaning from the gaps in his speech, from the valleys of what he does not say.

"You learn by watching, Felipe. The water, the *kala*, Mr. Choy, everything will give up, then you see the true nature. Sometimes takes long time to see, so you must know how to wait."

"Give up what? What do you mean, Dad?"

"I mean, they come out from hiding because is much tiring to hide for long time." I get the feeling as I hear his voice fall that we are not talking about *kala* just then, but because I am tired, because I cannot bear the thought of asking him to explain what he means, because I understand I am entering a country I am not prepared to see, I whisper, "Okay, I get it."

We drive in silence the rest of the ride home.

My five-year-old sister, Tessa, runs up to the Jeep when we pull into the garage.

"What'd you guys catch?" she asks. She steps on the tire's rim to get a better look.

"A whale," I say.

"No," she says, laughing. "You're tricking me, Felipe." Her laughter trills, unexpected, fluttering up like joy. "Lift me up, Felipe. Let me see, please."

I grab under her arms and lift her up.

"Oh! Eels! And crab! And *tako*!" she says, pointing to the octopus that slides along the floor of the floater in a foot of salt water. One tentacle pokes through the heavy wire screen, searching. I set her down.

My father and I hang the nets along the wall of the garage and rinse out our tatami shoes and legs with the garden hose. The salt and the sand converge into little rivers on the garden's gravel walkway and empty into the grass.

"Where is your mother?" my father asks. He is in perpetual motion, tidying the Jeep, washing the fish, now sweeping the garage: quick, stabbing gestures. It strikes me that my father is graceful only in the water.

"I don't know," Tessa says. "I think she went for a walk again."

She frowns, her eyebrows knitting together, her face intent with remembering.

"What's the matter, Tessa-nee?" I ask. She loves my nickname for her, which sounds like a flubbing of that southern state.

"Mommy was mad at me," says Tessa.

"What for she is mad?" my father says, a loose pile of dry fish scales like blue-gray half moons at his feet. He sweeps the pile into a dustpan and walks over to Tessa.

"She said I'm a noisy pain-in-the-neck."

Tessa looks suddenly small and unkempt sitting there, her feet under her, wearing a colorful muumuu faded past cheerfulness.

"Your sister?" my father asks, as he scoops her up.

"Reading," Tessa answers, the rest of her words muffled in the hollow of my father's shoulder.

My father slips out of his rubber thong slippers at the door, a Japanese practice of tidiness taught to him by my mother, and carries Tessa inside. I follow them in and leave the screen door ajar.

Tessa and I wait for our mother on her sofa. I turn on the TV and promptly turn it off; I switch on the radio, searching through the stations in static fits and starts until my older sister Delia asks me to lend a hand with the *pansit*. I help my father julienne the carrots and green beans, blanch the *harusame* noodles, steam the octopus delicately, and toss it with a delicate oyster sauce that my father makes from scratch. I am grateful for these tasks.

Delia enters the kitchen through the back door that leads to the garden, her arms full of plumeria.

"For Mom," she says, when I ask her why we need flowers.

"What's the special occasion?" I want to know.

"For Mommy," Tessa echoes. Delia sets the flowers in a deep bowl filled with water. Tessa nudges the floating blossoms, then holds them underwater with her small hands. By the time we gather around the table for dinner, the petals are swollen, half drowned.

Pansit is our favorite dish, but we are quiet for most of the meal, as if we are all waiting, straining, to hear the door open.

My mother has done this before. Her absence in our family is growing. But it is spotty, so that if you string the time away—the hours she says she spends walking, or the odd errands to my aunt's house—you would have less than twenty-four hours in your hands, barely a day missing altogether. That is not enough time to feel lonesome.

I hear the lemongrass shushing near our kitchen window. Our neighbors, the Jacañas, are arguing again, a throaty grumble, not serious.

The phone rings.

Delia runs to get it. "Hello?" she says, already flustered. She stands straight, narrow shoulders square as she leans forward.

"Mom!" she says. "Where are you, Mom? Dad made *pansit* for dinner. The *tako* was juicy and tender, just the way you like it. Do you want me to keep it warm for you? Tessa ate all of her dinner. I told her she could have ice cream for dessert. Just one scoop. That's okay, right? What? Where are you, Mom? We're waiting for you. Are you at Aunt Mina's? Wait, wait, what? I can't hear you, Mom. Where are you?" She says this in one breath, her words collapsing and falling, cramped and pinched, in this house that has become too small to hold them. I squeeze my eyes shut.

"Um, okay," I hear Delia say. Her voice is flat. "Dad, she wants to speak to you."

My eyes spring open. My father gets up from the table and takes the phone from Delia. He waits until she returns to the kitchen table before he speaks.

"Akiko?" he says softly. He walks to the hallway and faces the wall, his back to us.

I turn to Delia. "You idiot! Why'd you go on and on like that! You didn't even let her speak," I whisper savagely. "What did she say?"

"She hardly said anything." Delia's face slowly crumples. "She wasn't at Aunt Mina's." I want to shake my sister until her glasses fly off her face. She removes them and wipes her eyes with the back of her hand and I realize how thin she is, and how her face is like complicated geometry: lines intersecting at odd points, an awkward beauty like my mother's. I wonder if Delia or my mother has ever noticed the resemblance.

I clear the table and begin washing the dishes. Delia gets Tessa's bath ready. My father is still on the phone. The extension cord is not long enough for him to go into their bedroom, where it would feel more private and secure. But that seems unnecessary. We are perfectly quiet. It is the sound of a family holding its breath.

"Wait! Don't forget to leave some *pansit* for Mom," Delia cries, agitated, grabbing the serving bowl from me. I have an overwhelming urge to slug her. Blood rushes to my face. Instead, I glare at her.

"What?" she snaps, an answer to nothing.

My mother and father are still on the phone long after Delia and I dry and put away the dishes. I have heard my father say only a few words. I look over at him and see his hands tighten around the telephone cord as he listens. As always, my mother does all the talking. But then, uncharacteristically, my father interrupts her.

"Come home," my father says. "No, Akiko, you no can ask this. No. I know, I already know, I see you——" His voice breaks, and then I hear it recompose itself when he repeats what he said, this time in Japanese, her native tongue, so there can be no misunderstanding him, *I'ihito o shitte riu:* I know who is your lover.

I hear my father tell her how he has followed her on one of her walks. As he recounts my mother's steps over the past few weeks, I realize my father is circling, drawing closer, trying to force her to shallow water. But it occurs to me, in the way he halts and stammers, the quiet sinking like stones in this too small house, that it is my father who is struggling to keep his balance.

"Why was Mommy mad at me, Delia?" Tessa asks when we tuck her into bed.

"She wasn't really mad, Tessa-nee. She was just distracted."

"What's that?" Tessa asks.

"Um, it's when you have a lot on your mind and you can't pay attention to it all."

"Oh," Tessa says, after a moment. "How did she get it, Delia? Can Daddy get it too?"

Delia is mute, fat tears ruining her long, pimply face.

"I want my mommy," Tessa cries, guarded now as she regards Delia with growing alarm. "Mommy's been walking for so long."

"She'll be home any minute," Delia tells her. She looks down at her lap.

"No! You're just tricking me, Delia."

Delia says something to Tessa that I can't hear, but Tessa will not be soothed. "Go get my mommy, Felipe," she bursts, her small hands clutching my face. I want to escape this airless room, to slam tight the door behind me and leave my sisters to themselves. But the moment passes, and there is a shift of light in the room that I take as a moment of grace.

I pull a book from Tessa's nearby bookshelf and slowly begin reading it. It is a simple story, but a long one, and I am grateful for this. My sisters fall silent, a captive, miserable audience. By the time I get to the end of the chapter, Tessa has fallen asleep, faint sobs catching in her throat.

My father has remained standing in the hallway. He places the phone in its cradle when he sees Delia and me emerge from Tessa's bedroom, as if he has just come to and realized where he is.

He tells us he thinks our mother will be home later tonight. He has the same expectant look that he had at the reef, before he cast the net, waiting for the clouds to move. When I ask him if he's sure, his lips tighten into a thin line, almost disappearing, and he says, "Felipe, please," and the way he says this, with his eyes and hands, I know somehow that I have trespassed into that wordless country. Delia stands between us with her arms crossed, fingers touching her shoulders.

I feel tired, the day breaking me like regret.

"Well, good night then," I say to both of them, because there is nothing else to say. My father looks dazed, as though he has stepped into a harsh, inconsolable light.

After a while, as I lie on my bed, I hear the house slowly settle into sleep. Delia knocks softly on my door and says my name, but I won't answer her. She gives up and goes to the bathroom, where she turns on the faucet to drown the sound of her sobbing—so much wasted water, I think to myself.

I hear my father leaving and returning several times. He lingers at the front door each time he returns. And then I hear him finally enter their bedroom. The walls of our house are thin and I hear the window shudder into place when he raises it open.

The Jacañas next door have long since made up. I hear Raul Jacaña singing. He has an awful voice, flat and reedy, unambitious, until he reaches the catchy chorus of "heartache, heartache, go away," when he lets loose and gives himself up to the music. In his thick Filipino accent, the lyrics sound like "harday karday go Hawaii." The words are meaningless, absurd, soothing. I wish the music could go on forever, that Raul Jacaña could keep singing his drunken, piteous serenade until morning, but after a while the song recedes, fading one note at a time until I hear nothing but my own breathing. I pass my hands in front of my face.

I lie awake in the dark. My shoulders hurt from the strain of trying to sleep. I feel the loneliness of the early morning, that chilly twilight when dawn is still a rumor. I prop an extra pillow under me and sit up. I have a full view of the street that dips into our driveway. I watch a gecko lizard scuttle along the window ledge; it takes no notice of me. I wonder if in my stillness I have become invisible. I focus my eyes on the street, on the darkness outside my window. I am patient. I know what it means to wait.

Wendi Kaufman
George Mason University

HELEN ON
86TH STREET

the play

I hate Helen. That's all I can say. *I hate her.* Helen McGuire is playing
Helen, so Mr. Dodd says, because, out of the entire sixth grade, she
most embodies Helen of Troy. Great. Helen McGuire had no idea
who Helen of Troy even was! When she found out, well you should
have seen her—flirting with all the boys, really acting the part. And
me? Well, I know who Helen was. I am pissed.

mother

Mother doesn't understand. Not that I expected she would. When I
told her the news all she said was, "Ah, the face that launched a thousand ships." She didn't even look up from her book. Later, at dinner,
she apologized for quoting Marlowe. Marlowe is our cat.

At bedtime I told my mother, "You should have seen the way
Helen acted at school. It was disgusting, flirting with the boys."

Mom tucked the sheets up close around my chin, so only my head
was showing, my body covered mummy-style. "Vita," she said, "it
sounds like she's perfect for the part."

horse

So, I can't play Helen. But to make it worse, Mr. Dodd said I have to
be in the horse. I can't believe it. The horse! I really wanted to be one

of the Trojan woman—Andromache, Cassandra, or even Hecuba. I know all their names. I told Mr. Dodd this, and then I showed him I could act. I got really sad and cried out about the thought of my husband Hector's head being dragged around the walls of my city. I wailed and beat my fist against my chest. "A regular Sarah Heartburn" was all he said.

mother

"Well, at least you get to be on the winning team," my mother said when I told her about the horse. This didn't make me feel any better. "It's better than being Helen. It's better than being blamed for the war," she told me.

Mom was helping me make a shield for my costume. She said every soldier had a shield that was big enough to carry his body off the field. I told her I wasn't going to be a body on the field, that I was going to survive, return home.

home

Mom and I live on West 86th Street. We have lived in the same building, in the same apartment, my entire life. My father has been gone almost three years. The truth is that he got struck with the wanderlust—emphasis on *lust*, my mother says—and we haven't heard from him since.

"Your father's on his own odyssey," my mother said. And so now it's just me and Mom and Marlowe, our cat, and the Keatses, John and John, our parakeets, or *pair of Keats*, as Mom says. When I was younger, when Dad first left and I still believed he was coming back, it made me happy that we continued to live in the same building. I was happy that he would always know where to find us. Now that I am older, I know the city is not that big. It is easy to be found and easy to stay lost.

And I also know not to ask about him. Sometimes Mom hears things through old friends—that he has traveled across the ocean, that he was living in the islands on a commune with some people she called "the lotus eaters," that he misses us.

Once I heard Old Farfel, the man that's hanging around Mom now, ask why she stayed in this apartment after my father left. "The rent's stabilized," she told him, "even if the relationship wasn't."

rehearsal

At school Helen McGuire is acting weird because I am going to be in the horse with Tommy Aldridge. She wants to know what it's like. "Is it really cramped in there? Do you have to sit real close together?"

I told her it's dark, and we must hold each other around the waist and walk to make the horse move forward. Her eyes grew wide at this description. "Lucky you," she said.

Lucky me? She gets to stand in the middle of the stage alone, her white sheet barely reaching the middle of her thighs, and say lines like: *This destruction is all my fault,* and *Paris, I do love you.* She gets to pretend to cry. Why would she think I'm lucky? The other day at rehearsal, she was standing onstage waiting for her line, and I heard Mrs. Reardon, the stage manager, whisper, "That Helen is as beautiful as a statue."

mother's date

At home Old Farfel is visiting again. He has a chair in Mom's department. The way she describes it, a chair is a very good thing. Mom translates old books written in Greek and Latin. She is working on the longest graduate degree in the history of Columbia University. *I'll be dead before I finish,* she always says.

Old Farfel has been coming around a lot lately, taking Mom and me to dinner at Italian places downtown and telling Mom jokes with weird punch lines—*vidi, vici, veni,* they laugh strangely when I tell them it's in the wrong order. I don't like to be around when he's over.

"I'm going to Agamemnon's apartment to rehearse," I told Mom.

Old Farfel makes a small laugh, one that gets caught in the back of the throat—laugh, laugh, gasp—and never really makes it out whole. I want to tell him to relax, to let it out. He smells like those dark cough drops, the kind that make your eyes tear and your head feel like it's expanding. I don't know how she can stand him.

"Well, the play's the *thing,*" Old Farfel said. "We're all just players strutting our hour on the stage." Mom smiled at this, and it made me wish Old Farfel would strut his hours at his apartment and not over here. I hate the way he is beginning to hang around all the time.

mother's urn

When I come home from rehearsal Mom is spinning Argos. It's what she does when she gets into one of her moods. Argos, our dog, died last summer when I was away at camp. My mother can't stand to part with anything, so she keeps Argos, at least his ashes, in a blue-and-white vase that sits on our mantle.

Once I looked into the vase. I couldn't resist. I did not see the gray stuff, like at the end of a cigarette, that I had expected. Instead, there was black sand and big chunks of pink—like shells, just like at the beach.

My mother had the vase down from the mantle and was spinning it in her hands. I watched the white figures on it turn, following each other, running in a race that never ends.

"Life is a cycle," my mother said, twirling the vase. The spinning made me dizzy. I didn't want to talk about life. I wanted to talk about Helen.

"Helen, again with Helen. Always Helen," my mother said. "You want to know about Helen?"

I nod my head. I always want to hear about Helen.

"Well, her father was a swan and her mother was too young to have children. You don't want to be Helen. Be happy you're a warrior. You're too smart to be ruled by your heart. "

"And what about beauty? Wasn't she the most beautiful woman?" I asked.

Mom looked at the Greek vase. " 'Truth is beauty, beauty truth'—that is all ye need to know."

She is not always helpful.

dreams of water

"Manhattan is a rocky island," Mom said at dinner. "There is no proper beach, no shore." My mother grew up in the South, near the ocean, and there are times she still misses the beach. Jones, Brighton, or even Coney Island beaches don't come close for her. I know when she starts talking about the water that she's getting restless. I hope this means that Old Farfel won't be hanging around too long.

Every night I write a letter to my father. I don't send them—I don't know where to send them—but still, I write them. I keep the letters in the back of my closet in old shoe boxes. I am on my third box; it is getting so full I have to keep the lid tied down with rubber bands.

I want to write: *Mom is talking about the water again. I think this means she is thinking of you. We are both thinking of you, though we don't mention your name. Are you thinking of us? Do you ever sit on shore at night and wonder what we're doing, what we're thinking? Do you miss us as much as we miss you?*

But instead I write: *I am in a play about the Trojan War. I am a Greek. I get to wear a short white tunic made from a sheet, and I ambush people from inside a big fake horse. Even though we win the war it will be many, many years before I will return home. Until I see my family again. In this way, we are the same. I will have many adventures. I will meet giants and witches and see strange lands. Is that what you are doing? I wish you could come to the play.*

That night I dream about a swan. A swan that flies in circles over the ocean. This is not the dark water that snakes along the West Side Highway or slaps against the shores of New Jersey, but the real ocean. Open water. Salty like tears.

travel

Old Farfel is going to a convention in Atlanta. He wants Mom to go with him. From my bed, I can hear them talking about it in the living room. It would be good for her, he tells her.

I know that Mom doesn't like to travel. She can't even go to school and back without worrying about the apartment—if she turned the gas off, if she fed the cat, if she left me enough money. She tells him that she'll think about it.

"You have to move on, Victoria," he tells her. "Let yourself go to new places."

"I'm still exploring the old places," she says.

He lets the conversation drop.

Mom said once that she traveled inside herself when Dad left. I didn't really understand, but it was one of the few times I saw her upset. She was sitting in her chair, at her desk, looking tired. "Mom, are you in there?" I waved my hand by her face.

"I'm not," she said. "I'm on new ground, it's a very different place."

"Are you thinking about Dad?"

"I was thinking how we all travel differently, Vita. Some of us don't even have to leave the house."

"Dad left the house."

"Sometimes it's easier to look outside than in," she said.

dress rehearsal

At play practice I watch the other girls dress up as goddesses and Trojan women. They wear gold scarves or fabric wound tight around their necks and foreheads. They all wear flowers in their hair. And flat pink ballet slippers. I wear a white sheet taken from my bed. It is tied around the middle with plain white rope. I wear white tennis sneakers. I don't get to wear the gold scarves or flowers. Mr. Dodd wrote this play himself and is very picky about details. Tommy Aldridge, my partner in the horse, was sent home because his sheet had Ninja Turtles on it. "They did not have Ninja Turtles in ancient Greece," Mr. Dodd said.

burning

Old Farfel is taking Mom out to dinner again. This is the third time this week. Mom says it's a very important dinner, and I am not invited. Not that I would want to go, but I wasn't even asked. Mom brought in take-out, some soup and a cheese sandwich, from the coffee shop on the corner. She left a note saying that she and Old Farfel would be back soon.

Alone in the kitchen, I eat my soup from a blue-and-white take-out cup. I remember once at a coffee shop Mom held the same type of blue-and-white cup out in front of me.

"See this building, Vita?" she asked. She pointed to some columns that were drawn on the front of her cup. It wasn't really a building, more like a cartoon drawing. "It's the Acropolis," she said. "It's where the Greeks made sacrifices to Athena."

"How did they make sacrifices?" I asked.

"They burned offerings on an altar. They believed this would bring them what they wanted. Good things. Luck."

I finish my soup and look at the tiny building on the cup. In between the columns are the words *Our pleasure to serve you*. I run my fingers across the flat lines of the Acropolis and trace the roof. I can almost imagine a tiny altar and the ceremonies that were performed.

It is then that I get my idea. I find scissors on Mom's desk and cut through the thick white lip of the cup toward the lines of the little temple. I cut around the words—*Our pleasure to serve you*—and decide to cut them out, too. Then I take the temple and the words and glue them to the back of my notebook. The blue-and-white lines show clearly against the cardboard backing. I get Argos's big metal water bowl from the kitchen and find some matches that say La Luna on them, from the restaurant Old Farfel took us to for dinner.

In my room I put on my white sheet costume and get all my letters to Dad out from the back of the closet. I know that I must say something to make this more like a ceremony. I think of any Greek words I know: *spanikopita, moussaka, gyro,* only food words. It doesn't matter. I decide to say them anyway. I say them over and over out loud until they blur into a litany, my own incantation: *spanikopitamoussakaandgyrospanikopitamoussakaandgyrospanikopitamoussakaandgyro.*

As I say this, I burn handfuls of letters in the bowl. I think about what I want: to be Helen, to have my father come back. Everything I have ever heard says wishes are granted in threes, so I throw in the hope of Old Farfel leaving—why not? Three things I want: to be Helen, to have my father come back, to have Old Farfel disappear.

I think about what I want, say my Greek chant, and watch as the words burn. I watch as three years of letters go up in smoke and flame. I see blue-lined paper turn to black ash; I see pages and pages, months and years, burn, crumble and then disappear. The front of my white sheet has turned black from soot and my eyes water and burn.

When I am done, I take the full bowl of black ashes and hide them in the vase on the mantel, joining them with Argos. My black hands smudge the figures in white, until their tunics become as sooty as my own. I change my clothes and open all the windows, but still Mom asks, when she comes home, about the burning smell. I tell her I was cooking. She looks surprised. Neither of us cooks much. "No more burnt offerings when I'm not home," she says. Mom looks upset and distracted and Old Farfel doesn't give that stifled laugh of his.

Pox

It's all my fault. Helen McGuire got chicken pox. Bad. She has been out of school for almost two weeks. I know my burning ceremony did this. "The show must go on," Mr. Dodd said when Achilles threw up the Tater Tots and when Priam's beard got caught in Athena's hair, but this is different. This is Helen. And it's my fault.

I know all her lines. Know them backward and forward. I have stood in our living room, towel tied around my body, and acted out the entire play, saying every line for my mother. When Mr. Dodd made the announcement about Helen at dress rehearsal, I stood up, white bed sheet slipping from my shoulders and said in a loud clear voice: "The gods must have envied me my beauty, for now my name is a curse; I have become hated Helen, the scourge of Troy."

Mr. Dodd shook his head and looked very sad. "We'll see, Vita. She might still get better," he said.

Opening Night

I still can't believe it—I am playing Helen!

Helen McGuire is feeling better but didn't want to do the part because of all the pockmarks that are left. Besides, she wanted to be inside the horse with Tommy Aldridge. Mr. Dodd insisted she still be Helen until her parents wrote that they didn't want her to be pressured, they didn't want to *do any further damage*, whatever that means. After that, the part was mine.

Tonight is the opening and I am so excited. Mom is coming without Old Farfel—*He wasn't what I wanted,* she said. I don't think she'll be seeing him again.

"What is beautiful?" I ask Mom before the play.

"Why are you so worried all the time about beauty? Don't you know how beautiful you are to me?"

"Would Daddy think I was beautiful?"

"Oh, Vita, he *always* thought you were beautiful."

"Am I like Helen?"

She looked me up and down, from the gold lanyard snaked

through my thick hair, to the short white tunic, to my too tight pink ballet slippers.

"You are more beautiful than Helen. You are going to make those ancient gods come alive again with envy. I wish your father were here to see it."

"What do you mean—come alive again? What are you saying about the gods?"

"Vita, Greek pantheism is an extinct belief." She laughed. And then she stopped and looked at me strangely. "When people stopped believing in the gods, they no longer had power. They don't exist anymore. You must have known that."

No. I don't know that. And I don't believe it. Didn't I get the part of Helen? Didn't Old Farfel leave? I made all these things happen with my offering. I know I did. I don't believe these gods disappeared, or don't have powers anymore. At least not Athena. Besides, I still have one more important thing I asked for. One more thing that *has* to come true.

"I don't believe you."

She just looked at me, confused.

She'll see. Tonight, when I step out from behind the thick red curtain and look beyond the glare of the bright lights toward the empty space, I know his familiar shadow will be standing there, watching me, waiting. He has to come back. I am now the beautiful Helen of Troy. My father, my swan. I know he will fly home to me.

Christina Milletti

University at Albany, State University of New York

THE RETROFIT

I.

"You're real Mexicans now!" Chencho-Mac laughed as he pulled over to the side of the road and toward a young couple, a young *American* couple he quickly surmised (knowing by sight, as any good cabbie would, the Yank from the Frenchman, or the Anglo from the Slav), who, with their luggage strapped on their backs, were walking away from San Miguel and toward the northern stretch of the island. The walk from the pier wasn't far, but they hadn't counted on the rain. Like most Yucatán storms, it had loosed in a panic from the clouds above and, quite simply, they were drenched. More than drenched, they looked exhausted. Who wouldn't be exhausted playing the part of a burro? he thought, waving to them as he stepped from the convertible Bug and, as though kindly, offering them each an umbrella before telling them his fare for a ride. It was hiked, of course, but they agreed without question, climbing in even as Chencho-Mac explained that he always drove with the Bug's top down, that the top stayed down even in the worst of weather because the vinyl had shrunk in the Mexican sun and would no longer snap in place. Wiping the rain from their chins, his new clients shrugged. It was no weather to bargain in and so, huddling close, they set umbrellas over their heads like helmets, then draped the damp blanket Chencho-Mac hid under the seat over their legs to keep them warm.

At heart, Chencho-Mac was honest. He had never cheated and had never stolen, and above all (he often told his wife): he had never told a lie he did not first believe himself—this being one of the many lectures he liked to thump eloquent before a meal, the others involving the bullfight (though he himself had never attended), and, of course, the allure of the American woman, whose hair always smelled of aged liquor as though this is what she washed it in and, dried on the stem, what set it in place. To all of this, his wife would snort and turn back to the stove. If she were in a particularly feisty mood, though, she might mutter loudly, "You're just a Chencho-liar." This reply, as rote as his lectures, reminded him, though there was no need, that she had learned to translate *him* as much as his words—for instance, his sudden desire for orthodontic devices, for the braces he'd had attached to his canines just the day before, and that he claimed he'd purchased for just slightly above cost.

"The Americans," he'd explained before he'd gone to the dentist, "they only trust a man if he can smile a bona fide smile like their own."

"They are, of course, quite stupid," she had remarked without thinking, having thought this many times over, and not expecting him to stomp his slight frame across the kitchen, trying hard to go heavy so his steps would resonate through the shack's thin walls. He only had succeeded in rumpling, in some cases tearing up, the newspapers he'd laid for her like tiles on the kitchen floor. She had smoothed them out after he left, added new sheets to patch up the holes, and when he'd come home three hours later he had shown off his grin and the wires that framed it. He kept rubbing each tooth, poking at the swollen gums to make them bleed.

"You're a crow," she'd said as she peered into his mouth. "Hiding jewels in that maw of yours."

Mouth open, he'd simply grunted as she'd sprayed water and lime juice over each tooth to cool off the gums and heal them more quickly. Then he winced, dipped a finger in the cup, and rubbed the juice on his teeth himself.

"You'll see," he had said. "These will pay off nicely."

Absently, she'd nodded (she often nodded absently) and brought him a cosmetic mirror—a birthday present from her mother, who frequently sent such gifts, hoping that her daughter would one day own as many trifles as the soap opera ladies she admired every day at noon. Instead, Chencho-Mac's wife had kept them packed in the boxes they came in, debating over her cooking whether she would pass them on to the daughter she did not have; whether her daughter would look at the gifts as she did and, if not, what then. Mirror in hand, Chencho-Mac had then parked himself on a kitchen chair and examined his braces as the evening wore on, wiping, with the hem of his shirt, the fug of his breath from the mirror's face before shoving it in his mouth again and, eyes somewhat crossed, staring down his nose at the glass, trying to see if his smile had begun to pull more broadly, if his teeth had moved the fraction the orthodontist had promised by the end of the month.

That night, before they fell asleep, Chencho-Mac had pulled at his wife's thigh and, happy, squeezed the flesh of her hip in his palm.

"I see a difference already," he'd told her.

"Yes," she had said. "You now have a Chencho-shrine."

Sighing, she had rolled toward the side of the bed farthest from him.

The next day, all trace of the heavy rain had evaporated in the sun by the time Chencho-Mac arrived at the docks to meet the first incoming ferry. He parked, he smiled, he stood up in his seat— "like a jack-in-the-Bug," he told the couple approaching, warily, which he liked. More Americans. He liked Americans, he told them. The blonde, though skinny, wasn't bone thin like some of the young girls who came to San Miguel and pretended to be women. Her friend, he was wiry and confident, and it was with the confident man that Chencho-Mac played his best games, taking advantage of the over-plumed ego and his own good nature.

They had a hotel? Why, yes, they told him, though they were staying for only two days. Just two? Why so few? Because they needed to get home—where it was snowing! said Chencho, to which they all chuckled. Yes, where they lived, it was cold all right. Imagine, the young fellow said, five feet of snow and ten-foot drifts if you were in the right spot. The woman coughed: *Our* home is in the right spot.

They were married, Chencho-Mac spied the rings. They weren't newlyweds, though; they no longer worried their rings as most new-lyweds did, like half-formed thoughts. He'd bet they'd been married for a year, but not less.

"Well, I will tell you," he said slowly, letting the sweat from his lip collect on a knuckle before wiping it on his shirt. "This island, as you know, is the largest in all Mexico. You'll need a car to get around, to the other side, to the north, the south, and into town for the night. The center, it's all jungle, nothing there but diving bugs." Chencho-Mac leaned toward them as though confidentially: "Now, I will take you to your hotel. You take a shower, make yourself at home in your rooms, unpack. And then at noon, I'll come back for you and show you around, your own private tour, to the best beaches, the best shops, or if you want the quiet place, you tell me and I'll take you there too. Best yet," he said when they began to blink quickly at each other, "I have no fee. At the end of the day, when I take you home at dusk or dawn, you and your pretty wife together think it over: then you pay me what *you* think is right." He waved his hand toward a small alcove in the stone wall that ran along the docks. "You go and talk it over, I won't be offended." He bowed slightly and closed his eyes. They waited for him to open them, as had so many others, then turned and walked a few steps away.

Chencho-Mac slipped out of the Bug and, as he would many times more in the days to come, began to shine the car with a soft terry cloth he stowed under his seat, buffing the paint slowly to give his clients the portrait of accustomed nonchalance they'd come to Mexico to see. In a few moments they returned. They were sold.

Chencho-Mac grinned, the wide-open grin the infidel shares with the infant, and loaded their bags under the hood as the woman leaned on the passenger door. "My name is Anne," she said, intro-ducing herself as she counted each bag with her eyes. Chencho-Mac smiled, he had a fine smile. "And my daughter," he said, "her name is Anna!" He pointed to a picture of his neighbor's daughter, which he'd pinned to the glove compartment. "Just five years old and already she counts the change her papa brings home at night." "How bright! You're very lucky," said Anne, who liked children—especially children in pictures—then she stepped back to admire the Bug.

"I didn't know Volkswagen made these anymore," she told him. "I used to have one in college."

Chencho-Mac smiled. "Maybe later I let you drive."

And then they were off to the Cozumel Club. Anne was a teacher, she told Chencho. And John, he was a dentist. John had just opened his first practice, bought it off a fellow who, whirring drill in hand, had a heart attack and, in the midst of his seizure, grabbed hold of the rinsing fountain, electrocuting himself before the patient, mouth stuffed with cotton, could knock him to the ground. Strangely, though, the fellow survived because the charge put his heart back to rights.

"My God," said Chencho-Mac. "Two days ago I went to the dentist. To the orthodontist." Chencho bared his teeth in the rearview mirror, weaving through two rental cars driven by tourists and a bus driving unusually slowly. "Look," he said, waving for John to sit up in his seat and look in the mirror, not toward the road and a truck filled with milk crates on which they were bearing too fast.

"Look!" Chencho-Mac said again, and cut sharply around the truck.

John looked. "Braces."

"Braces!" said Chencho-Mac, smiling as they caught up to another taxi, which abruptly took a right onto a small, unused road. In the backseat of the car—a shiny convertible Bug much like his own and one he recognized as belonging to Papa José, the young man the ladies called Papa because he'd had so many girls—sat a woman who looked like Chencho-Mac's wife, balancing a frying pan on her knees, pushing the long dark hair blowing around her face with one hand from her eyes.

"One moment," said Chencho-Mac, pulling the car to the side of the road, choking the Bug's gears, and running over a sign fallen to the pavement long ago when a tourist knocked it over.

Chencho-Mac quickly explained to the Americans that he had passed a turnoff to an attraction of such a subtle nature that he often didn't show it to the tourists he escorted around the island. Anne and John, however, were different. They of course could see how unlike they were from the tourists with whom they arrived on the ferry; being refined Americans, they no doubt could bridge the unpredictable discourse between a Mexican and his neighbor.

"There is something I'd like to show you," he said.

Making a U-turn at the next break in the median, Chencho-Mac returned to the small sand trap of a road down which Papa José had driven his taxi, setting the Bug's wheels in the taxi driver's tracks to avoid the shifting sand that threatened to stall the convertible. Fifty feet down the road, the uncut jungle blocked their view to the sides and, as though down a chute, Chencho-Mac rolled the car and its occupants slowly, commenting quickly on the various insects stunning themselves on the windshield, on the sounds of the geckos chirping, on the seabirds cruising in line over others rustling the mangroves. His clients were content as he carried on; after all, they were on a tour of the Mexican jungle, which, they had surely read in their guidebooks, was home to the jaguar and manatee, to the crocodile and wild boar, forgetting, because of the denseness of the brush and the small fierce trees, that they were no longer on the mainland, that the chief predators of the island jungle were stray tomcats and large birds—as well as mosquitoes, of course, which they'd begun to swat at briskly.

Around a bend, the road came to a halt. Confused, Chencho-Mac put the Bug in neutral and considered the duplicity of Papa José and the cleverness of his wife. Evidently, they had seen him and had quickly broken off their rendezvous. Even now, Papa José would be dropping off Chencho-Mac's wife and the frying pan she had brought with her. They certainly weren't hiding; the jungle was impassable, the brush far too thick for such a light car, even a durable one like the Bug, to roll into and hide.

No one, Chencho-Mac thought, is here.

II.

When the knock came that evening, it was not on the front door, which was not a door but a curtain. Nor did it come on the door frame that framed the curtain and to which Chencho-Mac's wife had pinned the dark fabric to keep it from blowing open much as someone might lock a door. Instead, her husband rapped his knuckles against the windowsill looking into the kitchen where Chencho-Mac's wife stood over the stove rotating the frying pan with quick sure movements above the burner's blue flame, banging the pan down sharply when it became too heavy for her wrist to bear. From the pan came the scent of garlic, of cilantro and lime masking the sweet sting of chile. She was cooking up a feast.

"Chencho-Mac," she acknowledged without turning around. "Your supper is almost ready."

He nodded. Though she did not see the nod, she imagined it, his nods being unusual and always the same, less a nod than a tick, a jerking of the skin by the corner of his mouth and which, so determined, gave the illusion that he had tossed his chin much as a stubborn horse will seem to shake its head at a pest when it has only blinked its eye. A moment later, she heard him wrestling with the pin and the curtain, and then refastening the curtain to the frame as he stepped inside their home. Chencho-Mac sat down at the kitchen table as his wife brought over a stew of conch and squid with a basket of tortillas.

"You've cooked a feast," he said.

"A strange thing happened today, Chencho-Mac," she said. "I have a story to tell. Will you listen while you eat?" He nodded and so she began.

"Today after you left in the morning, I did, as I always do, the wash and the dishes, I fed the chickens and your father's mules, I pitched the barn and watered the garden, planted some chiles. At noon I came in to rest and make myself some chocolate. I was standing at the stove when the knock came much like yours this evening, a knock rapped not on the door but on the sill of the window looking into the kitchen where I was standing melting the chocolate. It was not you, of course. I knew it was a stranger by the way he rapped his knuckles: firm so I would hear the knock over the sound of the pot pinging from the burner and the boiling milk. But the knock was yielding too, so I wouldn't be angered by the intrusion, as though I would be flustered by a neighbor's arrival if the neighbor didn't call first.

"'My name is Schnee,' he said, and so I invited him in, how could I not invite him in after I began to stare at him like the town children stare at tourists, as if they weren't really tourists but performers on a stage who fail to see their audience. And so the children run after the tourists, dodge them just to get close, to smell them, to touch their clothing, to pick their pockets like some of the older ones do. They know they'll be ignored, that the tourists are less interested in the attention than in their own dismissal of it as they study them from afar. And there I was staring at this man—Schnee he said his name was and so I took him to be German, though not just because of the name; he also held himself as Germans do, as if his shoulders were linked by bone to his hips. There he was, then, not in the square but by my house, nearly in my kitchen, at least part of him, the hands on the sill, the head and neck leaning in. I would not have it: Chencho-Mac, I have my pride.

" 'My name is Schnee,' he said again as though I had not heard the first time, and so, because I wanted to study him but not stare at him, I invited him into our home.

"Now this man, he was not overly handsome, he was not tall, nor did he look particularly strong. Quite simply, his head was far too large for his body, which was not so small itself, the head just over-sized for the average broadness of his shoulders and his neck to bear. The man was a hopeless carnival, one of the traveling kind with fine equipment gone shoddy, not with age, but lack of care. This Schnee, he wore his linen pants like that—with the hems let down—and his shirt, it was clean but of a pattern long since passed out of fashion. And though he walked with his head held high—I can only imagine the effort—and with that stride so common to his race, his head wobbled, shimmered really, a sound ship tossed on a gross rebelling sea, up and down it went as we sat together. My God, it was a sight.

"Would you believe he was a salesman? A scout sent to evaluate the Mexican market for retrofitting light fixtures? He was a lightbulb salesman, Chencho-Mac, selling a long-life, energy-efficient light-bulb that costs as much as three regular ones, but lasts as long as six."

" 'Would you, Señora Mac, be interested in such a product?'

He asked this somewhat coyly, and, if he'd had a hat, I think he would have tipped it then. As it was, he did something queer with his fingers, as though on their way past his nose and up toward the hat that was not there, he realized he'd forgotten it and so, startled, his fingers cramped and he dropped the hand to his side.

"At any rate, that's when I told him we only have one lamp, and suggested, to be helpful, that he'd be better off inquiring at the hotels on the coast whose managers worry about such expenses far more than we do.

"And then, this Schnee, he looked around the room, at the love seat and the rocker and the little stand with our one lamp, and nodding—he was so polite this German with the great big head—he rose from where he sat, said, 'Thank you for your time' as most salesmen do, and quietly passed through the curtain."

"He went next door, to Papa José's house?"

Chencho-Mac's wife shook her head. "No. He simply walked down the road as though he'd been to all the other homes already. But when I asked the neighbors if the German had paid a visit, none of them had seen him."

"Perhaps he picks homes randomly?" Chencho-Mac suggested.

His wife shrugged. "Who's to say? I watched him to the corner. The hems of his pants dragged up the sand in the street and it must have got into his shoes because, before rounding the corner, he took them off, tucked both shoes under one arm, and, barefoot, walked back toward town. For a man with such a large head he moved quickly, because no one on that street saw him either. I am, it seems, the only one."

For Chencho-Mac, there remained the matter of confirming his wife's story, which is to say, he wondered, could not sleep for wondering—which was rare for him and so, he thought, unhealthy—when to trust one's wife and not one's eyes? There was also the question of proof: his was the glimpse, his wife's, the tale—which was he to trust?

So Chencho-Mac went to see his friend the fisherman, Gordo. He brought along his clients, Anne and John from the day before. At the front of the fish store he dropped them off, leaving them with Gordo's son, Pepe, who began to show off the morning catch in the buckets around the counter—the fresh squid marinating in its own ink, shrimp, and clawless lobsters. Meanwhile, Chencho-Mac found Gordo in the back room, smoking a cigarillo and reading the morning paper. Chencho-Mac joined him as he often did and, sweeping the table free of the ash that always collected on it, he leaned in on his elbows, retelling his wife's story, though not why he told it to him.

"Have you seen such a man?" he asked his friend. "I myself would have liked to. My wife, she said it was something, to have this strange man in our house, to have his great big head bobbing outside the kitchen. This island is not so big that a man with such a large head can remain unnoticed. I would like to find him."

Gordo shrugged. "But how large is large, my friend? Like a cut from the cheese wheel? Like a ball? Like the bosom of Papa José's latest girl?" He chuckled. "Perhaps his head was not so large. Perhaps this German's neck was simply small. Perhaps it is your wife who is lacking in a sense of proportion."

"Are you suggesting my wife made up this story?" Chencho-Mac pulled over a section of the newspaper and began to study its headlines while Gordo carefully formed his words so as not to insult his friend.

"Now Chencho-Mac," he began, "the lie usually comes in the plain package, no? A quick trip to the market, for instance, when the feet in fact intend to take the liar somewhere else. Now this story— your wife, she would have to be foolish to make up such a tale. I merely suggest that she perhaps sees things not as they really are."

"And how are they really?" his friend wondered.

Gordo laughed. "You are Chencho-Mac. Things are as you see them."

At the front of the store Anne and John were debating whether to buy squid or lobster. But their hotel room, they realized, did not have a kitchenette.

"We'll cook it here for you," Pepe explained. "And tonight, for dinner, you pick it up. Chencho-Mac will bring you."

"I have a better idea," Chencho-Mac interrupted, as he and Gordo emerged from the back room. "Tonight you will eat at my house. My wife, she has only one skillet, but she uses it exceedingly well. It is, of course, why I married her."

Pepe nodded. "It's true."

Chencho-Mac stepped back and bowed. "I would be honored to have you visit my home for the evening, unless, of course, you have other plans."

"No plans," Anne said after her husband nodded. "We'd love to come. At what time should we expect you?"

"Why wait?" said Chencho-Mac. "Let's go now, have an early supper, and then I will take you to the best place for dancing. Is this not your last night in San Miguel?"

III.

By the time the knock came that afternoon, Chencho-Mac's wife had pulled off her apron and rinsed her mouth with lime juice; she had already wiped her face of sweat and oil and pushed the loose strands of her long dark hair back behind her ears.

"Chencho-Mac," she acknowledged without turning around. "Who have you brought with you?"

"The Americans," he said, unsurprised.

"Tell me."

"You will cook them dinner, there is a cooler from Gordo under the hood of the Bug. We will pin the curtain and the shades. We will light candles by the love seat, where they will sit and eat their meal."

She paused and turned. "You've never brought tourists before to our home."

"Until yesterday, a German never stood in the kitchen."

After a moment, she nodded. "Bring them."

"We haven't put you out I hope?"

"Of course not, we have so few guests."

"And as you know I like Americans."

"He's always liked Americans."

"We like your stories! The way you tell them."

"Of course! He tells them well!"

"As does my wife."

"Your daughter, too?"

"Our daughter?"

"And where is she?"

"At school, of course."

"On Saturday?"

"Because of the strikes."

"Bliss for the parents!"

"Oh, she's never a chore."

"And so bright says your husband."

"I'm not surprised," nodded Chencho-Mac's wife. "He's always been proud of his family."

*   *   *

334

"You must be tired," Chencho-Mac said an hour later—after he had given his guests a tour of the barn, showed them his mules and the garden, the chiles his wife grew there, the serrano and chipotle, the jalapeño, the habanero. "Of course you're tired," he said when Anne and then John protested. "Now come inside!" and began to pull at them, John by the elbow and his wife by her arm. "Here you will take your first real siesta, here in my home. You honor me." Through the small living room, they followed him, giving in quickly because they were in fact tired, drained by the heat of the afternoon sun. Into a dark cool bedroom, Chencho-Mac allowed them to yield and, pushing his guests to the bed, he gave them a sheet and a knit blanket too; they soon would feel chilled without the sun on their skin. Plumping their pillows like a maid, he helped them take off their shoes.

"I will come to wake you," Chencho-Mac assured them, "when the meal is ready." He shut the door behind him softly and went to find his wife.

She was leaning on the kitchen sill, looking out beyond the Bug and toward the tracks the car had made in the sand, her gaze fixed, it seemed, on the places where Chencho-Mac's footsteps obscured the car's tracks, tossed up the sand unevenly so that the seabirds came down hunting for crabs, crosshatching the sand once again with their new and hasty prints. She might have been thinking, he thought, about the nature of time, how to mark its passing when the events that seem to imprint it, in fact obscure even older markers, unsettling them and so displacing the very ones she relied on. She might have been thinking, in short, that her affair had been found out, that Chencho-Mac, as a man of action, surely had a plan, a scheme, because there always was a scheme. Certainly, she was wondering why he had brought the Americans, why he had invited tourists into her home and made of it a stage.

She did not turn when he entered, acknowledging him by ignoring him as she always did, by turning her back so that he would know that she knew he was there.

"A strange thing happened today," he said, sitting down at the kitchen table. "My wife," he said, "I have a story to tell you. Will you listen while you cook?" She nodded and, turning slowly to face him, returned to the pan sitting cool on the stove. With a match, she lit the pilot and watched the metal begin to flex against the heat.

"When I left this morning," he began, "I drove, as I always do, directly to the Pemex station where I filled the Bug's tank and washed the tires, checked the oil, and swept the backseat free of sand. I bought a cola and a chocolate, and though I ate the chocolate right there at the station I saved the soda for later. I hid the bottle under my seat because you never know where you'll get stranded when there are Americans about. By ten, I was off to the hotel where my clients are staying, and though we had made an appointment for noon, I went over early to talk business with Old Pinto, the hotel's concierge. I was en route, driving not too fast since I had room enough in the back to give someone a ride, when, to my surprise, I spied a fellow who looked like the German you described last night, the lightbulb salesman with the great big head, sitting by the road, his knees pressed up into his chest as if he'd been folded like a box. In his hands he held a lightbulb. Without thinking, I pulled over. I wanted to ask him about the product he had walked so far to sell just the night before.

" 'It is the lightbulb you're selling?' I asked. He was lethargic, unaware, it seemed, of my presence and of the nearby car, of the dust I kicked up when I got out. He didn't answer and so I sat down by him, waiting because there is always time, too much of it, and finally he responded as if he had not made me wait.

" 'One needs the fixture for the light and, here, there are few fixtures. That is what I wrote.'

" 'What you wrote?' I asked.

" 'In my report.' And a moment later, 'Is it better to be fired sooner or later?'

" 'Why wait?' I counseled because, as you know, I am a man of action, but my answer only made him sigh and, pulling his knees to his chest even tighter—I can only imagine the effort—he balanced the bulb on his left knee as if the bone were a pedestal and not a joint, though it did well enough for his purpose.

" 'Since dawn,' he said slowly, 'I've been thinking on this question, whether to go, whether to stay. If the moving makes a difference. As yet, I have come to no conclusions.' He paused and looked me over. 'You, on the other hand, are clearly a man of action.'

" 'Of course,' I said because it was true.

" 'That is a gift,' he said. 'It is a gift to know something, to *know* it, you understand, beyond all the doubts that are among the knowing.' He nodded to himself in agreement and, uncertain what to say, I simply nodded back as he began to contemplate once again the light-bulb on his knee. He was silent for a long while, but I was in no rush—Old Pinto would remain where he was, at the hotel where he has always worked, smiling at guests who would continue to come, borrowing favors and hopefully giving some business to me.

"Finally, the German spoke up.

" 'I see you have a car,' he said, his chin jerking toward the Bug, his eyes lingering on it before resting again on me. 'I will make you a deal,' he said. 'I will loan you this lightbulb now if, in one hour, you return to see if I'm here.' During that hour, he explained, he would contemplate his future, if he had such a thing, and if his future were bright, what he should expect from it, which is to say, if one should in fact hope for a bright future at all, this sounding to him, he said, far too luminous and in need of retrofitting. He laughed halfheart-edly at his joke as I bent to take the lightbulb, assuring him that I would return to drive him to the ferry. In exchange, I gave him the cola. Snapping off the cap with a coin, I sat the bottle by him in the sand.

"He nodded his thanks, and like an old door, began to move, shaking out one arm and extending it toward the cola. Wrapping his hand around it, he raised the bottle to his lips, drank, and poured the rest of it over his feet."

"His feet?" asked Chencho-Mac's wife.

"To be sure it was strange, but the German quickly explained that he abhorred dirty feet.

" 'I've not always hated them,' Schnee said, nodding slowly to himself. I even imagined he smiled, although, if in fact he did smile, it was only fleeting and covered with dust. 'As you can imagine, a young woman's involved, a young woman's always involved when a young man's lost. It is how we tend to remember the ladies. But per-haps you know this already.'

" 'I'm not sure what you mean,' I said, which also was true. I had never met a German who did not get straight to the point.

"Schnee paused for a moment, his pauses took time and, to my eye, sapped his strength. At last he sighed and leaned over, resting his chin on the knee that was not supporting the lightbulb.

" 'My friend,' he said as though he meant it, 'recollections are all that we have, memories not like pictures, but like little myths. They gain strength over time as we retell them. But by then, one need never tell them again, because they've become *understood*.'

"After a moment, I shrugged at him. 'I'm afraid I don't understand,' I said.

"But this didn't seem to concern him. Quietly, he slipped his feet—still wet with soda, but not yet sticky—back into the shoes sitting by his side.

" 'I have not always been a failure,' he added before I drove away, and I must admit, I believed him because he spoke the words without inflection as though he'd never had to convince anyone of the fact before.

"I returned as promised an hour later, but without the lightbulb he gave me in good faith and which I gave to Old Pinto in much the same way, to seal our arrangement. Even as I helped the German into the back of the Bug, he asked for it, however, as if it were the lightbulb's return and not the ride to the ferry that he'd been looking forward to while I was gone.

" 'I'm afraid I don't have it,' I admitted, explaining that I broke it tripping over a vine. He said nothing for a moment, though it seemed to me that his neck was suddenly thinner, that under the weight of his massive skull, his neck curved and his shoulders bent. I've never seen a man look so uncomplicated and sad.

" 'It is wise perhaps,' he finally said, 'to every so often lose a thing one holds dear in just such a fashion.' He sighed then and quite suddenly I felt sad, though I couldn't say why.

" 'Let me make it up to you,' I told him. 'Why not join my wife and I for dinner tonight?'

"The German thought this over for a moment, and then agreed. 'That would be kind,' he said. 'I am, after all, quite hungry.'

" 'Excellent,' I said. "And in fact, I was pleased, far more curious about the salesman, his lightbulbs, not to mention his large head, than I had imagined. So I drove him into town and dropped him at the plaza. Before he left, though, he promised to come for an early supper tonight. In fact, he's late," Chencho-Mac said, looking at his watch. "He should have been here by now."

"More guests?" said Chencho-Mac's wife.

"Indeed," her husband replied. "It's a regular dinner party."

By the time Anne and John woke from their nap, the table was set, the candles were lit, Chencho-Mac had stuffed extra pillows beneath the love seat's cushions to make their guests' seat more comfortable, there was water in the glasses, and, at the table's center, an ashtray filled with scented straw. Chencho-Mac had washed his face, his wife had changed her dress, above all, the warm scent of fish and lemon was hanging in the air and everyone was hungry.

When Anne and John emerged, Chencho-Mac guided them to the love seat and, sitting them down, pulled over the table and tucked its edge beneath their ribs. He then gave John a bottle of wine, explaining, as the American unscrewed the cap, that, though their meal was ready, they were still waiting for a tardy guest. He was a German, Chencho-Mac said, a very unusual German, a salesman, but more than a salesman, an average-sized man with a great big head out of scale with the rest of his body. His name was Schnee, and to this Schnee, he was indebted for reasons he'd rather not say, since the salesman was not only a private man, but a modest one as well.

"He's a salesman, you say?" Anne asked.

"Of lightbulbs," Chencho-Mac said. "A long-life energy-efficient lightbulb that costs as much as three regular ones but lasts as long as six."

"Ah," said John. "He's a retrofitter."

His wife nodded. "Germans often retrofit."

"Do you know many Germans?" Chencho-Mac asked.

Anne took a sip of her wine. "Who doesn't know Germans?"

"I know Germans," John said. "In fact, many of my patients are Germans, if not German, which is to say, from Germany, then certainly of German origin, their parents or grandparents having been German and having brought their culture with them. I can always tell a German by the way he lays back in my chair and shows me his teeth."

"Do they all have such large heads?"

"They certainly have large teeth," said John.

"Well," said Chencho-Mac, tapping the table slowly. "I imagine a man with such a large head must also have large teeth."

John nodded as he poured himself another glass of wine. "That would only make sense." Then he smiled and tapped his rumbling belly. "Perhaps when your German arrives in a few minutes, we can take up the matter with him."

There is always the question of hunger, which is to say, how hungry one may be at any given moment, how much food one requires to alleviate one's innards, the abject sensation of their movements. Such questions must be ignored, however, when one is a guest, as Anne and John were guests (one might even say tourists) in their cabbie's home. They, of course, had read at length about Mexico and its people—how hospitable they were and, it was said, how friendly, how they always doted on the guests they invited to their homes. Though, as the Americans sat an hour later staring at their hands around the empty table, they could not help but think that their guidebooks had been wrong or, at the very least, left out essential points—idle thoughts made worse because the Americans were drunk. How could we not be drunk, Anne thought, with so much wine, so little food, with the smell of squid and garlic hanging damply in the air. Chencho-Mac's wife looked around. Her guests were hungry, it was clear to see, toying with their knives and forks, as they considered, she imagined, the nature of food and time, above all, the punctuality of Germans. This is no way, she thought, to start a dinner party.

"I'm sorry for the delay," Chencho-Mac said. "I'm sure Schnee will be here soon, let's wait a few more minutes."

"It's the least we can do," Anne said politely.

"Yes," John added. "The least."

"Are you sure Schnee is coming?" Chencho-Mac's wife asked when a half hour had passed and still Chencho-Mac would not allow her to put the meal on the table.

"You understand," he told the Americans, "our rules of hospitality."

"Of course," Anne said quickly while John smiled, as though good-naturedly, through the candle's flame and toward their hosts.

Chencho-Mac returned the gesture, his lips pressed and curling as he looked at each of them in turn, last of all at his wife, who glanced away when his eyes fell slowly on her.

A while later, John was finishing a story about a patient who, after taking pain medication John had prescribed, became convinced he was a dentist himself. "Can you imagine?" John said. "And when his wife had him call me—she was worried, you can see why—he thought I was his patient. Needless to say," he went on, "the fellow was fine once he stopped taking the stuff, though he's now enrolled in the dental school I went to myself—in fact he graduates next month." John began pounding his fists on the table, teeth bared as if he were laughing, though he made no sound. Anne tried to grab his arm but, overshooting the mark, missed and spilled a glass of water. Chencho-Mac's wife rose and brought her a dry towel.

"How much longer must we wait?" Chencho-Mac's wife whispered to her husband.

"As long as it takes," he whispered back.

"And how long will it take?"

"How long is the walk?"

"The walk is not long."

"Then the wait will be short."

"But the wait *has* been long," she snorted.

"Then Schnee must walk slow."

"But I've seen him walk fast."

"Perhaps today he is tired."

"He had enough time to rest."

"No doubt, it's perplexing."

"Which means something's wrong."

"Which means," her husband corrected, "he'll be hungry when he finally arrives."

Fifteen minutes later, Anne sent a pleading look across to their hostess, who abruptly stood up.

"Come with me," Chencho-Mac's wife said to her husband, pointing to the kitchen. He followed her and found her standing at the stove, back turned to him as she tapped the frying pan on the burner. "This cannot go on," she said as he pulled the curtain after him to block their guests' view. "Chencho-Mac, what are you and the German scheming?"

"Why, I have no scheme, wife."

"Then why do we wait?"

"Because Schnee has not come."

"You still think Schnee's coming?"

"And why not?"

"Because he is late."

"Guests often are late."

"But not Schnee."

"How do you know?"

"He told me last night."

"He told you last night that tonight he'd be prompt?"

"Last night he told me that a good salesman's never late, that a salesman who wants to make a sale must always be on time and that, because a salesman always likes to sell, he is *always* on time."

"Schnee said that?" her husband, frowning, said. "He told me that, though a salesman always likes to sell, a salesman sometimes *should* be late, that selling is in the timing."

"Much like a meal!" she added, banging the pan.

"Perhaps."

"We should take the Americans out to eat, the meal by now is ruined."

"But what of Schnee?"

"Schnee is not coming!"

"But how do you know?" her husband asked almost gleefully.

They paused an unkind pause, stepping back from each other as John rustled then pushed through the curtain into the kitchen. He studied his hosts' flushed faces. "I don't mean to interrupt," he said flatly, "but I thought you should know that your German just stopped by." Unsteadily, he leaned against the kitchen wall. "What I mean is that your Schnee just stopped by and then left in a great big hurry. Would you like to know what he said?"

"I didn't believe it, you know," John told Chencho-Mac and his wife after they all sat down and began to eat the tepid meal, the squid ceviche that had shrunk, as meals often do, when they've sat too long.

"Frankly, a German with such a large head was hard to imagine. But your salesman, this Schnee we waited for this evening, my—what a fellow—I've never seen anyone like him. He was—" he paused, searching for words.

"He was mammoth," Anne said.

"Mammoth," John nodded. "Yes, that's it. We'd never seen anything like it."

"Now I must admit," John went on, "your Schnee was in a rush, he couldn't stay long, he said, not even long enough to apologize to you personally for holding up our meal."

"He was rude," Anne said.

"No," John corrected, "not rude, in a rush. Anne and I were talking softly when we first heard the knock, the knock was soft at first, at first I didn't hear it. It's not so late, but late enough—I imagine your German thought you'd gone to bed. At any rate, I got up, I got up quickly because I knew it was him, who else could it be? Who else were you expecting? I was right of course, and there he was when I pushed the curtain aside, there he was, your German, the retrofitter you'd described. How quiet he was, too quiet for such a large man, engrossed in bearing that enormous weight on his neck. Then again, he just might have been thinking about what to say, because when he at last spoke, his message seemed rehearsed."

"Like lines someone's practiced," Anne said.

"Exactly," said John. "He had poise, I'll give him that—wordless but with his poise—standing just outside the door. After a moment, he stepped inside and let the curtain fall behind him. He looked around, at the table all set up, at the wine, the empty plates, at the rocker where Chencho-Mac is sitting, finally at the lamp.

"'How kind of you to wait for me,' he said at last, 'but I must leave at once. I'm late, you see, I'm going home. You'll witness for me, won't you? You'll pass on my apologies? You'll tell our hosts I'm sorry, that it's unavoidable that I must go?' He paused and studied us, nodding his thanks as though we'd agreed. 'We all must go home eventually,' he added. 'And I'm tired of my time here, all the lovely vistas. I'm tired of translating.' He stepped close to me and held out his hand. 'As Americans,' he said as I gave him my own, 'you must know what I mean.'

"He didn't wait for me to answer and, to tell the truth, I wouldn't have known what to say. But then he nodded and, shrugging, said simply, though with apparent effort, 'Thank you for your time.' Just like that! 'Thank you for your time,' as most salesmen do, and that was all he said. Then he turned and walked out the door, pulling the curtain after him, and it was as though he'd never stopped by at all. It wasn't until I heard his steps fading, in fact, that I realized how final his words seemed. You know how salesmen are when they thank you for your time, how they say it meanly because it's not what they intend. But your Schnee, he wasn't at all like that. How serious he was, melancholic even. In his words was something final, I'd bet on it, as though the time he spent with you was over, a finished thing, as though he stopped by to take *back* his time, to take it with him on the ferry, to rescind it and take his time back with him all the way home."

John paused and then looked at his hosts.

"I suspect you won't see him again."

IV.

The next morning, Chencho-Mac found Gordo in his office at the fish market. As usual the fisherman's feet were on the table, a paper on his knees, in his fingers the cigarillo he smoked while reading, and on the table the soot he left behind. Chencho-Mac sat down and swept the table free of ash, pulling toward him a section of the paper Gordo had cast aside.

"Did you find the man you were looking for?" Gordo asked, folding the pages neatly before he offered the cabbie his full attention. Gordo would finish reading the news after Chencho-Mac left; he always finished the paper before giving it to his friend when he returned in the evening to pick up meals Pepe cooked for the tourists.

"My friend," Chencho-Mac said slowly. "I have a story to tell you. Will you listen while you smoke?" Gordo nodded and so the cabbie began.

"Last night, as you know, I invited the Americans into my home, I asked them to meet my wife, and sample her cooking. Even the German, that salesman I told you about, was going to come. I wanted to see him for myself, to study him, but not stare at him, to share some stories perhaps over a glass of wine.

"But when Schnee at last arrived—my friend, there is no other man like him—I stepped back from the door, I stepped aside, I moved out of his way to give him more room, though he was not big, not tall, nor overly strong. No—it was the head, just as my wife explained. The head, like a fat squash on a doll, as if a sleepy seamstress had sewn the two together as she was nodding off. There he stood, the handiwork of weary dreams—an average-sized man with a great big head, held high less by strength than by pride. That didn't stop it from wobbling on his neck, of course, as if he were standing on a ship always out at rough sea.

"Now the German, he didn't stay long, he just dropped by to pay his respects, a polite man, there's no doubt. After drinking his glass of wine, he left us, tipping a hat that was not there and saying, as most salesmen do, 'Thank you for your time,' that was all, nothing else. Even the Americans noticed how final his words were, how formal he seemed when he left. Schnee didn't just thank us, you see, he thanked us for our *time*, as though that time was now *his* time and he was taking it with him like loose sand in a jar. There it was between us, the time we shared, and as Schnee collected it up as a serious man would, I knew he'd take good care of it, our time, and so I relinquished it to him, as did my wife, even the Americans who, you'd think, wouldn't have known any better.

"We gave him our time willingly, and he took it in much the same way. It's his gift, I think, this taking of time, and so we gave it to the German with the great big head and he took it to keep."

Chencho-Mac fell silent as Gordo continued to smoke, blowing smoke rings that grew and enclosed them, then dissolved.

"Soon your Schnee will be legend," Gordo said at last, shaking his head slowly.

Chencho-Mac shrugged. "Legends are always made of such men."

Gordo thought on this a moment, then laughed a soundless laugh as he crushed his cigarillo beneath his foot. "My friend," he said, cutting the smoke with his hands, "did you think legends are ever made from men such as us?"

Daniel Noah Halpern
University of Texas at Austin

THE GOLEM'S RECORD

The pen in his hand becomes loose until it seems to slip; its weight lessens inside his clasp, its substance fading. Until all that is there is the place it occupied. Then the fingers, once impressively knuckled: they are emptied steadily, until they are only borders, with nothing inside. So too the thick tendons beneath his thumb, disappearing; so the flesh of the palm; so the bright bones beneath; and so the skin. The visible forms of his hands, dissipated, leaving only the indefinite trace of their patterns. Now: up the arm. And without hesitation through the elbow. To the still muscles of his shoulder: his body does not resist the progression.

And now: the stoop upon which he sits and writes, and the street beyond. As if on a yellowed map that, in crumbling, leaves no dust, the neighborhood fades, even the city is gone; the drooping miserable suburbs and the long blind eyes of the quiet country, until all that is left are the ideas called borders, and then those gone, and on . . .

Even the patterns are gone.

1.

There: that's Josef, that fool, on the step across the way, just as he always is. Confess it before God: the creature surely takes up his share of the earth! How does he expect anyone to get past him, with that endless and lumpy fortress wall, all iron and corded wire, masquerading as a set of mismatched shoulders? His feet are used as a pair of stages by local vaudeville troupes; his head controls the orbit of three small moons with the faces of children! The fastest automobiles would take weeks to travel from one of the deep scars of eyebrow on his forehead to the other. And there he sits, in the way, on the top step.

Three elderly ladies sit around a wooden table, considering the case of Josef the fool and playing cards. A small girl sits, considering her feet. An elderly man, also sitting, chooses this moment to stand. All he's considering is how it is that he always ends up as the dummy. He can't remember the last time he got to play one damn hand.

When he gets to play he makes bad decisions, and losing, calls the ladies bullies and looks as if he will cry.

He does not yet remember that Josef is not alive.

2.

I was a child actor. It's true, I was a star. I played multiple parts often. All the child roles in certain productions. Often I was a girl. I played Juliet when I was thirteen, one week after being bar mitzvahed: How now! Who calls? I leapt upon the stage. At the time I thought the play was a comedy. Maybe it was. This was the Yiddish theater, when I was a boy. Our translation was by a man named Horowitz. That's what I think, I'm not sure. Perhaps Mr. Horowitz wrote his later. Time is hard. *The Complete Works of Shakespeare*, translated and improved by Mr. Horowitz.

How now! Who calls?

Here's a line I got to say: They say, Jove laughs. At lovers' perjuries, is what he laughs at, if you want to know. I liked saying that. I was right about it. Proverb: Man thinks, God laughs. So I was right. Juliet was my favorite role. I liked the girls, I was best at them. You could have seen me in *Shulamit, Moyshe the Tailor, Kol Nidre, Mr. Harry and the Aristocrat*. I think I remember it. I think you could have seen me. Wasn't I someone in *Orpheus in the Underworld*? I think so. I played the parts. But I liked Juliet best.

How now!

3.

Eva Dancing, leaving her international reputation in her pocket, loses all the hands. All her bids are outlandish. All her trumps are ill-considered. She doesn't care at all. She gets drunk unobtrusively on expensive vodka, feeling each potato that went into the alcohol slip down her throat, and tries to get someone to argue with her, even about whether there are fewer pigeons in New York in March or in October, but all this in some likeness of good nature.

The two other ladies are not so interested in pigeons. Neither is she. The little girl won't argue because she tends to agree with Eva. The elderly child actor does not know how to argue.

What about Josef? Would he argue with her? He is silent. His lips are sewn shut. Does argument require an open mouth? Perhaps she should try to know him. What does anyone know about him, after all? Isn't it true that he went to America?

Tell me, Josef, you fool, she says to her own ears, what you are.

Josef went to America, say her ears. Don't you know? These are his secrets. Everyone knows them. In America he was a gangster. In New York City, where the gangsters are kings and the kings are gangsters (this is not exclusive to New York, she tells her ears, who ignore her). The famous names: Big Jack Zelig, Mother Rosie Hertz. Josef's name was not so famous. The Rabbi, Monk Eastman, Waxey Gordon, Gyp the Blood. Stiff Rivka. Josef was a killer. A *shtarker*, they were called: strong-arm men. There was Dopey Benny Fein, the pickpocket who sang high and clear when the law pinched him, and Dutch Schultz, who lived with the *alrightniks* of West End Avenue (enough, enough, she tells her ears, who know there is no such thing). Dangerous men, and sinister ladies. Their business was loans, gambling, women, and thievery. Horse-poisoning and arson. Politicians in their deep, deep pockets. Josef strangled men who were not agreeable. Everyone must be agreeable (agreeable, she tells her ears, is the most measured death in life one can face). Casually mentioning the name of Arnold Rothstein was good enough to fix the 1919 World Series, though the criminal czar himself had nothing to do with the eight men from Chicago who threw the game. Josef's hands ruled the city for his bosses. They were terrible hands. Hands that issued from the mists on their own like leering basilisks. He did not mind. He lived in America as a pair of hands, and did not speak.

Eva would like to know why he came back across the sea to live here, and the stunted old man once a child actor who is her partner in cards gets the bid, the pigeons on the street scatter for no reason whatsoever! And she doesn't know that Josef does not live at all, anywhere.

4.

Dr. Eva Dancing was a slight woman with a small limp on the left side. She had thick white hair and dark eyes and hands that were uneven: one large, one small. She was sixty, a staff obstetrician/gynecologist at Barnard College, and had lived in New York since 1949. By birth she was Polish, though she had lived in Poland ten years only. Having spent four of those in a closet belonging to a Catholic woman who was paid for that service, though not paid enough, in the woman's mind, to provide the girl with the closet, at her own peril and inconvenience. Having been thrown over the Warsaw Ghetto wall in a sack with thousand zloty bills taped to her thighs, to be collected by the woman who owned a closet, who put the girl (though not the money) into the dark place and kept her there the four years until the war was over, strictly forbidding Eva to come out into the open when the woman was not at home, working.

Eva had come out, of course, each time, immediately upon assuring herself that her savior had left the house. Although numerous back surgeries during later years suggested that her spinal vertebrae remembered the closet best, most of what she remembered was not the closet but rather the little Warsaw apartment and the woman's daughter, Milena, who was slow. A plump, blond girl, always in pink dresses, Milena lived at home and did not attend school. Rarely allowed outdoors, she was bored and lonely. The same age, the two children became playmates, carefully staying away from the windows (a child, Eva could no more explain to the retarded girl why this had to be than Milena could have explained it to her), but when Eva decapitated one of Milena's dolls one afternoon, Milena had wrathfully confessed to her mother that Eva was used to emerging from her hiding place, in the hope that Eva would be punished. Which she was, as well as threatened on pain of death not to come out again, though the event did not do Milena any good: after first whipping the little Jewess and sending her to her closet, Milena's mother spanked her own child with a hairbrush and forbade her to leave the house at all, afraid that the stupid child would forget that the girl in the closet was a secret.

In 1945 Eva was taken away from the woman, who, with the German defeat, tried to sell the child to a Russian general. The general threw the Pole out of his makeshift Warsaw office and took the ten-year-old Eva from her, disgusted. He then brought her with him to Berlin, where he had been newly assigned, but he was a single man and unprepared to be a father, and so he gave the girl with his best prayers to a friend, who promised to find her a good home. The home this friend found was in Paris and belonged to a rich family named Barrault, socialites who had fled France for Montreal and returned with the downfall of the Vichy government. They taught the girl some French and loved her cautiously but were well into their sixties, and when Madame Barrault suffered a debilitating stroke, and a great deal of money they had believed would still be theirs after the war turned out to be gone, Monsieur Barrault had told the girl that they simply could not care for her anymore. She was fourteen; it is possible she could have been of use to them. But the old couple sent her away. Perhaps because the teenager frightened them: like an animal, possessed of only physical reaction to only physical stimulus, she spent hours staring blankly at the street from the tall apartment windows, her eye occasionally twitching here; there; there. She was given at times to the unconditional impulse to begin running as fast as she could, no matter where she was, dashing suddenly into the street, or from one end of the kitchen to the other, or out of the *boulangerie,* stopping just as suddenly as she had started. Her body blinked to the second hands of clocks. She slept for days at a time. She wouldn't look them in the eye. They sent her to America.

In retrospect, she forgave them without hesitation. It was a strange time in Europe. America seemed like a good place. And things did not turn out so terribly there. A childless Hungarian couple had found her sleeping in a gutter, and the husband, who possessed enough French and Polish from his experience in the camps to communicate with her, had decided to take her home. And so she was given another family. Eva learned both Hungarian and English, as well as Yiddish. These things she did not find difficult. By working as a seamstress she managed to put herself through City College, winning scholarships and fellowships, and received her medical degree from Columbia University. In time she had become a doctor known around the world, in certain circles, a reputation for methods of research no one else would have imagined. Certainly it was an astounding success story.

She was grateful to her new parents, if cautious. Though it was not until after their deaths that she found herself wondering if she had loved them. If she was the type of person who could do such a thing. A natural result. After all: too much stolen already. Her first parents were lost ciphers, never to be recovered: the child is called Eva, the Polish woman had told the Russian, when asked; this is Eva, the general had said to his friend; her name is Eva, said the friend to the French couple. It was not until after she reached New York that she would realize dully that she did not know her own family name.

5.

Josef, Josef, thinks Malka, don't I know you? Haven't I known you for a long, long time? Wasn't it Josef who brought her water, before he had fled with everybody else, perhaps to Grodno or Bialystok or Minsk or, more likely, somewhere much farther away? It had certainly been someone very large. A behemoth. The biggest Jew in the world, hadn't that been what they called him?

She looks out onto the street, but not at him. She pities everything that surrounds him, the diseased pigeons, all of whom have three legs or one leg or none at all; the unhappy grimacing buildings; the bored, fallen-in chimneys, their single living eyes pointing always toward the sky. But not the senseless, mute piece of rock, sitting on the stairs. The Vilna of the past has never left her and she pities what surrounds her now for its benefit. She does not pity Josef, for he is a fool, and not to be suffered, therefore.

Wasn't he the one, after all? The one who had brought her the water to fill her kegs; the one who had overflowed her house when she was short of help before the Passover feast; the one who had brought with him floods of imbecilic divinity that her kegs could not hold? He had kept filling them, bringing more and more, long after they were full up. Enough water, enough water, her husband had cried upon his return and seeing the disaster; and she, discovering the flood, cowered in rage. The fool!

Eva rattles on incomprehensibly about some political issue in which even Eva has no interest, and Malka vaguely plays the wrong card and looks at Josef. She has no idea he is dead.

6.

I was a great beauty in my day, though I never worried myself about it much. But that's what they said about me, that I was a beauty. My father, of blessed memory, was a very learned man and very wise, and he gave all his children both a religious and a secular education. When I was thirteen he married me to my beloved husband. He could not have chosen a better man. My husband was a pious Jew, a clever businessman and a faithful husband. Also, and most important, a good father. We always took counsel with each other: my husband listened to me when it came to the business, and in turn did not leave the children all on my back. We shared everything, the good and the bad. He was a very hard worker; he knew the importance of a little bit of good Jewish sweat, my husband. In addition, he took my own mother into our house when my father died, and put food in front of her and a warm bed beneath her to the end of her days. He gave me eight children, three sons and five daughters. There were three more children lost early in their lives, and I grieved for them, but on the whole God was much kinder to me in this than to many women and in Him I place my trust. There are moments when I wonder if I would recognize my children if God saw fit to take me to the Holy Land and to place them before my eyes, and I weep bitter tears at my loss. But I know I am only a poor sinning woman, and my weak faith is shamed, and once again I know God's graciousness and His greatness.

For when there is wrong done us, in truth we have no one on the good green earth to forgive but ourselves, and even this is not enough; when there is wrong done us, the only hope we have of forgiveness is that which is granted us by God.

7.

The third elderly lady knows exactly what cards the other players hold without wishing to. Her mind traps the progress of the cards and keeps them still: she knows exactly which spades have been played, which hearts, diamonds, clubs; she knows the patterns beneath the other players' throws. The simple mathematics are achieved in her mind without realizing. She would like to leave all this aside, or move aside herself. Live outside it. It cannot be.

But then there is Josef, who lives in precisely this manner. Across the street his monstrous form is blurred, monolithic and without feature; she cannot see anything but mass. But, a moment. Is she seeing him? Is that his face in his hands? What wounds are covered up? Is that his blood, seeping through his fingers? He hides his scars. She dreams that he holds his face in his hands so it will not fall into the street, the wound with which he lives, both scarred over and open, an unspeakable void. She does not even look at the card she throws.

She does not understand that the wound is fatal; she does not know that he is murdered.

8.

Papa, you know, was a singer, and what I say is that he sang the music of time, about which perhaps more later, this music, if I am up to it. He sang to my mother. She, Felice, listened and seemed very small. The six-point star in gold around her neck and her hair dark like his. György sang to her and she was very small next to him, and people might call what he sang to her Gypsy folk songs but the mistake is understandable, his lovely ridiculous Romany bearded lips like a thousand taut strings and then not like that at all, not like that one bit. What do I know about these two, after all? Are there photographs? Are there documents, recordings? All a blank. I am myself from Budapest, although that fact can be considered as negotiable in that I cannot be bothered to recall the exact day I managed to get myself born, though I am quite sure of the year, which, you know, was the very one that the cities held in chastity by the so-called Blue Danube cast aside that sword laid between them, the sword that had ensured their continuing virginity. I achieved birth during this very year, the year these two cities called Pest and Buda crossed the river blade that separated them, the former of the pair the developed, the moving, the metal city, and the latter, its hilly, belated counterpart, the two together, consummating and kissing in order to conceive, well, me. But not to forget Obuda, the third parent, closer kin to Buda than to Pest, small and, as they say, quaint, but still part of the genetic construction, essential to the whole hilarious confabulation.

Look: there I am. I'm five, in Budapest, the three cities that have become one. Papa sings. Mamma sings too. Yes, she sang to him, and he listened. Did I say the music of time? Hers, I think, the music of history. Felice is standing by—what? A castle? Old kings with dead ears in the ground? As she prepares to sing. György is sitting. He makes sounds with grass, his cheeks, anything. All for a laugh. Then he sings, and she sings too.

Already I know that these musics, time and history and whatever else, are not for me, five years old, and I go home to play the piano.

9.

His name was Daniel, although he was known by another name. To the great world he was Shloyme Shtickel, which is to say, give or take, Shloyme the Little Bit. This was his stage name. In time it was the only one. Although there were great actresses in his time, he often played female roles when there were not children in the script. His eyes were those of an image an adult creates when thinking of the unspoiled wholeness of childhood. His tiny body, never developed, a reminder of a time when there was no time. False images, false reminders. He was a child who was never a potential adult, but also never a child.

For much of his life he had only two expressions, which were communicated through not only his face but by the manner in which he moved and the manner in which he breathed as well: first, a beseeching, terrible cry: *Save me!* and second, a perfect contentment, the surety that there had been nothing before and would be nothing later, but only now, which could not have been improved upon in any way. These two modes of visible feeling were all he had to show the world of his life. They were all he had.

But not onstage! Onstage there was more. Onstage the characters' faces and limbs acted the emotion he did not know himself. It was inexplicable.

10.

I treated an old gangster once. I know what he was because his granddaughter told me. He had a gash in his forehead and never opened his mouth, but he was dressed in a long-out-of-fashion suit, thin lapels, the old cut. His vest underneath the brown jacket was buttoned perfectly. It was me who took care of him by a mistake; old men with cuts is not typically in my line, obviously. But one does what is required.

In the clinic room, I had to step on a chair to wipe away the blood from his enormous bald head. He was an enormous man. I was trained as a gynecologist, and although I have known men, I found that I had not known the tops of their heads. Little flecks of blood had gotten into the coarse white hair cut short in a ring around the middle of his head over his ears, and I touched one of the flecks with my finger.

How did this happen? I asked him.

He did not answer.

I asked him his name, his age. No response. I repeated my questions, addressing them now to the room. Waiting again.

A nurse led into the room a little girl.

This is the patient's granddaughter, said the nurse, she would like to watch you stitch him up. Is that okay?

I bent my head down to look at him. He turned his eyes away, nervous.

How did this happen? I asked the child.

The bookcase, she said, it fell.

What was in it?

Russians, she said directly. Then a pause. I think, she added. That's what he calls them. They're really books.

I would expect nothing less from them, I said, the Russians.

You're Dr. Dancing, said the girl. My name is Gertie. I'm going to call you Adela.

Yes?

Yes, she said. You have an accent. Adela has an accent.

So do you.

The little girl didn't even bother to deny the joke. My name is Gertie, she said. You don't know me. Do you?

I don't know, I said.

Are you a dancer?

No.

I'm a dancer, said Gertie. I'm eight.

So be a dancer, I said. Maybe it will be fun.

After this she told me the date of her birthday, the number of friends she had, how often she got ear infections. That she liked strawberry ice cream. That her grandfather had been a thumb breaker who had gone straight. The words, memorized from an overheard conversation between, one supposes, the child's parents, shocked me. Not because he was a criminal, but because he was a criminal and was loved; because he broke thumbs and went straight and she loved him. She loved him, I thought; one day she will develop the linguistic capacity to put thumb and breaker together and know what it means. I thought she would love him still.

How old are you, Gertie? I asked, though I knew the answer.

Eight, Adela.

Eight! I said. Do you know, I was just now thinking about the time I was eight. Just now, before you came, I was thinking about it.

You were?

Yes, I was.

When were you eight, Adela? she asked.

A long time ago, I said. There was no TV and no cars and no toilets, it was so long ago.

No, said Gertie.

Well, I said, you're right. Maybe there were some of those things. But it was very different.

How?

We had pickle barrels, I told her.

What's a pickle barrel?

What's a pickle barrel? Oh, the shame, I said. You don't even know what a pickle barrel is. I must be very old.

You're not very old, Adela, Gertie said. She giggled.

You might as well live on Mars, I said. You don't even know what a pickle barrel is.

Martians live on Mars.

That's true, Gertie, I said.

Adela?

Yes, Gertie?

Is a pickle barrel just a barrel with pickles?

I sighed. I felt very much, at that moment. Yes, dear, I said. That's exactly what it is.

11.

I may be wrong to speak such a truth, but it was not during the years when the terrible Ukrainian came with his murderous armies that my troubles began in earnest. History will perhaps record Bogdan as the scourge of those times, and he will take his place in the list of the Jews' great miseries, from Pharaoh to the destruction of the Temple, to, God forbid, the future; but for him I have nothing but pity. He hated us for who we were and God knows we survived, together, as we always have. My own hatred is reserved for another.

I do not know the number of years left behind us since the day we were forced to flee Vilna that talk was first heard of Shabbetai Z'vi. Like a contagion, spreading by air, water, earth, and fire, this man fell upon us. I do not know but the will of God decreed it so; how or why are too much for my poor woman's mind. Whether your people of Israel were unworthy for your grace, Lord; whether we had done some wrong unto you; whether we had betrayed the holy covenant, I cannot know. Abram raised his knife to Isaac, and it is possible that we were not of such faith; but of a truth, I know in my heart that the matriarchs in *Gan Eden* wept for us.

We went to the Sephardic synagogue like the rest when the news came from Smyrna. Like the others, we expected at any moment to be transported to the Holy Land. Must I even say that it did not happen? My husband, blessed be his memory, had been slower than the others to believe that the Messiah had truly come, that this man was indeed that for which we had waited and prayed, and I chided him severely. May I be forgiven. Shabbetai Z'vi did not arrive and take us away with him. We were deceived; we were as brides at an altar without a groom in sight.

But my misery did not end there. With great suddenness my husband became ill and soon began to cough up blood, so weak that he could hardly leave his bed. The evil days were far from over, had I known it! He was very sick, but awake. He bade me bring each child to him, and kissed them each in turn, and when he had kissed them all he bade me come close, and whispered in my ear that he believed now that the pretender was true, and that Shabbetai Z'vi would heal him.

God save us from the miseries of false prophets! My husband was indeed cured; but it was the doctor who cured him, not the villainous pretender championed by his cursed apostle, Nathan of Gaza. Yet my husband insisted that he had been saved by the power of the Messiah come from Smyrna, and on this he was adamant; and he began immediately to make preparations to travel to Gallipoli.

For it so happened that in Gallipoli at that time Shabbetai Z'vi was imprisoned in the palace of the sultan, who demanded of the pretender that he convert to the ruler's religion, or die. So my husband set out for Gallipoli, with a young man named Binyomin, to reach the man who called himself the Messiah. Of what occurred in their travels, Binyomin told me thus: "We traveled the road, but it was a long, long way, and Gallipoli seemed never to get any nearer. But one day we met a traveler who had come from the very city we desired, and eagerly we begged of him any news; and he told us that, faced with death, the pretender had converted to the Islamic faith. Your honored husband disbelieved the traveler at first and called him a liar; the man told him to think what he wanted, but it was true, Heaven and Earth his witnesses. At this your husband fell to his knees and grasped at his hair in agony, and as I rushed to his side to help ease his grief he toppled over and fell to the ground, and when I came to him he was dead."

These are the words that held my husband's death. Most just and bountiful Lord, forgive us our sins, as I cannot forgive the Jew who said he was what he was not; forgive me my memory, that I remember what happened and cannot forget. Forgive me for the wrong done to me, for I have not the strength to forgive myself.

12.

It has been said, or if not, it will be said, that music derives from a specific sort of encounter with time. A typical example, it seems to me, might be an isochronic meter played against an irregularity, be it of meter, of rhythm, etc. This creates a double strand. One way to phrase this might be as follows: a straight time coupled with a crooked time. Through time, music thus captures the essence of the abstract real as well as the essence of the practical relative (which is of course also real), and in this union thereby achieves some existence roughly corresponding to the tension between the two. This is what my father thought.

Pish!

That is not music.

13.

A second way of considering music: music gives structure to time, which has none. Thus music is as human history seems to be, discrete and advancing. The fabricated caesuras we insert into the past, centuries and eras and so forth, we use also to make a music. Music and history: mechanisms to slice up time so that we may attempt some understanding of it. Forms overlaid on something utterly vast, arranging for us the pretense that we have reined it in. This, from my mother.

Again, pish!

This is not music either.

14.

Malka, formerly a beauty, of unusual education, the mother of daughters, the mother of sons, speaks:

We are the children of Father Abram, it is said. We are the chosen people. Perhaps there has been a mistake: perhaps we were meant instead to be the children of Cain, he who slew his brother. Cain, the murderer and the wanderer, who built a city, which he called Enoch after his first child. To this book of generations came Jabal, the father of such as dwell in tents; and his brothers were Jubal and Tubal, the musician and the artificer.

Their father was Lamech, and it is written that he said:

> I have slain a man to my wounding
> And a young man to my hurt.

If Cain shall be avenged sevenfold.
Truly Lamech seventy and sevenfold.

We are the children of the city builders, perhaps, not of Abram father of Isaac; the children of the tent dwellers, as well; children of the musician and the artificer.

Children of he who would be avenged of the wrongs done him in the past.

15.

At Ellis Island, guessing that they were asking her what she was called, she had said as quietly as she could, Eva. She spoke no English. When they asked for her Christian name, she told them Eva; when they asked for her surname she had said, Eva. And when they repeated and repeated the question, she had said, terrified and without any idea of what they wanted, Warszawa, Warszawa, naming the city of her birth. When that did not seem correct, she had tried other cities; if they did not like Warsaw, perhaps another place would satisfy them. What is your name? Cracow, Cracow? What is your name? Lodz? Your name? Lublin? Danzig? And so it was: they chose for her. In her terror she had named the Hanseatic seaside town Gdansk, otherwise called Danzig, and was registered then and forever in America as Eva Dancing.

16.

Shloyme Shtickel's last performance. His role: the Rebbitsin, wife of the Maharal. The story: an old, old tale. Rabbi Judah Loew of Prague, the Maharal, creates a being from clay to defend the Jews from their enemies. This creation is achieved through the power of the sacred Name. In this play, unlike the legends that precede it, the Golem speaks.

At first he can only repeat what he is told: his name, that he is a man, that he lives. Then, his own words: *Rabbi.* And: *I want to leave this place.*

Shloyme Shtickel, dressed as the Rebbitsin, offstage, fell as if

struck by a blow upon hearing the Golem's voice; as if the actor playing the rabbi had indeed created life from clods of earth; as if he
knew that a mistake to end mistakes, in causing the Golem to speak,
had been made. His knees shook; his hands trembled; his fear was
that of someone who learns that nothing is ever forgiven, nothing is
ever remembered. His face became fits of terror. Daniel, once
Shloyme Shtickel, curled up in a ball and did not uncurl.

17.

I loved Juliet, I did. Where is my Romeo? she says. I was Juliet. For a
while, I was her. That was good times. When I was her. I was Juliet,
and then I was nothing.

18.

Eva turns off Broadway onto West 116th Street and enters her apartment. She will not come out again.

19.

Malka's children cannot bury her next to her husband, for he lies
somewhere beneath the ground along the road to Gallipoli. Her
youngest daughter, copying her older brother, says Kaddish at night.
She can see the moon; it seems to have her mother's face.

20.

Then I opened the door and saw him. He had shot himself in the
face, and he was dead. Mamma's death was too much for him. It
made me happy to imagine that no one had ever heard his songs
except her, and no one had heard her songs except him. And me.
What was music to me then? The attempt to stop time? The attempt
to stop history? I do not know; perhaps the attempt to have nothing
to do with either of them. I had finished a fugue I had been working
on for some time, that morning, and I knew then that not one of my
scribbled clefs on the white page would be read by a conductor, not

one of my smeared notes would emerge from clarinets or violas or pianos, not one of my carefully placed rests would be respected by a musician who knew what silence was.

I was not angry with him. Later, I would choose no more and no less heroically. In my case gas, and not gunpowder. Silence. I feared the noise of a gunshot would cause me to look backward, as Orpheus did.

Josef the Golem, created by man and uncreated by man, unable to speak, knows only what is written. But what is written is erased as fast as his pen can work. Sitting on the step, his massive body blocks the way to nothing: blocks the way to no flesh and bone, no concrete and wood. For he is a memory come alive; come alive to find that there is nothing to remember. All across nonexistent borders stories are told, in concert with each other and in argument, and Josef writes. But to read these records is impossible.

To read his records, that which he records would have to be gone.

Across from Josef the players bicker and are bored and make bad decisions at bridge. All that exists of them is the Golem's record. Once, the story goes, the creator gave his creation the word; now, the creation withholds what he has written from the creator.

Meanwhile, we live.

Naama Goldstein
Emerson College

PICKLED SPROUTS

In fifth grade comes the call to duty. A new uniform over the old, another layer. White apron to cover the pink school blouse and the gray skirt, actually a skirt of black and white, but the houndsteeth so tiny, the eye tires and cheats. And on the head—pull back the hair, every hair—a tiara of white cotton pleats. You've never eaten in the cafeteria, but you will prepare the food when your turn comes, without strands of you shed into the mix. And in your hair a coarsening begins. At the temples and the nape still the fine-spun auburn of babyhood, but something tougher and darker threading through at the crown. There is talk of blood, with every girl's lunch break knowledge without exception secondhand, never from the source. Her? Her, really? Yes, all down her legs.

It will be some years before you understand this thing that makes pants wetters of grown girls. There are myths, the slide show in the darkened classroom will tell you for the meantime.

" 'There are myths,' " the nurse reads the words beamed onto the backward map. "Don't you believe them," she says. "For instance, when you're in your period, don't worry; you can, too, cook and bake, and there is absolutely no need, whatsoever, to be concerned that everything you touch will foul up the recipe when you're in your period. Because that, for example, is a myth, an old wives' tale."

Her voice is as cool and soothing and reiterative as her chiming glass wands, dipped in milky disinfectant, which have before and will times again frisk your scalp for lice. In the nurse's wake (the crawling skin after, by mere suggestion, licey or no, truth or myth), the map is flipped over, back to Homeland studies. The shape on the map a ram's horn curving along the Mediterranean, only the wide trumpeting end sawed off to Egypt of late, though neither old map colors nor teacher will address this. You imagine the heralding sound of the hacked-off horn, without the Sinai not much more than the mouthpiece kissing Lebanon and the scrawny neck craning against Jordan, and it's a sound as thin and hysterical as a stifled baby's. The nurse's white-shod footsteps clop down the tiled hall.

The gray schoolyard is dappled with faces of many colors, the sounds as variegated: the depth of color corresponds with the throaty depth of pronunciation. You are pale and you have a pale sound. Your mother sends you to the grocer's to teach you how to speak up, but it's not working. It's because of coffee. Your mother won't let you drink it, says it stunts the growth, though it's more than clear to you it does the opposite. To witness, the children here all drink it, and they are sharp and bothered as grown-ups. You drink milk. You speak soft and slow. You have parents from elsewhere and they say you, too, came from there, though you've no memory to support this and you are nothing like your parents, Hebrew syllables like storm-blown sand in their throats. Your language is bland, but unaccented. Neither here nor there, your own self; fine with you. These days your nowhere flavor, though, wants vigilance. Cafeteria duty is a threat.

"When's your turn up?"

"Do I know? What letter on the name list are we up to now? *Tet?* *Yud?* Doesn't matter. Listen." What you want to know, more importantly, is will you have to eat in the mess hall once you're done with cooking duties. By fifth grade you are less the picky eater, but still your repertoire isn't wide. "Listen, do you have eggs a lot? I can't stand them hard-boiled, or soft-boiled, or poached, or sunny-side up. Does she make you eat olives? Or sour pickles? Vinegar tastes like poison. I think it's poison. What if there's fish with the skin? She really crazy, the cook?"

"If you fall on a Friday, there'll be schnitzel. Other days it's always something different, but on Friday, it's without exception schnitzel."

"With ketchup? I can taste the vinegar in ketchup."

"Ketchup, it's up to you."

Your fifth-grade friend with dry, gray knees, frayed boys' under-shirts, as pregym strip-downs tell, and a meal plan card. First grade, second, so forth, she'd been too tizzied a one for you, she not mean, no tussler, but a bolter and a brayer, with a mouth so wide as to unhinge her face. Marionette face, Shlomtzee Ateeya, with big-jointed stick limbs to match. Shlomtzee six, seven, eight, nine, ten years old as likely an ally to you as a road runner to a play-dead coney. But now, in the fifth grade, there is a certain collapsing in the wilder girls, like balloons finally caving in to circumferential pressures, whereas in some of the softer girls there is a tautening. For the first year ever, you're thrown out of class. Twice already you've been ousted for garbling answers through a smirking mouth full of sandwich, or spit-softened vanilla wafers, or titters, or all three. Shlomtzee approves. Shlomtzee, your back row partner at one pale-green Formica desk, one of twenty to a classroom, is also curious. Your meals alluring not only in their covertness but in that their absence of flavor astonishes her. She makes fun of it; she can't resist it: the exotic cuisine of nowhere.

Your first exchange, Prophets class, words hissed, her long lips as motionless as a prisoner's:

"Give, give a *beess*, Neetsah."

A bite given, bread broken over chubby pink knees and slipped onto her bony ones, and her whispering again through crumby lips:

"What kind of sandwich do you call this?"

Your writing penciled on the margins of Joshua, VI: MAR-GARINE. QUIET.

"Neetsah Lustig and Shlomtzee Ateeya, is there something you would like to share with the rest of the class?"

No, nothing, but with each other, yes. After the teacher catches you eroding Joshua with your eraser and has you kiss the holy text and leave the class, after, in days to follow, there are your strawberry jam sandwiches with all the strawberries picked off for a pleasing, textureless texture, your cream crackers, limpened with sweating sliced cheese, your sponge cake, your hollow pita, your cold, peeled baked potato. The two of you stuff your craws like single-minded hatchlings, your skulls, for all the chewing and the scheming, admitting nothing of the lesson. An ongoing secret banquet on the event of big-mouth Shlomtzee and tongue-tied you finding a sneaky common language in forbidden foods. You eat such baby food, she says, and keeps on eating. Mornings your foods buffer her bitter coffee breath, afternoons they mask cafeteria traces. And though Shlomtzee never contributes to the feast, she sees that you partake of inside information from the lunchroom. *Lamed* for Lustig, your letter approaching, your turn in the kitchen up very soon, and you've only ever been inside the cafeteria for school rallies in bad weather, and you've never seen the crazy cook.

"So tell me what today."

At the end of every lunch period Shlomtzee emerges from that place with her school clothes putting off sour food smells.

"Spaghetti in sauce."

"The sauce on top or mixed in so you can't dig out the plain spaghettis?"

"Of course mixed in. That's how she cooks it in the pots till the spaghettis go orange like they're supposed to."

You offer her a bite of ripe banana, too fragrant for classroom eating. She accepts, absolutely always hungry, and still the eating is clandestine; there is no lunching allowed in the yard. The civil defense man at the school gate, someone's granddad with a rifle and a hankie on his head against the sun, he doesn't care, but there are health monitors from the sixth grade who will tell on you. They get to carry the first aid kits on school trips. They hold weekly meetings with the nurse and carry out her law: eating, only organized. Cloth napkin out, food on top, hands washed, nails inspected, grace before and after. Casual eating means contamination. There've been other slide shows.

A few secret bites facing a windowless section in the coral stucco wall of the old building where you go to see the principal or get shots, get psychotechnically tested, or fetch the janitor when somebody throws up. And as bell time nears you walk together across the glaring cemented yard to your classroom in the new concrete-slab building, slithery banana peel squeezed inside your fist.

"My baby brother eats spicier than you."

"I eat what I eat."

"Besides," she says, "mixed in or not, you still have to eat everything in your plate or she goes crazy."

"You seen that happen?"

"Everybody knows."

"Maybe it's a myth."

There are sixth graders stacked against the fence looking out on the street and the boys' school across it, the girls shoulder to shoulder in their uniforms, a pink-and-gray wall with their heads the merlons, glossy in the sun. The two of you count the bra-strapped backs and snicker. Nothing like that has started up in you, and nothing will, because, you know, it's in the coffee and their food.

"So funny," you say, "everyone eating disgustingness like they have to and meantime it's all a made-up myth that she goes crazy."

Shlomtzee's hair is black frizz, and this year she parts it down the middle and bunches it into pigtails like frazzled pom-poms over each ear, the hair across her scalp so tightly drawn her eyes are stretched. There are little golden loops in her ears, instead of the tiny studs she's had since first grade and, also new, a narrow pink belt she wears over her skirt waistband, with a heart-shaped plastic buckle, opalescent, that never stays in place but migrates round and round. It's on her back now.

"Disgustingness, you yourself, what you eat," she says, and in the sudden rubber-bandiness of her gait there is a remnant of what this year has given way in her to a reining in of limbs, to timid looks at the stately older girls who know how grown girls behave, and will let you know.

"I got cookies left," you say, "in my hand."

"One for me?"

Next thing she's got a handful of wet banana tentacles, and you're bounding around the side of the building, she after you, but only for a moment before she catches herself, tosses you an adult scowl and heads for class, her luminous belt buckle riding on her hip. You do have cookies, in truth, only in your dry hand, and now Shlomtzee is gone, you work on them all yourself, kicking through the dirt and weeds behind the classroom building, along the edge of the bomb shelter. When a health monitor sees you and your cookies, you walk past her quickly, taking flight when she yells she's going to tell the nurse, and your thigh snags on a fraying fence link and you'll use your own spit to treat the bleeding and that will be a scar to stay.

There is a problem with something you were given.

It's go home time. Outside the school, you step over turmeric yellow *amba* stains, the trampled cucumber cubes and red pepper paste on the pavement, and hold your breath while Shlomtzee sucks in the air and eyes the goods inside the stainless steel tubs. It's a new thing in town, a self-serve falafel stand. The vendor hands out slit-top pitas and customers cram the bread with the fried chickpea balls, with fine-diced salad, saucy *shakshooka* eggs, fried potatoes, pickled peppers, things purple, orange, red, and bitter green that you cannot name. Times, you've slipped into the disorder to buy a pocket, fill it with fries. There are those who understand self-service in a way the vendor didn't intend. They empty out the pita, eat the stuffing, chins burrowing into the bread, and then step back over to the stand to serve the self again these tastes of here. At busy times the vendor doesn't notice, but other times there have been shouts.

The acrid smells of this new phenomenon thin out and fade as you walk on.

"Look, Shlomtzee." You slip your book bag off one shoulder and show her the problem you've kept hidden.

"What is it?"

"A lunch box."

"A lunch *box*?"

"Yes, a box for lunch."

It's crammed into the bottom of your pack, squashing books and notebooks out of shape. It's where you hid it soon as you left the house this morning. It's tin and painted red and has hinges and a clasp. A birthday present.

"A box for lunch?" Shlomtzee doesn't understand.

"My mother bought it for me."

"Who uses boxes for lunch?" Shlomtzee uses nothing but a meal card, but those who eat home food tote it in stenciled leatherette or plastic bags strapped round their necks. "For tools, maybe," she says. "Is it for tools? Looks like a toolbox."

"My mother said she had one like this when she was little, for her food, for school."

"In this country?"

"Not in this country. She said it keeps your food in better shape than what they use here."

"You from there, too?"

"No."

"Did you tell her no one else does?"

"I told her."

"It's stupid looking," Shlomtzee says, and you know it. It's a problem.

You sit under a bus stop shelter and wait with Shlomtzee for her bus.

"We had chicken soup today at lunch," she says. "You like chicken soup."

"Strained." You buckle up your book bag, shut the foreign thing away, and kick the air with both your feet.

"There's a girl from fourth grade whose dad drives her to school every day in his truck," Shlomtzee says.

"So?"

"It's a garbage truck."

You look at each other and make embarrassed monkey faces for the garbage girl. Try hiding a Dumpster truck in your bag.

"You know," she says, festive suddenly, "the terrorists are for sure very stupid."

"Right, stupid," you say. "Why?"

On TV there are public service ads showing watermelons, loaves of bread, dolls, split open to reveal ugly coils and clocks. You must touch nothing you find on the street.

"Look up," she tells you, and you do. The two of you crane your necks and stare at the corrugated metal roof over the backless bench from which your legs dangle and kick. "If they were smart they'd put bombs on top of every bus stop. Who would see them up there?"

Shlomtzee gets up, and you too, and together you stalk around the bus stop trying to get a full view of the roof. An old lady with bowed legs wheels her groceries by and tries also to get a good look at the shelter top.

"You lost a ball?" she says. "You shouldn't play on the street with a ball."

It's a risky feeling, the both of you making fun of the old lady's waddle behind her back, but you want to laugh, so you do. The more distance between you and the old lady, the more you laugh. Then you prowl around the bus stop a little longer, and sit down.

"You're right," you say, "you couldn't even see it up there, at all, even."

"They're so stupid," she whispers. And then it's time to talk about new bleeding rumors until the bus comes.

In the gymnasium dressing room there are some strange new shapes, and many turned backs. There is great prowess at dressing through and under layers without ever completely disrobing, secret transformations managed through narrow openings. Shlomtzee hides nothing and has nothing much to hide, unless it is the swelling nipples pushing at her tattered boy's undershirt, but she doesn't seem to care. You are drawing gym pants over good, straight hips when the teacher comes in with a note. Lustig, Neetsa, she reads, and she says it is your day, today.

"On Wednesdays, what?" you whisper to Shlomtzee as you leave, grabbing your school bag.

"Always something different." She shrugs.

The hair goes back; with rubber bands and bobby pins from a jar, every strand is kept in place. The head is crowned with starched white cotton. There are giant whisks and spatulas hanging alongside colanders and pots like drums; one tap could set off a racket like a band of maddened cymbalists. Everything is scoured steel and white enamel tile, and on the shelves there is no food package you could carry with only one hand, if you could carry it at all. Behind the kitchen door, you apron up and wash down.

"To the elbows. Hygiene, hygiene."

The cook looks like someone's grandma, pinafored, the fabric a light orange with pale blue stripes. She is lovelier, though, than any grandma. Her skin is white as wax and she has eyebrows and hair you can't stop watching, beautiful, brows fine as pencil strokes and hair a purplish copper, teased up and glittering inside black mesh. She doesn't smile. She doesn't look crazy, either, only blank, with dark eyes hooded in that smooth, waxy skin. There is no need to be afraid.

She says to call her Miss Altbroit. She says you're baking fish today, and fixing vegetables to go with it. To you fish tastes like nothing to be eaten, and of vegetables, only potatoes, and cucumbers without the seeds, so long as there's no bitterness. Miss Altbroit speaks with an accent. You want to know if you'll be eating in the mess hall. Beyond the white kitchen wall the cafeteria floor is acreage of scuffed black tile, with rows of long Formica tables, outsized versions of your classroom desks.

"What? Eat where? Such a soft speaker, this child," she says. "Oh no-no, of course you don't eat there."

You hold the sieve, she pours the flour, salt, some pepper, and some sand-colored and orange spices. She says she could proportion all of it by sight, but how would you learn like that? She measures everything. She shows you how to dredge the fish, and starts greasing desk-sized baking sheets with a peeled stick of margarine.

"After all this work," she says, "why should you have to wait to eat? We'll eat together after we set the tables, and then we'll be good and strong to serve up and clean up. With all the labor we deserve to eat what we want, when we want, no?" Her eyes narrow, and it's a sort of kindness that makes her narrow them at you. Though she moves briskly and with utmost efficiency around the giant kitchen, it's like she's sleepy or weak; all her expressions are partway. She tells you to wash your hands again, after the fish, and you rush to the sink and breath in lungfuls of the pink school hand soap with the medicinal smell to get the fishiness out of your nose.

The scent of baking fish isn't as bad as the raw, but still you're glad when your nostrils adjust and no longer register anything. You peel potatoes, stopping now and then to shake clingy parings like damp cuffs from your wrists, and they fall in with the rest, into a large black garbage pail. Miss Altbroit is cutting up tomatoes. She has a little gadget, which she's let you hold and examine, for gouging out the hard green scar without any wastage. You were very careful not to stare at her forearm, and not to touch her when you handed her tool back. She hums a little. Otherwise, only the gentle sounds of blades. You could have been in and out of Gym by now and in Mathematics; you hate both Gym and Maths. Miss Altbroit isn't crazy, you don't think. You will explain about your taste and she will say no problem; what you want, when you want. She lets the red pieces drop onto a mountain of cubed cucumbers and purple cabbage in a big white tub.

"We call this vegetable salad," she says, "isn't that right?"

"Yes, Miss Altbroit."

"So-so quiet and respectful," she says. "More children in our country should be like you."

She takes the peeled potatoes from you and drops them in a vat of boiling water, then hands you a knife. You work on the tomatoes together.

"When really," she says, "a tomato is a fruit, not a vegetable. Did you know?"

You did not.

She says, of course, when most adults don't, how would a child. But as for her, it is her job to know what goes onto the plate. "And what makes a fruit a fruit?"

You don't know.

"It is the ripened ovary of a seed plant. Do you know what is an ovary?"

"From the nurse." Though you don't know, really, just remember the word from the slide show, and the footsteps down the hallway. You remember that. You will tell Miss Altbroit you'd prefer no salad, please, no fruit, please, none, please.

"Good. So. We are putting fruit into a vegetable salad. Funny, no?"

Her laugh is an awful, out-of-practice sound. She says she likes to make this a learning experience for the girls. The tomato juice burns your fingers where you chewed the nails too far down. You used to be a thumb sucker; not supposed to do that now.

The cloudy, steaming water is poured off the hot potatoes, and into the vat you and Miss Altbroit add some milk, some salt, five sticks of margarine, and crush it all up with coil mashers. The tables are set, bread baskets put out. There are kümmel seeds in the bread, which you don't like.

"Now," says Miss Altbroit, "food for the workers." She puts a slice of bread on a blue plate. "We serve ourselves," she says, and hands you the plate and a giant metal spoon. Then she holds your wrist and guides it, her dry forearm against yours.

You scoop up mashed potatoes, and she lets go.

"And fish for protein," she says. "And for the vitamins the salad. Always for a growing girl some salad."

You choose the smallest piece of fish you can find, and a little salad.

"We eat," she says, and she narrows her hooded eyes at you.

Small, cubed vegetables can be swallowed like pills. With the breath held, flavor can be censored to salty, bitter, sour, and so forth. But before long, you'll have to breathe. The food goes down in slow-traveling, half-chewed lumps. You hide bits of fish in forkfuls of mash, and that helps. Miss Altbroit eats with the efficiency and industry of her kitchen work and she does not seem to see you there, with her, at the table in the back of the school kitchen. And then, she does.

She says, "You are my best worker, so far. I tell you. It's not often, now, I see a girl so quiet and well-bred. The children here. Ah. What is this culture from? This pushing and the shoving." She wipes her plate immaculate with her bread, and chews. "I was a good, quiet girl, like you. I had respect. There were ways," she says, "well, they're gone now. Well."

She watches you, or at least her eyes rest on you, while you chew slowly, trying hard not to taste. "Some more of anything?" she says. "Why don't we first wait till you're done. I tell these girls," she says, "I tell them, what they put on their plates, they must eat. There must be an appreciation. It cannot just be assumed." Then she serves you a story. Her expressions are no longer partway; they are gone. A talking old lady doll: waxen, still face, glimmering net of hair, pencil brows. Only the lips alive. Partway through the episode about famine within walls, there is a fleeting coming-to of Miss Altbroit. She says, "And at that point I had the prettiest legs I would ever have, they were so thin," with a certain shyness, like a girl. This is one thing you will always remember, that fond narrowing of her eyes, thinking of her pretty, starving legs. And it all takes place somewhere that won't bear understanding, and then there is something about finally freedom and Russian liberators forcing something you ought not understand yet on the girls in the trains going somewhere, away from that someplace, and this is the second thing you will not forget.

"Here only it is safe," she says, "here only, and this do not forget."

And now Miss Altbroit has taken away your plate, as you have chewed and swallowed her food without stopping, like a machine, all the while she told her story, and now your plate is empty and your palate stunned.

"What I have forgotten!" Miss Altbroit says. "What have we forgotten! The special treat!" She beckons with her tattooed forearm in your view, and you follow her to a door you hadn't noticed, and it opens into the deepest pantry, lined with the longest shelves, which are bearing the vastest collection of pickle jars you have ever seen. Some of the glass is clean, and some crusted with dust. In the murky brine in the jars there is every possible vegetable, and fruit. Now you know—those are fruit. "So? Impressive, no, my collection? Preserving is my specialty. There is a recipe I am developing, and you get to try, for being such a fine helper." In the jar she takes down, what look to be tiny dark green cabbage heads bob around, and there is a slow process of disintegration evident in detaching leaves. "Everything was so mild, and what the meal was missing we forgot. Some zing. How about these?" she says. "Or there is baby eggplant, tomatoes, broccoli, cauliflower. You can see. Which?"

After the tears, after she seats you back at the table, brings a glass of milk, and sits opposite you, peering; after Miss Altbroit's awkward, fingertip pats on your shoulders, more like a tap-tapping to awaken than a consoling touch; after she tells you there was no need to cry, she never makes anyone eat what they don't like, only what's on their plate, that she's no monster, after she tells you that; after this, you are the server, eyes dry but pinched feeling, apron only a little stained, nauseous stirrings below your waist from the unfamiliar foods. Girls in pink and gray walk up to the steam table, and you serve, with Miss Altbroit prescribing the balance. Then from behind the kitchen door, you watch Miss Altbroit stroll along the dining tables in silence as the girls eat. And there is Shlomtzee, looking at you with her stretched eyes as she consumes a second helping of the fish you helped prepare.

There is an incident some days later. There are soldiers in the yard, and all the girls are evacuated to the boys' school across the road, an invasion of pink shirts. It's an occasion. Though the boys are in session, sixth-grade girls preen in the sandy soccer court on the chance they're being watched. It's all settled rather quickly, to general dismay, and the lot of you are shepherded back to your classes, the soldiers in olive holding up traffic as you cross the street.

The civil defense man with the hankie on his head has given Miss Altbroit his chair by the front gate, and holds a glass of water to her lips, while pressing his big, old man's hand onto her shoulder and speaking in a language you don't understand. The nurse approaches. Miss Altbroit's face looks as blank and white as you remember, but she rocks, faintly, back and forth, and murmurs back to the guard, in the same language. You duck into the throng so she won't see you.

It's over. It's over, now, the Prophets teacher says in class. Done. She says to settle down if there is to be an explanation. A Suspicious Object, she says, in the cafeteria pantry. Just an empty red toolbox as it transpired, some worker's oversight. Who knows how long it had been there before poor Miss Altbroit noticed it in her pickle pantry. Now, as for Joshua.

"I'll never tell anyone," says Shlomtzee, "but what about your mom?"

"I said I lost it."

"You leave it there on purpose?"

"They shouldn't let crazies next to children."

You stretch your legs along the bus stop bench as Shlomtzee slides down the pole holding up the corrugated roof.

"Was your mom mad?" she asks.

"I had to wash everyone's dishes that night when it wasn't even at all my turn, even."

"It was stupid looking," she says. "What do you need a thing like that."

"So I used lots of soap on the dishes on purpose and I didn't rinse them good."

"So you showed them."

The bus will come soon and take Shlomtzee home. In sixth grade she will wear a bra and sometimes in gym she'll have a note from the nurse; you will have a different friend. Over the course of months and years your palate will coarsen, so that you'll seek out flavors more and more assaulting. For now, you and Shlomtzee eat airy white bread, brand-new, baked-today fresh, that you let soften to nothing on your tongue. There is no one on this street but you and Shlomtzee, beside you now on the bench, the two of you kicking out softly and to a rhythm so placating, even the growl of the approaching bus is as a baby cooing her own lullaby, in no one's language, and with no one's memories.

Julie Otsuka
Columbia University

EVACUATION ORDER NO. 19

Overnight the sign had appeared. On billboards and trees and all of the bus stop benches. It hung in the window of Woolworth's. It hung by the entrance to the YMCA. It was nailed to the door of the municipal court and stapled, at eye level, to every other telephone pole along University Avenue. Mrs. Hayashi was returning a book to the library when she saw the sign in a post office window. It was a sunny day in Berkeley in the spring of 1942 and she was wearing new glasses and could see everything clearly for the first time in weeks. She no longer had to squint but she squinted out of habit anyway. She read the sign from top to bottom and then, still squinting, she took out a pen and read the sign from top to bottom again. The print was small and dark. Some of it was tiny. She wrote down a few words on the back of a bank receipt, then turned around and went home and began to pack.

When the overdue notice from the library arrived in the mail nine days later she still had not finished packing. The children had just left for school and boxes and suitcases were scattered across the floor of the house. She tossed the envelope into the nearest suitcase and walked out the door.

Outside the sun was warm and the palm fronds were clacking idly against the side of the house. She pulled on her white silk gloves and began to walk east on Ashby. She crossed California Street and bought several bars of Lux soap and a large jar of face cream at the Rumford Pharmacy. She passed the thrift shop and the boarded-up grocery but saw no one she knew on the sidewalk. At the newsstand on the corner of Grove she bought a copy of the *Berkeley Gazette*. She scanned the headlines quickly. The Burma Road had been severed and one of the Dionne quintuplets—Yvonne—was still recovering from an ear operation. Sugar rationing would begin on Tuesday. She folded the paper in half but was careful not to let the ink darken her gloves.

At Lundy's Hardware she stopped and looked at the display of victory garden shovels in the window. They were well-made shovels with sturdy metal handles and she thought, for a moment, of buying one—the price was right and she did not like to pass up a bargain. Then she remembered that she already had a shovel at home in the shed. In fact, she had two. She did not need a third. She smoothed down her dress and went into the store.

"Nice glasses," Joe Lundy said the moment she walked through the door.

"You think?" she asked. "I'm still not used to them yet." She picked up a hammer and gripped the handle firmly. "Do you have anything bigger?" she asked. Joe Lundy said that what she had in her hand was the biggest hammer he had. She put the hammer back on the rack.

"How's your roof holding out?" he asked.

"I think the shingles are rotting. It just sprung another leak."

"It's been a wet year."

Mrs. Hayashi nodded. "But we've had some nice days." She walked past the venetian blinds and the blackout shades to the back of the store. She picked out two rolls of tape and a ball of twine and brought them back to the register. "Every time it rains I have to set out the bucket," she said. She put down two quarters on the counter.

"Nothing wrong with a bucket," said Joe Lundy. He pushed the quarters back toward her across the counter but he did not look at her. "You can pay me later," he said. Then he began to wipe the side of the register with a rag. There was a dark stain there that would not go away.

"I can pay you now," she said.

"Don't worry about it." He reached into his shirt pocket and gave her two caramel candies wrapped in gold foil. "For the children," he said. She slipped the caramels into her purse but left the money. She thanked him for the candy and walked out of the store.

"That's a nice red dress," he called out after her.

She turned around and squinted at him over the top of her glasses. "Thank you," she said. "Thank you, Joe." Then the door slammed behind her and she was alone on the sidewalk again and she realized that in all the years she had been going to Joe Lundy's store she had never once called him by his name until now. Joe. It sounded strange to her. Wrong, almost. But she had said it. She had said it out loud. She wished she had said it earlier.

She wiped her forehead with her handkerchief. The sun was bright and Mrs. Hayashi was not a woman who liked to sweat in public. She took off her glasses and crossed to the shady side of the street. At the corner of Shattuck she took the streetcar downtown. She got off in front of J. F. Hink's department store and rode the escalator to the third floor and asked the salesman if they had any duffel bags but they did not, they were all sold out. He had sold the last one a half hour ago. He suggested she try JCPenney but they were sold out of duffel bags there too. They were sold out of duffel bags all over town.

When she got home she took off her red dress and put on her faded blue one—her housedress. She twisted her hair up into a bun and put on an old pair of comfortable shoes. She had to finish packing. She rolled up the Oriental rug in the living room. She took down the mirrors. She took down the curtains and shades. She carried the tiny bonsai tree out to the yard and set it down on the grass beneath the eaves where it would not get too much shade or too much sun but just the right amount of each. She brought the wind-up Victrola and the Westminster chime clock downstairs to the basement.

Upstairs, in the boy's room, she unpinned the One World One War map of the world from the wall and folded it neatly along the crease lines. She wrapped up his stamp collection, and the painted wooden Indian with the long headdress he had won at the Sacramento State Fair. She pulled out his Joe Palooka comic books from under the bed. She emptied the drawers. Some of his clothes—the clothes he would need—she left out for him to put into his suitcase later. She placed his baseball glove on his pillow. The rest of his things she put into boxes and carried into the sunroom.

The door to the girl's room was closed. Above the doorknob was a note that had not been there the day before. It said, "Do Not Disturb." Mrs. Hayashi did not open the door. She went down the stairs and removed the pictures from the walls. There were only three: the painting of Princess Elizabeth that hung in the dining room, the picture of Jesus in the foyer, and, in the kitchen, a framed reproduction of Millet's *The Gleaners*. She placed Jesus and the little princess together facedown in a box. She made sure to put Jesus on top. She took *The Gleaners* out of its frame and looked at the picture one last time. She wondered why she had let it hang in the kitchen for so long. It bothered her, the way those peasants were forever bent over above that endless field of wheat. "Look up!" she wanted to say to them. "Look up, look up!" *The Gleaners*, she decided, would have to go. She set the picture outside with the garbage.

In the living room she emptied all the books from the shelves except Audubon's *Birds of America*. In the kitchen she emptied the cupboards. She set aside a few things for later that evening. Everything else—the china, the silver, the set of ivory chopsticks her mother had sent to her fifteen years ago from Hawaii on her wedding day—she put into boxes. She taped the boxes shut with the tape she had bought from Lundy's Hardware Store and carried them one by one up the stairs to the sunroom. When she was done she locked the door with two padlocks and sat down on the landing with her dress pushed up above her knees and lit a cigarette. Tomorrow she and the children would be leaving. She did not know where they were going or how long they would be gone or who would look after the house while they were away. She knew only that tomorrow they had to go.

There were things they could take with them: bedding and linen, forks, spoons, plates, bowls, cups, clothes. These were the words she had written down on the back of the bank receipt. Pets were not allowed. That was what the sign had said.

It was late April. It was the fourth week of the fifth month of the war and Mrs. Hayashi, who did not always follow the rules, followed the rules. She gave the cat to the Greers next door. She caught the chicken that had been running wild in the yard since the fall and snapped its neck beneath the handle of a broomstick. She plucked out the feathers and set the carcass into a pan of cold water in the sink.

By early afternoon Mrs. Hayashi's handkerchief was soaked. She was breathing hard and her nose was itching from the dust. Her back ached. She slipped off her shoes and massaged the bunions on her feet, then went into the kitchen and turned on the radio. Enrico Caruso was singing "La donna è mobile" again. His voice was full and sweet. She opened the refrigerator and took out a plate of rice balls stuffed with pickled plums. She ate them slowly as she listened to the tenor sing. The plums were dark and sour. They were just the way she liked them.

When the aria was over she turned off the radio and put two rice balls into a blue bowl. She cracked an egg over the bowl and added some salmon she had cooked the night before. She brought the bowl outside to the back porch and set it down on the steps. Her back was throbbing but she stood up straight and clapped her hands three times.

A small white dog came limping out of the trees.

"Eat up, White Dog," she said. White Dog was old and ailing but he knew how to eat. His head bobbed up and down above the bowl. She sat down beside him and watched. When the bowl was empty he looked up at her. One of his eyes was clouded over. She rubbed his stomach and his tail thumped against the wooden steps.

"Good dog," she said.

She stood up and walked across the yard and White Dog followed her. The tomato garden had gone to seed and the plum tree was heavy with rotting fruit. Weeds were everywhere. She had not mowed the grass for months. Junior usually did that. Junior was her husband. Junior's father was Isamu Hayashi, Senior, but Junior was just Junior. Once in a while he was Sam. Last December Junior had been arrested and sent to Missoula, Montana, on a train. In March he had been sent to Fort Sam Houston, Texas. Now he was living just north of the Mexican border in Lordsburg, New Mexico. Every few days he sent her a letter. Usually he told her about the weather. The weather in Lordsburg was fine. On the back of every envelope was stamped "Alien Enemy Mail, Censored."

Mrs. Hayashi sat down on a rock beneath the persimmon tree. White Dog lay at her feet and closed his eyes. "White Dog," she said, "look at me." White Dog raised his head. She was his mistress and he did whatever she asked. She put on her white silk gloves and took out a roll of twine. "Now just keep looking at me," she said. She tied White Dog to the tree. "You've been a good dog," she said. "You've been a good white dog."

Somewhere in the distance a telephone rang. White Dog barked. "Hush," she said. White Dog grew quiet. "Now roll over," she said. White Dog rolled over and looked up at her with his good eye. "Play dead," she said. White Dog turned his head to the side and closed his eyes. His paws went limp. Mrs. Hayashi picked up the large shovel that was leaning against the trunk of the tree. She lifted it high in the air with both hands and brought the blade down swiftly on his head. White Dog's body shuddered twice and his hind legs kicked out into the air, as though he were trying to run. Then he grew still. A trickle of blood seeped out from the corner of his mouth. She untied him from the tree and let out a deep breath. The shovel had been the right choice. Better, she thought, than a hammer.

Beneath the tree she began to dig a hole. The soil was hard on top but soft and loamy beneath the surface. It gave way easily. She plunged the shovel into the earth again and again until the hole was deep. She picked up White Dog and dropped him into the hole. His body was not heavy. It hit the earth with a quiet thud. She pulled off her gloves and looked at them. They were no longer white. She dropped them into the hole and picked up the shovel again. She filled up the hole. The sun was hot and the only place there was any shade was beneath the trees. Mrs. Hayashi was standing beneath the trees. She was forty-one and tired. The back of her dress was drenched with sweat. She brushed her hair out of her eyes and leaned against the tree. Everything looked the same as before except the earth was a little darker where the hole had been. Darker and wetter. She plucked two persimmons from a low hanging branch and went back inside the house.

*   *   *

When the children came home from school she reminded them that early the next morning they would be leaving. Tomorrow they were going on a trip. They could only bring with them what they could carry.

"I already know that," said the girl. She knew how to read signs on trees. She tossed her books onto the sofa and told Mrs. Hayashi that her teacher Mr. Rutherford had talked for an entire hour about prime numbers and coniferous trees.

"Do you know what a coniferous tree is?" the girl asked.

Mrs. Hayashi had to admit that she did not. "Tell me," she said, but the girl just shook her head no.

"I'll tell you later," she said. She was ten years old and she knew what she liked. Boys and black licorice and Dorothy Lamour. Her favorite song on the radio was "Don't Fence Me In." She adored her pet macaw. She went to the bookshelf and took down *Birds of America*. She balanced the book on her head and walked slowly, her spine held erect, up the stairs to her room.

A few seconds later there was a loud thump and the book came tumbling back down the stairs. The boy looked up at his mother. He was seven and a small, black fedora was tilted to one side of his head. "She has to stand up straighter," he said softly. He went to the foot of the stairs and stared at the book. It had landed face open to a picture of a small brown bird. A marsh wren. "You have to stand up straighter," he shouted.

"It's not that," came the girl's reply. "It's my head."

"What's wrong with your head?" shouted the boy.

"Too round. Too round on *top*."

He closed the book and turned to his mother. "Where's White Dog?" he asked.

He went out to the porch and clapped his hands three times.

"White Dog!" he yelled. He clapped his hands again. "White Dog!" He called out several more times, then went back inside and stood beside Mrs. Hayashi in the kitchen. She was slicing persimmons. Her fingers were long and white and they knew how to hold a knife. "That dog just gets deafer every day," he said.

He sat down and turned the radio on and off, on and off, while Mrs. Hayashi arranged the persimmons on a plate. The Radio City

Symphony was performing Tchaikovsky's *1812 Overture*. Cymbals were crashing. Cannons boomed. Mrs. Hayashi set the plate down in front of the boy. "Eat," she said. He reached for a persimmon just as the audience burst into applause. "Bravo," they shouted, "bravo, bravo!" The boy turned the dial to see if he could find *Speaking of Sports* but all he could find was the news and a Sammy Kaye serenade. He turned off the radio and took another persimmon from the plate.

"It's so hot in here," he said.

"Take off your hat then," said Mrs. Hayashi, but the boy refused. The hat was a present from Junior. It was big on him but he wore it every day. She poured him a glass of cold barley water and he drank it all in one gulp.

The girl came into the kitchen and went to the macaw's cage by the stove. She leaned over and put her face close to the bars. "Tell me something," she said.

The bird fluffed his wings and danced from side to side on his perch. "Baaaak," he said.

"That's not what I wanted to hear," said the girl.

"Take off your hat," said the bird.

The girl sat down and Mrs. Hayashi gave her a glass of cold barley water and a long silver spoon. The girl licked the spoon and stared at her reflection. Her head was upside down. She dipped the spoon into the sugar bowl.

"Is there anything wrong with my face?" she asked.

"Why?" said Mrs. Hayashi.

"People were staring."

"Come over here."

The girl stood up and walked over to her mother. "Let me look at you," said Mrs. Hayashi.

"You took down the mirrors," the girl said.

"I had to. I had to put them away."

"Tell me how I look."

Mrs. Hayashi ran her hands across the girl's face. "You look fine," she said. "You have a fine nose."

"What else?" asked the girl.

"You have a fine set of teeth."

"Teeth don't count."

"Teeth are essential."

Mrs. Hayashi rubbed the girl's shoulders. The girl leaned back against her mother's knees and closed her eyes. Mrs. Hayashi pressed her fingers deep into the girl's neck until she felt her begin to relax. "If there was something wrong with my face," the girl asked, "would you tell me?"

"Turn around."

The girl turned around.

"Now look at me."

She looked at her mother.

"You have the most beautiful face I have ever seen."

"You're just saying that."

"No, I mean it."

The boy turned on the radio. The weatherman was giving the forecast for the next day. He was predicting rain and cooler temperatures. "Sit down and drink your water," the boy said to his sister. "Don't forget to take your umbrella tomorrow," said the weatherman.

The girl sat down. She drank her barley water and began to tell Mrs. Hayashi all about coniferous trees. Most of them were evergreens but some were just shrubs. Not all of them had cones. Some of them, like the yew, only had seedpods.

"That's good to know," said Mrs. Hayashi. Then she stood up and told the girl it was time to practice the piano for Thursday's lesson.

"Do I have to?"

Mrs. Hayashi thought for a moment. "No," she said, "only if you want to."

"Tell me I have to."

"I can't."

The girl went out to the living room and sat down on the piano bench. "The metronome's gone," she called out.

"Just count to yourself then," said Mrs. Hayashi.

". . . three, five, seven . . ." The girl put down her knife and paused. They were eating supper at the table. Outside it was dusk. The sky was dark purple and a breeze was blowing in off the bay. Hundreds of jays were twittering madly in the Greers' magnolia tree next door. A drop of rain fell on the ledge above the kitchen sink and Mrs. Hayashi stood up and closed the window.

"Eleven, thirteen," said the girl. She was practicing her prime numbers for Monday's test.

"Sixteen?" said the boy.

"No," said the girl. "Sixteen's got a square root."

"I forgot," said the boy. He picked up a drumstick and began to eat.

"You never knew," said the girl.

"Forty-one," said the boy. "Eighty-six." He wiped his mouth with a napkin. "Twelve," he added.

The girl looked at him. Then she turned to her mother. "There's something wrong with this chicken," she said. "It's too tough." She put down her fork. "I can't swallow another bite."

"Don't, then," said Mrs. Hayashi.

"I'll eat it," said the boy. He plucked a wing from his sister's plate and put it into his mouth. He ate the whole thing. Then he spit out the bones and asked Mrs. Hayashi where they were going the next day.

"I don't know," she said.

The girl stood up and left the table. She sat down at the piano and began to play a piece by Debussy from memory. "Golliwogg's Cake-walk." The melody was slow and simple. She had played it at a recital the summer before and her father had sat in the audience and clapped and clapped. She played the piece all the way through without missing a note. When she began to play it a second time the boy got up and went to his room and began to pack.

The first thing he put inside of his suitcase was his baseball glove. He slipped it into the large pocket with the red satin lining. The pocket bulged. He threw in his clothes and tried to close the lid but the suitcase was very full. He sat on top of it and the lid sank down slowly as the air hissed out. Suddenly he stood up again. The lid sprang open. There was something he had forgotten. He went to the closet in the hall and brought back his polka-dotted umbrella. He held it out at arm's length and shook his head sadly. The umbrella was too long. There was no way it would fit inside the suitcase.

Mrs. Hayashi stood in the kitchen, washing her hands. The children had gone to bed and the house was quiet. The pipes were still hot from the day and the water from the faucet was warm. She could hear thunder in the distance—thunder and, from somewhere deep beneath the house, crickets. The crickets had come out early that year and she liked to fall asleep to their chirping. She looked out the window above the sink. The sky was still clear and she could see a full moon through the branches of the maple tree. The maple was a sapling with delicate leaves that turned bright red in the fall. Junior had planted it for her four summers ago. She turned off the tap and looked around for the dish towel but it was not there. She had already packed the towels. They were in the suitcase by the door in the hall.

She dried her hands on the front of her dress and went to the bird cage. She lifted off the green cloth and undid the wire clasp on the door. "Come on out," she said. The bird stepped cautiously onto her finger and looked at her. "It's only me," she said. He blinked. His eyes were black and bulbous. They had no center.

"Get over here," he said, "get over here now." He sounded just like Junior. If she closed her eyes she could easily imagine that Junior was right there in the room with her.

Mrs. Hayashi did not close her eyes. She knew exactly where Junior was. He was sleeping on a cot—a cot or maybe a bunk bed—somewhere in a tent in Lordsburg where the weather was always fine. She pictured him lying there with one arm flung across his eyes and she kissed the top of the bird's head.

"I am right here," she said. "I am right here, right now."

She gave him a sunflower seed and he cracked the shell open in his beak. "Get over here," he said again.

She opened the window and set the bird out on the ledge.

"You're all right," the bird said.

She stroked the underside of his chin and he closed his eyes. "Silly bird," she whispered. She closed the window and locked it. Now the bird was outside on the other side of the glass. He tapped the pane three times with his claw and said something but she did not know what it was. She could not hear him anymore.

She rapped back.

"Go," she said. The bird flapped his wings and flew up into the maple tree. She grabbed the broom from behind the stove and went outside and shook the branches of the tree. A spray of water fell from the leaves. "Go," she shouted. "Get on out of here."

The bird spread his wings and flew off into the night.

She went back inside the kitchen and took out a bottle of plum wine from beneath the sink. Without the bird in the cage, the house felt empty. She sat down on the floor and put the bottle to her lips. She swallowed once and looked at the place on the wall where *The Gleaners* had hung. The white rectangle was glowing in the moonlight. She stood up and traced around its edges with her finger and began to laugh—quietly at first, but soon her shoulders were heaving and she was doubled over and gasping for breath. She put down the bottle and waited for the laughter to stop but it would not, it kept on coming until finally the tears were running down her cheeks. She picked up the bottle again and drank. The wine was dark and sweet. She had made it herself last fall. She took out her handkerchief and wiped her mouth. Her lips left a dark stain on the cloth. She put the cork back into the bottle and pushed it in as far as it would go. "La donna è mobile," she sang to herself as she went down the stairs to the basement. She hid the bottle behind the old rusted furnace where no one would ever find it.

In the middle of the night the boy crawled into her bed and asked her, over and over again, "What is that funny noise? What is that funny *noise?*"

Mrs. Hayashi smoothed down his black hair. "Rain," she whispered.

The boy understood. He fell asleep at once. Except for the sound of the rain the house was quiet. The crickets were no longer chirping and the thunder had come and gone. Mrs. Hayashi lay awake worrying about the leaky roof. Junior had meant to fix it but he never had. She got up and placed a tin bucket on the floor to catch the water. She felt better after she did that. She climbed back into bed beside the boy and pulled the blanket up around his shoulders. He was chewing in his sleep and she wondered if he was hungry. Then she remembered the candy in her purse. The caramels. She had forgotten about the caramels. What would Joe Lundy say? He would tell her she was wearing a nice red dress. He would tell her not to worry about it. She knew that. She closed her eyes. She would give the caramels to the children in the morning. That was what she would do. She whispered a silent prayer to herself and drifted off to sleep as the water dripped steadily into the bucket. The boy shrugged off the blanket and rolled up against the wall where it was cool.

In a few hours he and the girl and Mrs. Hayashi would report to the Civil Control Station at the First Congregational Church on Channing Way. They would pin their identification numbers to their collars and grab their suitcases and climb onto the bus. The bus would drive south on Shattuck and then turn west onto Ashby Avenue. Through the dusty pane of the window Mrs. Hayashi would see the newsstand on the corner of Grove. She would see the boarded-up grocery and the sign in front of it—a new sign, a sign she had not seen before—that said, "Thank you for your patronage. God be with you until we meet again." She would see the thrift shop and the Rumford Pharmacy. She would see her house with its gravel walkway and its small but reliable rosebush that had blossomed every May for the last ten years in a row. She would see Mrs. Greer next door watering her lawn but she would not wave to her. The bus would speed through a yellow light and turn left onto Route 80, then cross the Bay Bridge and take them away.

Three years and four months later they would return. It would be early autumn and the war would be over. The furniture in the house would be gone but the house would still be theirs. The sunroom would be empty. The stovepipe would be missing from the stove and there would be no motor inside the washing machine. In the mailbox there would be an overdue notice. Mrs. Hayashi would owe the library $61.25 in fines and her borrowing privileges would be temporarily suspended. The bonsai tree would be dead but the maple would be thriving. So would the persimmon tree. Six months later Junior would come home from New Mexico a tired and sick old man. Mrs. Hayashi would not recognize him at first but the girl would know who her father was the moment he stepped off the train. The following summer Junior would have a stroke and Mrs. Hayashi would go to work for the first time in her life. For five and sometimes six days a week she would clean other people's houses much better than she ever had her own. Her back would grow strong and the years would go by quickly. Junior would have two more strokes and then die. The children would grow up. The boy would become a lieutenant colonel in the army and the girl would become my mother. She would tell me many things but she would never speak of the war. The bottle of plum wine would continue to sit, unnoticed, gathering dust behind the furnace in the basement. It would grow darker and sweeter with every passing year. The leak in the roof has still, to this day, not been properly fixed.

PARTICIPATING WORKSHOPS

UNITED STATES

Abilene Christian University
Graduate School of English
ACU Box 28252
Abilene, TX 79699-8252
915/674-2252

American University
MFA Program in Creative Writing
Department of Literature
4400 Massachusetts Avenue N.W.
Washington, D.C. 20016-8037
202/885-2972

Arizona State University
Creative Writing Program
Department of English
PO Box 870302
Tempe, AZ 85287-0302
602/965-3528

Bennington College
Writing Seminars
Bennington, VT 05201
802/442-5401 (ext. 4452)

Boston University
Creative Writing Program
236 Bay State Road
Boston, MA 02215
617/353-2510

Bowling Green State University
Creative Writing Program
Department of English
Bowling Green, OH 43403
419/372-8370

Brooklyn College
M.F.A. Program in Creative Writing
Department of English
2900 Bedford Avenue
Brooklyn, NY 11210
718/951-5195

Brown University
Program in Creative Writing
Box 1852
Providence, RI 02912
401/863-3260

California State University, Long Beach
English Department
1250 Bellflower Boulevard
Long Beach, CA 90840
562/985-4223

California State University, Northridge
Department of English
18111 Nordhoff Street
Northridge, CA 91330-8248
818/677-3431

California State University, Sacramento
Department of English
6000 J Street
Sacramento, CA 95819-6075
916/278-6586

City College of the City University of New York
138th Street at Convent Avenue
New York, NY 10031
212/650-5408

Cleveland State University
Creative Writing Program
Euclid Avenue at East 24th Street
Cleveland, OH 44115
216/687-3950

Colorado State University
Department of English
359 Eddy
Fort Collins, CO 80523-1773
970/491-6428

Columbia College Chicago
Fiction Writing Department
600 South Michigan Avenue
Chicago, IL 60605
312/663-1600 (ext. 5611)

Columbia University
Writing Division
School of the Arts
Dodge Hall
2960 Broadway, Room 415
New York, NY 10027-6902
212/854-4391

DePaul University
M.A. in Writing Program
Department of English
802 West Belden Avenue
Chicago, IL 60614-3214
773/325-7485

Eastern Michigan University
Department of English Language and Literature
612 Prayharrold
Ypsilanti, MI 48197
313/487-4220

Eastern Washington University
Creative Writing Program
705 West First Avenue
MS #1
Spokane, WA 99204
509/623-4221

Emerson College
Graduate Admissions
Writing, Literature, and Publishing
100 Beacon Street
Boston, MA 02116
617/824-8750

Florida International University
Creative Writing Program
English Department
North Miami Campus
North Miami, FL 33181
305/919-5857

Florida State University
Department of English
Tallahassee, FL 32306-1036
904/644-4230

George Mason University
Creative Writing Program
MS 3E4
Fairfax, VA 22030
703/993-1185

Georgia State University
Department of English
University Plaza
Atlanta, GA 30303-3083
404/651-2900

Hamline University
Graduate Liberal Studies–MFA in Writing
1536 Hewitt Avenue
St. Paul, MN 55104
612/523-2900

Illinois State University
Department of English
Campus Box 4240
Normal, IL 61790-4240
309/438-3667

Indiana University
MFA Program
English Department
Ballantine Hall 442
Bloomington, IN 47405-6601
812/855-8224

Johns Hopkins University
The Writing Seminars
135 Gilman Hall
3400 North Charles Street
Baltimore, MD 21218-2690
410/516-7563

Kansas State University
Creative Writing Program
Department of English
104 Denison Hall
Manhattan, KS 66506-0701
785/532-6716

Long Island University
Brooklyn Campus
1 University Plaza
Brooklyn, NY 11201
718/488-1000 (ext. 1050)

Louisiana State University
English Department
213 Allen
Baton Rouge, LA 70803
504/388-2236

Loyola Marymount University
Department of English
326 Foley
Loyola Boulevard and West 80th Street
Los Angeles, CA 90045
310/338-2954

Manhattanville College
Office of Adult and Special Programs
2900 Purchase Street
Purchase, NY 10577
914/694-3425

Mankato State University
English Department
Box 53, Mankato State University
Mankato, MN 56002-8400
507/389-2117

McNeese State University
Program in Creative Writing
Department of Languages
P.O. Box 92655
Lake Charles, LA 70609
318/475-5326

Miami University
Creative Writing Program
Department of English
356 Bachelor Hall
Oxford, OH 45056
513/529-5221

Michigan State University
Department of English
201 Morrill Hall
East Lansing, MI 48824-1036
517/355-7570

Mississippi State University
Drawer E
Department of English
Mississippi State, MS 39762
601/325-3644

Naropa Institute
2130 Arapahoe Avenue
Boulder, CO 80302-6697
303/546-3540

New Mexico State University
Department of English
Box 30001, Department 3E
Las Cruces, NM 88003-8001
505/646-3931

The New School
Office of Education Advising and Admissions
66 West 12th Street
New York, NY 10011
212/229-5630

New York University
Creative Writing Program
19 University Place
New York, NY 10003
212/998-8816

Northeastern University
Department of English
406 Holmes Hall
Boston, MA 02115
617/373-2512

Ohio State University
Department of English
164 West 17th Avenue
Columbus, OH 43210-1370
614/292-6065

Oklahoma State University
English Department
205 Morrill Hall
Stillwater, OK 74078-4069
405/744-9469

Old Dominion University
Department of English
BAL 220
Norfolk, VA 23529
757/683-3991

Pennsylvania State University
Graduate Admissions
MFA Program in Writing
Department of English
University Park, PA 16802
814/863-3069

Purdue University
Office of Admissions
1080 Schleman Hall
West Lafayette, IN 47907-1080
765/494-1776

Rivier College
Department of English
South Main Street
Nashua, NH 03060-5086
603/888-1311

Saint Mary's College of California
MFA in Creative Writing
P.O. Box 4686
Moraga, CA 94575-4686
510/631-4088

San Francisco State University
Department of Creative Writing
College of Humanities
1600 Holloway Avenue
San Francisco, CA 94132
415/338-1891

Sarah Lawrence College
Program in Writing
1 Mead Way
Bronxville, NY 10708-5999
914/337-0700

The School of the Art Institute of Chicago
MFA in Writing Program
37 South Wabash Avenue
Chicago, IL 60603-3103
800/232-7242 or 312/899-5219

Sonoma State University
English Department
1801 East Cotati Avenue
Rohnert Park, CA 94928
707/664-2140

Southwest Texas State
University
MFA Program in Creative
Writing
Department of English
601 University Drive
San Marcos, TX 78666-
4616
512/245-2163

State University of New
York at Stony Brook
Creative Writing Program
Department of English
Stony Brook, NY 11794-
5350
516/632-7373

Syracuse University
Program in Creative Writ-
ing
Department of English
Syracuse, NY 13244-0003
315/443-9469

Temple University
Graduate Creative Writ-
ing Program
English Department
Philadelphia, PA 19122
215/204-1796

Texas Center for Writers
University of Texas at
Austin
FDH
702 East 26th Street
Austin, TX 78705
512/471-1601

University at Albany,
SUNY
Writing Program
Department of English
Humanities Building 333
Albany, NY 12222
518/442-4055

University of Alabama,
Tuscaloosa
Program in Creative Writ-
ing
Department of English
P.O. Box 870244
Tuscaloosa, AL 35487-
0244
205/348-0766

University of Alaska,
Anchorage
Department of Creative
Writing and Literary
Arts
3211 Providence Drive
Anchorage, AK 99508
907/786-4356

University of Alaska, Fair-
banks
Creative Writing Program
Department of English
P.O. Box 755720
Fairbanks, AK 99775-5720
907/474-7193

University of Arizona
Creative Writing Program
Department of English
Modern Languages Bldg.
#67
P.O. Box 210067
Tucson, AZ 85721-0067
520/621-3880

University of Arkansas
Department of English
333 Kimpel Hall
Fayetteville, AR 72701
501/575-4301

University of California,
Davis
Graduate Creative Writ-
ing Program
Department of English
Davis, CA 95616-8581
916/752-2281

University of California,
Irvine
Program in Writing–Fic-
tion
Department of English
and Comparative Liter-
ature
Irvine, CA 92697-2650
714/824-6718

University of Central
Florida
Department of English
P.O. Box 161346
Orlando, FL 32816-1346
407/823-5254

University of Cincinnati
Creative Writing Program
Department of English
and Comparative Liter-
ature
P.O. Box 210069
Cincinnati, OH 45221-
0069
513/556-5924

University of Colorado at
Boulder
Creative Writing Program
Department of English
Campus Box 226
Boulder, CO 80309-0226
303/492-6434

University of Denver
Creative Writing Program
Department of English
Pioneer Hall
Denver, CO 80208
303/871-2266

University of Florida
Department of English
4008 Turlington Hall
Gainesville, FL 32611-7310
352/392-0777

University of Georgia
English Department
329A Park Hall
Athens, GA 30602
706/542-2659

University of Hawaii
Writing Program
Department of English
1733 Donaghho Road
Honolulu, HI 96822
808/956-7619

University of Houston
Creative Writing Program
Department of English
Houston, TX 77204-3012
713/743-3015

University of Idaho
Creative Writing Program
English Department
Brink Hall, Rm 200
Moscow, ID 83844-1102
208/885-6156

University of Illinois at
  Chicago
Program for Writers
Department of English
(M/C 162)
601 South Morgan Street
Chicago, IL 60607-7120
312/413-2239

University of Iowa
Program in Creative Writ-
  ing
Department of English
103 Dey House
Iowa City, IA 52242-1000
319/335-0416

University of Kansas
Creative Writing Program
Department of English
3116 Wescoe Hall
Lawrence, KS 66045
913/864-4520

University of Maine
English Department,
  Room 304
5752 Neville Hall
Orono, ME 04469-5752
207/581-3839

University of Maryland
Creative Writing
Department of English
3101 Susquehanna Hall
College Park, MD 20742
301/405-3820

University of Massachu-
  setts, Amherst
MFA in English
Bartlett Hall
Box 30515
Amherst, MA 01003-0515
413/545-5497

University of Michigan
Hopwood Room
1176 Angell Hall
Ann Arbor, MI 48109-
  1003
313/763-4139

University of Missouri,
  Columbia
Creative Writing Program
English Department
107 Tate Hall
Columbia, MO 65211
573/882-0854

University of Missouri, St.
  Louis
Department of English
8001 Natural Bridge Road
St. Louis, MO 63121
314/516-5541

University of Montana
Creative Writing Program
Department of English
Missoula, MT 59812-1013
406/243-5231

University of Nebraska,
  Lincoln
English Department
202 Andrews Hall
Lincoln, NE 68588-0333
402/472-3191

University of Nevada, Las
  Vegas
MFA in Creative Writing
Department of English
4505 S. Maryland Park-
  way
Las Vegas, NV 89154-5011
702/895-3533

University of New Mex-
  ico
Creative Writing Program
English Department
Humanities 217
Albuquerque, NM 87131
505/277-6347

University of New
  Orleans
Creative Writing Work-
  shop
College of Liberal Arts
Lakefront
New Orleans, LA 70148
504/280-7454

University of North Car-
  olina, Greensboro
MFA Writing Program
Department of English
Greensboro, NC 27412-
  5001
910/334-5459

University of Notre Dame
Creative Writing Program
365 O'Shaughnessy Hall
Notre Dame, IN 46556-
  0368
219/631-7526

University of Oregon
Program in Creative Writing
Box 5243
Eugene, OR 97403
541/346-3944

University of Pittsburgh
Creative Writing Program
526 C.L.
Pittsburgh, PA 15260
412/624-6506

University of San Francisco
M.A. in Writing Program
Program Office, Lone Mountain 340
2130 Fulton Street
San Francisco, CA 94117-1080
415/422-2382

University of South Carolina
English Department
Office of Graduate Studies
Humanities Building
Columbia, SC 29208
803/777-5063

University of South Dakota
Creative Writing Program
Department of English
Vermillion, SD 57069
605/677-5229

University of Southern California
Professional Writing Program
Waite Phillips Hall, Room 404
Los Angeles, CA 90089-4034
213/740-3252

University of Southern Mississippi
Center for Writers
Box 5144
Hattiesburg, MS 39406-5144
601/266-4321

University of Southwestern Louisiana
Creative Writing Program
Department of English
P.O. Box 44691
Lafayette, LA 70504-4691
318/482-6906

University of Texas at Austin
English Department
PAR 108
Austin, TX 78712-1164
512/471-5132

University of Utah
Writing Program
English Department
Salt Lake City, UT 84112
801/581-6168

University of Virginia
Creative Writing Program
Department of English
Bryan Hall
Charlottesville, VA 22903
804/924-6675

University of Washington
Writing Program
English Department
P.O. Box 3543300
Seattle, WA 98195-4330
206/543-9865

University of Wisconsin, Milwaukee
Creative Writing Program
Department of English
Box 413
Milwaukee, WI 53201
414/229-4243

Vermont College
MFA in Writing
Montpelier, VT 05602
802/828-8840

Virginia Commonwealth University
MFA in Creative Writing Program
Department of English
P.O. Box 842005
Richmond, VA 23284-2005
804/828-1329

Warren Wilson College
MFA Program for Writers
P.O. Box 9000
Asheville, NC 28815-9000
704/298-3325 (ext. 380)

Washington University
Writing Program
Department of English
Campus Box 1122
One Brookings Drive
St. Louis, MO 63130-4899
314/935-5190

Wayne State University
Department of English
Detroit, MI 48202
313/577-2450

West Virginia University
Department of English
230 Stansbury Hall
P.O. Box 6269
Morgantown, WV 26506-6269
304/293-5021

Western Illinois University
Department of English
and Journalism
Macomb, IL 61455-1390
309/298-1103

Western Michigan University
Program in Creative Writing
Department of English
Kalamazoo, MI 49008-5092
616/387-2572

CANADA

Concordia University
Department of English
Creative Writing Program
LB 501
Montreal, PQ H3G 1M8
514/848-2340

University of Alberta
Department of English
3-5 Humanities Center
Edmonton, Alberta T6G 2E5
403/492-3258

University of British Columbia
Department of Theatre, Film and Creative Writing
Creative Writing Program
Buchanan E462–1866 Main Mall
Vancouver, BC V6T 1Z1
604/822-2712

The University of Guelph
The Department of English
Guelph, Ontario N1G 2W1
519/824-4120

University of New Brunswick
Department of English
Box 4400
Fredericton, NB E3B 5A3
506/453-4676

University of Windsor
401 Sunset Avenue
Windsor, ON N9B 3P4
519/253-4232